STITCH

TRADING STITCHES BOOK ONE

TIMOTHY COLLINS

To my wife, who never questioned our crazy "conversations" that involved me debating plot points with myself while she patiently waited for me to come to a solution. And to my three little Stitches, who are the best beta readers a dad could ever ask to have at his side.

ONE

W e live in a flawed design. A failure of the greatest magnitude: the human body. It provides little protection from the elements, beasts of nature, and sharp objects. I conclude it's cursed, however, not flawed. At least mine is. Mind *and* body.

Staring into Mom's sink, I watch the bubbles circle the drain, following the water to the depths below. Cracked porcelain left in its soapy wake.

Flawed. The unknown female voice whispers in my mind. It's not the first time she's talked to me.

I rescue a black-handled silver blade from the surviving bubbles.

She's not coming back. Seven years dead.

The knife's uncaring, razor-sharp edge presses against the smooth underside of my wrist. I hesitate, but my wrist beats back logic with painful pressure on my skin. More pressure than last time.

The pulsating blood peaks in the same spot, horizontal on my wrist, creating a black, bumped line. My living tattoo has returned, longer and stronger than the times before. Possibly even controlling me, I can't be sure. It might never stop happening if I don't do something.

Seven years is long enough. Your mom misses you.

The urge possesses immortality my body lacks and stamina greater than my will.

"Cut along the dotted line," I say. "A simple solution."

I slide the black-handled knife across the dotted line on my wrist. The line that appeared with the voice, same as before. Searing pain radiates the length of my forearm. The fingers on my injured arm twitch uncontrollably. The knife bounces off the edge of the sink and clatters to the ground, christening the white linoleum floor with my crimson blood offering.

My eyes turn to the red trouble flowing from my wrist.

Flawed design. Check.

Blood spurts from my wrist, flowing freely across my palms and down the length of my fingers. On the bright side, I can't see the dotted line on my wrist any longer. Vanquished after a seven-year on-again, off-again relationship, as if I broke a mirror rather than having my mother killed.

Regret floods my every thought. *What have I done?*

"Dad!" I scream between rapid breaths until my throat hurts. Scorched by my desperate and sudden need for help.

I twirl, leaving behind a red circle on the floor with the artistry of a second-grader. I grab for anything I can use to cover my wrist. The barren kitchen offers nothing more than a greasy dish towel.

If the cut doesn't kill me, the bacteria might. I wrap the towel around my wrist, holding it as tight as I can. It only takes a moment to soak it. *Oh, God.*

The red puddle turns my head inside out. A sludge of bile attacks the back of my throat. My legs crumple as I reach for the phone, landing me a seat in a pool of blood.

The knife lays next to me, taunting me. The red soaked towel falls to the floor with a sloppy slap.

Not a butcher's knife. Not even a steak knife. Nothing manly. Child's play.

A glorified fucking paring knife.

Clyde, my furball mastiff, dances around me, licking my face and shedding burnt orange fur in the river of red. He shifts from one foot to the other, getting blood on his paws. He refuses to leave my side.

Loyalty. Clyde's gravity.

I pull on the dangling curly cord on the phone to dislodge the receiver. It stretches and strains, but the stupid hook won't release its grip. It remains in the cradle, joining the knife in taunting me.

Out of the corner of my eye, Dad's soiled hand catches my attention. Finally, some help. My panic temporarily subsides.

I extend my uninjured arm, but he brushes it aside to grab the wobbly handle of the banana-yellow refrigerator.

He shakes his shaggy, black hair away from his eyes and reaches deep into the fridge. Same clothes he wore yesterday. Maybe I don't want him touching me. I might be able to smell the sweat and beer on him if not for the overpowering stench of my own death in my nose.

Bottles clink a familiar alcoholic's melody as he unearths a Coors Light from the dark interior. Dad twists the cap and finger-snaps the bottle cap toward the trash can in a single motion.

"Damn. Light burned out again," he mutters between gulps.

"I'm dying!" Panic overwhelms relief. "I'm going to pass out." My body lurches left as I try to grab his blue jeans.

He stumbles around the island out of my reach. "I'm

out of coffee. Gonna head to the store to pick some up. I'll leave the door unlocked. Let's hope you got my genes and your mother's good looks."

Guess Dad needs a steaming hot cup of morning hangover juice. You know what they say, gotta be alert while you watch your son bleed out.

I think that's what they say.

He staggers around the island and leans every inch of his six-six frame across the expanding pool of blood. Dad snatches the receiver from its hold. A happy twenty-second birthday card precariously balanced above the phone loses its balance, and flutters end over end through the air.

"Before I go. Here." He punches three numbered buttons and tosses me the phone.

Every time he speaks, his face highlights the litany of scars crisscrossing his cheeks and neck. Even three days of stubble can't hide them.

I grab the phone, creating a crimson handprint on the receiver. My head dances in circles. A long stream of blood flows down my arm, collecting on my shoulder. Memories escaping via a blood conduit. Memories of loved ones. They live in the heart, not the head. The heart pumps blood. Irrational or not, I believe it.

Tears hit my cheeks. More memories leaving. I have none to spare.

The phone trills. I stare into the pool of red, hoping for Mom's face, but I see only hatred for Dad. How can he stand there?

My head bobs.

"Nine-one-one. What's your emergency?" a calm, female voice asks.

I blank.

"Watch your wrist." Dad points to my drooping arm. A small drop of beer crests the mouth of the bottle. "Damn."

"Hello? Do you have an emergency?" Her voice changes tone three times.

"I'm cut . . .my wrist . . . bleeding bad . . . need help." I probably sound like a Geico spokesperson. A few grunts and I'd have myself an audition tape. I focus on Dad's pine green eyes and gather myself.

"Can you tell me your address?" she asks.

More information? I want to scream, send help. "Allison Road. Small yellow house. Two. Zero. One." I lose the last number somewhere in the puddle of blood.

"Five," Dad shouts as he walks down the hall.

"Okay, we're sending help to two-zero-one-five Allison Road. Please—"

I let go of the phone and watch the stretched curly cord call the receiver home.

"Why?"

I lean back against the island and stare at the kitchen light, failing to muster additional thoughts with my angry question.

"Why what?" Dad resurfaces with a fresh plaid shirt and an empty bottle. He steps around me and fishes the phone out of the blood before placing it back on the hook. He doesn't even wipe it clean.

I attempt to show him a single finger, but my arm weighs a million pounds. Surely it should be lighter given all the blood I've lost.

"Why are you going to watch me die?"

"Don't insult me," he says. "We'll talk later."

"But . . . " Everything in my narrow field of vision turns cloudy.

"But nothing. Just remember, whatever doesn't kill you makes you stronger." He claps twice. "Come on, Clyde."

His silhouette fades with Clyde in tow, but I hear his voice as he walks toward the front door. "Milt?" Dad sees fit to call his best friend during the morning's excitement. "No, I'm not calling about the money. No clue what I'm gonna do about that. The boy cut his wrist. Really thought it skipped him being an adult and all, but we gotta let it play out. No more stepping in front of potential trouble."

Dad slams the door so hard it bounces back open. A subtle winter breeze joins my pity party. Nothing left but to hope death doesn't ride on the wind today. If so, he better be a kick-ass, fire-breathing skeleton riding atop a nightmare.

Silence.

The blood clinging to the edge of my elbow, cedes its grip and falls to the floor rhythmically.

Drip. Drip. Drip.

I opt to lie flat on my back and bring my arm to my chest.

"There are two ceiling lights burned out," I yell to no one. "I'll make sure to remind you when I haunt you." I laugh. Delirious and alone, but not crazy.

I consider making a blood angel on the floor so that it will be memorable for the paramedics. Humor. Humor and delirium offer small victories.

Okay, maybe I'm a little crazy.

The cold November air offsets my warm pool of blood. I wonder if Mom's last moments were like this. Lying freezing in a wrecked automobile after our neighbor's Christmas party.

I miss her.

Six feet underground in the most exquisite vinyl casket, Dad's alcohol drained bank account could buy.

"Mom's blood is on your hands!" I scream as my thoughts drain down a black hole. "And so is . . . "

I die for the first time.

TWO

A sharp syringe pierces my arm.

"Ow!"

"Sorry." The young nurse holds up the needle. "Tetanus shot."

But I washed the knife. Bet it was cleaner than your needle.

I expect massive bandages on my wrist, but when I raise my head off the starched pillowcase, nothing more than a thin white wrap protects my forearm.

"Not one drop of red," I say.

"That's because you tried to leave it all on the kitchen floor," a deep voice says. The whisker-heavy doctor hovers over the foot of my bed. A smirk flashes on his face while faint creases pollute an otherwise clean dress shirt.

"Hilarious, Doc. Didn't you swear an oath that keeps you from making fun of your patients?"

"Yes, but I make an exception for anyone I bring back from the dead. It's a shortlist, and everyone on it shares your last name," he says. "Interesting fact, most guys in their early twenties spend their birthday in a bar, not a hospital."

"And miss my chance to dine in the hospital's cafeteria? This place has the most five-star food reviews of anywhere in town."

"Even though you're joking, it wouldn't surprise me."

I raise my arm. "How long before I'm discharged?"

"Not long." He moves to the bedside and examines my wrist. "Excellent. Should heal fine." He pulls a rolling seat under himself. "I have concerns about the incident in the kitchen. We both know you didn't come for the food, and," —he looks toward the ceiling— "you see, the men in your family suffer from certain, ah, tendencies."

"Tendencies?" I ask.

"Poor decision-making skills. Evel Knievel Syndrome. Adrenaline junkies. Attempted suicide." Doc counts on his thick fingers. "Those thoughts crossed your mind?"

"Suicide?" Such a heavy word to breathe. I sink deeper into the bed from its weight. The line on my wrist appeared dozens of times before, every time begging to be split. This time demanding.

"Not just suicide," he says. "Your body, well, your body is unique. Like your dad's."

"Doesn't make it unique then, does it?" I say. Anything to move the conversation away from suicide.

"Clever," He smiles, his pearly white teeth matching his lab coat. "But I'm talking about how your body reacts. For whatever reason, it holds adrenaline and testosterone."

"I don't get it."

"Well, let's take today. When you cut your wrist—"

"Accidentally." I curl my uninjured hand around the blue blanket.

Touch blue, make it true.

"When you *accidentally* cut your wrist, your body experienced a surge of adrenaline, the same as an average person." He punches his tablet and swipes the screen three times. "And twelve hours later, your levels have barely changed."

"Is that bad?"

"Like I said, it's unique. Your levels should've returned to what those in my profession consider normal, but your body, like your dad's, retains adrenaline as well as testosterone."

"What gives?"

He shrugs. "Well, if you can answer that question, you're smarter than me. We have people that can help you if—"

"Hey, kiddo." Dad's gruff voice startles me. He slides in behind Doc and places a hand on his shoulder. "Can you give us a minute, Malcolm?"

"Sure."

The guy seamlessly jumps into the flow of the hustle and bustle of bodies navigating the hallway outside my door.

Dad nudges my foot. "Still mad?"

"Kiddo? Please don't patronize me. And what do you think?" I cross my arms. "Are you insane?"

"Well, I'm pretty sure all Cheeks men are made that way."

"I could've died." I dig my top teeth into my bottom lip, fighting the urge to punch him. Dad walked out while I was bleeding to death. Not sure how I justify that to anyone, let alone myself.

"Technically, I think you did," his hesitant smile begs for a positive response. "Besides, whatever doesn't kill you makes you stronger."

"Not helping, Dad," I stress each word.

"Still calling me Dad. That's a plus. Besides, you weren't going to die," he says.

"Technically, I did."

"Well, you weren't going to die, like, permanently."

"Can you hear yourself? You sound crazy. You belong in a mental institution," I say.

"Wouldn't be the first Cheeks."

"What?"

"Marc, I understand you're pissed, but listen, if I loaded you into my truck and drove you to the hospital, it would've taken twenty-five minutes. The ambulance arrived in twelve." Dad stares at his shoes. "Sometimes, we have to make tough choices."

"Rough?" I say. "I died. Does it get any rougher than that?"

"It kinda does." Dad's head drops, and he picks at the frayed cuticle on his index finger. "Why did you clean the knife before you cut your wrist?" he asks.

His detour surprises me.

"Why would you think that?" I tuck my wrist under the cotton blanket.

"It's just you and me here. Believe me, when I tell you, I understand." He yanks the plaid flannel sleeves up to his elbow and flips the underside of his wrists for me to see. A barcode of scars decorates his wrists and forearms. Nothing I haven't seen before. "See this one here?"

He points to a zigzag scar running diagonal away from his wrist. "Accident. Jagged. Thick outline in some parts and barely visible in others."

"But these" —The grungy fingers on his right hand slide lower to two other scars, one on top of the other— "Straight. Smooth. With a purpose. A Cheek's special. I suspect yours looks identical."

First thing I'm doing when these bandages come off is scratching the edges around my scar.

They'll still know.

"Shut up," I shout, slapping my hands over my ears.

Dad pulls my hands away with the ease of placing a baby bird back in its nest.

"I get you might not want to talk about this, but it's important," he says. "Some days, it feels as though you're trapped inside an exoskeleton. Some dark part of your brain decides you can cut your way out. Whatever it is inside of us, that's better than other people."

"Better?"

How is hearing voices better? I want to ask, but I might find myself in an entirely different kind of hospital if I do.

"Stronger. Smarter. Better. There's something inside the Cheeks men that fights to emerge. Different for every one of us, but also the same. These little incidents, well, they will make you stronger in a way."

"Because I don't die?"

Because you do.

She's faster than him.

Dad shakes his head. "Because you do."

"That's messed up," I say, still not entirely sure what he means.

"You could say that, but Doc says we're unique. Grandpa called us cursed."

"And Mom called you crazy," I snap.

Dad buries his hands in his pockets. "Mom called me lots of things. Good news is Doc said you'll be able to come home tomorrow. Guess you'll need clean clothes."

"You think?" I roll my eyes. The childish part of me wants to leave in blood-soaked clothes, so people ask questions. "Jeans and my Steelers jersey."

Mom bought me that oversized jersey. I wore it for a year straight, despite it being two sizes too big for an average adult, let alone a teen. Pretty sure it was the last thing she ever bought me. Only Dad understood why I wore it to her funeral.

"Steelers, huh?" Dad says. "I think this is their year." He walks over to the bedside, leans down, and kisses me on the top of my head. "See ya tomorrow. We got a lot to talk about."

A kiss? Am I twelve? What the hell? A terrible apology, but hospitals have a strange influence on people. It's their chance to act kind in front of God. I peg hospitals as the third most popular place people show off for God, just behind churches and cemeteries.

I don't utter another word as he leaves.

"Marc Cheeks, ladies and gentlemen, the new walking poster boy for crazy," I mutter as I close my eyes to chase sleep. "I came close to my own vinyl casket today."

You sure did, but now we can start.

THREE

I slouch low in the dry, cracked leather passenger's seat, seeking refuge from judgmental eyes. Nothing better than having Daddy drive you to work. He didn't even give me time to dry my hair after my shower this morning.

He won't survive if I'm not around to take care of the day to day for him, but I can't seem to grow up unless I'm away from him—which I never am.

Maybe that's why I chose a college a bus ride away from home. Maybe that's why I'm spending my senior year student teaching at the same school responsible for four years of teen torture. Maybe leaving the hospital wasn't the best idea, but I can't prove I'm not my father if I stay in a hospital bed.

Besides, there's no such thing as a curse.

"Goddamn, these bandages are itchy. A masochist probably designed them. You think I need to change them?" I tug the tape away from the spot on my wrist, which is now rubbed raw.

"I don't know, Marc." Dad flutters his whiskey-chapped lips and leans his shoulder into the driver's door. "That would've been a question for your mom."

He only mentions her when he wants to end a conversation abruptly. Isn't there a rule about not leveraging a dead wife to your advantage against your kid? Dad didn't get the memo.

I cringe as our Nissan's balding tires skid into the school's gravel parking lot. The truck's rickety fender clings by a single rusty screw, a painful daily reminder of the past seven years. It begs to be fixed, but Dad ignores it.

He seeks refuge in denial.

We jerk to a stop, and Dad leans back, pinching the bridge of his crooked nose. "Do you bitch like this to the other teachers? Hierarchy doesn't end after high school. Even worse, students can smell fear. They'll make fun of you without hesitation."

"How's that different from any other day?" I pick at the exposed yellow padding brushing against my thigh. Anything to keep from pawing at my wrist. "I'm the only twenty-two-year-old that needs his daddy driving him to work. And why is that? Oh, that's right, because I took the fall for your DUI, so you didn't end up in jail."

"Can you call an unpaid internship work?" His stare follows a teacher's skirt.

The broken handle jiggles in my palm as I struggle to open the door. "It's called student teaching. In eight months, I'll have a college degree and a job waiting for me next fall, but what does it matter? It's not like you care."

"Wait a minute!" He slams the faded dashboard. I don't flinch because I'm numb to it these days. The dash showcases a fresh crack when he removes his hand. "I do care. Besides, whatever doesn't kill you makes you stronger. Right?"

I roll my eyes. "That was a great pep talk in the hospital, but no one believes that."

"I do. Your grandfather did." He squeezes the steering wheel until his knuckles turn white. "One day, you will, too."

Dead grandfather card for the win.

I never knew Grandpa. Another Cheeks man settled into an early grave. Mom said cancer tore through his body like hot shrapnel, and Grandpa didn't even try to fight it.

"We'll talk about this tonight. There are things you need to know, but right now, you better get moving before we're both late," Dad says, pointing a dirt-encrusted fingernail in the direction of the school. "Here. Take this."

No hug goodbye, no fist bump, no *have a good day*. Just an empty bottle of Rebel Yell whiskey chucked my way for disposal after I hop out of the truck.

"What do you want me to do with this?" I ask. "Pretty sure they don't put Boxtops on liquor bottles."

"Toss the damn thing in the trash, smart-ass."

I wrap my fingers around the bottle's smooth neck. The natural fit comfortably nestles in my fingers. I remind myself I might have Dad's hands, but I don't have to have his devotion to drinking.

I cock back my arm but hesitate. The trash can sits ten feet away, nestled inside a brick facade on school property, no less. "There are students around. With my luck, I'll miss."

And let's not forget about the potential parole violation.

"Then throw it underhand." Dad revs the engine. It turns over and dies. It takes two attempts before smoke billows from the exhaust, and the engine sputters to life. "Will you just get rid of it? I need to get to work."

I take a giant step toward the trash can.

"I said, throw it." His words escape through clenched teeth.

"But there's a student right there and—"

Dad reaches over and slams the passenger side door shut. The truck tires spit up gravel and leave me hacking up a lung in the massive gray cloud. No doubt he'll be complaining to his bar buddies later tonight about his uncoordinated son.

I toss the bottle, and it makes an unapologetic clang off the side of the can.

A slender, overdressed senior picks up my misfire from the ground. Glenn Lang was never one to wear casual clothes. Since the first day I started tutoring him almost ten years ago, he dressed per his mother's direction. He claimed he needed help with math and reading, but all he truly wanted was a friend.

"I'll grab it, Marc. I mean, Mr. Cheeks."

"Thanks, Glenn."

Susan Lang, assistant volleyball coach and Glenn's older sister, takes the bottle from Glenn.

"You rebel." Usually, a woman like her wouldn't talk to me, but tutoring her little brother had its perks. "See what I did there?" She winks. "You look a little down. I have something that will cheer you up. Watch this." Susan balances the Rebel Yell on her middle finger and spins it. "Adult fidget spinner!"

The bottle teeters on the first pass but completes another revolution before Glenn snatches it from his sister.

"Two seconds left on the clock—Lang steps back and launches a three." Two large steps back, followed by a hop, and he launches the bottle high in the air toward the trash can.

"Rejected!" The self-anointed social leader of the senior class, Kyle Arrington, swats the bottle back in

Glenn's direction, forcing him to shield his face for protection.

The bottle ricochets off Glenn's forearms before bouncing into my arms. I immediately drop it into the grass, as if it's on fire.

"With a short-armed shot like that, I'd stick to chess." Kyle impersonates a limp-wristed T-Rex. A small posse trails close, invading the space between Glenn and me. Donnie, never one to leave Kyle's side, signals the group to begin a Munson Marauders football chant.

Glenn's head dips, and he catches a few subtle elbows and hips as he shuffles through the beasts to my side.

High school beats you with her cruelty every chance she gets.

Do something.

The thought gnaws at the back of my brain.

"Guys." I wave my hand. "All right, fellas, I need you to quiet down." My voice disintegrates in the wave of vocal testosterone.

"Get to homeroom!" Principal Evans booms. His wide shadow of brown polyester and a misshapen comb-over ends our fun.

The players shuttle their way down the pathway to the school's entrance in double-time. Evans' six-four frame carried the weight of his high school linebacker years when he attended Munson, but Father Time exchanged ab muscles and bulging biceps for a beer gut and a second chin. He still scares the shit out of most of the student body.

"Mr. Cheeks, if you want the students' respect, you need to earn it. Until that time, demand it!" Evans says with fists clenched.

"Sorry, sir." I nod as if I understand what the hell he's talking about.

Evans pivots toward Glenn. "And I'll need you to come with me, Mr. Lang. Alcohol is prohibited on school grounds. Now pick that up."

"But—"

"No buts!"

No sooner does Glenn scoop up the bottle than Evans confiscates it from him and hands it to me. The damn thing keeps finding its way to my grasp.

"Marc, I mean, Mr. Cheeks," Susan growls. "Do something."

Yeah, do something.

Now, I have two women commanding me.

Doing nothing created dotted lines in my life, not just on my wrist.

"Kyle Arrington threw it on the ground, sir. Glenn tried cleaning it up, but Donnie stopped him," I say. It's as if someone else speaks through me.

I double-down on my lie.

"And you saw this, Mr. Cheeks?" Evans asks, grimacing his caterpillar unibrow.

"I did, Principal Evans."

"Kyle Arrington and Donnie Hauck, huh? I'm walking a fine line here, Mr. Cheeks. Coach Throgmorton has received offers to coach from Alabama, Oklahoma, USC, Ohio State, and UT. Texas, not Tennessee. Despite those chances, he continues to grace us with his coaching prowess and small-town spirit. We are blessed to have a man of such high standing in our community. Are you certain?"

"Totally."

"Mr. Arrington, Mr. Hauck, and I need to have a few words. Guessing Coach Throgmorton won't be thrilled about this situation, especially with the superintendent on school grounds today. This is bad. Very, very bad." Evans storms into the swarm of students buzzing around the school's entrance.

Susan brushes a few strands of golden hair from her eyes. "Well, that's one solution."

"What?"

"Are you trying to get me killed?" Glenn tugs at the collar on his plaid perfectly pressed shirt. "Not only is Kyle's uncle a cop, but Donnie supplies beer for every underage kid in town."

"I'm only trying to help, Glenn. And how do you know about the party thing? Have you been to a party with underage drinking?"

"Well, no—" Glenn kicks a pebble across the ground— "That's what I heard. All I'm saying is I'm screwed if they catch me alone."

Susan sighs. "Evans might suspend them."

"Sorry. I'll try to straighten things out. I'll see you in class, Glenn. We still on for tutoring after school?"

He nods.

"I'll meet you by the side entrance as usual, and we can hit the library. Sound good?"

"I guess," Glenn says.

Susan puts her arm around his shoulder and ferries him away.

I stare at the bottle in my hand. Never had a drink, yet this is the second time an empty bottle put me in a hole. I pray this one isn't a grave.

FOUR

I discreetly dispose of the bottle and shuffle toward the dilapidated building.

My workbag sags at the corners, and the zipper strains to hold my books and lesson plans. Even my shadow drags its feet. The town labeled the building historical, which simply meant they didn't want to repair the damn thing. They'd rather spend the money fighting the Audubon Society. Dad claims they are "some bleeding-heart group that cares more about wildlife than people." The group fights to protect a dozen peregrine falcons nesting in the ruins of the otherwise abandoned factories. A battle rages between saving an endangered species and saving an endangered town.

Being back at this school makes me feel like an endangered species most days.

I walk to the cracked concrete stairs. My hands tremble as I reach for the rusty handrail.

Kids helicopter around me, pointing and whispering. My name slips off their lips, and their words hang in the breeze. I can hear every snipe, every untruth. They aren't lies, but their words lack facts.

The doors resist. I lean my shoulder into the brown beast and leverage the full power of my legs.

"It's pull, not push, genius." A junior gremlin chides me.

I rear back, pivoting my hips, and throw a fist at the door with every intention of stopping. At least, I think I intended to stop.

The thud of my wrist echoes around the school's parking lot. Wood splinters around my knuckles embedded in the door.

"Dang, Mr. Cheeks." The gremlin breaks the overhanging silence. "You been hitting the gym?"

I pry my hand loose. A few small splinters litter the valleys between my knuckles, but no damage to my hand. I peer at the door. "Rotten wood. See the fungal decay around the imprint of my hand? Now I can take a picture and use it in today's lesson."

"TMI," he scoffs before scurrying away.

I slip inside. Students part to each side of the hall as I walk toward my shared office. I am Moses of Munson High School.

Although Evans labels my planning area a shared office, it acts as a community dumping ground for unwanted flyers, Kleenex boxes, confiscated paraphernalia, and anything else a teacher wants to keep out of Evans' sight.

The other thing better than hiding something with someone good at keeping secrets is hiding contraband with someone too afraid to speak up.

Seconds tick the countdown to my demise after I learn Kyle and Donnie are suspended for three days, which includes missing the football team's biggest game of the season with county rival West Allegheny, or W.A. as the locals call them. Probably the first time in forever, Munson has a chance of winning.

Last time we beat W.A., Throgmorton intercepted a late-game pass and returned it for a touchdown for the win. It's the only game folks in town still discuss. He's a hero. Their hero. Since that day, he can do no wrong. Even went on to a big-time college, won fancy awards, and would have gone pro had he not blown out his ACL twice in two years.

I know the boys don't deserve a suspension for the bottle incident. For being assholes, that's another story. After school, I'll figure out how to tell Evans about the misunderstanding and make things right without anyone else getting into trouble.

Susan sticks her head in my classroom and warns me; Coach Throgmorton is on the warpath. Unfortunately, shit rolls downhill. From Evans to Throgmorton, and I can guess who's next.

As if that isn't bad enough, both Kyle and Donnie take my last period Business Management class, and their suspension doesn't start until tomorrow. I wait until after the starting bell before I head into class.

"Good afternoon," I announce as my entrance into the room is met with snickering. "Hope everyone had a good day. Who's ready to learn about debits and . . . " I pause as my eyes catch the two dozen Bic safety razors strewn across my desk.

Rumor spreads faster than wildfire around this school.

"Didn't anyone tell you? The proper gift for a teacher is a shiny red apple." I open my center desk drawer to sweep my desktop clean, but it's filled with more razors. Drawer after drawer filled to the brim. A note sits neatly folded among the convention of blades. I unfold it, stand tall, and read it to the class.

Mr. Cheeks,

We heard about the accident with your wrist, and we didn't want you to cut your neck shaving. Please accept this gift.

Sincerely,

Members of the Senior Class

Laughter erupts from a cadre of students. Donnie laughs so hard he snorts, which causes everyone else in the class, except one student, to join the ruckus.

Glenn sits front and center with hands folded and foot bouncing. As the laughter finds another level, Glenn jumps to his feet and turns to the back of the room.

"Kyle and Donnie did it!"

Kyle throws his chair out from under him and flies toward the front of the room, "You're dead, Lang! Dead!"

I scramble across my desk and leap in front of Kyle.

"Cool it, Mr. Arrington." I hold an open hand out.

"You gonna send 'im to the office again? Try 'n get 'im suspended fur next week's game too?" Throgmorton's froggy voice shouts across the room.

Most of the students shout a greeting his way.

"Everything is fine, Coach Frogmorton," I say before I can stop myself.

"What did ya call me?"

Coach waddles his wrecking ball frame with surprising speed for a man who stands as wide as he is tall. His red polyester sweatpants swish with each stride. Coffee crests the edge of his Dunkin' Donuts cup. He refuses to use a lid because, as he says, a man of his agility and coordination does not require such a hindrance. I may be paraphrasing and editing out bits of profanity.

I backpedal, forcing Glenn to do the same until we find ourselves in the corner enjoying a spit shower as Coach reigns down every bit of jargon slang his southern upbringing has to offer.

"Relax, Coach. I'm sorry about the slip, and I am not sending Kyle, Donnie, or any of the kids to the office. Just a harmless prank," I force a chuckle and slide around him to get to my desk. "Do you need a razor? I see you shave your head."

"What in the hell are you talking about?" Coach asks.

I pick up a Bic and display it like I'm a spokesperson. "These might come in handy. Why don't you take one? Heck, take as many as you like."

I figure some light-hearted humor, then a request for a sit down to straighten things out with him and Evans.

"You disappoint me, Cheeks," Coach says. "Kyle. Donnie. You're officially excused from this class. Come with me."

Throgmorton casually swats a half-dozen razors onto the floor as he passes my desk; although he does it with such grace for a big man, it looks as if he did it on accident.

It's not.

He stops at the door, spins, and throws his coffee cup, short hopping it less than a foot in front of me. Coffee splatters the front of my pants.

"Clean that up for me, will ya?" he sneers.

"Coach, there's still a lesson that needs to be taught, and I want to—"

"Damn right there is," he says. Throgmorton slams the door behind the three of them, not giving me the chance to request the opportunity to talk later.

FIVE

I excuse myself from class and duck into the bathroom to clean off the coffee stains before they set. My disgusted twin glares back at me from the looking glass side of the mirror. He refuses to make eye contact despite sharing my eyes.

"What's your problem?"

The silent twin in the mirror continues unfairly judging me. He mocks with mimicry before running his finger across the dotted line on his throat.

Do something. Her voice merges with my thoughts.

I rear back and throw my fist into his smug little face.

The glass shatters, cascading pieces of my doppelganger into the sink. Blood drips from my fist, splattering as it hits the grimy, beige ceramic. I inspect the cuts on my knuckles.

"These aren't even stitch worthy," I say to my scattered reflection.

They're . . . disappointing.

Several broken mirror pieces find their way to the floor

while the rest lay in the sink. Seven years of bad luck might be an early release program for me.

A single eye gazes upon me from the sink. I reach for the pizza slice shaped piece of glass. Smaller pieces crunch as I carefully ease the triangle free.

I rotate it, reflecting prisms of light into every corner of the bathroom before focusing on the dotted line on my jugular.

That bastard in the mirror taunts me from his shattered prison.

My hands tremble. Slight pressure unleashes a tiny stream of red from my neck, not strong enough to make its own path across my skin, so it follows grooves and curves around unshaven hair.

Electricity crackles throughout my body.

I push a steady flow of air from my mouth.

Rattling in the pipes and gushing water snap me from my trance.

"What the . . . ?" I ask myself, dropping the glass and throwing my hands in the air like I'm under arrest. My breathing races with the water in the old pipes. Blood trickles onto my pants.

I shake my mind clear and focus on cleaning my pants. They refuse to come clean and now showcase blood and water.

Marc Cheeks, ladies and gentlemen, the walking poster boy for spreading disease.

And cursed, let's not forget that little bonus.

Mom always said to me, "God doesn't give curses, only gifts. It's up to us to figure out how to use them."

I'm pretty sure cutting my own throat isn't what she had in mind.

I snatch a piece of mirror from the floor and stare at the fading dotted line on my throat.

Dad wears a scar on his neck in virtually the same place. Scratch that. He wears two. One with jagged edges and one perfectly smooth.

The period ends, and the bell rings. I drop the glass into the sink and head for the administrative office.

I spend the rest of the school day hiding from Throgmorton and my mirrored self. Evans buys my excuse about the stress of the first day back and has me running files most of the day.

When the end of the day comes, I'm one of the first people outside. Fresh air. I need fresh air, and to be anywhere but here. Screw hanging around after school to prep for tomorrow's classes. I'm not getting paid to put up with this shit.

SIX

I'm two steps out the school's back entrance when the ugliness of the situation hits me. Coach Throgmorton is everything to the lifers in this town, which is practically every person over the age of thirty.

Glenn meets me out here every day. The rear exit gives us a straight shot up a grassy hill and through the trees surrounding the school's property without worry of running into other teachers or students. I answer any questions he has about his classes, upcoming graduation, or college while he obliges with little tidbits that might help me get to know his sister, Susan, better. The teacher's lounge makes for a lousy get-to-know-you spot.

The crisp air carries the stench of two-day-old sloppy joes from the trash bins. My gag reflex attacks full force, but I power through. I suppose it's a fair tradeoff for my earlier stupidity.

"He's not coming." A deep voice booms behind me, one I often hear when Dad brings his drinking session and best friend home in the wee hours of the morning.

I spin around and find myself face-to-overgrown-beard with said friend, Milt. I can barely see his nose or mouth through the black hairy mess. "Who?"

"Squirrely kid. Says you're his tutor." Milt pushes his hands deep in the pockets of his faded blue jeans and rocks back on the heels of his snakeskin boots. "Couple of hefty-sized boys grabbed him and dragged him away. Got him pinned in the trees. Think I heard Coach call them Kyle and Ronnie. Maybe it was Donnie."

"What?" I swivel my head in every direction. "This is my fault. And you didn't do anything? We have to tell someone who can help."

Milt nods. "Just did."

"No, I mean someone who can actually do something," I say. Opening a jar of pickles most days equals the height of what I can do.

"Like I said, just did," Milt says. "Might want to hurry, though. Them boys seemed pretty agitated. Here." Milt pulls back the camouflage trench coat, revealing his own version of Batman's tool belt. Two pairs of brass knuckles, three different sized knives, and an old-school Colt 45 revolver. Milt unhitches a pair of black brass knuckles with a crimson coating wrapped around the middle and tosses them my way. "Your pops and I can't protect you any longer. You're gonna wanna take these."

"But my parole . . . " I didn't earn it, but I stepped into it. When my drunk father wrapped a car around a tree, squeaky-clean no-criminal-record Marc took the fall. I'm not sure what was worse, getting processed and spending a few hours in the sheriff's office or having to chug down whatever cheap ass whiskey he had in the backseat. Why Dad insisted we turn it into a DUI is beyond me. To this day, he argues it was about plausibility. Like father, like son.

"You prefer to have a death on your hands?" Milt asks.

I examine the steel in my hand. "Is this dried blood?"

Milt shrugs. "Sure as hell don't use it to cut tomatoes."

"Are you friggin' crazy? I've never fought anyone in my life," I protest.

"Gotta pop your cherry sooner or later. So this will be your first, but it sure as hell ain't gonna be the last." Milt turns and whistles an upbeat tune as he strolls toward a black Cadillac Escalade without a license plate. "My money is on you, so don't disappoint me."

"What?" I yell. "I don't understand—"

A quick tap on the shoulder steals my attention.

"Susan," I stammer. Big hazel eyes and a bouncy blonde ponytail splash nervousness over my words.

"Glenn needs help." She points in the direction of trees. "Kyle and Donnie have him cornered. We screwed up, Marc. Big time. Even Coach Throgmorton is out there."

"Go call the police." I put a hand to my forehead as if I'm going to pull a solution from my brain physically.

"They already came, Marc. It was Kyle's uncle." Susan drags me two steps. "He talked to the coach for two minutes, then left."

"Shit."

Do something.

I clench the brass knuckles tight around my fingers before tucking them into the blood-stained front pocket on my jeans. "I'll try reasoning with everyone so that I can get Glenn out of there." I suppose it's the least I can do since this is my fault.

I race to the tree line where a half-dozen guys stand in a semi-circle between two giant maple trees.

"Look who it is." Coach holds out his python-sized

arm, preventing me from reaching Glenn and Kyle. The two teens stand center stage in an out-of-balance human circle of high school kids with smartphones at the ready.

Kyle steps to Glenn, the brim of his Mason County Police Department hat grazes Glenn's forehead. He never passed up a chance to remind folks his uncle is a cop. "Are those Garanimals? Did Mommy dress you?" He sneers. A chorus of laughter erupts. The girls in school fawn over Kyle's asshole camouflage of jet-black hair and bulging biceps. His only method of cloaking his inner moron is rarely opening his mouth.

"There's been a mistake," I say.

This is my fault. I can't stand idly by and let a kid take the blame.

I try to push past the impregnable arms of Throgmorton, but he doesn't give ground.

"Why don't we let the boys work things out?" Coach suggests, chewing hard on his Skoal tobacco. His jaw oscillates side to side with each chomp while the hat on his head undulates in rhythm.

Donnie and four other football players fall in behind him. The stench of Axe body spray citrus mixed with sweat assaults my nose. My confidence wilts like a flower caught in an early season freeze.

"That's not how things work," I say.

"You've been here for four months. I've been here for fourteen years, and you're going to tell me how things work?" Coach pulls a handful of my shirt closer to his face, his off-center brown eyes surveying my body. I smell every minute of this morning's football practice and all-day weight room workouts on his body.

"Careful Coach, he might tell his mommy about you," Donnie says. "Shit, I almost forgot. She's dead."

The boys in my high school class didn't get the dead mother memo either.

"Donnie, we do not disrespect the dead," Coach says.

"Thank you," I say.

He smirks and twists the handful of my shirt. "Of course, if you want to talk about his old man, I don't think anyone will stop you."

"Shut up." I swat at his arm but come up empty as Coach pushes back during my swinging motion. The momentum causes me to stagger back a few steps.

"Gotta be faster than that, Cheeks." A two-armed shove sends me face first into the ground. "And stay down. There's no one here to protect you now." Coach flattens my face with a foot on my lower back. Dirt and pebbles infiltrate my every breath.

He wrangles his legs free from mine. I turn my head to the side to catch my breath when I lay eyes on Kyle.

Kyle growls. "Think you can just lie about me with no consequences just because you're the teacher's pet, Glenn?"

I rake my nails across my injured wrist, spilling blood across my fingertips and into my palm. Pain surges throughout my body.

But it's not pain. It's energy.

Adrenaline.

Testosterone.

Life.

My heart races. At first, I struggle to breathe fast enough to keep up with my body's needs, but I adjust within moments. I regain my footing.

"Back down, Mr. Arrington!" I yell.

Looking to create a distraction, I slash a bloody palm at Coach's sweaty meathead, knocking loose his Marauders hat and leaving a trail of my AB negative in his eyes.

Like I said, I'm the model citizen for spreading disease.

I wave my arms in a summoning motion, trying to get Glenn to come to me. He's too focused on Kyle, so I shout at him. "Glenn—"

Coach's elbow finds its way between my ribs and cuts off my communication attempt. The oxygen in my lungs abandons my body as I fold in two.

"Fight. Fight. Fight." The chant gains power with each repeated word. Over the past decade, violence transformed the town to survival of the fittest. I joke the school should be renamed Darwin High.

I resist as Coach hoists me to my feet. Donnie joins him, and the two drag me to Glenn at the circle's center. Unfortunately, I'm not the first teacher working here to receive this treatment.

"Ain't high school great?" I scoff.

"Best years of my life," Glenn rolls his eyes.

Coach rushes with the power of a bull.

I picked a terrible day to wear a red jacket.

His head meets my nose. Firecrackers set off on an explosion of pain and blood on my face. I crumple to the ground, taking Glenn with me.

Another rush of adrenaline.

I pop back on my feet, not wasting time wiping the blood cascading from my nose.

Guess red wasn't the wrong choice jacket after all.

"I've got good news for you, Mr. Cheeks," Coach says. "I could use an assistant to help the football team. We need another tackling dummy."

"I think there are enough dummies on the team already." I fire back as I turn to help Glenn stand.

"Donnie," Coach says, nodding.

In a flash, the gray sky spins above me. My work as a tackling dummy starts immediately, courtesy of Donnie. I clamor to my feet, despite my ankle screaming the same sentiments as my nose.

"You have to bend your knees, Mr. Cheeks. Give a hit as you're taking one," Kyle says.

"Hell yeah!" Throgmorton says. "That right there is solid coaching. Now watch closely, boys."

Throgmorton swings wide and puts his full weight behind a punch. I'm sure he knocked my stomach out of my ass. My chest rolls forward, and I crumble to my knees at the base of a towering oak.

"And that's for being a smart-ass!" Throgmorton spits tobacco juice on the back of my head. The warm, chunky liquid oozes down either side of my neck.

Laughter echoes from every direction. The voices around me join Kyle's taunting. *Loser. Loser. Loser.* I swear my father's voice chants the loudest.

Fear hugs Glenn's face as he staggers back two steps. The patrol car circles close by but doesn't stop. The faculty makes a beeline for their cars, refusing to even look in our direction.

No one is coming to help.

Do something. Her voice pushes.

The heckling continues as I square myself on my hands and knees. I see a small, black, dotted circle appear on Throgmorton's temple.

My left hand tugs at a large tree root. *No use.* My right hand slides the brass knuckles over my fingers. I find a jagged-edged, baseball-sized stone nestled under a small arch in the tree roots. I cradle the cool surface in my palm under the steel and regain my feet.

"Look, we're sorry. We'll make it right." I extend my left hand.

"Where's the lesson in stopping now?" Throgmorton smacks my hand away. "Way I figure, my boys are going to miss three days of practice—plus a game. You owe them more time working as a tackling dummy."

I give the man credit; he put all his weight into the swat. Hips pivoted, giving him maximum power as he twists. And the textbook exaggerated follow-through. Just like a coach teaching a player.

The fortitude of action leaves him exposed and prone to retaliation.

As his follow-through reaches its apex, I wrap my left hand around the tree's low-hanging branches. The noose shape grants additional leverage as I unload a right cross. My trajectory changes three times as I try keeping my aim on the dotted circle on the side of Throgmorton's face. I don't extend my arm or follow through the way Coach did, but the knuckles combined with the rock hidden in my palm deliver a crippling blow.

Throgmorton's head whips backward into Donnie's jaw, sending Donnie's bicuspids flying and rolling his eyes white.

Coach staggers backward while Donnie collapses from the blow to his jaw. A two-for-one.

The large tree root cuts short Donnie's fall before he can whimper. Coach lashes out twice before his knees buckle, and he joins Donnie on the ground. Neither move an inch.

I contemplate sliding the noosed-branches over the coach's bloodied skull—serving up public vengeance for all those still haunted by enablers like Throgmorton and dicks like Donnie and Kyle.

Do something?

Nope.

Done something.

This isn't me. None of this.

Seizing pops Throgmorton's body three times. Blood

pours from Donnie's mouth, but he doesn't move, doesn't even blink.

What if I killed Throgmorton? Worse, what if Donnie's dead?

Panic sets in as I focus on Donnie's chest. A rise and fall. I see it. Slow and labored, but there. Throgmorton too.

Throgmorton rolls to the side. He spits out a wad of tobacco chaw and a few ounces of blood.

I release my grip on the bloodied stone and scan the crowd.

Kyle slugs Glenn across the shoulder with a backpack. Glenn's head whiplashes almost ninety degrees before the rest of him follows. His body hits the ground so hard it bounces two inches.

Kyle snakes his hand into his back pocket.

Fear dances in the eyes of the boys standing across from me. I mouth, "Donnie isn't dead," as Throgmorton yells, "Do it!"

A blinding white fire steals my sight. My back burns. I reach for the pain. The flames race up my spine toward my brain.

I flail aimlessly for the handle of the knife in my back but can only muster a single scream before joining Donnie on the ground. The blade remains firmly planted, a new addition to my fallen body.

"Run!"

The pounding of feet fills my ears. My vision returns but offers me only glimpses of shoes fleeing in every direction. Crimson stained dirt sprays across my body courtesy of the heels of the shoes closest to me trying to outpace the spilling blood.

"Marc!" Susan races to my side and kneels. She puts one hand on my back and another on my cheek. I imagine a halo gracing her beautiful blonde hair while her warm, caring hands cradle my bruised and beaten body, but truthfully, I'm numb.

Her words. Her touch. Not perfect, but enough to quiet my pain and anger. A soft kiss on my cheek.

This isn't such a bad way to go.

And so I go. Again.

SEVEN

No white light. No wings. No harp accompanying a singing choir. Only rhythmic beeps. Our pastor will be so disappointed.

Beep. Beep. Beep.

The constant beeping drives me bonkers.

Am I in Hell? Did I kill Donnie?

That would explain it. I crushed his skull. And now I'll rot for eternity.

Beep. Beep. Beep.

With only a beeping sound keeping me company.

I'm in Hell.

That settles it. I killed Donnie.

He deserved it. A female voice, but not one I recognize, and certainly not Mom's, interrupts my self-pity.

Are voices after death healthy? *Healthy.* Ha! I laugh at my stupidity. There's nothing healthy about being dead, but is it normal? I have no clue. It's not like I'd been given the book *An Idiot's Guide to Life After Death*.

I fear spending eternity alone more than I worry about

conversing with a disembodied voice. Best to roll with the situation rather than question it.

Throgmorton deserved it more, but Donnie had it coming too.

He was a jerk. He deserved it, she says.

Asshole is more like it. I counter. You know what they say: when in Hell, talk like the damned.

Bet your dad is proud of you. I imagine Susan's strawberry lips speaking. *Probably boasting about you at Milt's Bar. After all, you defended him.*

You think they threw me a parade? I ask.

No doubt, she quips.

You think Susan came?

The parade was probably her idea.

Death makes maintaining a grasp on reality difficult, but this conversation helps me stay grounded rather than afraid.

Beep. Beep. Beeeeeep!

A male voice shouts, "Clear!"

A shock of pain surges through my being. I peer into the dark and find myself alone.

My Hell is loneliness, and my punishment is electrocution.

"Again!" The voice yells.

Another surge of electricity.

"One more. Clear!"

I miss the beeps. They annoy me, but pain doesn't accompany them. This Hell isn't for me. I figure it best to find a way out.

Everything fades to nothingness. The beeps. The pain. The voice.

My thoughts.

Everything.

A WHITE LIGHT.

Not that I care, but the Church will be so relieved.

"Ah, there he is. I thought we'd lost you." The voice speaks again, but without the electric encore.

My eyelids fight the brightness. After a few blinks, the light dims as the rest of my senses sharpen. With some luck, my voice will return, but for now, I only communicate with my eyes.

"Calm down, Marc. You've been through a traumatic experience, but we're going to take excellent care of you." The man in the white coat stands over me, annunciating each word with care.

So, I'm not dead? I doubt he possesses the power to read my mind. *Did I kill Donnie?*

I try raising my arms. What little strength my body retains lifts them a few inches.

"Good, Marc. Good." He pushes my arms back down. "But you need to rest."

Two sets of feet shuffle across the floor, and then the room falls silent.

Well? Did you kill him? My disembodied lady friend returns, insistent.

I miss the beeps.

No handcuffs, so I guess I didn't kill him, I reason.

There's hope for us yet.

You think Dad is proud of me? I grasp for a reason to be alive.

Proud. So, proud. Devil be proud. That's how proud he is.

I can practically hear her Cheshire grin.

"And tomorrow everything will be back to normal," I speak to an empty room.

As I drift back into the darkness, I glance one last time at my wrists. Dotted lines cross in every direction.

Horizontal.

Vertical.

Diagonal.

And they pulse as if they have no intention of leaving anytime soon.

EIGHT

"Can we see him?" Dad's gruff voice cuts short my daily twelve-hour nap. Outside of my daily meals and a sponge bath, it's the first interaction I've had in three days.

"Hey, buddy, how ya feeling?" He manages a straight line from the door to the bed, which means it's either early morning or less than an hour before his shift starts. "You know what they say, whatever doesn't kill—"

"Don't say it."

He smiles wide. "I brought someone with me."

Susan emerges from his shadow. Her pink Reebok shoes carry her with small, timid steps. I need her confidence, but only see a girl, not a woman, more comfortable standing in the gray. It isn't the Susan I know.

The greeting fights its way from her mouth. "Hey, Marc." She bites her lip and hesitates, moving closer until I lift my hand at the wrist, which is disguised as a crimson, bandaged, stitched appendage.

It isn't the warm welcome she needs, but I impress myself.

"The doctor said you'll be okay. Good as new by Christmas." She stares at her Reeboks the entire time she speaks.

"You'll be your old self in no time." Dad shelters in the frame of the room's window.

Susan inches closer before passing over a plate of gooey chocolate chip cookies I hadn't noticed her holding. "I made you cookies."

"You made these?" I welcome the plate and chomp into a treat.

"Me. Target. Tomato. To-mah-to."

Dad fumbles with the television remote while waiting for Susan to finish.

"Now those smell delicious. Right hand to God, I could eat the entire plate." He waves his hand toward his nose as he inhales. My cue to surrender the plate. I squeeze the white-flowered plate tight, but it is snatched from me with ease.

"Coach?" I ask.

Susan leans in over the side rail, "You broke his nose, and I think he lost a couple of teeth. The district placed him on administrative leave for two weeks."

I struggle with the next name. "Donnie?"

"Bad. Really bad. Concussion. Skull fracture. Over-heard someone say his jaw is wired shut. His parents are threatening to sue. It doesn't help that Kyle and Donnie were kicked off the football team. Both already filed appeals." Susan's voice flat lines. "Glenn had an in-school suspension."

I point at myself. "And me?"

"Evans said there would be a hearing when you return to determine your role, but no one's talking about what happened. They're afraid. It probably won't end well for you."

"Shocker," I say, expecting nothing less from a town that often looks the other way rather than addressing the real problems.

The sound of her sobs fills the room. "I'm sorry. I shouldn't have asked you to help. This is my fault. That situation was way beyond you." Susan breaks down, burying her face in her hands.

Dad stuffs an entire cookie in his mouth. "Hey, whatever doesn't kill you makes you stronger. Right? Damn, these are good." Crumbs spew with his muffled words as he ducks into the hallway with the cookie plate in one hand and a ringing cell phone in the other.

"I hate the way Throgmorton and his band of followers think they run the school," Susan speaks faster than usual. "Those kids tortured my cousin. The others drove her crazy. They had to leave town. That was ten years ago. She's your age now and still can't be around people."

She reaches forward and places her fingers on my forearm. I watch my heartbeat spike ten ticks on the machine next to my bed. "I gotta go. Feel better."

Doc slides into the room while Dad makes good on his promise to eat all the cookies. He details my ruptured kidney. I also suffered from septic shock. He mumbles about the knife piercing my intestine because I fell at a wrong angle like it's somehow my fault.

Is it too much to ask someone to stab you in the back properly so you can collapse without worry? Where are the dotted lines when you need them?

"So, I'm stuck here awhile?" I ask.

"Nah, you'll be right as rain in time to carve the turkey tomorrow. We're discharging you today. In a few minutes, matter of fact. Just remember when you're carving the bird to keep the knife clear of your wrists." He winks.

Inappropriate much?

I chuckle uncomfortably. "That was bad, Doc."

Dad saunters, sugar-high, around the room, and sets the empty plate on the vinyl powder-blue visitor's chair. "He ready to go, Doc?"

"Seems your boy is a quick healer, Dan. Just like his old man."

My jaw clenches while I listen to Doc's words, and though I believe him to be a smart man, given he's a doctor and all, I hope he's wrong. I don't want to be anything like him.

He shakes Dad's hand, pats him on the back, and looks him in the eyes with a warm smile. No one looks Dad in the eyes anymore. Respect for him is an artifact buried so deep I doubt Indiana Jones could unearth it.

They chat for a few minutes before acknowledging I'm still in the room with them.

"Ready?" Dad asks.

I slide out of bed. The icy floor jolts my feet back under the covers.

"I know that look." Dad passes a bag containing my clothes to me.

I shake off my expression, "What look?"

"Your mother had the same look when she couldn't figure something out. Usually something beyond my comprehension."

"I'm not thinking about anything. Just nervous about the hearing."

Dad pauses. "Well, I believe you. The real question is, do you believe you?"

I don't know what to believe anymore. Am I crazy?

I gotta be different. Different from Dad.

But here I sit in the hospital, the same place where I

visited him fifty times while growing up. Times when I thought he was dead. Hell, the hospital staff prepped Mom and me for that possibility a dozen different times, but somehow he'd pull through. Every time.

Just like me.

NINE

"Did you seriously buy cranberries?" I shake my head as Dad kicks the snow off his Wolverine boots. Principal Evans instructed me to rest until the holiday break ended, so two weeks on the couch binging television weighs on my nerves a bit.

"Yeah. I thought we'd cook up one of those traditional Thanksgiving meals." He smirks. Only his left cheek puffs up when he impresses himself with a joke. I call it the dyslexic chipmunk smile.

"I hardly think cranberries, canned yams, a store-bought pie, and cold cuts qualify as a traditional Thanksgiving dinner."

"It's the thought that counts."

"That's Christmas, not Thanksgiving."

I guess I should give my old man credit. He usually treats holidays as if they are any other day.

"One holiday's the same as the next. Plus, I have something for you."

He sets a rectangular box on the counter. The newspaper wrap job showcases sloppy corners and barely covers the one-inch thick sides. "Stash that in my room for now. Milt's outside bringing in the last of the stuff. I don't want him to see it."

"I have a tentative tutoring session set up today," I say, not knowing how to react to a gift. Outside of Christmas and my birthday, he hasn't given me a gift in seven years.

"On Thanksgiving?"

I shrug. "Didn't think we'd be doing anything."

Dad's protest drowns in his cold beer.

One text to Glenn, and he's on his way. The boy will do anything to get out from under his mother's wing.

I need to apologize to him, and maybe he can help me unwrap dad's mystery.

As I stare out the window above the sink watching for Glenn, I think about how I'd give anything to have mom back. This was her window, and I understand why. It paints the most beautiful picture of the world. I guess that's why she always washed the dishes by hand.

Mom loved snow. It weighs on me since she died. Now, I see it as rain too lazy to melt. I can't enjoy it.

She loved Christmas, too. Thanksgiving, not so much, but this was the kickoff weekend when she put up the tree and decorations illuminated our house. Twinkles of white light blinded anyone within fifty yards of our home.

Most of the neighbors didn't mind until she started decorating a few lonely pine trees on the side of the road. They petitioned to have it stopped. I remember her dragging me to the town council meeting. She destroyed argument after argument against her. It was almost as if she could read their minds.

We stopped to decorate the first tree of the season on the drive home. "To celebrate her victory," she said. "No, to celebrate *our* victory" were the words she used as I placed the star on top.

The tradition grew year after year with her. It also died with her.

A frisk of air proceeds a light sprinkle on the back of my neck. I turn to find dad holding a beer cap between his front teeth.

"You're going to ruin your teeth opening bottles like that. They make bottle openers for a reason. Or buy cans. They're cheaper."

"And that's why people want to kick your ass," he says.

"Seriously?" I push anger into my trembling fists.

"Too soon?"

I pinch my shaking thumb and pointer finger together. "A bit."

"Well, don't worry about me, my teeth will be fine. Besides, whatever doesn't kill you makes you stronger." He opens another bottle to prove his point.

"Enough with that stupid saying already."

He swigs from the bottle of Michelob Light. The muscles in his throat vibrate in harmony, releasing an eardrum-rattling burp.

"Gross." I pretend I'm not impressed. "Don't we have anything to drink in this house besides beer?" I eye the fridge contents.

"Whiskey!" He bursts out laughing.

"I gotta get out of these tight clothes." Dad dances around the boxes down the hall. He packed them seven years ago after Mom died. He hates the house, her house, too many memories, yet here we sit.

I grab two slices of bread.

He wheels around the corner of the kitchen in black sweatpants, snatches two slices, and tosses them on a faded ceramic plate. "Make me a sandwich."

"You want cranberries on that?" I wiggle the can in the air.

"Hell no. Who eats that crap? Although I will say cranberry juice mixed with vodka is tasty. And it gives you a whole day's supply of vitamin C."

I shake my head and toss the can of store-brand cranberries on the counter.

"Did I hear somebody say vodka?" Milt's raspy voice proceeds him as he enters. Blue flannel shirt with blue jeans. A juicy, fat blueberry to pair with my cranberries.

And his super-utility belt flush with his Colt, two hunting knives, and two pairs of brass knuckles, including a shiny new pair probably to replace the ones he'd given me for the fight.

His boots track muddied snow from the front door to the kitchen, where he deposits a twelve-pack of beer and a ginormous bottle of vodka.

I stare at the 1.75-liter bottle of Tito's Vodka. "Think you got enough?"

Milt smiles. "For me, but I don't know what your old man is gonna drink."

"Before we sit down to eat, can you grab the bag of dog food out of the truck? I didn't have enough hands to carry it in." Dad tosses me the keys to the truck. "Figure Clyde should feast with us."

Clyde is short for Clydesdale. We all agreed his father must have been a horse due to the size of him. A beast of a dog. There is something comforting in not having to bend down to pet him. I pat his cashmere-soft head on the way out the door.

I kick up some wintry soldiers, only to watch them fall back to Earth. As I walk to the truck, my mood drops, spying naked pines along the sidewalk. They need garland, a few dozen ornaments, and a star. They need Mom. Hell, I need Mom.

The truck's passenger door swings open with its usual

objections before relenting, exposing Clyde's passion. All-natural lamb and potato dog food. The big boy loves to eat.

"Eighty pounds?" My wiry frame immediately rejects the idea of lifting this. "Where the hell do you even find a bag this big? No way I can't carry that with my recent injuries."

I swat a low hanging icicle off the gutter. If I drag the bag through the wet snow, the local cops will think I'd hauled a body into the house. Wouldn't be the first time they came around to our place. Most of them know Dad on a first-name basis, but not for friendly reasons.

I crouch low and dig my hands deep under the bag.

"Lift with the knees, Cheeks," Glenn mocks me from behind.

I free a hand temporarily, flashing a middle finger in his direction before going back to work.

Here goes nothing.

"One. Two. Ahh!"

In a blink, I find the bag nestled against my chest.

"Dang, Mr. Cheeks. You been working out behind my back?" Glenn flexes and groans with a look of constipation. The kid has never seen the inside of a weight room.

"You're a tremendous help," I grunt. "Really."

One step. Then two. Before I know it, I'm standing at the door staring Dad in the eyes.

"Knew you could do it." He holds the door open.

"Glenn's gonna eat with us," I say.

"You like cranberries, Glenn?" Dad asks.

Milt and Dad laugh so hard, small waves of beer cascade over the edges of their bottles.

I wonder if a drink would dull my urge to open the scar on my wrist.

Focus.

I shake the thoughts from my mind.

"What do you have to drink in this place?" Glenn asks.

I shush Dad when he opens his mouth.

"Don't ask," I say.

The only question that needs answering is: why would dad give me a present?

TEN

The snow stops falling as I cut into the store-bought pie. I prefer cake, but asking Dad to bake is like asking a preacher to sing *Shout at the Devil* at service. We haven't been to the sinner sanctuary since Mom died. He lost faith when she died, and I can't get behind the lack of science and logic of it all.

I gaze out Mom's window, washing the plates from our feast and watching Glenn beat a path back home. The kid comes over, and we spend two hours of tutoring consisting of him finishing my questions for me, then spouting out the answers as if we shared a brain.

When I'm able to pull myself away from how lowly Glenn must feel to hang with me, it strikes me.

"Dad, how did you know I could lift the bag of dog food?"

Dad stares into the cup. "Like the doctor said in the hospital, you take after your old man."

He leans deep into the lumpy couch cushions, closes his eyes, and inhales the coffee's steam.

"And that means what, exactly?" My voice cracks. "Is this like charades? Or is it more like twenty questions? Either way, it's stupid."

"Let's just say I experienced a few growing pains, but they helped me excel, especially in college." He kicks his feet up on the wobbly coffee table and seemingly gets lost in a sigh. "Ah, those were the days."

"Until you got expelled," Milt says, laughing before he tosses back another shot of vodka.

Dad lurches forward on the couch. "That guy started it!"

"And you ended him. Booted from college in three days. Gotta be a record," Milt said. He leaned in closer to Dad. "What do you think? Is the kid ready for us to take him out on a test-drive?"

My eyes burst wide. "You buying me a car?"

Dad glances in my direction. "No." He stares harder at Milt. "And no." I never heard Dad talk that hard at Milt.

"Come on, Dan. He's old enough. Never been able to mold an adult from scratch. Plus, we could use some new energy,"

"Marc, time for bed," Dad says.

"I'm twenty-two, you can't tell me—"

"This isn't a debate." He points a stiff arm toward the hallway. "Get your ass out of my sight right now."

Neither Milt nor my dad speak until I enter my room. I press my ear hard into the wooden panel door.

"What the hell is your problem?" Milt asks.

"Not him. We're not doing this with him."

"That hurt kid's parents are leaning hard for money. It's making more dangerous folks lean harder. They'll take my bar." Milt's gruff voice breaks. "And they'll take more than that from you."

"I'll figure something out. I always do."

"We can't go faking deaths for insurance money. What few connections we have left are bailing on us," Milt says. "Marc is the key. We can rebuild everything around the kid the way it used to be. Better even."

"No!" Dad shouts. The sound of shattering glass follows two seconds later. "This needs to end with me."

"And it's going to happen if we don't do something. This isn't a random two-bit bookie knocking on the door. I'm desperate," Milt says. "You should be too, so get your head out of your ass and get the kid in the game."

"Get out, Milt. Get the hell out of my house."

A slamming door jars my concentration, and I jump back from my eavesdropping, hearing Dad's heavy footsteps approaching.

He swings open my door.

"You can come out now." He scratches his head and rolls his eyes toward his forehead. "Sorry about sending you to your room. You're right. You're too old for that."

I inch closer. "Everything okay?"

His shallow nods say yes, but his weight shifts back and forth. Not the drunk, uneasy shift I've seen too many times. This is something else. "I'm gonna call it a night."

"Hey, what about my present?"

Dad's chin hangs below his shoulders. "I don't feel up to it right now. Tomorrow."

He zombie barrels through the boxes in the hallway toward his room.

The headlights on Milt's truck stare into our front window for ten minutes after Dad adjourns to his room. Milt doesn't leave until I pull back the curtains and our eyes meet.

Milt points his finger and thumb at me like a gun. A

click of his thumb, a wink of his eye, and then a blast of exhaust as his truck races down the road.

I spend the next three days thinking about his smile while shooting his finger gun. It was genuine, but not kind.

Milt won't be receiving an invitation to Christmas dinner if I have anything to say about it.

ELEVEN

"**W**ake up, Dad." I jostle his shoulder. Saliva drips off his chin, forming a puddle on his pillowcase. *He's still drunk.* Despite the hunting knife nestled under his pillowcase, I grab his truck keys from the antique end table. First day back after break, no hot water in the shower, and I'm going to be late. A great way to kick off December.

It's only two miles. I'll go slow. It's more tank than truck, after all. I should probably be more worried about him sleeping with a knife under his pillow.

The morning dew licks my Nikes as I jog to the old pickup. I climb into the driver's seat and toss my workbag onto the passenger's seat. The beast feels more intimidating from the driver's side. I've watched Dad drive this donkey a thousand times. I can do this. Twenty-two and no license because fifteen-year-old Marc got busted for a DUI and reckless driving the day before his sixteenth birthday.

But it wasn't you.

She's right. Dad needed me to cover for him. His idea, not mine, but I followed the logic. Him in prison meant an orphaned Marc. Probation and a suspended license outweighed the idea of a foster home. In this town, foster kids never found a new home or found their way back to their old home.

Goosebumps tickle my arm as I click the key forward. The truck always resists Dad, but the engine revs to life on my first attempt for me. The sudden pounding on the windows causes me to test my seatbelt's resistance when I startle at the loud sound in the cold silence.

"What the hell do you think you're doing?" Dad yells. "Open the goddamn door and get out of my truck." His bloodshot eyes and morning breath greet me as he yanks open the door.

"Sorry." I duck in case his anger level matches my nervousness. "I can't sit in the house another day. I'm fine. Besides, I need to get started with my disciplinary hearing. They won't wait around for me forever."

"Go around the other side and get in. I'll drive your ass to school." Dad plops into the driver's seat.

I knock on the passenger side window. "Umm, hello? Can't open the door."

He lights a cigarette. The white end turns a fiery orange before fading to gray. His exhale resembles death's final kiss. I doubt smoke will ever stop fuming from his mouth. Finally, the dragon unlocks my door, and I grab the seat next to him upfront.

Dad steers us away from school and toward an old highway seldom used by locals. It connects our town with more vibrant places.

"How about we stop for coffee?" Dad's unsteady voice needs more than caffeine.

"I don't drink coffee."

"Ha! But I do." He punches my shoulder. Hard.

"Hey, injured man here." I rub my arm and furrow my eyebrows.

We toil the streets endlessly following a red car. Right. Left. Right. Right. Dad stays right on the car's bumper until he has an opportunity to pass. Then, we slow to ten miles an hour below the speed limit.

"See that?" Dad stops in the middle of a narrow road and points to the road in front of us. "Your mother would've loved it." Snow covers every lawn, and tacky Christmas decorations adorn porches and rooftops.

A loud honk from behind us makes me jump in my seat, but Dad doesn't budge off the brake pedal. "Well?"

The honking blares in a pattern this time. Beep-Beep-Ba-Beep-Beep. Pause. Beep-Beep. Dad bobs his head from side to side with each beep.

I guess the guy is tired of waiting. He pulls his red Nissan Maxima next to us with his driver-side wheels popped onto the curb, completely disregarding the rules of the highway. The driver rolls down his window, eyes of fire, and cheeks to match. He hurls insults at Dad, who answers with an extended middle finger.

"I wish he hadn't done that." Dad shakes his head. Two of his dirty fingers rub the bridge of his nose.

"You get your ass out of that piece of junk right now!" The man points at us.

My hand reaches for my phone, but Dad grabs my arm.

"Let this play out. It's time for you to start to understand who you are. What you are. And how you can use it, what you are, to pay off your debts from time to time. Okay?"

The wrinkles in his forehead and pause after his question make me believe he's asking, not telling.

"I don't have any debts," I say.

"That kid from your high school that wound up in the hospital. We, well you, racked up a pretty big debt to him and his parents. Unfortunately, they owe a shitload of money to a rather unpleasant person who happens to be the boss of the man driving that red car. In a few minutes, your debt and theirs are going to disappear. Hell, Coach Throgmorton might even forgive you."

"Really?"

Dad chuckles. "I wouldn't hold my breath."

I don't recognize the driver of the car. His three-piece suit, proper haircut, and lack of a winter beard are a dead giveaway he's from out of town. He pauses from his shouting to blow air into his fists.

"Stay here a moment while I welcome this gentleman to this lovely town of ours." His voice is both civil and refined, but his fists sport dotted black lines around every knuckle. I've seen that skin tone before. On my wrist. Moments before I sliced it. On Throgmorton's temple, right before I smashed it.

Dad hops out of the truck as I roll down my window.

"Howdy, stranger. I'd appreciate it if you didn't use that kind of language."

"Well, I'd appreciate it if your redneck ass would learn the rules of the road." A little spit foams up at the side of his chapped lips.

"My bad. Just a little reminiscing about better times and teaching my son a quick life lesson." Dad opens his arms in what some might call a prayer peace gesture.

Apparently, the stranger isn't the religious type. "How about we teach him the lesson where I shove my Italian leather shoe up your ass?" The out-of-towner leans into the Nissan's front seat and emerges with a long, gray steel rod.

My arms tense, and my clenched fists bounce in my lap. A few faint dotted black lines bloom on my knuckles. I fight the urge to jump out of the truck.

"Not sure where you're from, Mister, but around here,

we call that a crowbar, not a shoe." Dad's body bounces as he laughs.

"We'll see who's funny in about two seconds." The stranger wheels around the front of the car, wielding the crowbar high at the apex of his extended arm. "Wait a minute. I recognize you. Dollhauser is going to pay me top dollar for taking you out of play."

He makes a line for Dad.

Although the Italian shoes may serve him well in the business world, they afford little in the way of traction on the icy roads. His planted foot slides a few inches as he whacks at Dad. The slip provides Dad with an opportunity to raise his forearm and block the blow. Without so much as a flinch, he absorbs the strike and returns a closed fist to the stranger's jaw. From my perch, I watch two teeth careen off the hood of his shiny, red car and trickle to the ground. The stranger's butt tags the concrete before the crowbar.

"Take that message back to Mr. Dollhauser."

Dad drags his body toward the front of the vehicles, punches him square in the face, and lays his unconscious body in the middle of the road like a speed bump. After a quick look around, Dad fishes the car keys from the man's pockets.

I wave him back to the truck, but he has other plans. Now it's my turn to look left and right for onlookers. Sweat builds on my palms as Dad circles the car and pops its trunk. I crane my neck to get a better view, but the grimy windows and popped trunk block much of my sight.

Dad steps back enough for me to see him scanning two pieces of paper before returning them to a briefcase he tosses back into the trunk. A minute later, Dad shuts the trunk and returns the keys to the stranger's pocket.

The grin on Dad's face stretches ear to ear as he hops

back into the driver's seat, "The best part is how pissed he's going to be when he realizes his suit is ruined from the ice and snow."

"Is your arm okay?" I try to grab it, but he pulls away before I can take hold.

"I'm fine. Where did we leave off?" He looks at the truck ceiling.

"Yeah, probably, but shouldn't we talk about what just hap—"

"Marc, focus. What just happened is part of this. Part of me. Part of you. Part of it. You need to use it. Feed it. Or you'll resent it. It will resent you. Resent will grow into anger. You get angry over the wrong things, and you end up like that idiot in the road." Dad flicks a finger in the direction of the unconscious driver. "Use it to your advantage."

"By it. You mean . . ."

"Being a Cheeks. Embrace who you are. Don't let anyone judge you or tell you what you should be. Don't back down. Do something."

Do something.

Like I said.

I place my hands over my ears. "Shut up."

The voice in my head needs to leave.

Dad pulls my hands free. "Calm down. I know this is a lot to take in."

Shame rips through my innards, "We should get him help." I toss my head in the direction of the stranger's car.

"Good idea."

Dad holds nothing back, slamming his foot on the gas pedal, gunning the truck. The chains on the tires catch the road deep, and Dad drives his side of the truck directly at the man's calf. A subtle thump bounces me in my seat, not once, but twice. I fling my head around and cringe. The stranger's barefoot points in an unnatural direction.

Dad scoffs. "I was wrong. That will be the best part when he wakes up."

"Wake up?" I can't resist glancing behind us. "You just ran over him!"

"Only ran over his ankles. He'll survive. Need him alive to convey a message to more influential people. We'll call for help down the road. Now, how about that coffee?"

I exchange glances between Dad and the now barefoot man that is shrinking more and more with every foot put between us as we drive on. Is this what it will take to connect with Dad? I want to feel bad for the stranger, but no matter how deep I search my soul, I find no sympathy, only satisfaction. Growing up or growing cold? I need time away from him to think. "I should get to the school, but can we talk later?"

The spark leaves Dad's eyes, but a small grin remains on his face. "Okay."

Dad pulls the truck up to the front of the school. "Hey." He stops me before I jumped out. "Sorry you got hurt. I should have told you that before, but I promise things will be different now. They'll regret it if they come after you again."

"Thanks." I fake a smile.

This is my best opportunity to reach into Dad's brain and understand what just happened, yet the best I come up with is, "thanks?" I guess I worry, the more I learn about him, the greater my chances are of becoming him.

"Get rid of that for me, will ya?" He tosses me an Italian shoe.

TWELVE

"Hey, Marc, I'm home." Dad pulls off his cracked, brown leather jacket as he walks through the door.

"Evening, Dan." The officer's voice snaps Dad's head around.

"Howdy, Dale. What can I do for you?"

"First off, I had to escort Marc here off school property." Dale exaggerates my suspension on my first day back. In this case, any teacher, or student-teacher, is escorted from school grounds when suspended, but I can explain that to Dad in private.

"Marc—"

"Please, let me finish . . ." Dale hoists his belt, pulling his pant bottoms a few inches above his ankles. Black socks, tan pants, and a belt with two, no, three extra holes Dale must have made himself so that the belt could keep up with an expanding waist. His jaw doesn't close quite right. And his coffee-brown eyes blink with a sense of independence rather than in sync. Everything about him is off.

" . . . there's been an incident."

Dad takes off his hat and scratches his head, "Incident?"

"Seems someone assaulted a visitor to our fine town," Dale says. "Run over by a truck. Witness puts your boy in that truck."

Dad pulls his head back at the neck. "You're kidding."

I jump into the fray. "It's not like that at all." *Witness? I didn't see any witnesses.*

"Son," Dale says. "Adults are talking here." Dale puckers his lips and looks around for a place to spit.

"I'm an adult."

"You're looking at serious jail time, Marc. Checked your records, and this won't sit well with your history."

I can't blink, can't breathe, can't move.

"Dale, if this is your way of getting back at us after what happened to your nephew at the high school . . ."

"Dan, this isn't personal." Dale points to the state emblem on the shoulder of his uniform. "This is about the law."

"Bullshit!" Dad encroaches the officer's safe space. "When has it ever been about the law with you?"

"I'm not going to stand here and argue about something that's already been decided." Dale's neck muscles flex. He clears his throat and continues in a normal volume, "I'm doing you the courtesy of telling you it would be in your best interest not to disappear in the next day or two."

"Give us a moment." Dad motions me toward my room.

I grab my backpack and sling it over my shoulder.

Dale peers over Dad's shoulder, "That's an interesting shoe you got in your bag there, Marc. Fancy for a guy who's swirling the toilet bowl of shit jobs."

"Jesus, Dale. First, you threaten jail, and now you're

making fun of his shoes. You are a prick." Dad defends me for the first time in a long time.

"Shoe, Dan, and, well, that's the thing. The victim is missing a shoe. One looks just like that one your boy has."

Dammit, Marc. Why did I keep the shoe?

"It's mine." I look Dale straight in the eyes. No one lies looking someone in the eyes.

Dale steps deeper into the house. He slides his hand down toward his hip. "Mind telling me where you were today?"

"Hand feeding the homeless."

"We got ourselves a comedian." Dale lifts his belt again in his never-ending battle against the bulge. "I'm going to need to take that shoe."

I retreat two full strides. "You can't. It's mine. It's special."

Dad holds up a shaky, open hand and steps in Dale's path, "You gotta be kidding me, Dale. You've upset us enough as it is. It's time for you to go."

"Come on, Dan. We both know that's the vic's shoe. You make me get a warrant, and you might be looking at aiding and abetting. Step aside. Your days of being a lousy father are over."

Dad lunges forward and unleashes a right fist pulsating with fury. Dale staggers back and grabs the railing on the front porch. His legs wobble as he reaches for his Taser.

"Marc, get back!" Dad waves both his arms.

"Now you're gonna pay!" Dale's eyes fill with anger as his face turns red. He squeezes the trigger on his Taser, sending wires filled with electricity into Dad's chest. "How do you like that, tough guy?" Dale refuses to let go of the trigger. Five seconds, then ten.

Dad's eyes open wide, and his body convulses. Dale fills his body with white lightning. I scream when Dad's eyes roll back into his head, morphing into egg whites. Streaks of red crisscross the white ovals. Clyde's barks challenge Dale's screams of triumph, but I'll have a zombie for a father and a soon-to-be dog corpse if this continues.

How did my home turn into a haunted house overnight?

Dale repeatedly triggers the Taser. He keeps one hand on the Taser and fumbles for his gun. "I'm going to put that mutt down right now and haul both your asses off to jail. Dead if I have to!"

Dad blinks twice, and his eyes return to normal. He smiles, even though I see sadness. Despite an electric current coursing through his body, he speaks, "You will do no such thing."

Before Dale frees his gun, Dad grasps the pulsating wires and yanks forward, bringing both the Taser and Dale into range.

He reigns down electricity-filled punches with every word, "You. Will. Not. Touch. My. Son."

I lunge forward, grabbing Dad's arm. His last punch comes with me in tow, sending his full force and my entire body into Officer Dale.

Blood pours from every inch of Dale's face. I count three teeth on the floor, two deep lacerations around the eyes. His nose has been relocated, and his forehead dented. Dale's blondish beard now the epitome of blood orange.

"Is he dead?" I stutter, barely able to get the words out. The question is becoming a running theme with him.

"He isn't dead, but we have things to do and not much time." He nods.

I high step over Dale's belly into the cold air. My thin white socks offer little warmth.

The color drains from my face. "But doesn't this make us criminals?"

"Me, Marc. It makes me a criminal."

I sense his impatience.

Dad slides his hands under Dale's shoulders and hoists his torso off the floor and over his shoulder with a jerk. For a moment, I'm in awe of the sheer brute strength before reality kicks me back to our current predicament. I glance around. "Where are we going with him?"

He directs us with a flick of his head. "To my room."

Dad bulldozes straight through the boxes in the hall, and I follow in tow.

The door to his room reveals every housekeeper's worst nightmare. Old pizza crusts, empty beer cans, dirty laundry, and a mattress without a bedspread.

The box spring creaks as Dad tosses Dale on the bed like an unwanted rag doll. He pushes aside a pile of clothes and pounds a hammer first on the floor. Each hit bounces Dale.

"Come on! Seriously?" Dad shakes his head and pushes another pile of clothes to the side.

Three more attempts, two more relocated piles, and a floorboard finally pops up, exposing a thin metal lever. Dad smiles before giving it a yank. The wood board next to my foot creaks open.

"Was the lever necessary?" I ask.

"No," he laughs. "But it's pretty fucking cool, isn't it?"

One by one, he removes floorboards, exposing a crawl space wide enough for two people.

"What is that?" I step back from the hole.

"Haven't you ever read *The Tell-Tale Heart*? Poe was surreal. A goddamn genius. These boards are soundproof." He winks at me.

"Are you enjoying this?" I ask.

"Well, kinda . . ." he pauses, "aren't you?"

I don't know how to answer him, and I worry that I want to say yes, even though every part of this is wrong.

Two wrongs don't make a right. I guess I used it with coach and Donnie and Kyle. But we are piling on the wrongs so thick I can't find right with a map and a flashlight.

Dad rolls Dale from side to side. It's the only way to remove his police jacket.

"Help me lower him down. Try to be careful, but if you're not, that's fine as well," he says.

I turn off my internal dialogue and do everything Dad asks. He places a pillow under Dale's head and even covers him with a blanket. We start repositioning the floorboards.

"Oh, wait!" Dad halts work and withdraws a rusty, metallic box tucked under the boards. "Let's finish up."

I hold the last board, but my arms don't cooperate.

"Will he die?" I ask.

"Not if you don't forget about him. Although, there's probably black mold down there."

Again, with the laughing. He is enjoying this.

I dust off my hands. "What now? Do we call the police?"

"You're kidding, right? This *is* the police, and they have no interest in helping us. None of 'em in this town. Especially if you're a Cheeks."

"Then what?"

"We act fast. I need you to drive Dale's police cruiser to Mr. Chavez's house. Pull the car into his garage. The code is two-thousand fourteen."

"Hate to spoil your cloak and dagger routine, but we just sealed the keys under the floor."

Dad holds up a dirty hand and jingles the keys. "Your old man still has a few tricks up his sleeve."

"How about the fact that I'm scared shitless right now? Got any tricks for that?"

He smiles and shakes his head. "No, I don't. But you're

a smart kid. I know you. I've known you your whole life. You're ready for this. *All* of it."

He flips the keys to me. They clatter on the floor after they pass through my butterfingers.

"Well, everything but catching. Don't drive too fast." He tosses me Dale's jacket. "Put this on. Mr. Chavez is in China on business. He asked me to watch over his place since he won't be back for a few months. What better way than to park a police car in his garage?"

I can't argue with his logic.

"Go." He points to the open door. "Now!"

I hobble to the front door but hesitate when Dale's car comes into my sight.

Another wrong, but no time to debate it.

THIRTEEN

Act like you're supposed to be doing this.

Whatever challenges I expect never develop. No PTSD. No nerves. No hesitation. I guess being convicted for a vehicular crime you didn't commit doesn't translate to future trauma behind the wheel.

I leave the car running in Mr. Chavez's driveway while I punch in the code.

Two. Zero. One. Four.

I wait, but the door doesn't budge.

Somebody's bound to pass sooner rather than later. We don't live on the busiest street in town, but enough people come and go that sweat builds on my palms as each second ticks.

I press each button harder until the skin under my fingernails turns dark red.

Two. Zero. One. Four.

Nothing.

"Stupid door." I kick the white paneling, sending vibrations from the bottom to the windows at the top.

A slow rumble fills my ears. I duck around the side of the garage and use the plastic green trash can as a shield. A white Toyota Camry cruises the road in front of the house. It slows behind Dale's car, and I see the driver crane his neck.

Everyone in town gawks at police cars, fire trucks, and car accidents. The driver is probably guessing what Mr. Chavez did wrong. This isn't the forgiving kind of town.

"Keep driving," I whisper, hoping the words will catch the wind in the gray evening sky and carry my message to his ears.

The car lingers before driving away, leaving me to finish my business.

One look at the security panel has me cursing.

Two. Zero. One. Four. *Enter.*

The garage door groans to life, tugging the white paneled gate higher.

No time to waste. I hop in the car. The garage is wide and forgiving, but I proceed with care.

Mr. Chavez maintains an orderly garage. Everything has a place. More lawn care equipment than sold at the local hardware store lines the wall. Not a single piece shows a scratch, a dent, or dried dirt.

Even though I'm swimming in Dale's jacket, it keeps me warm. I hate to admit it, but it comforts me. I like the jacket.

The weather isn't conducive to a leisurely stroll without a jacket, but I don't want to be seen sprinting away from Mr. Chavez's house, so I head down the driveway and cross the road.

After a few steps, I turn my walk into a limping jog. The steam from my mouth increases with each stride, fogging my view until my house comes into view.

"Home sweet home."
It's not where you belong, she chimes.
This time I happen to agree with her.

FOURTEEN

"Dad! Where are you?" I chase my own words down the hall, finding him in his room.

He scoots back two steps from a spreading yellow puddle before zipping his pants.

"Seriously?" I shake my head less than he shakes his, um, thing. "Did you pee on Dale?"

"Don't judge me. The guy's a jerk. He deserves it."

Dad retrieves his down-jacket from the closet as he leads me to the front door.

"What about Clyde? Where is he?" I turn toward my room. Dad snatches my arm and pulls me close.

"Clyde is fine. Milt came and grabbed him along with a few items. But we need to leave. Now." He stares hard into my eyes. Every feature of his face showcases a subtle droop. Sadness or exhaustion? I can't tell, but his words are calm and calculated.

"Where are we going?"

He clears the hard stare with a soft blink and puts his hand behind my neck, pulling my forehead into his, "I'm proud of you, Marc, but it's time for you to grow up."

"And *where* do we go for that?" I feel awkward talking to the ground.

Dad releases his grip, "Not where. How." He walks to the old Nissan. "Come on."

"Why does everyone seem to forget I'm an adult already?"

"I'm not talking about age, Marc."

"If you want me to move out, then say so, but who's going to take care of you and these little situations of yours?"

"Would you get in the truck?"

"What's with all the pillows?" I open the passenger door and discover my seat occupied by a half-dozen feather-filled pillows. "Dad, there's no room for me." I squash the pillows.

"Back. You're in the back." He pulls a pillow into his lap.

I know he can be strange, but this takes the cake. "What the hell's the deal with all the pillows?"

"People sleep on them." Dad fakes a laugh.

"Very funny, but I can do without the sarcasm."

"I'll explain on the way." Dad twists the key, and the truck guts out a start.

I nestle into a group of pillows in the backseat.

"What do you call a group of pillows? A herd? A murder? A flock?" I try getting Dad to talk. Nothing he says makes sense. He sounds nuts. No, he sounds insane. I start to worry about my safety as well as his.

"What?" Dad's voice strains over the struggling engine noise.

"I'd go with a flock because of sheep. And people count sheep when they want to fall asleep," I say.

The truck reverses out of the driveway. I sit back in the

flock of pillows, satisfied with my conclusion, needing the small victory because I'm getting nowhere with him.

"Eat this." Dad tosses me two energy bars.

"But—"

"No buts. Just eat the damn things."

The truck tears down our quiet street as I choke down The Quest Hero Vanilla Caramel bars.

Hero. I like the idea, but doubt that entails taking down a cop, crooked or not.

The pillows make it difficult to sense how fast he is driving or where he is taking us, and the handful surrounding him keeps the dashboard hidden.

The passing trees signal backroads, while the lack of mailboxes led me to conclude we're heading to town's commercial side.

"My friends and I used to drive on these roads when we were younger," he starts. "Honestly, it was more racing than driving. Only a few houses out here and the deer population thinned out so much over the years. There was never a concern that Rudolph might end up doing a belly flop onto your windshield."

The trees quicken their pace in the windows. I try counting how many we pass every ten seconds, but it makes my stomach turn.

"We'd race on this road almost every night. My dad was none-the-wiser. I loved this road until the night we lost your mother."

The cab of the truck falls silent. Even the engine quiets, despite trees flying by faster.

"How can you pass it off so casually? You wrecked. She died. Or were you so drunk you don't remember?" I hammer-fist the pillows. He never apologized or even acknowledged what I did—what I'm still doing—for him.

Why should I expect him to talk about what happened with Mom?

"People talk, Marc. They talk without knowing. I didn't kill her. She tried to help, but it should have been the other way around. Your mother is the only person who was ever able to help me."

He wipes away a few rebellious tears.

My mind races with the thought my last seven years have been one big lie. Misplaced anger. Wasted time. And now, more anger. Different anger. "If you didn't kill her, then who did?"

"The whole night is a blur. I can't remember a goddamn thing." Dad smashes his fist on the steering wheel, deforming the circle. "And it's not the first time." He sighs. "Piranha, the Cheeks men. All of us. Put us together, and it's a feeding frenzy." Dad inhales deep, recoiling snot escaping his nose.

"When I was about your age, I fell off the roof. Broke my back. Bone from my arm poked through the skin. I screamed. It was the only thing I could do. My dad comes running out of the house holding a pillow. I tell him I can't feel my legs. Every breath was a fight. I blubbered, hyperventilating and scared. My dad tells me everything is going to be okay. He mumbles he's sorry, but he has to do it.

"Everything goes black. Breathing became impossible. I wanted to kick, but my legs wouldn't move. I wanted to push him off me, but I only had one good arm. I wanted to scream, but the pillow smothering my face prevented any sound. It didn't take but a minute or two before I passed into the void. Not dead, mind you, but somewhere beyond life."

I push every pillow as far from my face as I can.

"Then I heard a voice. Cold and uncaring at first, but she convinced me not to quit. I flailed with the last bit of my soul. Fortunately, the bone protruding from my forearm had splintered. The sharpest pieces sliced my dad's face, cutting across his forehead, and coming to a rest in his eye.

"I woke up in the hospital. Whatever happened after my father released his grip on that pillow is a mystery to me. I never saw him again. My mother sent him away. I guess part of him still loved me enough to stay away. I was told he and my uncle shared a house until they died."

He glances over his shoulder. "I've done dark things. Things I'm not proud of. I made so many mistakes, but not this time, not with you. Not again. A mistake with you would be one too many."

Sweat drips from my palms. Grandpa tried to kill him . . . or grandpa did kill him? I swallow, but my mouth has gone dry. I want to know more, but I don't ask. His sudden increase in speed distracts me. The engine strains on every level of its being as Dad floors the accelerator.

"Dad, what are you doing?" I push pillows to the side, hurrying to find my seatbelt. "Stop! We'll figure it out." The button to release it jams. I bloody my fingertips scratching the metal.

"You're stronger than you know, Marc. I couldn't beat the curse. Mom couldn't help me. Milt tried but failed. But I think I can help you. Right here. Right now.

"Every man in our family has failed, but you're smarter than them. Smarter than me. I never learned from my mistakes, but you can. Every single one of them. I wrote them down."

The trees blur together as the truck fights to hold its integrity.

Dad punches three numbers on his phone, followed by the speakerphone.

"Nine-one-one, what's your emergency?" A voice asks.

"There's been a car accident on Route Eight, near the

corner of Route Eight and Munson Pass. Send help," Dad says.

"We'll get help, Dad. You don't have to." My stomach tightens. Tears cascade down my face. My begging morphs into whimpers.

"Marc, you'll need to bring me back."

"Back? What do you mean back?" I ask, but I understand. I've been brought back, but never by non-medical personnel.

"This will work. It has to. Tomorrow you'll just be Marc, and I'll just be your dad finally able to protect you." Dad lowers his head. "Remember. People talk without knowing all the facts."

He rips the wheel left, sending my head into a pillow bank. The feathered flock does little to stifle the high squeal of the motor. Seconds later, the sound of twisting metal shatters both my eardrums and sense of well-being. Dad wraps the old truck around the same massive oak tree that claimed Mom.

The collision frees snow nestled in the most prominent branches high above the ground. The oak stands its ground as if to say; no human-made machine will end its one-hundred-year reign in this county. Within seconds, the roof of the truck peels back, exposing the bright morning sky. My body contorts in ways reserved for circus performers, but I never lose consciousness.

It takes a solid thirty seconds for me to catch my breath and rattle reality back into my brain.

"Dad?" I push bloodied pillows aside.

"Under your seat. Bandages. A medical kit. Water." His wheezing breath makes him difficult to understand. "Patch yourself first, if you need it. Then get the portable defibrillator out of the case in the back. Instructions are on the box. It's simple. Zap me back to life once I'm gone."

"Gone? No, I'm not letting you go. I don't want to be alone." I stretch toward the front seat. "Argh!"

Pain radiated from my thigh to my toes.

My leg doesn't follow my body. A piece of the truck impaled my thigh into the floorboard. Feathers mimic falling snow turned burgundy as they land on my leg. A few more clog my mouth with every deep breath.

"Dad?" My quivering voice fills the quiet sky as far as the eye could see. "Dad, I can't reach you. What do I do? What do I do!"

His silhouette forms beyond the tufts of floating white. As my vision focuses, the sunlight illuminates what's left of his upper body and face. His eyes stare over my shoulder.

"Dad?" My voice drops. I'm not sure I even said anything.

A blink.

My heart quickens.

He labors for breath between his broken words. "Milt. Lest. Her. Be careful."

"I don't understand. What should I do?"

His eyes close but don't reopen.

"Marc, find your Kismet." He gasps one final time, "It doesn't have to be a curse."

FIFTEEN

Dad died a week ago, and I have yet to go home. Glenn's folks put me up in their spare room. A week of being force-fed vegan and healthy food has me thinking Dad is the lucky one. I'm catching a sniff of freedom today, visiting my father's lawyer.

"Thank you for coming in today, Mr. Cheeks. Let me start by saying, I'm sorry to hear of your father's passing. He was a good man." The attorney points to the plush, black leather chair, caddy-corner to his desk. "Please have a seat. I'm your attorney, James Layer."

I survey the room. I could comfortably live in his office for the rest of my life. A big-screen television, two leather chairs, a couch twice my length, and a mini-fridge tucked neatly in the wall.

The tall city buildings flood the window behind Mr. Layer. I can't help but marvel at the pointed towers as I limp to the chair. My whole life, I only knew the four walls around me, the schools I attended, the local hospital I called my vacation home, and the mountains shrouding our town in shadows.

"Care for a soda or snacks?" He points to the fridge. A basket of chips, pretzels, candy bars, and breakfast bars fill a leather basket.

I'm not shy about grabbing one of everything, sitting back down, and stuffing my face. An ice-cold Mountain Dew works perfectly to wash down all the salty and sugary goodness.

"Where is everyone else?" I ask the man wearing a suit that probably cost more than my house while wiping my mouth clean with the sleeve of my sweatshirt.

"You're the only one, Mr. Cheeks. You and your uncle are the only people named in your father's will. We've already informed your uncle of what he needs to know. Well, as best as he could comprehend, anyhow."

"Wait." The new leather crunches as I lean forward. "I have an uncle?" The importance of the city fades in the background. For the first time since Dad's death, an ember of hope emerges in my life.

"Yes."

Questions fly from my lips. "Why isn't he here?"

His eyes study every word on the papers in front of him with youthful vigor. No wrinkles on his face nor a single whisker. Every hair lay precisely where you'd expect. "I'm afraid I don't know. And it wouldn't be my place to say even if I did." His dry voice doesn't fit his youthful appearance. It never pauses when it isn't supposed to, nor goes too fast when it shouldn't.

Mr. Layer and his manicured fingernails tap the papers' edges on his mahogany desk, lining up the documents until they are perfect. I imagine he doesn't want to risk a paper cut to his soft skin. "May we continue?"

"Yeah." I sink into the chair defeated and can't decide how to bring up the cop, but what if I imagined it? Maybe shock from my dad dying.

Dad's dead.

"Don't worry. Your father has taken care of you."

Those were words I've not heard since Mom died.

"That'd be a first." I struggle to find sentences longer than a few words. Regular guy or not, I feel intimidated.

"I understand this is a difficult time for you, Mr. Cheeks. We're going to cover a lot here, so I'm happy to answer any questions you may have when I'm done," He pauses and folds his hands. A gaudy diamond ring adorns his pinky finger. "Until you are satisfied." I raise my eyebrow at his patronizing tone as if I am nine years old. But I keep my mouth shut.

The man sounds like he cares, which I believe is rare for a lawyer. And he's right. He rambles on, stressing words like estate and bequeath and in-perpetuity and trust as if I don't know what they mean. It's common sense stuff, and I'm impressed my parents took the time to plan anything out, let alone something advanced.

I stare out the window, pondering the excitement of a jump from this height until he utters the name Nellie Cheeks.

"Nellie Cheeks. Who's that?" I doubt my uncle's name is Nellie. Then again, my family doesn't make the best choices.

Mr. Layer presses a red, circular button on his phone. "Barbara, please hold my calls." His voice drops lower, losing its robotic tone. "The conversation we are about to have never happened. Okay?" Mr. Layer pops to his feet and scoots a butt cheek onto the corner of the desk, balancing himself with a single straight leg. "Your father trusted you."

I nod.

"He trusted me as well, but I'm afraid he didn't tell me

why he did what he did. Although your father wasn't a rich man, he was insured."

"Wonders never cease," I sneer.

He bobs his head in agreement. "Your parents owned sizable insurance policies. When they passed away, the life insurance company sent the proceeds to an offshore trust fund. You are its beneficiary.

"The fund has money to pay for necessities like groceries and clothes. You can GrubBud or GrocerDash what you want online to have it delivered to your door since you can't drive to the grocery store. Like the gas, water, and electricity, everything else will be handled on your behalf by us. You're not lavishly wealthy by any means, but you won't have to worry about your necessities. We're waiting on the insurance company to finish their review of your father's death, but I'm confident you'll receive the funds."

"Can I ask how much?"

"Seven-hundred thousand dollars."

My head swirls. "So, I can get a new car? Or a nice used car? It won't be Ferrari stupid or anything, but it would be nice to drive something more metal than rust."

"Let's hold off on that until you get your license reinstated," he says. Guess he knows more about me than I realized.

"Cable? High-speed internet? All the streaming services? A smartphone? That should be no problem, so that's a plus." The thought of quiet nights alone scares me. I didn't sleep much before Dad died, and I'm not sure I'll ever sleep again with my parents gone.

Mr. Layer's face hardens around the eyes, birthing wrinkles on his brow. "We'll get to that, but Marc, we have more pressing matters to discuss."

I smash my fist against his mahogany desk, or whatever

expensive wood a fancy lawyer would buy. "I need an answer, dammit!"

Mr. Layer juts backward.

Forcing a calming breath, I manage to fight the tears trying to escape. "I'm sorry. I don't know what just happened." I exhale.

He straightens his shirt and cracks his neck side to side. "Continuing on. It's fair to say your dad didn't trust many people. Fortunately, we could assist each other with challenging situations, so he and I established a strong rapport."

Dad helped someone other than himself? That's a new one.

"Like what?" I ask.

"Unfortunately, I'm not at liberty to say, but please know I think highly of your father." Mr. Layer smiles. "He was a good man."

It is the kindest thing anyone has said to me about him since his funeral. Probably since Mom's funeral.

"The best part for you is the trust pays an ongoing retainer fee for my legal services. In short, I am at your disposal whenever you need me."

Mr. Layer withdraws a key from his pocket and approaches a shiny wooden cabinet behind me. With one turn of the key, he exposes the inside of the cabinet.

He turns my way and holds out his hand.

I grab the long black metallic cylinder. It's lightweight, thin, and smooth, with two colored buttons in the middle. "A flashlight?" I ask.

"No, not a flashlight."

He scurries to his desk. For a man of calm demeanor, he transforms into a kid on Christmas morning.

Mr. Layer flashes a plain white sheet of paper in front of me. "Here. Take this" After I take it, he continues.

"Now point that at the paper and hit the green button," he instructs.

"It's only a flashlight."

"Look closer."

I inspect the light. "Nellie Cheeks?"

The name Nellie Cheeks illuminates in black within the white circle of light. The light tingles my fingers, warming them the longer I hold it.

"I don't understand. What is it?" I ask.

"Here, you better . . . " Mr. Layer clears a spot on his desk and beckons me over, indicating I'm to set the paper down.

"Okay, press the green button."

I follow his direction, and the name illuminates once more.

"Now hold down the black button for five seconds. Keep the light steady."

Steam rises off of the paper after I press the button. Five seconds later, a bright flash blinds me.

"Let go of the button," Mr. Layer's voice squeaks.

I blink a few times to regain my vision. The once blank piece of paper reads Nellie Cheeks in perfect cursive print.

"Voila. Your trustee." Mr. Layer's pearly whites flash every dollar of his high hourly fees.

"I'm afraid I don't understand, Sir." I hold up the paper to examine it closer. The handwriting is the same as Mom's, but her name isn't Nellie.

"Who's Nellie?"

Mr. Layer clears his throat. "Someone who exists only on paper and in the legal system. Son, your father knows you are old enough to care for yourself. Unfortunately, he's worried there are those out there who might try to take advantage of you. Use you. The trust protects the money until your thirty-fifth birthday. It's located offshore and sheltered from civil suits, a problem your father encountered with his many, ah, altercations. The day after your thirty-fifth birthday, Nellie Cheeks will sadly pass away." He uses air quotes around the last two words.

I quickly realize I've underestimated Dad's intelligence and planning.

"With this device, you possess the ability to sign almost anything you need, provided you are out of sight. When you require a witness or something notarized, you'll come here to my office." Mr. Layer lifts himself onto his desk. "Unfortunately, if you abuse this power, then you're likely to get caught. If that happens, we'll all end up in court."

"Don't abuse the signature power." I sigh and drop my head. "Got it."

Mr. Layer scribbles a few notes on a scrap of paper and folds it in half. He holds it out. "Give this to my secretary. We'll hire a housekeeper to come by and clean the house, do the laundry, that sort of stuff. Now here's what I need from you." He counts out my tasks on his fingers. "Stay out of trouble. Go to work. Stay out of trouble. And stay out of trouble." Four fingers.

"I'm sensing a trend."

"A trend your family has trouble avoiding."

"About the housekeeper . . . " Visions of a decaying zombie cop corpse bursting through the floorboards and tearing some old woman's limbs from her body flood my mind.

Mr. Layer raises a silencing hand. "I'm aware of the incident. While solving one problem, it created another. I'm examining solutions, but it's complicated with your father gone. Milt has been attending to your guest and keeping him comfortable. Most importantly, alive. You can live in the house but stay out of that room. We'll hold off on the housekeeper until I figure out what to do, but you might want to load up on air fresheners and stick towels under the door. It's in all of our best interests if we can handle this on our own. Understood?"

My conscious gnaws at my gut. Nothing about this feels right, but anything I do will probably land me in jail. What choice do I have? He's a lawyer. He knows about this stuff. He's on my side. Follow the plan.

I grip the device in my hand. The cold steel frame fits my palm as though it belonged only in my hand. "Is this stuff legal?"

"Sometimes, it's better to ask forgiveness rather than permission." He winks.

Even his wink is high class.

"Gotcha. Lie low, stay out of trouble, and keep my mouth shut." I try to wink back, but both eyes slam shut. "Is that everything?"

"One minute." Mr. Layer extends his wrist, fully exposing his shiny gold cufflinks. "May I see it?"

I hand the device to him.

He walks around his mahogany desk. Five seconds later, a flash brightens the room. After flipping over a few papers, he repeats the same action.

"There we go." Mr. Layer grabs a manila envelope from his top drawer and slides it across the desk.

"What's this?" I ask.

"You'll see when you open it," he answers. "But maybe wait until you're on your way home."

"So, that's it?"

"Yep. That's it." He hands me the device. "You'll hear from me again, but until then, best of luck, Marc. He extends his arm and offers his well-manicured fingers.

I fumble for a proper goodbye but awkwardly offer a fist bump for no reason.

He smiles. "I'm down." Mr. Layer punches rather than bumps.

On my way to the door, I watch him shake his hand, top teeth on his bottom lip, fighting back a few choice words to deal with the pain.

"Marc, Milt asked that you swing by and visit him. He may be able to help you, but I wouldn't rely too heavily on the kindness of strangers if you know what I mean."

SIXTEEN

"Milt's Bar, please." I settle into the cab, trying my best to touch as little of the sticky, faux leather seat as possible.

The cabbie looks at me cockeyed. "You ain't the first person to go straight for the bottle after meeting with your lawyer." His smoke-and-onion-filled breath seeps through the glass separating passenger and driver. "I recommend bourbon. If you're gonna drink yourself onto the floor, do it with American liquor." He reaches forward, punches a few buttons on the meter, and eases the cab into drive. "Get comfy. GPS says it's gonna be a slow trip."

Dad believed in me. It's time to grow up. The words rattle around my head. I guess age didn't matter. Staying at home made me still a kid in the eyes of many.

I peel open the manila envelope.

A single sheet of white-lined paper remains nestled in the envelope. I fish it out, nestle my body deep into the vinyl backseat, and read.

. . .

Marc,

I think these letters are supposed to start: if you're reading this, it means I'm dead.

Unfortunately, I've known you'd be reading a letter like this since the day your mother died, so we can skip the cliché.

You need to know I didn't kill your mother. It's important you believe that. I've spent the last few years working with Milt trying to figure out what happened that night. Every avenue has been a dead end.

I wish I could give you answers, but I can only offer you hints. Hints about who you are and what you are.

You're a Stitch, like all the Cheeks men. No matter how badly we get banged up, we can be stitched back together. Like new. No, better than new.

I've wanted to tell you so many times, but I was afraid of losing the hope this might have skipped you. I needed that hope to keep going after your mom died.

That hope died on the kitchen floor. At that moment, I realized you were like me and my brother.

Remember our conversations, and you'll find the phrase you need to understand. Clichés come from a buried truth. We are that truth.

Whatever doesn't kill you DOES make you stronger. It's a wonderful gift, but a slippery slope. The stronger you get, the more you'll want.

I left you something. It tells you everything I know. Everything I can't put in a letter.

I'm sorry to leave you with so many questions.

*Don't mourn me. My tortured soul rests. Be wary
of the tortured souls still around.*

Make your own path. My path failed.

*Your mother and I couldn't be prouder to call
you our son. You're ready for this.*

Love,
Dad

*P.S. – Find people you can trust. Start with Milt. He'll know what
to do to help you until you find yourself. He's the only one who was
ever able to help me.*

THE P.S. IS RAGGED and hurried. My dad must have been in a different state of mind because the handwriting appears off. My guess is he was near the end, near the final time in the truck.

I read the letter four times before we pull up in front of a rickety building twice condemned by the health department. Milt's stays open, not only because he offers cheap wings and cheaper beer, but serves alcohol two hours later than any place in town. Every other place shuts off their lights at midnight. They say nothing good happens after midnight, and our town is living proof, mostly thanks to my dad.

I sit in the back of the cab staring at the bar's red door; showing years of wear, the bottom is worn worse than the middle. Probably from all the drunks kicking it open. Milt's thrives as the last stop on any drinking tour. No normal sober person dares to walk in the place, other than Dad.

Poor Clyde lay somewhere inside. I imagine Milt tossing him scraps of fat from leftover chicken wings, but a little indulgence might be a good thing.

The driver presses a button on his meter. "Here you go."

"Thanks." My jeans stick to the seat as I try sliding out the door. I can't get much push from my injured leg, so the process takes a minute, rather than seconds. Puncture wounds seem to require longer to heal than my other injuries. A tetanus booster accompanied this wound. Lucky me. Damn thing stung like a bitch.

"Come on, man, I've got other fares. Move it along."

"I'm sorry. I'm trying." I strain, but the stitches pop in my thigh.

Stitched back together and better than new? Bullshit.

A deep purple stain soaks my jeans.

"You better not get any blood in my cab! I have a strict no bleeding policy."

I press both palms hard against my leg. The warm, crimson liquid detours away from my hands and down my calf.

"Shit," I mumble, lifting my leg in a futile effort.

Blood drips onto the worn gray carpeting of the cab.

"You're going to pay for that!" The driver points to a sign reading: *Bodily fluid stains - $150 fee.*

"I don't have any money." I raise my hands, attempting to look innocent but only succeed in freeing the blood flow.

I glance at the darkening carpet under my foot. A circular black hole encompassed by a silver rim meets my eyes when I look back toward the driver.

"I suggest you find some money—" he eases back the gun's hammer with a metallic click— "quickly."

I yank the tattered camouflage wallet from my back pocket, but it only contains Mr. Layer's business card, my license, and a Polar Ice Caps Frozen Yogurt rewards card good for two medium-sized cups.

"You're not a frozen yogurt fan by any chance?"

The driver waves the barrel in my face. "Do I look like I eat any goddamn yogurt?"

I don't know what to say or do. Mr. Layer's card might offer a solution, but patience doesn't seem high on this guy's list of traits.

A rapid tapping on the driver's window redirects the tension.

The hunter becomes the hunted.

The driver stares into not one but two barrels. Milt stands square, resting the butt of the shotgun against his broad shoulders. A faded brown outline on his leather jacket hints this isn't the first time he's nestled the gun there.

"Your business here is done," Milt shouts through the window. "Put the gun down. Let the kid out. And get the hell off my property."

Milt flicks his head in my direction. The pain. The blood. The sticky seats. None of it matters. I scurry from the back of the cab and tumble into the dusty parking lot. Nice to have someone looking out for me, someone Dad says I can trust.

The driver guns the gas pedal before I finish closing the door. The cab's black tires kick up rock-salt as the car beats a path down the narrow lane.

Milt chuckles, "That there is a big mistake. He's going to hit a patch of ice on that turn before the bridge and lose traction." He aims at the cab. "Just in case, I'll help him along."

Milt steadies himself and fires a blast of shells toward the cab. The back windshield explodes in a cloud of glass, reflecting rainbows as the pieces fall to the earth. The gun's recoil, combined with the ice patch on which he stood, sends Milt sprawling to the ground and the weapon bouncing a few feet out of his reach. The cab veers hard right and fishtails into Munson's Creek, which locals know is more river than creek.

Old Bud Munson didn't want townsfolk fearing floods during the rainy season, so he opted for the friendliest sounding name he could conjure. Unfortunately, over the decades, the creek has grown angry, swallowing up several houses she deemed too close to her banks.

A thin sheet of ice covers the top. Not quite thick enough to skate on, but enough to protect the fish below. Amazing how ice can form on such fast-flowing water. Most folks argue it isn't natural, but the bitter cold and early winter snow give them little to contemplate. Munson's Creek is as mean as ever, and right now, she has her sights set on the crappy cab and its driver.

"Where's the phone? I need to call an ambulance!" I shout.

"He's squeezing down on family. You. So, here's what we are going to do. First, you're gonna help me to my feet. Then we're gonna check on that piece of garbage. If his car is down on the banks, then we'll deal with it. I got a feeling Munson swallowed him up in her belly. Nothing for us to do if that's the case."

I tug on Milt's arm, unsure of his words. "But we could call for help. They might—"

"NOTHING for us to do." Milt's voice drops an octave. "After that, I believe I'm going to have myself a drink, and then we can get down to business."

I take hold of Milt, marrying our dirty hands, and help him up.

"Here." I offer the shotgun I had retrieved from the ground.

He shakes his head. "Don't want it. It's yours now. Wasn't mine no-how. Belonged to your old man. Check the barrel."

I trace my fingers across the roughly carved letters.

CHEEKS

We follow the tire tracks off the road to the banks of the river. The shotgun works exquisitely as a cane, although a part of me is afraid I'll accidentally pull the trigger and launch myself three feet into the air.

"Don't get too close. She's bound to try for us as well," Milt warns.

"I don't understand. Where's the car? I get it's a deep creek and all, but shouldn't there be something? There's not even a hole in the ice."

A frothy wave invades the banks where we stand. Milt jumps back while I'm forced to throw myself to the ground to avoid the creek's reach. The white foam top increases six inches, and the water roars as it picks up speed.

"It's not our problem now, Marc. He won't be the first dark secret buried in Munson's Creek, and he's not nearly the worst. But we need to remove any traces of the cab being here. I think I have a couple of shovels that should do the trick."

Is this my life now? Nothing but death?

Dad trusts Milt, but every inch of me wants to run away. But I need answers, and I'd even take a haunting from Dad to get them if I could.

"Not that I don't appreciate your help, but don't you have a bar to run? Customers? People to shoot?" My hands shake.

"Not today," Milt answers. "Closed to train a new employee."

"Who's the unlucky victim?" I ask.

"Name's on the gun."

SEVENTEEN

"Where do I start?" I glance around the kitchen. A grill stained brown from twenty years of frying burgers. A prep station with more roaches than metal. A cutting board wearing deep cuts courtesy of Milt's anger. Or maybe from Dad. And a fryer that churns out crisp wings and peanut-oil shoestring fries that draws every drunk from three counties like moths to a flame.

I snatch a spatula from the counter and bounce my shoulders to keep pace with my racing heart, as if I'm preparing for a competitive cooking show, but I have no clue what I'm doing. Worse, I'm not sure why I'm here.

"Not here." Milt points to the storeroom. "There, but first, we gotta take care of something."

Woof. Woof.

His massive paws clatter across the sticky wood floor, leash trailing behind him.

"Clyde!"

I drop to my knees and let him plow me over. Pain. No pain. I don't care.

"I missed you, buddy. Who's a good boy? Who's the best boy?"

He flops to his side and surrenders his belly.

"All right, you've said your hello, but now you have to say goodbye," Milt says, waving a shadow into the room.

A pair of fur-covered, knee-high brown UGG boots hug Susan's familiar blue jeans. Her pink down-jacket and matching knit hat are more suited for the white-collar ski hills than our town.

"Hey, Marc," Susan says.

"Hiya, Susan."

"Seems like we can't get away from each other," she laughs uncomfortably, not cute. Almost fearful.

"What are you doing here?" I ask.

"She's going to take care of Clyde." Milt jumps in. "While you're training."

"But . . ."

Susan's soft fingers touch my neck and shoulder. "I'll take great care of him. Won't let him anywhere near Glenn."

"I know you will, but he's all I have left," I say.

"And that's why I'll give him attention every day and all the treats he can stomach without throwing up on my carpet." Susan winks.

"You'll go broke before you find his limits." I force a laugh.

"I'll come back around once he's settled," Susan says.

"Marc, we gotta get started. Clock's a-ticking," Milt says.

I hug Clyde one last time before I follow Milt into the back. A full bathroom sits with a door ajar. For a hole-in-the-wall establishment, I have to admit the shower, sink, and countertop appear top of the line. A twin bed hugs the far wall with a small reading light attached to a metal frame.

Kegs and cases of beer litter the floor. The wobbly, metallic shelves hold dozens of sauce jars: buffalo, teriyaki, something called The Flame Thrower, honey BBQ, Thai sriracha, and one labeled Sh*t Your Pants.

"This sounds like it tastes awesome," I say, pointing to the profanity titled jar.

"It's my best seller," Milt replies.

"Seriously?"

"I shit you not." Milt laughs. "You see what I did there?"

How Dad was friends with this guy, I have no idea.

"So, am I supposed to do a keg stand or something?"

Milt rolls his eyes. "Like you've even done a keg stand."

"Well—"

"I didn't think so."

Milt pushes aside a pile of soda syrup, uncovering a huge, seven-foot-tall safe. It included a narrow one foot long by four inches wide window about eye level for an adult.

And no combination dial.

"Keep something valuable in there?" I ask.

Milt eases the handle lower and struggles to open the cast-iron door.

He takes a minute to catch his breath.

"Get in."

I glance around, looking for someone else in the room. No way I'm getting in there.

"Umm, why?"

"Part of your training means helping me out around the bar. The other part is trusting me," Milt says. "I'm asking you politely to step inside."

"But . . ."

"Your dad never questioned me. He'd tell you to do exactly the same as I've asked you to do." Milt squints his eyes and stares directly into mine. "He's not here though, so you listen to me now, and we call it even for me helping you with the cabbie."

Nothing like putting this trust thing to the test on day one.

"Fine." I walk into the three-foot-wide opening. The darn thing has to be three or four feet deep as well.

"Here. Take this." Milt hands me a thermometer.

"A thermometer? You gonna cook me?" I stare at the glass and mercury as the door slams shut with a boom that reverberates through my entire body. "Milt?"

I run my hands across the rough walls searching for a latch, but the rugged cast-iron surface covers every inch of the interior other than the window.

A hissing sound permeates from the floor.

I slam my fist against the door.

"Milt! Let me out of here!" I shout until my throat turns raw. "Milt."

I throw my shoulder against the door, but the box doesn't move. Breathing the thickening air becomes difficult. Sweat trickles from my brow as the sweltering air consumes me.

The constant hissing assaults my ears and my eyes.

My skin singes and turns pink when I push against the quickly warming door. I center myself in the hot-box and rip off my shirt.

Tapping on the window interrupts the hissing.

Milt holds a sign for me to read.

What's your temperature?

Oh my God, he is cooking me. Am I going to be served as wings tonight? I wonder what sauce will make me taste best. What if I'm a Sh*t Your Pants guy?

Get it together, Marc.

I flip Milt my middle finger.

He turns his back to me as sweat pours through my eyes. The salt burns. I consider breaking open the thermometer and drinking the mercury to end it quicker.

Milt turns with a new message.

Need to know when to pull you out before it's too late.

Underneath it a single word.

TRAINING.

You have to be freaking kidding me.

I poke the thermometer at my mouth. Motor functions, even simple ones, become a struggle. It requires three attempts to stab the thermometer into the Sahara Desert that has become my mouth.

I swallow the last of my saliva. It goes down like two pounds of wet sand.

The hissing pushes harder. I sway right. The cast-iron wall brands my shoulder with a red blob. Overcorrecting my body left, and I force a hand against the wall to protect the side of my face. My fingers surrender their top layer of flesh.

Milt pounds on the window.

I balance myself in the center of the hot-box and yank the thermometer from my mouth. The silver metal pushes the upper limits of its glass casing. I shove it back in my mouth and finger one-zero-four.

Another blast of heat follows, increasing hissing. My legs buckle, and I sacrifice the knuckle skin on my injured hand for a temporary retrieve of balance. Milt's eyes dart into view through the window. A familiar What's your temperature? sign flashes.

I signaled one-zero-five despite the thermometer pushing one-o-six. My left hand no longer functions, so one-zero-five was my limit.

Unfortunately, my bladder-control loses function, but on the plus side, I don't notice much difference given the sweat filling my jeans.

A mangled, bloodied body appears next to me. I would fall back to get away, but there is no place to go. I'd gasp, but I can't breathe anymore. "Welcome to Hell. I've been waiting for you."

"Dad?" The word comes out strangled.

"Officer Dale is here as well."

Dale's blue skin matches his blue officer's uniform.

"He looks blue. Shouldn't he be red?" I ask.

"No, Marc. You did that. He suffocated under those boards in our house." Dad pats me on the shoulder. "I couldn't be prouder. We should throw you a parade. Now hug your old man."

I lean in, and Hell's fire rolls up my entire chest.

Pain snaps me back to reality. My body sizzles against the door of the hot-box. Blisters push the surface of my skin to their breaking point. Blood boils underneath each as I struggle to center myself and figure out what is real.

A single click interrupts the hissing.

A whoosh of cold air sweeps in on all sides as the seal breaks. My body crumples onto the cool storeroom floor as Milt releases me from Dante's prison.

"Holy shit! Four-twenty-five! Your old man never made it to four-twenty-five in the hot-box!" Milt screams. He snatches the thermometer from my mouth. "One-ten! How in the hell are you still alive?"

Thirty seconds later, I'm not.

EIGHTEEN

"What in the actual fuck, Milt? You just tried to kill me!"

"Why are you worried about something that happened yesterday?" Milt asks without so much as a change in tone.

"I was out for a day?"

"Get over it. I'm making you stronger. You need to live up to your pop's legacy."

"By becoming fried chicken?" I stare at the beet-red skin on my arms, pushing a fingertip deep into my forearm. The spot turns bright white before fading to a burgundy red. "Planning on serving me on wing night?" My left hand hurts like hell. The skin grows back by the minute while the red coloring refuses to let go.

"I peg you more of a Thanksgiving turkey."

"Ha. Ha."

"I didn't kill you, kill you. Besides, whatever doesn't kill you—"

"There's no qualifying killing. This isn't a fucking middle-school relationship. You guys and that ridiculous cliché."

"When are you going to realize that saying is life for you? Your dad and I pulled that hot-box trick at least a half-dozen times a year, but heatstroke isn't his thing. He called the rush a let-down." Milt glances at my hand. "His skin grew back faster and never got so red. Besides, the off-duty EMTs brought you back in under a minute. Barely broke a sweat, unlike you. Check your drawers. You slept in that."

"You let me sleep in this last night?"

"Two nights." Milts flicks his chin in my direction. "New pair of pants and underwear along with a dozen wings, fries, and four rolls on the plate behind you. Figure you're hungry."

I soaked my jeans thoroughly, but I couldn't care less. Every muscle in my body pulsates, flexing with newfound strength blossoming from the pain. After I change my clothes, I wolf down the entire plate in two minutes. Milt tells me how the hot-box can hit two-thousand degrees if left unchecked, but Dad rigged it with a heat regulator.

"So, is there a point to all this training? Do I have a future in power-lifting?" I ask.

"You're going to need it. We're both going to need it."

"If you think I'm going to carry your kegs all around this place—"

"There's a bigger picture here. Your dad saw it when he was your age, but then he lost sight and couldn't find his way back in time." Milt signs the cross. Not something I've seen him do before. "You gotta trust me. There's a time when you're gonna need that strength, all of it, and more. When people find out what you are, what you can do, they'll come to challenge you, to use you, or to kill you if it comes to that. A lot of those scars on your pops weren't self-inflicted if you get what I'm saying."

I remember plenty of nights with slow passing trucks in

front of our house, random calls in the middle of the night, broken windows accompanied by messages my parents never let me see. They happened before Dad left town on what Mom called business trips. Never saw, hell, I never heard of a man who experienced so many accidents while traveling. But every time he came home, the trucks stopped passing for months, no windows were shattered, and we slept through the night in silence.

Guess I let naivety rule my youth. "Dad never left town, did he?"

"What happened to your dad was no accident," Milt says.

"No shit. I was right there in the truck. He drove straight into that tree on purpose."

"And you think that was the first time he's ever done that sort of thing?" Milt asks.

"Um." It's hard to see after living in the dark shadow of lies for so long.

Milt shakes his head. "See, you don't know a goddamn thing. That tree may be the taker of most lives, but it gave him the biggest strength boost of anything that ever done your pops in. Your dad wouldn't do himself in that way. Not for good. Whatever plan he had, someone sabotaged it, and I have a good idea who."

Considering no airbags deployed and his seatbelt broke, I assumed something was wrong.

You know what they say when you assume. She chimes in my head after a long absence.

"Get out of here!"

Milt assumes I'm yelling at him.

"I'm serious. Your dad constantly borrowed money from the wrong people. Then, he made some bad bets, Marc, and he lost. Worst damn gambler I've ever seen, and stubborn to boot. He couldn't pay. They sent a guy to collect, not only from your dad but a few other deadbeats. Your dad got to this fancy out-of-towner first."

"He didn't happen to wear Italian shoes, did he?" I dread the answer.

"Pretty good chance."

I let it happen. I watched it play out from the front seat of the truck.

"Who's they?"

"I'm not one-hundred percent sure, but I'll find out, and when I do, I need you to be ready.

WE REPEAT the process six times over the next two weeks. Each time becomes easier, and I come out of the other side feeling better and more focused, once the light-headedness wears off.

I don't love it, but I don't hate it either. It requires three showers to cool my skin from lobster red to a pale ivory. Milt suggests bath bombs, but I'm not sure if he's being literal with the bomb part or talking about the scented stuff from Bath 'n' Body Works.

In between, I spend as much time eating wings as slinging them out to customers. Shamefully, I admit the *Sh*t Your Pants* sauce is pretty damn good. Eating the day before getting in the hot-box is not so good. I avoid that mistake a second time.

Bright lights challenge me constantly, so most afternoons, I sleep on a cot in the bar's dingy storeroom, only visiting my birth house to shower. Milt assures me he's addressed my *flooring* problem but asks that I don't go in dad's old room, and I take no issue adhering to the request. Wish he'd figure out a way to stop my pupils from going rogue after every training incident. Damn things open so wide I can practically see in the dark, but sunlight is a bitch. He tries to nickname me Vamp, but I refuse to answer him for a week, and he finally quits trying.

On Christmas Day, I visit the hot-box two times in one day. I hit five-hundred-twenty-five degrees. Five-twenty-five! The second trip, I sneak a bow in and tie it around my head when Milt isn't paying attention.

He doesn't appreciate the humor. At least, the EMT gets a chuckle from my mistletoe belt buckle, but Milt greets me with a scowl when I return from my medical evaluation.

"It's time to switch things up a bit," Milt ransacks his desk, tossing papers from drawers while cursing all the while. "Where the hell did I put it?" He snatches a shiny, silver forty-five from the bottom drawer. "Here it is."

Milt cocks the hammer and points the gun at my chest.

"Through the heart and you're probably dead. For good." He shifts the barrel away from my heart and slightly higher. "But here and you'll survive. Sure, it'll hurt like hell, but you'll come out of it stronger than before."

I'm bored with the hot-box. Whatever growth it offers may have maxed out before Christmas. Maybe I've built a tolerance to it. Can that even happen?

Pull the trigger. Do it. Shoot me!

Milt eases back on the hammer and laughs. "Another time, perhaps. Your old man hated getting shot. He preferred blades or overdosing."

Anger sears my skin. I can't decide if the fact he threatened me pissed me off more than the fact he didn't pull the trigger.

Neither instills joy.

"You ready for your Christmas present?" Milt asks.

"What?"

"Revenge." Milt loads up his weapons belt and pushes

through the back exit of the bar. "They say it's best served cold, but they're wrong. It's best served in the aftermath of the hot-box. Your body is juiced up right now."

I trail behind as we enter the dining area. My heart pushes hard against my chest twice every second.

"Revenge?"

"I have a lead. If you think you're up for it."

"What do we do?" I ask, clenching my injured hand for another rush of pain.

"You sure you wanna do this?" Milt crosses his arms. "You can't half-ass this."

"Are we going to kill someone?"

"Does it matter?"

It should, but . . . dad.

"Okay, I'm in."

Milt grabs a bag from the counter, and we head outside. I drop a pair of knock-off Oakley sunglasses over my eyes as we exit the dark bar, the light raging against my overexposed corneas. A high-pitched beep unlocks the doors to Milt's Escalade. "Get in. I'll explain on the way."

The tires spray rocks high into the air as Milt buries the pedal into the floorboard. My body whips hard left, fighting the road with the fishtailing Escalade as we exit the parking lot. The road for the entrance stopped being a road twenty years ago, but the SUV manages adequately.

Milt turns hard right onto a road without a name. The road leads two places and two places only: the dump and old mining housing. Second thoughts overwhelm my thinking. We can't really be going to kill someone.

"Please tell me we're going to dig through trash," I say, focused on the fork ahead. "Looking for old winning lottery tickets or something."

"And what would be the fun in that?" Milt's smile lights his eyes like sparkling diamonds.

I pick at the leather seat, but this is a quality vehicle, top of the line. The seat gives nothing. Old habits die hard, but that didn't mean I'll be successful with them.

We race past two dilapidated towers struggling to stand in the slightest breeze, the lookout spots for collapsing shafts long since sealed. About two miles into the towering maples, old box houses come into view. Many without doors, some without a fourth wall, opening themselves up to the passing traffic, which consists mainly of deer and rabbits. I grip the side of my seat until my knuckles turn white.

Staring out the truck's window is like watching the world's worst yard sale pass before my eyes. A sink, a toilet, a mattress frame, and maybe an old chair or rotted sofa. Gutted houses with frames stripped of any copper wiring they once held. The houses stretch another two miles to the county line's edge into an area nicknamed the DMZ. Drug manufacturing zone.

I reach over my right arm and lock my door before sliding my fingers across my wrist. The pain intensifies. The pressure pulsates. My rubbing turns to a hard massage, pushing so hard I expect blood to geyser any minute.

"Wrist hurt?" Milk asks. His eyes focus on my wrist.

"From time to time. Doc said there might be long-term nerve damage," I lie. A small surge crackles through my body.

"Seriously? You ain't making that up?" Milt furrows his brow.

"There's some fancy medical term for it."

"In the future, let's not lie to each other. Okay?"

"But—"

"For Christ's sake. Look down. You're rubbing the wrong wrist." Milt rolls his eyes.

My head doubles in mass. I can't hold it above my shoulders.

"Your old man was the same way, although his pain always seemed to be in his lower back. It took him years before he stopped lying about it. Denying it made him light-headed. You too, it seems." Milt chuckles. "I remember this one time he wouldn't stop bitching about the pressure in his back. Usually, four or five drinks and some time on the heavy bag would get him through, but this one day, nothing worked. So, he downs five shots of Jose Cuervo without so much as a breath in between and hands me an aluminum baseball bat. Aluminum, mind you, not wood. And he says, I want you to hit me as hard as you can right here. The crazy SOB points to his kidney."

Now he has my attention.

"I hesitate, so he slugs me across the jaw. Well, I take to swinging like I'm chopping down one of them giant redwood trees out in California. Smack. Smack. Smack." Milt bangs the steering wheel with a flat hand.

My eyes bleed dry from staring.

"Did it work?" I ask.

"Hell no. And neither of us could figure why. Shit like that always worked. Pain usually relieved his pressure when alcohol failed, but not this time. By now, his left side is every shade of purple imaginable. He unearths the boning knife out of my tackle box and tosses it at my feet. Told you he preferred the blade. Well, I jam it in his back and —" Milt pulls his open palm across his face and appears to wipe away a thought he no longer wants in his head— "luckily, he passed out, so I hauled his drunk ass to the hospital. Told them he was in a bar fight. Doc said he should've been dead with all the damage I'd done. You wanna hear the kicker? It was a kidney stone. A tiny freaking kidney stone. Can you believe that?" Milt's laughter ricochets off the Escalade's interior. The SUV's wheels flirt with the rumble strips on the road. "Oh man, we laughed about it for years."

"Right up until he died," I say.

Milt nods, signs the cross, and says, "Does put a damper on conversation."

He slides the SUV off the side of the road fifty yards short of the DMZ. He reaches across my lap and pops open the glove-box. Two pairs of shiny brass knuckles tumble to the floor. "Grab those, will you?" He points between my feet. "I know you're already familiar with what those can do."

"What's our play?" I maintain a steady voice but can't keep my hands from shaking enough to pick up the brass knuckles.

"First, stop worrying. Uncle Milty ain't gonna let nothing happen to you." Milt pats a bulge in his waist. "And remember, you were born for this."

NINETEEN

"All you gotta do is get inside," Milt says before sliding on a black mask.

"And how do I do that?"

"Act lost or something. Just get him talking, and I'll be right behind you. Simple."

Simple.

A kiss of death word if I ever heard one.

"No mask for me?" I ask.

"Would you answer the door if someone was wearing a mask?" He flicks a backhand into my forehead.

"Good point."

I drop the brass knuckles into my pocket and head toward the front of the one-story boxed house with a crumbling black number three above the door. For an abandoned section of town, a front door with three dead-bolt locks seems excessive. The house next to number three doesn't even have a front door, nor anything inside it with less than six legs and a creep factor of eleven.

Milt disappears behind the white shack labeled number

one as I stutter step my approach, trying to think of what I'll say.

Hi. I know you don't know me, but I'm pretty sure you had something to do with my dad's death. I mean, I don't know how, but I'm hoping you'll tell me.

What the hell did I get myself wrapped up in? This is stupid.

Milt peeks his head around the side of house number one and uses his gun to wave me forward. Because that's reassuring. I may have to have a chat with Milt about his social skills and means of encouragement.

"You're doing this for Dad," I mutter.

My hands shake, but I find surprising comfort in the brass hand-piece in my pocket. I slide my fingers through the cold, metallic circles. The cool steel makes my heart skip a beat.

"Keep one hand in your pocket and remain calm," I repeat as I shuffle past discarded beer bottles and an old tire toward the front door.

Knock softly? Pound with authority? Kick the fucking thing in and go guns-a-blazing?

A traditional approach wins the day.

My bare-knuckles bounce off the oak door. It looks as though it'd be easier to barrel through the rotting wood walls than the solid oak door. I rap harder, shaking the door in its fragile frame. The locks refuse to loosen their grip. The corner of the window's blue and black striped curtain retracts. It still covers most of the onlooker's facial features, but two squinted eyes work their way up and down my body before ducking away.

"Hello?" I consider using the brass knuckles on the door, but it may scare a jittery occupant. "I need your help. I'm lost. My car broke down."

Appeal to their good nature. Living out here, I'm sure they're full of it.

The only thing full of it is Milt expecting anyone to answer the door.

"Please."

"Get the hell out of here," a muffled voice yells from the window.

He hesitates long enough for me to get an unobstructed view of his hippy face. Brown, shaggy hair dangling over a huge forehead and unnaturally round eyes along with a handlebar mustache. A face firmly entrenched in my memory. A face no kid from AP calculus could forget.

"Mr. Dudak?"

"Who's there?" His voice squeaks. "How do you know my name?"

"Marc. Marc Cheeks." I step back, stand straight, and present a full-frontal view, smile and all.

Three clicks and the door creaks open four inches.

"Cheeks, huh? I remember you. Good student. Hung around with that squirrely younger kid. Greg."

"Glenn," I correct him.

Dudak snaps out of rhythm with his speech. "Yeah, that's him. Good looking older sister. Shit. That explains why you tutored him for years. God, I can be so blind sometimes. Anyhow, always thought you would amount to something after high school, but sounds like you're stuck in this hellhole with the rest of us."

My smile fades. "Thanks for reminding me."

"What do you want?"

"First, Merry Christmas. And second, I'm here to settle up for my dad."

The door whips open. Dudak's bangs flutter off his gargantuan forehead.

He buys my lie. Hook, line, and sinker.

"Grab a seat. Can I get you a drink?" Dudak kicks a Domino's pizza box from his path as he crosses the room. "Pardon the mess. Maid's week off." He arches back with laughter.

The square room offers life's necessities, but little else. A stained mattress off to my left and an out-of-date velvet love seat to the right. Some might argue vintage, but this is the crap sold cheap in the local shops. Dudak's toilet hugs the far wall, exposed to the naked eye. I'd rather use the trees across the way.

He lined up a hot plate and a small toaster oven on the lone counter in the corner I figure is the kitchen in the one room. I doubt the faucet works, but the mini-fridge next to the counter hums an icy tune.

"You get electricity and water here?" I ask.

"Gas-powered generator out back. There ain't been power or water here for a decade, but the realtor called this part of the county up and coming." More snickers. I believe the wave of nauseous gas spewing from the toilet is driving him crazy. "Orange soda?"

"Sure," I say.

Dudak hands me a lukewarm can. "So, on to business. You got the money?"

"Yeah. Of course. I mean, Dad wasn't quite sure of his balance, so how much?" If I'm here to pay him, I should have an idea of numbers, but I make a bet of my own that Dudak will be too excited by the thought of collecting he won't notice.

Dudak turns his back and digs through a pile of blankets on the floor. He turns toward me with a pen and notebook in hand.

"Let me see, with interest that comes to——" Dudak's high-pitched whistle reverberates deep in my ears. "154,182 dollars. Let's call it an even one-fifty. For Christmas, you get a teacher's discount." He winks. "That offer expires today, and judging by the lack of a briefcase, paper bag, or even bulge in your clothes, I'm guessing you might be a bit light. Unfortunately, my employer doesn't accept checks."

Holy shit!

"Marc, your dad's been dead for more than three weeks."

"You knew?"

"I do now." A Cheshire grin overwhelms the bottom half of his face. "I bet most of the folks in town are still celebrating, so unless you inherited a shitload of money and want to make good on his legacy, now might be a good time to tell me why you're really here."

TWENTY

My cover disintegrates faster than cotton candy in water.

I crack the pop-top on the can, and orange carbonation sprays in every direction.

"Damn!"

I drop the can, spraying a shower of orange-sugared sweetness, and roll it toward Dudak. He tosses his notebook behind him and throws his body on it as if it's a live grenade.

Milt bursts through the door, knocking me onto a pile of Chinese food containers. My backside flops in General Tso's chicken while Broccoli and Beef snakes its way down the back of my pants.

"Knock knock," Milt yells.

Milt's bulbous thumb eases back the Colt revolver's hammer. A click. Metallic. Evil. Offensive, not defensive. The gun's barrel partially disappears in Dudak's hair.

"Ain't many places to hide cash in this joint, but why don't you make it easy on everyone and just tell me," Milt says.

"I have no clue what you're talking about." Dudak tries to turn his head, but Milt smashes Dudak's nose into the wood floor using the gun's nozzle as leverage.

"Don't lie to me," Milt says.

"Look, man, I'm just a retired teacher working on writing a novel. Ask the kid. He knows."

"For a teacher, you're a dumb, mo-fo," Milt bounces Dudak's whimpering face off the wood floor a few times. "Where's the money? And the list."

I shake the last noodles and pieces of beef out of my pants. Chinese food is off the menu for a few weeks.

"I got no problem shooting you, buddy. Might take longer to find the dough, but the result will be the same." Milt smirks. "Except your head won't be a part of your body."

"But Mr. Dollhauser . . . "

"Three."

"He'll kill me . . . "

"Two."

"The freezer. Okay? The freezer." Dudak forces his head sideways.

Milt motions his head toward the mini-fridge. "Check it out."

I navigate the empty to-go cartons and pizza boxes. Both Milt and I will need tetanus shots after this.

"Got it!" I grab a stack of chilly greenbacks from the small compartment on the top side of the fridge. "Is this what they mean by cold-hard cash?"

"Seriously?" Milt gives me a disappointed parent look. "How much?"

A bit of the rising sunlight peeks between the gun and Dudak's head. We are deep into the morning, and I want to be far away from this place.

I whip through the bills. "25,000. It's mostly hundreds."

The light between Dudak's head and the Colt's nozzle vanishes.

"Where's the rest, Teach? Something's not adding up."

Part of me wants to shoot Milt because there's more than money not adding up. If Dudak had a hand in Dad's death, he would've known about it. There would not have been a need for the cat-and-mouse game earlier. Dad told me to find someone I can trust. Can I trust Milt just because Dad wrote it in a letter on his deathbed? What if he wrote it long before he died? Before the argument with Milt in our house. After I find the rest of the money, Milt needs to answer my questions.

I peer deep into the fridge. Cans. Nothing but cans. Fanta. Coke. Jolt Cola.

"Jolt?" I turn to Milt. "You ever hear of Jolt Cola?"

"We served that trash in the bar before Red Bull. Total caffeinated crap. Perfect for a piece of shit like this guy. No one in the world will drink that these days."

Milt rams a knee into Dudak's back, forcing the professor's body flat onto the floor.

Dudak's too smart to hide the money in plain sight, but what about inside crap no one would touch? I snake my arm deep into the fridge and snag a can. I crush it without trying.

"What the?" I mutter. Light as a feather. I grab a second with just a finger and a thumb. Then a third.

"What the hell are you doing?" Milt yells.

I lift one to my ear and shake. "No sound. No liquid inside."

Milt raises the gun arm's length and smashes hell across Dudak's skull. A soft grunt and Dudak's body goes limp.

"Toss me a can." Milt offers a big-targeted paw.

My throw flutters wide of Milt and donks Dudak on the head. Milt grabs the can and turns it over a few times in his hand.

"Son-of-a-bitch." Milt sets the gun on the ground and twists the bottom of the can. He pries a wad of cash free from the inside. "Gotta be ten-grand in here." He points to the fridge. "Empty the cans. Take it all." He claps his hands together. "Now. Move!"

Milt and I roll through a dozen cans before I stumble across a real can of cola.

"One for the ro—"

Aluminum disintegrates in my hand. A whizz-pop hollows my ears.

"Die, you bastards!" Dudak rises from the floor, waving the gun and screaming obscenities.

I roll hard left as another shot misses Milt and tears through abandoned cans.

Milt's silhouette fills my vision as he leaps onto Dudak's back. The intertwined pair roll until Dudak gains the upper hand courtesy of three forks and a few knives left scattered on the ground, jabbing Milt in places better not discussed.

He sits atop Milt with the gun hovering inches above his throat.

"After I kill you, I'm taking care of your new partner." Dudak glances in my direction. Black dotted lines crisscross the entirety of his face. "Dollhauser will overlook my indiscretions with last summer's roll if I serve up Dan's boy over there as settlement for his dad's losses and Dollhauser's missing man. Finally, I can come out of hiding and go back to living like a king."

I fumble for the brass knuckles, but the roll knocked all

the wind from my lungs. No matter how deep I inhale, my body can't find the oxygen it wants.

Panic.

Hyperventilation.

A small surge of energy as my fingertips touch the metallic circles of silvered-brass.

Milt stares into Dudak's eyes without a single flinch. No fear.

"You made a big mistake coming here. It's my list now, and soon this will be my town!" Dudak closes his eyes. His body tenses with every muscle flexed as he pulls the trigger.

Click.

No bang.

No time to figure out why. I lunge forward and connect a loaded right cross. The crunching sound of shattered cheekbones frees Milt.

My breathing morphs into a high-pitched wheeze as I drop to my knees. Dudak resembles a baby deer on ice trying to get to his feet. Drooling strands of saliva-soaked blood, more pink than white, cling to his chin.

"Grab the notebook," Milt says, reclaiming his gun. "I'll get the cash." He scrambles across the floor, scooping cash and stuffing a black duffle bag he found in the corner of the room.

"Notebook." I cough blood of my own, matching Dudak splat for splat.

Our hands meet on the frayed edges of paper. Waves of Dudak's fear, along with his fingertips, rake skin clean off my hand. Curled strands of flesh and red collect under his nails.

Great. More bacteria.

I swivel right and release a metallic barrage of fury. My left hand strains to steady my failing body. Dudak's facial bones fail to hold its structure. His skin slumps, ready to slide off his face. The black dotted lines blob together into a blood Rorschach of a splayed spider.

He flails two aimless slaps.

Milt cheers from the corner. My brass knuckles hide their silver under Dudak's blood.

"This is for my dad!" I cringe with every punch.

One more punch, then I'll stop.

The splatters of red and gurgling sounds from Dudak reinvigorate me.

Okay, one more.

My body chugs adrenaline and yearns for more. Black lines dance across Dudak's lips and cheeks, ebbing and flowing with troughs begging to be punched.

I don't stop when his front teeth clatter on the floor like a pair of dice.

Snake eyes.

Or his bottom teeth.

Boxcars.

I don't stop until my shirt is drenched with blood.

Not his.

Mine.

TWENTY-ONE

"Press hard," Milt says. He hands me two towels from the backseat of the SUV. Yellow towels become orange. "Stay awake. I know a guy. He'll fix you up good as new."

My side aches. Short, quick breaths like a dog on a hot summer's day. Music blares. The Foo Fighters: *Everlong.*

First time getting shot, and I can say I'm not a fan. Each time the weight of my head becomes too much for my neck to bear, I fight. The sun ducks behind the winter clouds, and I lose track of time. My heart pounds as if it's trying to make its own getaway. With each beat, blood does a loop-to-loop around the bullet hole and squirts from my body in a small fountain.

"Why won't the bleeding stop?"

"I coat all my bullets with anticoagulants. Expensive as hell, and nearly impossible to get, but fortunately, I have a legit connection."

"Fortunate is not the word that comes to mind. Why would you do that?"

"You saw how crazy it got in there once the shooting started. Now imagine five guys. Or ten. You don't have to hit center mass. Once they start bleeding and don't slow down, they panic and lose sight of the fight. Eventually bleed out. Can't have anyone identifying you if things go to Hell."

I press harder on my chest, determined to beat the blood thinner. The bleeding doesn't stop, but I hear a crack. Pain radiates across my chest. "Mother fucker! I broke a rib."

And then a wave of relief covers my mind. I can focus.

My bleeding slows but refuses to quit. I blink faster and faster. I can't stop it. It's as if my brain is taking clustered photos.

The weight of my head overpowers my neck. The world spins and spins, haloed trees highlighting each pass. Milt slams the breaks, and our seatbelts fight to hold us upright. I try to straighten my body, but nothing works.

"Where is he? How bad is it?"

A familiar voice greets us.

"You've seen worse, Doc. Kid's tougher than his old man. Should be no problem—" Milt spins the revolver in his hand— "And it will make all your problems go away."

"I do this, and my name disappears from that book. Permanently. You understand?"

"Doc, have I ever lied to you before?" Milt asks.

"Plenty," Doc answers. "And if this were you, I'd let you bleed out. That's no lie."

I flop my head back and smile at the man standing outside the open passenger door of the SUV. "Doctor Malcolm."

"Got ourselves in a little trouble?" He fakes a smile.

"Like father, like son," I scoff.

"Let's hope not," Doc answers.

"Let's." I cough thick liquid from my mouth. "You know what they say. Whatever doesn't kill you—"

A gray veil covers my world.

The Foo Fighters sing me out.

TWENTY-TWO

Milt sits at the greasy counter of the bar and flips through the pages of the notebook.

After two days of sleeping it off, as Milt calls it, I'm finally ready to move about again. After a single bullet, I conclude I'm not a fan of getting shot. The wound leaves a splatter scar I find myself staring at in the mirror any time I have my shirt off.

"What's so goddamn special about that book that I had to take a bullet?" I toss a pile of crusted dishes into the soapy sink water and turn toward the bar top. I'm no closer to knowing why what happened to my dad happened or why all the training, even if I didn't hate it.

"See for yourself." Milt slides it over to me.

I flip open the notebook. "And what exactly am I looking at? All I see are names on different pages, a bunch of codes, and a dollar figure."

"Names. Yup." Milt nods. "Whoever controls that notebook controls every name in there. Athletes. Celebrities. Politicians. Law enforcement. Judges."

Dudak was a bookie?

"Dad's killer in here?" A small glimmer of hope, if you can call the darkness of revenge such a thing.

"In there? No, but we need it. Trust me."

The notebook reads like a who's who in Munson County and every known name in the state. I recognize a slew of teachers. Anthony Birdsaw, Irene Phillips, Dorothy Cunningham, and Markese Donteet.

Dudak drew a cross next to Pastor McCann's name. Judging by the big negative next to his tally, the collection plate might be passed around twice during the next service.

Mayor Stanski appears to place the occasional wager, but he is either incredibly lucky or getting inside information. The guy never loses.

"So, we help these people, and they help us find the folks responsible for my dad's death? Like, erase their debts?"

"Erase?" Milt shakes his head. "Hell no! Leverage. That notebook is power. Complete power. It's like the One Ring of Munson County. Shit, the entire state. Unfortunately, the owner is gonna come calling soon, and he'll want his share." He lowers his voice and looks toward the bar's front door. I think I hear him mutter. "And I've got no intention of letting that happen."

"Huh?"

"Nothing."

"If this is so valuable, why was Dudak living in a shithole?" I ask.

"He tried blackmailing the wrong people, including the bank behind all those bets. Guessing there was a price on his head, but not one we can conclude. What happened in our case was an accident."

I'm growing uncomfortable with the number of *accidents* that leave folks dead around here.

"What's up with this one?" No name on the page, only a bunch of X's followed by a gold star.

Milt glances at the page. "Star? Means he's in law enforcement. Cop or a judge."

My heart sinks when I see Doc Malcolm's name grace the top of the next page. A big red hospital emblem dwarfs the big red hole Doc dug himself. That explains him helping with the gunshot wound outside of hospital grounds. There are only two people with bigger losses. One was Dad. The other is Susan and Glenn's dad, Mr. Lang.

"What if you don't pay?" I ask.

"They usually end up doing things they wouldn't, or they end up like—"

"Dad." Did Dad run his truck into that tree because of this? He mentioned a debt before he beat up that out-of-town guy, but he said it was my debt. My name's nowhere in this book.

"Figure we got ourselves a week of free rein to collect."

"And why should I care?"

"Because 10% of this book now belongs to you." Milts rubs his bulbous thumb and index finger together.

"Twenty." I don't flinch.

He straightens his back and stares hard, a yellow hue growing around his iris. "Twelve-half."

"Fifteen and Mr. Lang's debt goes the way of Doc Malcolm." I extend my hand. "So, we have a deal?"

A shit-eating grin overtakes Milt's face. "Fuck no. You still owe me for Doc fixing you up."

"I got shot because of you!" I grab a dirty plate from the counter and wing it against the wall. Cheap, white ceramic pieces spray in every direction.

"You got shot because you were sloppy. And you're going to pay for that plate."

"Then collect everything in that book yourself, asshole. I'll sit back, take my 10%, and eat all your wings."

"There's the Marc I need! Eleven, I ghost Lang, and we're in business. But he ain't getting no free passes in the future. He loses, he owes. As a gesture of goodwill, we'll call Doc a belated Christmas gift from me to you."

"Deal." I reach a hand into my jean pocket. "And I have a present for you too." I whip out my hand and hold my middle finger high.

Milt rolls up the notebook and tucks it under his arm. "Keep that fire. Grab your knuckles." *I don't need them.* "We'll start at the church. Watch your back, though. Most everyone in that place is packing."

"What about my dad?" I ask.

"Once we been doing this a week, they'll come to us." He flicks off the lights as we head out to his Escalade. The bastard doesn't even bother locking the front door. "Let 'em come. Let 'em try."

I clear my throat. "And what about the cop in my house? You think he's dead? I see him, you know, in the oven with Dad. That guy had to starve to death or bleed out by now. Can't imagine the air under that floor allowed for easy breathing. Should I do something?" Doubt creeps into my head.

Milt glances at me but turns away before I could make eye contact. "Focus on your training. Your pop wouldn't leave without making proper arrangements, so don't you worry. Once we take care of the book, we'll relocate the very alive cop somewhere far away, so he'll never be an issue for you again. I need you to focus on getting fully up to speed."

"Up to speed, what does that mean?" I scoff.

Milt holds out an open palm and lowers it slowly. "It's different with everyone. Guess you could say, understanding what it means to be a Stitch. Learning how to die, but not really die."

"Why don't you bring me up to *speed*?" I ask. "I'm not a big fan of you killing me over and over again without telling me what the hell is going on."

"You need to balance that anger with your intellect. You ain't ready yet."

―――――――――

I SPEND a week helping him clean up the largest of the past due debts from the notebook. The sit down on New Year's Eve with Glenn and Susan about their dad is awkward, but they need to know. Milt watches our conversation from a tree stump in the distance, cleaning under his fingernails with a hunting knife. Shortly before midnight, I drag myself back to the bar with Milt. Something about telling your closest friends their dad is a loser makes the food and drink of the evening tasteless.

Most of the collection sessions start with me getting beat up and end with Milt cocking back the hammer on his gun. My reward for helping Milt is eleven percent of the collected cash and the occasional walk down the Great Beyond's hazy red carpet.

I hide most of my share in Mr. Chavez's garage. If it's safe enough for a police car, then it works for cash. I count the hours toward the end of the week. Something better materialize, or I may use the knuckles on Milt for lying to me.

According to him, I should be thankful; thankful for the easy money, thankful for the boost in strength, and thankful for "learning how to take a bullet like a man."

While he may own a hole-in-the-wall drinking establishment, Milt rocks this sparkling Cadillac SUV. Tinted windows, chrome wheels, a kicking stereo system, power everything, and leather seats, which quickly heat both your back and your butt on a cold winter's day.

His prior explanation that "I'll find out soon enough and be grateful" for his training techniques continues to ring hollow in my soul, but everything feels hollow these days, especially my mouth. Three permanent teeth gone missing. Guess those don't heal. *At least I have the money to go to the dentist.*

I can't decide if he's an idiot, full of shit, or simply using me. Probably all the above, but I need answers, and I'm willing to look in the craziest places to get them.

Literally.

The term crazy isn't politically correct, but nothing about my life is. It's time for me to visit my only living relative, and Milt isn't thrilled with my request.

"What do you want to see your uncle for anyhow?" Milt asks.

"Because I'm not exactly loving my training. Ten days now, and we're no closer on the truth about what happened to my dad. Where's this phantom lead you keep talking about?" I stare out the window. "And what's the point of my training? Make me strong. Why? So I can be your heavy? A punching bag to collect gambling debts. If shit goes wrong, you're not too worried because I'll probably survive even if I have to die a little first. Might be time to renegotiate our contract because this is bullshit. I don't need you. You need me. How do I know you aren't making up all this cloak and dagger shit about Dad's death so you can keep using me?"

"That's a hell of an insinuation. And after all I've done for you," Milt says. "What about your buddy's dad? I spared that lousy excuse of a man from the humiliation and pain that comes from owing me money."

Humiliation is Milt's way of saying beating.

"You said we shouldn't lie to each other."

Milt huffs. "A little white lie now and then probably wouldn't be bad."

"Your wings taste great," I smirk.

"Now you're just being mean," Milt says. "If you think you'll find answers with your uncle, you may be beyond help."

"He's the only family I have left." *Despite Dad never mentioning him.* I marvel at the vast emptiness of the drive. A few scattered trees but mostly barren farmland. "What's the name of this place?"

Milt's voice stammers through his answer. "Piedmont Plains Psychiatric Rehabilitation Clinic. Folks call it P3."

Milt turns the Cadillac into a long, single-lane drive-way. A steel gate with bars wider than the spaces between the blocks the entrance to P3. A baby-butt smooth, white stone wall fifteen-feet high with another three feet of barbed wire fence weaves around the top. The smell of freshly spread Dillo Dirt seeps into the Cadillac.

"All of this for a psychiatric hospital?" I ask.

"No." Milt shakes his head. "All of this is for a first-of-its-kind, state-of-the-art privately run asylum, home to the lost, the hopeless, worst of the worst. Murderers, rapists, child molesters, and—"

"My uncle." I bow my head. It's not bad enough Dad was notorious in town, but it sounds as if my uncle one-upped him.

"And, yeah, your uncle."

"Did you know him?" I ask. "Why is he here?"

"Your uncle? Yeah. I know him. Know him better than your father ever did, but that's a story for another time."

"The time when you bring me up to speed?" I ask. Milt's avoidance routine grows tiresome.

Milt rolls his eyes. "Yeah, smart-ass, when I bring you up to speed."

An armed guard approaches the Cadillac and lets us through without much conversation.

Milt parks the SUV in the spot farthest from the asylum despite a lot virtually empty of vehicles.

"You coming?" I ask as I fumble for the door handle.

"Not my uncle." Milt punches a button on the front console. The Rolling Stones *Paint It Black* rocks the vehicle.

I cup my hands around my mouth. "You sure?"

He points at his ears and gives me the universal I-can't-hear-you face.

I can hear the music the entire walk to the front of the building. The P3 entrance doors echo the hollow dread in my soul. Plexiglass blocks my way. High-tech cameras in both corners spy my every step. Out of reach, but not out of sight.

I crack each knuckle on both hands before summoning the courage to approach the front desk.

"I'm here to see my uncle."

"Oh, how unfortunate," The young male attendant mutters. His face shadowed by long, uncombed black hair dented across the top of his head by the recently removed Bose headphones contrasts his bleached white uniform top.

"What?"

"What is the patient's name?" he drones.

"Cheeks."

"First name?"

It dawns on me that I don't know his first name. "Is there more than one person with the last name Cheeks in here?"

"Do you have an appointment?" He clacks the computer's keys.

I nod. "I called this morning."

"Second left. End of the hall. Ask for Dr. Gehringer." His fingers dance across the keyboard. "Follow the designated lit path on the floor. Yours will be the red line."

"Don't I need an escort?"

"Not if you follow the red line and only the red line," he says. "I'll be alerted if you step from the path. Now go." He shoos me with a flick of the wrist and pops the Beats headphones back on his ears.

A buzz accompanies the release of the door. I step across the threshold into a sterile white environment. Floors, walls, doors, and the ceiling are all stark white. Not cream. Not eggshell. White. I'm walking through a cloud. A creepy cloud housing the angels of Hell with a single red line running down the middle of the floor to guide me.

As I plod down the hall, I notice there are no windows on any doors. Step off the red line, and I may end up a patient myself going insane trying to find the exit.

"Red line. Second left," I mutter. Something straight ahead of me, far in the distance, catches my eye as I turn. I squint to get a better look at the all-black figure. The eyes. Its eyes. Both glow lapis lazuli blue before one melts to chartreuse.

"Ahh!"

A scream and a fall.

"Watch where you're going," a female voice scolds me.

I hop to my feet and extend my hand to help her up.

"Susan?" I blink twice to make sure I'm not imagining things.

"Hey, Marc. Sorry for yelling, but you scared the crap out of me." She straightens her blouse. "Now I'm wrinkled, you jerk." She giggles. She always laughs when she insults me.

"Yeah, I guess I am." I peek around the corner, but whatever had caught my eye vanished. "So, what are you doing here?" I scratch my head. "Those prom committee kids finally drive you insane?"

She parts her ruby red lips with a smile. "No, silly. I'm here to see my grandmother."

My heart sinks into my stomach. "Oh my God. I'm so sorry."

I hope she isn't next to my uncle.

"Jeez, Marc, she isn't a patient. She works here as a nurse. I grab part-time hours when they have them. They pay way better than student teaching. Then again, what doesn't?" She laughs. "It's been a while, but out of the blue, I got a call this morning that they were short-staffed and paying double. Sometimes my grandmother will let me do rounds with her when she passes out meds to the patients."

"No way. That's kinda cool, but I heard most of these people are crazy."

"Insane, not crazy," she corrects me.

My world freezes. "What did you say?"

"Yeah, it's crazy," she says. "That she lets me do it. It breaks like twenty rules, but she's been here forever. Also, don't use the word crazy."

Maybe I heard her wrong. I bury my hands in my pockets and rock back and forth on my heels. "My bad. I'm new to all this. Feeling a little ragged myself."

"Ragged. I like that." She smiles, helping me forget my ignorance. "The best part is it looks great on my resume and in my checking account. I'm thinking of nursing, or anything to get out of teaching and away from this town. Anything that gets me out of the apartment over my parent's garage and away from my mom. Some days I'd do just about anything." She waves a hand at me. "You aren't here to listen to my problems. Besides, I have to take these notes down the hall." Susan points in the direction of where the black figure stood.

I gulp. "That hall?"

"Yup. Let's talk soon, okay?"

"Totally."

Should I go in for a hug?

She puts her hand on my shoulder and stares deep into my eyes. "This place is a giant square. Stay on your line, and you'll be fine. That's the slogan, but if you do get lost, keep walking straight until you can only go left or right. Follow the outside walls until you get back to the front."

"Only left or right. Got it."

"Because they keep all the murderers near the middle. Sometimes one will get loose and RAH!"

I jump back and hit the wall as she lunges her upper body at mine.

"Gotcha!" Susan bends over laughing.

"Dammit." I smack the air and bow my head. "You win this round." I try to laugh it off, but my hands won't stop shaking, and I think I pissed myself a little.

"Sorry, but I had to." Susan smiles. "Check ya later, scaredy-cat."

TWENTY-THREE

I gather my senses by the time I reach a door at the end of the corridor.

A square sign reads *Dr. Gehringer, Clinical Psychologist.* A thin rectangle of light escapes the room from the partially open door.

I move to give the door a little knocking tap and slam my fist into it instead. The door flies open, bouncing off the doorstop and back at me. I throw up my arms in defense.

"What in the hell?" Gehringer yells.

"Knock. Knock." I push the door gently open and pop my head in. "Sorry about that. Kinda lost my balance." Lost my balance. Lost control of my strength. Tomato. To-mah-to.

A frail man, no less than seventy in age, sits behind a cubic desk punching away with two fingers on the keyboard. Wispy gray hair does little to cover liver-spotted, bald head. His glasses have become one with the bridge of his nose, the stark white frames matching his oversized wrinkled, white doctor's jacket.

"Please try to be more careful in the future." The doctor's deep voice catches me off guard.

"I will, Sir."

"Is there something I can help you with?"

I slide inside the room. "My name is Marc Cheeks, Sir. I'm here to visit my uncle. I called earlier." I walk over to the desk and have no choice but to remain standing. His office is the antithesis of Mr. Layer's. One desk, no chairs, an equal-sided window with so many bars it resembles a chessboard. All overlooking plain fields of grass and a frail older man wearing yesterday's wrinkled clothes.

"Cheeks, huh? No one informed me. He doesn't get many visitors."

"Many?" I ask.

"By many, I mean one."

"Oh." I look around the office, which sits bathed in white, broken only by pictures and plaques on the wall behind me. It reads, "Jonathan M. Gehringer, PhD., Johns Hopkins University."

"Blue Jays, huh?" I point to the plaque. "You play lacrosse or anything?"

Silence pollutes the air. A full minute passes. I crack my knuckles in every way imaginable but to no avail.

Another minute passes, so I turn to inspect the pictures.

The first one showcases a much younger version of Dr. Gehringer receiving a medal being hung around his neck by President Bill Clinton.

"Holy shit. You received the Presidential Medal of Freedom?"

"Language, please," Doctor Gehringer says.

"Sorry. Hey, that's you deep sea fishing with the Governor." Gehringer, the Governor, two large men, and a teenage boy are standing on a wooden dock overlooking clear blue water. The group seemingly struggles to hold a huge swordfish. "How big is that freaking thing?"

"Nine-hundred pounds. Give or take a few."

I shift to the next picture. Gehringer stands with Coach Throgmorton behind two Heisman Trophy statues. Each man is pointing to their name on the award.

"You and Coach Throgmorton both played football at Notre Dame? Wow. Small world."

The shrink ignores me and focuses on the computer screen, pausing only to scribble notes on a pad of paper or glance to the ceiling while tapping the eraser end of a pencil against his chin.

"Well, can I see him?" I ask.

The doctor relents. "Why?"

"I don't understand."

"Why do you want to see your uncle? Do you know why he's here? The things he's done to other people? The things he would do if he ever left this place?"

He talks like I should know.

I probably should.

"I was hoping for answers," I say.

"Try church," he says.

Doubt's shadow creeps up my back. Despite the doctor's warnings, I can't resign myself to believe this path offered nothing.

"I'd like to try," I say.

Gehringer sighs, "Fine." He presses a button on his phone. "Can you have Hallsy and Conley escort Mr. Cheeks to visit Lester Cheeks? Yellow line." He releases the button. "They will explain our procedures for visiting a guest in this facility. Good luck."

Guest? I hardly think my uncle is here by choice.

I stand and extend my hand. "Thank you. You won't regret it."

He dismisses me from his office with a wave of the hand. "I know I won't, but you might."

TWENTY-FOUR

Hallsy leads us down the corridor, following blinking yellow lines along both sides of the hallway. His partner, Conley, walks beside me with his mouth moving faster than his legs.

"First time here?" Conley's six-four wiry frame towers over mine, but I'm confident a stiff breeze would blow him over. He talks with unbridled excitement as he explains a list of dos and don'ts. The list is almost exclusively don'ts. "We don't get many visitors here, especially for folks like your uncle."

"What do you mean, folks like my uncle?" I ask.

"No offense or nothing, but the folks who have lost touch with reality and don't understand the value of life. I mean, these guys would do terrible things if given a chance. No guilt. No remorse. No hesitation. This is the only sanctuary left for them."

I'm second-guessing the family reunion idea.

"So, is this a prison or an asylum?" I ask.

"It's neither, and it's both," Hallsy says. The exactness of his every step throws me for a loop. I watch with a measured look, noting every step appears to be virtually the length as the one before it. For a guy probably pushing two-fifty and nowhere near six-foot-tall, he has the precision of a well-trained soldier and the hair of a hippie from the 1960s. Back straight, arms swinging in harmony with leg movements, hair bouncing in the same rhythm, and the ability to navigate the hallway dead center.

Conley jumps in. "What he means is that we're a voluntary, private rehabilitation center."

"Voluntary?"

"Voluntary so much so that if anyone here chooses to leave, they will head straight to prison. Some to death row," Conley says. "Doc Gary, that's what we call Doctor Gehringer, created this facility about forty years ago to study the psyche of criminals. A few grants from the right state agencies and a brother with more money than God, better political influence as well, and you have P3. When a hospital can't handle them, and a government doesn't want them, we get 'em. The best part is that the government and the regulators basically ignore us since we handle their problems. Being private has its perks."

"We still have rules," Hallsy says without turning around or breaking stride.

Conley taps me on the shoulder and shakes his head no while laughing without making a sound.

He breaks his silence a moment later. "Hey, I heard you talking to Susan earlier. You trying to hit that?" He pops his eyebrows higher a few times.

"Me?" I point at my chest but stumble on my answer. "No. We're friends. Besides, I teach her younger brother. Could get messy."

"I read you loud and clear." Conley's left side of his mouth rises as he nods a few times and throws a solitary wink. "I'll put in a good word for you, bro. She's here from time to time."

"Yeah, I know. Visiting her grandmother."

"And her cousin," Conley says.

"Her what?" My mouth hangs open. I can't seem to close it.

"Her cousin. I'm pretty sure her grandmother still works here only to keep an eye on her cousin." Conley throws his hands up. "It's the craziest story!"

"Hey!" Hallsy shouts. Conley stops and watches as Hallsy moves a finger across his throat.

Defeated, Conley's excitement fades. "Anyhow, right this way."

As we turn left, for the first time, the stark white walls hold contrast. Black handprints mark the walls surrounding the doors. Some doors showcase dozens, while others only four or six.

"What's with the handprints?" Some showcase so much detail, I can see the wavy fingerprints on the largest samples.

"Creepy, huh? It's a symbolic thing. Doc Garry has all the patients put their handprints on the wall before they go into the room."

"Why would he do that?" I pause and hold my hand up against one small print with fingers half the size of mine.

"Don't do that!" Conley lunges for my hand, and I withdraw it from the wall before making contact. "It's bad luck to touch the handprints."

"That one is a kid's, isn't it?"

"Insanity doesn't have age limits. There are no signs around here saying you must be this tall to ride the crazy train." Conley laughs as he holds his open hand a few inches over my head. "Doc Garry thinks the hands offer an escape for their soul because once you're placed in this place, you're here forever."

"Some patients die here?" A shadow blackens my mood.

"No." Conley shakes his head. "All the patients die here, eventually."

"All of them?"

"Yup. This is one place you don't want to end up," he says. "We say rehab, but the reality is research."

"Why the heck would anyone work here?" Our walk slows to a crawl as we move away from the door with the smallest handprints.

"Doc Gary pays us well and provides benefits. Steady job. Hopefully, one day the research will lead to treatments that can help folks. Then we can look back and say we helped do that. And it ain't so bad when your best friend works here. Hashtag BFF." Conley tags Hallsy with a backhand.

"More than that. We'll be family in six months," Hallsy says.

"Hashtag he's doing my sister," Conley says.

Hallsy's return backhand to Conley sends him two steps back.

"Too far?" Conley asks. He looks at me. "Yeah, too far."

We pause by one door with a wall showing very little white.

"Damn, that's a lot of handprints." I run my fingers around the outline of the door but don't make contact.

"The Black Hole. That's what we call it. Worst of the worst rot here. More patients have died in this room than all the other rooms combined. These patients have also killed more patients than all the other rooms combined as well. Rumor has it folks see a black shadow wandering around these halls shortly before someone dies in that room. Death incarnate or something."

I struggle to swallow. "Black shadow with blue eyes?"

"That's the legend. No idea about the eye color. This place has gotta be haunted, but I've never seen anything." Conley looks at Hallsy, "You?"

"Nope. Never." He speaks his words fast and taut. "Urban Legend. Cliché. Besides, ain't only patients that die in there. Why? You see something?"

Clichés and I don't get along.

"Well, I . . . "

The duo breaks out into laughter.

"You got Conned-ley! Hashtag prank king." Conley crossed two fingers on each hand, trying his best to form a hashtag.

"Sorry, kid," Hallsy said.

"Susan saw your name on the guest list and put us up to it," Conley says. "Totally her idea."

My heart beats a normal rhythm again. "Respect. Anyhow, moving on." I have no intention of spending any more time than necessary by the door. I pick up the pace but find myself alone three steps later.

"This is your stop, bro." Conley motions toward the door.

"The Black Hole?"

"Yeah. Sorry, man. Piece of advice. If you want to get through to him, you need to be a smart-ass."

"Excuse me?"

Conley flashes three fingers. "Lester respects intellect. Humor. Sarcasm. Outwit him, and you'll get through that great wall of crazy."

"Okay. Be smarter than crazy. Got it." Maybe in my next life, I can find people who don't talk in riddles.

"And don't use the word crazy," Conley says, shaking his head in tandem with Hallsy.

"But—"

"Great, now that we're clear, here's the rest of the list of things you do not want to do." Conley breathes deeply before he begins.

I stand listening as the two men trade turns explaining fifty shades of insanity. No touching. No hugging. Don't get too close. Bring nothing into the room. Don't help him loosen his jacket, which apparently, he wears for my protection. Don't yell. Don't swear.

And finally, don't listen to a word he says.

TWENTY-FIVE

Conley leads me in. After taking two steps into the room, I conclude the architect of this establishment must also be a resident. The room hosts a mattress mounted on a hard rubber frame, two blue-harden rubber chairs, a stack of paperback books in the corner, and a curtained off area in the far corner I assume to be a bathroom setup.

My uncle remains motionless. Balding but with good posture, Lester sits crisscross on the floor and stares at the room behind us, refusing to acknowledge me.

Frosted glass walls allow light through from the surrounding cells, but I can't see into any of the rooms. Beautiful art shimmers in the glass. I recognize several famous paintings. After a few seconds, they fade out with new works coming to life.

"Wanna see something cool?" Conley asks, but he doesn't wait for me to answer before he spins to a computerized pad on the wall by the door. He punches in a four-digit code. "James Conley Eckstrom requesting permission for daylight."

About twenty seconds later, the frosting on the glass disappears, allowing me to see in the cells surrounding my uncle. Left, right, and center. Every room is set up the same. All the occupants have their hands on the same mounted computer pad as Conley.

"Residents have to grant bio-permission to defrost," Conley says.

"That's crazy tech!"

"Yeah, Doc Garry has made connections. His brother is this high-tech mogul worth billions. Hashtag blessed."

"Do they always defrost when you request?" I ask.

"Depends, but few pass up the opportunity to peer into the Black Hole. Speaking of which, I'll leave you to it."

I jump as Conley slams the door behind me. Several locks click into place.

"Uncle Lester, I'm your nephew." No sense beating around the bush.

I look to my right and watch the glass re-frost as the occupant scurries to a far corner of the room. He moves so fast I fail to get a decent view of him.

I glance to the left and notice a younger girl, probably close to my age, fixating on me. Her head tilts left and then right as she stares. I smile and wave my hand from the waist level, not wanting to make any sudden moves. She giggles and returns a small curtsy.

As I wait for my uncle to respond, the girl moves closer to the glass wall separating the rooms. She inches forward and waits. I exchange glances between her and my uncle but maintain my position. She resumes her approach with a larger step, never taking her eyes off me. Her long amber hair bounces with each step but comes to rest in perfect concert with her body. The eyes show spirit, not something I expected in this place. They are predominantly black but flash an emerald green that highlights a few carefully placed freckles on her cheeks.

She extends an open palm against the glass when she reaches the wall and motions to it with her eyes before returning her focus to me.

I don't want to take my eyes off my uncle, but curiosity gets the better of me, and I do my best imitation of a crab sidestepping to the glass. She giggles all the while and keeps exchanging glances between her hand and my face.

I think she wants to compare hands. The attendants mentioned how rare visitors are in this wing, so I have a chance to do something special for the girl. Something right.

Not something wrong for a change.

I place my hand against the glass opposite of hers and watch her eyes twinkle like a Texas sky in the summer.

"Great. Now you're her soul mate," A melancholy voice chimes in.

I whirl and find my uncle standing a few feet in front of me with his arms tucked close to his chest inside a white jacket. I can't believe anyone still uses these things. It's gotta be a violation of his rights. Maybe that's what Conley meant about this place being able to do what it wants.

I swallow nervously as my hand comes off the wall and stagger two paces backward, attempting to catch my breath.

The girl's sparkle turns to darkness. I betrayed her by removing my hand, and she lets me know it by taking a single finger and running it horizontally across her throat, pointing first to my uncle and then to me.

"My advice would be to avoid visiting her in the future. As rumor has it; ten years ago, her dad blamed her for her mom's death, and she retaliated a year later by strangling him, castrating him, and feeding his manhood to her stepmother until she choked to death," Lester says, a crooked smile unbalancing his face. Only the left side lifts.

"But she's my age. And a girl."

"I said rumor has it. There are a lot of crazy stories floating around this place." My uncle steps closer. I respond with a step back. "While the state may care about our gender, Gallagher doesn't. Girl. Boy. Man. Woman. He operates within his own rules."

"Well, he sure as hell can't make you wear that jacket. It violates your rights. I'll—"

"Relax. I requested it. No doubt, you've heard stories, and when I found out I would receive a young gentleman caller, I wanted him to feel safe in my presence." Lester winks and blows me a kiss. "Besides, you think this place gives a shit about human rights? We're guinea pigs served world-class food, surrounded by the finest art, and sleep on the softest mattress. It's delightful. You want to give it a try?" He motions his head toward the bed.

"Thanks, but I'm good."

"Sooner you realize Gehringer's family practically owns the police force and the state politicians, the better off you'll be. They should call this place Vegas, because what happens in Vegas . . . "

It takes me a second to realize he's waiting on me. "Stays in Vegas," I say.

My uncle carries a decade more on his shoulders than Dad. The wrinkles on his cheeks outline a weary road through a life filled with difficult choices, or maybe it is this place I see on his face. The eyes are dark and dead, devoid of any discernible color.

"If you don't like art, we can watch a movie. You might think me *A Clockwork Orange* guy, but I'm more of a *Better Off Dead* fan, myself."

I bow my head as I talk. "I guess you heard Dad died." Not the greatest segue, but you work with what you got.

"Not a shock. Your old man was past his expiration date."

"That's not a nice thing to say." I stop to remind myself where I am and who I'm talking to. This is about getting answers, not getting emotional. "What do you mean, expiration date?"

"Like when you buy some milk and let it sit in the fridge too long," my uncle says.

"Sorry. I don't drink milk."

He cranes his neck back. "What? Everyone drinks milk."

"Not me." I shake my head. "Lactose intolerant."

"You're kidding."

"Why would I kid about that? It's not like my friends buy me a milkshake and dare me to drink it."

"Well, do you eat meat? Don't tell me you're a freaking vegan." He lowers an eyebrow.

"Damn right, I eat meat. I'm not a monster." The irony in my statement is almost too much for my brain to handle, but I'm nailing this witty sarcasm thing.

"You know the number they put on the package."

"Yeah. SKU numbers." I cup a hand over my mouth and lower my voice, "Although I think they have a secret meaning."

"No, not the damn SKU numbers!" Lester bites his lip. "Sorry. I didn't mean to get upset." He adjusts his crossed arms several times until he finds comfort. "The numbers that look like a date. Hell, they are a date."

"Oh, those numbers."

"You little shit," he sneers. "Conley?"

I offer a broad smile. "How'd I do? Nailed it, right?"

"Let's just say I'm annoyed, but also relieved."

"Give me some credit. I may be crazy, but I'm not stupid." I reach my hand out as if I can grab the word crazy and stuff it back in my mouth. My body freezes, waiting to see if he noticed my mistake.

"I guess not, but you can never tell with this stuff. It affects folks differently. It's driven me to do things society frowns upon." He looks down at the locks on his jacket. "And let me tell you, all it takes is putting one P3 mate into the infirmary, and they get a little hesitant on visitors."

I sense his sadness. There can't have been many things worse in this world than to be sane enough minutes of the day to understand you're not sane the rest of the time.

"One?"

"One. A half-dozen. Infirmary. Cemetery. Who can keep track of these things nowadays?"

And my moment of almost feeling sorry for him vanishes quickly.

"But my dad wasn't crazy."

"No, he was perfectly sensible, right up until the time he died. Let's just forget about the drinking, fighting, and gambling. He'd kick the crap out of total strangers for stupid things like cheering for the other team or looking at him the wrong way. There's a reason every cop learned his name, and every doctor recognized his face. The fighting, that's one thing common to a Stitch."

"That is what dad called it. What is that? Stitch?"

"A stupid moniker, but true. No matter how badly we were broken, you could stitch us back together, good as new. Hell, better than new, but assholes never stop trying to give us a fresh set of stitches."

"Why couldn't we attract pretty girls instead of assholes?" I scoff.

"You're an alpha male now. It's like we give off a pheromone that triggers aggression in other men." My uncle blinks a cumbersome blink, "You met your Kismet yet? I smell mine in the air. Haven't smelled that stench for quite a while. You need your Kismet." His tone becomes high-pitched and whiny. "You complete me." He puckers his lips. "Mwah. Mwah. Mwah." I shudder at the kissing sound.

My heart races. Dad used the same word.

"What do you mean, Kismet? You guys all act like I should know this shit."

A slight twinkle flashes in his eye. "Let me see your eyes."

I step closer. I fear my uncle will hear my chest thumping.

"Your eyes are still the same."

"So what?"

"It means the clock ain't ticking yet. An eye will change. Tick-tock. Countdown. Clock. Tick-tock. Happens to all the men in our family. At some point, it gets the better of us. History. The special something that makes a Cheeks man a Cheeks man. It gains speed like a freight train and takes over. Slow at first, but building, always building. Choo choo! Until it gathers enough momentum that stopping it becomes impossible. You keep accelerating until you jump the tracks."

"Terminal velocity," I mutter.

"What?"

"Sounds like hitting terminal velocity. I student-teach this experiment—"

Used to this experiment.

His chest heaves. "Call it what you damn well want!"

I clench my fists.

"Sorry. Just sometimes."

"It's cool." I stand up straight. Leaning in close no longer feels safe. "How did my dad beat it?"

"He didn't beat it. He's dead. Remember? You're kinda stupid for a smart guy," he scoffs.

"How did he last longer than his expiration date?"

"Booze."

My jaw gains a thousand pounds of weight. The right side of his face lifts in a smile while the left side remains lower. No matter what he tried, one side rose, and the other side fell. The Sisyphus of smiles.

"Booze?" I ask, not believing his first response.

"Yup. Beer. Bourbon. Tequila."

"I know what booze is." *Crazy and dumb?* "Did you drink, Uncle Lester?"

"Nope. I'm alcohol intolerant." Laughter erupts from deep inside his chest. "Where's me Lucky Charms? The leprechaun stole all the marshmallows from my cereal again! I'll kill that vile little green maniac if I ever catch him!"

"How do I find my Kismet?"

The door opens. Conley and Hallsy shuffle in. "I'm afraid you'll have to leave now."

"And he pees in the milk. The dirty bastard!" Lester dances in circles as he screams at the ceiling.

I look back at the shell of the man claiming to be my uncle one last time.

My uncle stops and stares wide-eyed. "Have you heard it yet, Marc?"

"The leprechaun?" I don't even know if I should have answered.

"Leprechaun. What?" He shakes his head rapidly, "No. No. No. It. Your Kismet. When you're into the sunset. Just about dead and gone. Kismets have a funny way of introducing themselves on your deathbed right before someone brings you back. Personally, it's not how I would pop the cherry, but it ain't my call." He leans forward, eyes so wide

I think they might pop out of his head. "Have you heard it? Man. Woman. Whichever. *It*." The emphasis on the last word sends chills cascading down my spine.

I understand precisely who he means. Her.

"You mean my Kismet?"

"First, you hear it. Then, you see it. After that, your clock starts to tick-tock. Tick-tock. Never stop 'til you pop!"

"Maybe. I don't know." I kick around my foot, searching for the correct answer.

"That's a shame," Lester says. "Better find your Kismet. Later they bloom, quicker they boom. Tick-tock goes the clock. Twice the speed. If you can't find your Kismet, you'll never be free." He tilts his head to the side; both sides of his mouth rise together. "I thought trying to kill people would be fun, but it's a pain in the ass. The screaming. The crying. The begging. The blood. I wouldn't do it if it weren't necessary. But there's one I need. No choice. No choice. Only chance to be free."

Free. There is a way to be free? I swallow the question in the presence of his manic break. Words tumble out of my mouth on their own. "It doesn't have to be a curse." My protest falls on deaf ears. "It doesn't have to be a curse." *Am I trying to convince him or me?*

"Tsk, tsk, naughty leprechaun. I see you." Lester freezes and stares at the back corner of the room. "The silly boy thinks he's cursed like you think everyone's after your gold. You're both paranoid. Someone should put you both out of your misery. Someone should." Lester says and then turns in my direction. His eyes click like a television changing channel and open wide. He refuses to blink again. "Someone like me."

Conley pulls hard at my sleeve, stretching the fabric until it pops at the seams. His eyes dart from wall to wall.

"Please, bro," Conley begs.

"What the hell is going on?" I point to the man behind us who abandons the dropkick for a flying elbow. The whole room quakes as he hits the glass wall a third time. "Can he break that glass? What if he breaks the glass?"

"Really, we need to go. The rooms have a way of keeping you here if you stay too long." Conley firms his grip on my arm. "It's time to go."

TWENTY-SIX

Milt blares music the entire ride back to his bar. I replay the hospital visit over in my head, but it's difficult with the bass thumping my every muscle. He lowers the volume to eight when we swing through McDonald's, but it didn't help them get my order correct.

Finding my Kismet tops my to-do list, but since no one will give me a straight answer, I have no idea where to look or what I'm even looking for. Despite this, the sense of urgency isn't lost on me. I'm not a big fan of this voice dancing around my head. I need to find out who owns it.

Dust kicks a cloud of darkness around the SUV as we pull into the bar's rear parking lot.

Milt turns down the music. "Saw you talking to an orderly on the way out. What was that about?"

"Conley? Nothing big," I say.

"Did he say anything about your uncle?" Milt asks.

"Not much, but get this. He said he'd be happy to help me with any of my needs around P3. Can you believe that? Gave me his card and everything. Five hundred bucks gets me whatever I need. Within reason." Conley quickly notes my uncle's file is not within reason.

"Go figure," Milt says. "What else did you learn?"

"That you have shit hearing. How about we turn it down to eleven next time?" I wiggle my index finger in my ear.

"Follow me inside." Milt flings open the driver's door the moment we pull into the bar's parking lot. "I've got more to show you. And you can help me get the place ready to open."

From intern teacher to bar back. Not exactly lighting the world on fire. I never thought I'd miss school this much, but I do. Unfortunately, I don't have any say in the matter as I wait for the School Board to decide my official fate. For now, I'm on an unpaid sabbatical.

I shuffle to the bar, confusion from my P3 visit, and depression with my current employment situation weighing on my every step. The backdoor on Milt's bar showcases more locks than Fort Knox. It requires three different keys, two combination locks, and Milt's thumbprint. He's never taken me into the bar this way. I figured the damn door simply didn't open.

"You have a thumbprint lock on the bar?" I ask.

Milt's hearty laugh echoes through the surrounding trees. "No. It's molded in the shape of my thumb to make people believe they need my thumbprint to open it. You simply have to press hard on it."

"Seriously?" I ask.

"Sometimes, answers are more obvious than they appear." Milt winks.

I return a wink.

"Why are you winking? You got some kind of condition?" He lowers one eyebrow and raises the other.

"Can we go inside, please?" I convince myself to write a book on the proper etiquette of winking when this is all behind me.

The smell of stale beer and mildew overpowers me as we enter the storeroom. A burning piece of my flesh clings to the open door of the hot-box. He slams the back door and leads me over to a dozen beer kegs.

I examine the caps. A couple of Budweiser, Bud Light, Miller Lite, Coors Light, Blue Moon, Sam Adams, Corona, and a single Keystone.

I shrug. "Afraid I don't know much about beer." Nothing like an alcoholic dad to turn you away from booze.

"Here's all you need to know. Keystone is garbage. Worst of the worst."

"Then why do people drink that?" I ask.

"They don't."

"Then, why . . . " The lightbulb clicks. Thumbprint lock. "You don't have beer in there, do you?"

A sly grin crawls up Milt's face, "If you tell anyone, I'll kill you. For good."

Milt rolls the keg out from behind the herd. He taps on the side a few times. Hollow echoes answer.

"Help me with this, will you?" Milt flicks his head. "Grab the bottom and hold it steady."

Milt holds the handles on the top of the silver barrel and challenges every muscle in his arm.

"Is something supposed to happen?" I ask.

"Why don't you give it a try?" Milt extends his open arms, leaving the keg solely in my clutches.

I clap my hands together and rub them up and down as fast as I can. If it worked for the old karate master on his student, I figure it will work for me.

One slight twist and the top half of the silver barrel

jars loosens. The smell of rank beer assaults my nostrils. My stomach pushes to rid itself of an afternoon gas station snack, but I manage to keep it down.

"That's awful." I wave my hand in front of my nose.

"Another line of defense. That smells renders mortal man incapacitated for a good ten seconds." Milt laughs.

"You were turning it the wrong direction," I say. "I appreciate the encouragement, but I'm not dumb. What are you trying to do here?"

"A confidence builder. At some point, you gotta start believing this stuff is real." Milt pushes his way over to the keg. "Here." He hands me a tarnished silver box that is more rust than anything else. Flecks of copper-colored metal encrust my fingertips. A black key fills the lock. "Open it."

I twist the black key, but it doesn't budge, so I jiggle the key a few times until the box finally clicks. I raise the lid, exposing a ratty brown journal held together by a single string tied in a double knot. The bunny ears on the knot look terrible. One side is big enough to drive a car through, but not a full-sized car, more like a Mini Cooper. The other loop isn't wide enough for my pinky. Only one man in the world ties a knot so poorly.

I brush my hand across the cover. "Dad."

"Sorry, but his wrapping was horrible, so I removed it."

"This was Dad's present for me?"

Milt nods. "Start by reading that. I think your old man left a few nuggets in there for you." He walks to the kitchen entrance. "I gotta turn the fryer on, prep the kitchen, and chop up vegetables. How 'bout you do a little reading, then come see me?"

"Milt?"

"Yeah?"

"There's still a man trapped in the floor of my house."

I hop up on a stack of cased beer. "I'd prefer it if we didn't leave a rotten corpse there. In fact, I'd prefer it if he were alive."

"He's still alive. I got it covered, and we'll get to it, but first things first. Read the journal."

TWENTY-SEVEN

Nerves tingle my fingers as I work the knots loose. The pages crackle upon each touch. Years of hiding turned the pages a banana color, but the smell is very much mildew and mold.

This journal serves as my Ouija board to Dad. Messages from beyond to guide me along my path.

Wild anticipation grows in my mind while a queasy feeling overtakes my stomach. I let out a deep breath before reading the first of the last words from my father.

MILK. Fat-free. Gallon jugs with the purple caps.
  Butter. Real butter, not margarine. Read the label.
  Wheat bread.
  Lunchables.
  Plain cheese pizza. Do not buy pepperoni. Marc won't eat it.

"MOM?" I run my fingertips over the dry black ink.

The first words aren't Dad's. They belong to Mom. I

guess she mistook his journal for a notepad and wrote a grocery list. Judging by all the notations, she didn't trust Dad's shopping.

I rip out the page and fold it neatly before stuffing it in my pocket. The rest of the journal can be gibberish, and I don't care. It may not be a hug or kiss, but when you never had the chance to say goodbye, the authentic, unexpected treats of life are the best.

I flip through the first few pages and shake my head. No Table of Contents. No synopsis. Heck, Dad rarely used headers.

Poorly organized, but the journal holds a wealth of information in short-hand form. I know where I need to start, and it isn't with the shopping list. One common word dominates every conversation: Kismet.

I don't have to dig deep. Two pages in and the scrawled word KISMET adorns the top of the page. I speak the words out loud. It helps my memory.

KISMET

-No rhyme or reason on pairing other than a birthday.

-Always thought the idea there's one special person for everyone was BS, but fate is fate. My Kismet happens to be the love of my life.

-Poor Les got stuck with a beer-swilling bloke for his Kismet. At least I can drink all I want for free. Alcohol helps, but I swear I see black dotted lines everywhere after a few beers.

-Dad never told me his Kismet. I'm not sure Mom knew either. It wasn't her. Probably why they split up.

-It seems as we get stronger, our Kismets get smarter, more in tune with our thoughts. This keeps up too long, Emily will realize she could have married better than me. Tough to say for sure though. Lester's Kismet appears to harbor darker and darker thoughts.

-At times, we can communicate without speaking

-We operate best around our Kismet both in terms of ability and maintaining control. Alone, my strength is spotty. Over time, I've

learned to harness my strength effectively, but **BE CAREFUL** *early on.* ***IT ISN'T ALWAYS THERE WHEN YOU WANT IT OR NEED IT.***

-It can be like a flickering light. On again, off again until you get the hang of it. More off than on during the first year, but kicked in easier after a few dozen RIPs.

-A hard knock on the head or hit to the family jewels can cause my strength to short circuit. Started wearing an athletic cup to elimi-nate one of two weak spots.

-Emily communicated with Lester telepathically. After a few tries, we realized Kismets can sometimes communicate telepathically with any Stitch. It's bad enough having one other person in your head. Not sure I could handle two or three. It's enough to drive a person crazy.

-Speaking of crazy, I'm worried about Lester

HE WAS dead on about Lester. I find the bigger, bold note less than reassuring. What use is this curse if being strong doesn't mean always being strong? On the other hand, it may explain Milt's training. Dad noted how long the para-medics, fire department, and police needed to arrive at any of a dozen locations around town. His crudely drawn map detailed the fastest route to the hospital, along with several emergency clinics and random spots with the name doc.

One sat close to the DMV.

I know the spot. The exact spot.

From home, it takes an average of twenty-one minutes to get to the hospital, but the paramedics arrive at our front door in twelve.

"Hey, here's Doc Malcolm's address," I say with a grin to the flies buzzing around my head. Malcolm's name and address headline a list of seven people that include Mr. Layer and Mr. Chavez.

I pull a prescription from my pocket. Earlier, Doc

Malcolm prescribed me light narcotics to help me sleep, but I hesitated filling the script for fear of addiction. If Dad succumbed to alcohol addiction, then I'm at risk. I find the drug prescribed to me listed under Dad's "preferred Rx to use 4 OD" list. I assume OD means overdose. He describes the hangover effects of each. Everything from raging headache to uncontrollable shivering to vomiting out the previous day's lunch.

A few of the words aren't in his handwriting. I analyze my prescription.

"No way." I can't believe my eyes. Doc Malcolm's handwriting sits on the pages of the journal.

Maybe my father wasn't the idiot I once believed.

I decipher Doc's notebook hieroglyphics the best I can.

WATCH your levels

Vicodin = 5 mg Hydrocodone, 500 mg Acetaminophen

90mg Hydrocodone = probably dead

7000mg Acetaminophen as well

Morphine – Limit to 200mg to start, may be able to work up to 3g per day with tolerance. Walk it up VERY slowly

OxyContin & Percocet □ Oxycodone

Dosage will differ. Know before you take the FIRST pill. (Seriously, I mean it) O/D range is 40—80mg, but you'll be in the upper range. Suspect you'll need 120mg by summer

Refer to Acetaminophen levels above

DO NOT MIX WITH ALCOHOL

DO NOT MIX WITH ALCOHOL

DO NOT MIX WITH ALCOHOL

"STILL DON'T THINK he got your message, Doc," I scoff.

I leaf to an untitled page with writing in every direction. Words and sentences cross. Parts of the damn thing read like a Mad Lib.

-*FIGHTS. No matter where I go, people want to fight me. I always hit back.*

    -*Men want to fight. Women seem immune to my "charms."*

    -*I killed someone. I should feel bad, but . . .*

    -*Emily calls the place between life and death "a sunset." Maybe the answer to ridding this curse lives there. She thinks so. She thinks if we're both there together, then we'll find the answer. I think I just need to send enough people into the sunset, and I'll gain control. Control = cure.*

    -*The first eye changed color all at once. The second is changing in pie slices. Same as Lester.*

    -*Blink in photos or pray for red-eye.*

    -*Develop pics in black and white just to be safe.*

    -*Lester said he'll kill my son if I write the name of his Kismet anywhere. Need to find a safer place for this. I think he knows.*

    -*It happened again.*

    -*There's a room in the city. Underground. Out of the light forever. People go there and never come back. People that know about us. It's easier that way. Emily doesn't feel their pain that way.*

    -*I think Lester wants to send me to the Underground. His pies are done. Now his eyes have lost all color. I worry about him.*

HOURS PASS. No matter how hard I try, I can't commit a damn word to memory. The journal acts as a guide to preventing your death after a suicide attempt. I can't decide whether to classify it as a thriller or a horror story. Hell, it's non-fiction. The last page leaves me no doubt. The journal should be filed under horror, even if it didn't frighten me.

Someone took the time to write a headline on this page: Side Effects.

I don't recognize the first two names on the list, but they both brandish the surname Cheeks. The third reads Cornelius Cheeks.

My grandfather hated his first name. Probably because people took to calling him Cornhole. He died before I was born. The words *pancreatic cancer* and *apathy* follow his name.

My uncle's name resides below my grandfather's. The word insanity follows Lester's name. My dad wrote "whack-a-doo" in cursive.

Hyper-aggressive is the term used to describe my father, but I never thought of it as something that could be a side effect.

I glance back to the first two names on the list. *Obesity, incontinence, and apathy* follow the first name while *loss of all five senses, apathy* is scribbled in pen next to the other name.

Toward the bottom of the page, the name Marc Cheeks sits with a question mark following it. I'm not sure I want to know the words that might one day follow my name.

TWENTY-EIGHT

M ilt sticks his head through the doorway. "Wanna help me with the dinner rush?"

I hold up the journal. "Is this stuff for real? I mean, like for real for real?"

"Seems you've had a taste of it. That's real enough, ain't it? We can talk about it while you're slinging hash and frying wings."

I flip open the journal to the back and point to tiny, jagged edges.

"Milt, why are there two pages torn out?"

Milt raises his eyebrows and purses his lips before snorting out a breath. "No idea. Wasn't my journal. I got folks to feed. Do you mind?" He motions me to the kitchen with his head.

I tuck the journal into the back of my jeans and pull my shirt down to conceal it.

Rock music blares from the jukebox while a couple of patrons play pool. Milt refers to his fryer and grill as a kitchen, but the area measures my closet's size. A small pass-through window separates the kitchen from the bar. I spy two men sharing a pitcher of beer at a table near the front door and another four guys seated at the bar.

"A bit of a sausage-fest, eh, Milt?" I nudge him with my elbow like we're part of an eighties sitcom. I look around at the peeling paint and faded neon beer signs adorning the walls. "How about a ladies' night? Or we could do a wine and trivia night."

"Wine? You're freaking kidding me, right?" Milt hoists a king-sized basket of wings out of the boiling oil. "Wing night. We'll go through a thousand wings before the night is out. It's still early. Ain't even dark out."

Milt fishes a handful of wings from the basket and tosses them into a bowl.

"Isn't that hot?"

"Nah, you get used to it." He tosses the breaded fowl in a spicy looking orange-red sauce before dumping them onto a plate. "Throw a few pieces of celery on here and take this to table seven."

"Do I need an apron?" I ask.

"Just take the mother frackin' plate." A sizzle replaces his harsh tone as Milt drops another batch of wings into the deep fryer.

I grab the plate, unsure if Milt is generous or stingy with the celery. Twelve wings, so twelve pieces of celery. Logic. Symmetry. Common sense.

I position a dozen green stalks side-by-side on the plate.

"Are you trying to fuckin' bankrupt me?" Milt stares at the plate. "Three." He snatches a handful of celery off the plate. "Three pieces of celery. I don't want them filling up on this garbage instead of wings."

"Sorry."

"You'll learn," Milt says. He peeks into the dining room when one of the patrons at the counter starts hooting so loud and stomping his feet so hard the jukebox skips.

"Hang on a sec. I'll be right back." He grabs the basket of wings and heads to the counter to drop them off to a regular. On his way back, a guy in a dark hat and dark glasses grabs Milt's arm.

"Rumor has it you're the man to talk to if a guy wants to lay down some action around this place," he says.

He lacks the subtlety I might expect for a guy making a bold move like asking a stranger about taking a bet.

"Afraid you have me confused with somebody else, my friend, but if you're interested in some wings, I'm your guy." Milt doesn't wait for an answer as he hurries around behind the serving line.

"As an eleven percent owner, don't I have a say in that?" I ask, joking, mostly.

"Keep your voice down and come here." Milt puts his oily hands on my shoulders.

I tense.

"Relax." Milt leans in close and gazes into my eyes. "Put down the plate." Waves of his hot breath wash over my face. The stench of a few shots of happy hour whiskey causes my face to scrunch involuntarily.

"You aren't going to kiss me, are you?" I ask.

Milt shushes me and continues to stare. "I need to know if you're ready."

Oil pops as the fryer continues to crisp tonight's special.

"You pluckin' the chickens before you cook 'em, Milt?" a voice from the bar shouts.

"Don't get your panties in a bunch!" Milt hollers. He lowers his voice. "Are you?"

I glance over his shoulder and look around the bar.

"What are you talking about?" I ask.

"Marc Cheeks, you're in luck tonight," Milt says.

"That's a first."

"That thing you've been waiting for, it just walked into

the bar. Two grabbed seats at table eleven and one at the counter. That guy asking me about taking a bet, he's fishing for the notebook. Dudak's notebook. By now, word has made its way to Mr. Dollhauser, and no doubt, Mr. Dollhauser wants his cut." Milt hands me the plate. "Blue cheese is fifty cents extra," he says before he shuffles the celery onto other plates. "Take these to table eleven, compliments of the chef."

"And say what?"

"Anything. Nothing. Treat 'em like regular customers. You do any different, and they'll know we have the book. Right now, it's all fairy tales."

Milt assembles two more wing orders and waves me away with the fryer basket. When hot oil hits my skin, I flinch but enjoy a little tingle as my skin sizzles then quickly dries.

I understand now that Milt waves me as an intimidation flag over those in the book from whom we've collected.

Snitches will get stitches. The term has a second meaning with me in the mix.

I approach two men sitting at a four-top. One sits low in his chair. He desperately needs a shave and a comb run across what little hair remains atop his head. The guy's jeans ride up past the ankle.

His tablemate brandishes tattoos from wrist to shoulder. A white tank top puts each muscular arm on display. His patch-filled black leather jacket drapes over the chair while Wolverine work boots hug his calves. The name Axe graces the back. Crossbones form the letter X.

"Wings?" I ask. "Compliments of the chef."

Axe raises his arm. I stare at his bicep. The tattoo of a man's eyes and cheeks nestle inside a Spartan helmet mesmerizes me. Across the forehead of the helmet are four notches.

"You gonna give me those wings or what?" he asks.

"Sorry." I set down the plate. "Cool tattoos."

"Thanks. This one's me as a Spartan warrior. Badass over in India inked this a few years ago. Sucks the guy tried to stab me in the back, literally. The dude tried to knife me when I was leaving his shop." Axe laughs. "He won't make a living doing tattoos now." He links his fingers together and stretches them out, cracking each knuckle one by one. "How about some blue cheese?"

"It's fifty cents," I say.

"Yeah. Yeah. Yeah." He slams two quarters on the table. "That's my jukebox money you're taking."

"I can just add it to your—"

"Take the damn money!"

His voice startles me, and I hurry to grab the coins. In my haste, my arm knocks his frosted mug of beer off the edge of the table. The glass bounces off his thigh, spilling the entirety of its contents into his crotch with a few splashes making their way onto the black leather covering his chest.

"Why you little dumpster humpster!" The guy launches his chair backward as he rockets to his feet.

"Come on, Axe. He didn't do it on purpose." Axe's friend paws at his arm. His uneven mutton chops make it hard to look at him when he talks. "Besides, we ain't here for some kid working in a bar."

Axe buries a meaty finger in my bony chest. "You owe me."

I retreat and put my open palms in the air. "It was an accident. I swear. How about I get you another beer? On the house. Maybe a Keystone."

"You ain't getting off that easy." Axe steps into my

personal space. "A little warm-up before the main event may be exactly what Axe needs."

A third-person talker. Seriously?

"How about I clean you off?"

I snatch the grimy dish towel hanging from my waist. My finger catches the loop in the journal's twine, and my quick motion forward inadvertently sends it flying.

Axe bends down and scoops up the journal. A smile lights his face.

"Well, what do we got here? A little old for a diary, ain't ya?" He smacks my arm with the papers, and I cringe, fearful it will fall to pieces.

I glance over my shoulder. "Milt, little help here."

Axe crosses his arms, tucking the journal in tight. As if the journal's smell isn't already rough, I have to add Axe's pit-sweat to the list.

The eyes from his tattoo stare at mine. "This yours?"

"My dad's."

"Name says Cheeks."

I nod.

"Dan is your old man?" Axe continues his line of questioning.

I nod again. "Was."

A wave of sadness washes over me.

"So, he's finally waggling with the worms," Axe says. "Couldn't have happened to a more deserving guy. I hope they eat his dick first."

"Jesus, Axe." His buddy hides his eyes under an open hand across the forehead.

"Tough break, kid. No offense, but your old man had it coming, and that makes my job all the easier. Thought I would have to go through him to get what I needed," Axe says. "It's his fault I had to come to this Podunk town no-how. Tell you what, you help me find the person squeezing down on my employer's, um, customers, and I'll forget this whole thing."

"I'm not a kid, and I'm smart enough to know when someone starts a sentence no offense; the words that follow are always offensive," I answer. "So, I don't think I'll be helping you find your stupid notebook, seeing how you disrespected my dad."

Shit. I can't take it back. I fell prey to my emotions.

"All I'm saying is you're probably better off without him."

Alone? No one is better off alone.

This is my chance to distract him from my mistake, but it's going to hurt. "No offense, but you're an asshole."

Axe puts his bulging biceps to the test, planting a right hook while my guard is down. Pain radiates from my jaw to my temple. The room spins for four or five blinks.

A wobbling glob of pickled color phlegm flies from Axe's mouth. I cover my face but feel the splash on my chin.

I crab-walk three or four feet away from the table before standing. It takes a few seconds to muster the courage to speak. My hands tremble as I look around the bar before returning my eyes to Axe. "I'm going to need my journal back."

I steady my arm and point to the only valuable thing Dad left me.

"The Journal. It belongs to me. Give it back."

Axe squeaks his voice, mocking my every word. "It's mine. Give it back."

DEFCON one averted.

Axe's tablemate waves his arms until we both look his way. "Axe, he mentioned the book."

"Yeah, so. I ain't giving it back."

"Not that book. *The* book."

Axe missed it, but his buddy didn't. DEFCON one reengaged.

"Shit. You're right. I never mentioned no notebook. I'm starting to think you know more about what I'm looking for than I first thought."

I edge closer. "I don't think you understand. That notebook, the one you're holding, is important to me. I need it." Power surges through my fists and thighs.

"You start talking, or I start chewing." Axe opens the journal and tears out a page. My heart sinks. Tears overwhelm my eyes, but I squint in hopes of not letting them escape. He's ripping apart the only piece of my family still with me. "So hungry, I could eat this."

Time to grow up. Not when. How.

Is this what Dad meant?

With one hand, he crunches the page into a ball and pops it into his mouth. My outstretched arm objects too late to stop him.

"Mmm." Saliva and tobacco juice creeps out the side of his mouth. "Pulpy goodness. You tell me where to find what I'm looking for, and maybe I give this back."

Power surges on and off through my fists and thighs like a light bulb struggling with electricity. Bright. Dim. Bright. Dim.

Bright!

I take two long strides and hurl my body into Axe.

Dim.

My shoulder connects with his midsection, but I bounce off him with little effect. Dad noted his early on lack of ability to harness his strength. It's probably something I should've remembered before I lost my temper.

"Hey!" Milt says. "No fighting in my damn bar."

"Damn, you're just like your old man. That's the same idiotic thing he would have done." Axe lifts his shirt to reveal a black fabric around his waist. "Kevlar. Specially made. My ribs couldn't take another punch from your old man. I came prepared." He digs his steel toe boot into my calf and spins my body half-way around. "You and me are gonna settle this on the bridge. No one attacks me! If it weren't for Milt's rule, I'd slit your punk-ass throat right here. You want this journal back, then you're gonna have to earn it. I win, and your ass better sing like a canary."

The small crowd begins a low, monotone chant. "Bridge. Bridge. Bridge."

"Everyone, calm down." Milt moves to the middle of the crowd.

Thank God.

"Stay out of it, Milt. Piece of shit lied to me, attacked me." Axe stands toe to toe with Milt. Their physiques match, but Axe is the taller of the two.

"I understand, but he's just a kid. Yellow line rules," Milt says.

I regain my feet. "What does that mean?" I ask. "What are you guys talking about?"

"You'll see," Milt says. A soft "bridge" chant plays as a background melody.

He puts his arm around my shoulder. "This is perfect. You beat Axe, and things will fall into place. I can negotiate from a position of strength for a fair split with Dollhauser. Hell, I'll even bump you up to fourteen percent on the book. Fucking everyone in this town will do whatever we say. That is, of course, if you get through this."

"If?" The word chokes me.

TWENTY-NINE

The bar patrons gather on the rickety old bridge. Its existence outdated the first settlers of the town, and its architect remains a mystery, but few people tamper with the structure. The previous mayor upgraded the safety rails and ordered the bridge repaved. He died the day after the safety rails were installed, and the new mayor halted additional work.

Milt doesn't speak a word as we walk toward the bridge. Axe chats with his friend and two other bar patrons. They laugh every few moments.

A sense of dread threatens to drown me. The journal hints at this being my future. Lester flat out told me. Fights. Men can't resist the urge to prove themselves, and I'm their siren's call. Kyle. Dudak. The Cabbie.

Now Axe.

I trudge alongside Milt to the bridge's midpoint. My feet become cement blocks, gaining weight with each step. I remind myself cement blocks aren't compatible with rivers.

Think light.

"Are you going to tell me what's going on here?" I ask. "Why don't you just shoot him?"

"Sure. I shoot him, and ten more guys show up with guns. A lot of 'em. And those guys won't be coming to collect anything other than bodies and blood. Mine. Yours. Doc's. Your buddy's dad."

"But we cleared them."

"Dollhauser ain't gonna care. He respects strength, not stupidity, and I'm guessing he's still pissed at what your old man did to the first guy he sent here to track down Dudak and pinch on a certain football coach," Milt says. "I'll explain the rules in a moment."

If I don't fight, I condemn Milt, Doc, and Glenn's dad to death. The alternative holds slightly more appeal, but not much.

My frustration spills into my words, and my body tenses. "Why don't I have a goddamn say in what happens?" *Why don't you ever tell me what in the hell is going on? What am I training for? Why do you refuse to clue me into anything before I'm neck-deep in it?* I swallow the questions, now is not the time.

"Keep that fire. You'll need it." Milt points to a thin corn-colored line. "Stand there."

I throw my hands into the air. For a moment, I think about punching Milt, but I need to find an escape. I dodge several potholes on the way to the yellow line. One hole measures about four inches deep by my best guess, and I imagine we'll be able to see the water through the hole in a couple of years.

Axe lines up on the other side of the bridge. I glance over my shoulder at the rolling waves sweeping under the bridge. A little white foam kisses the top of the gray-green water as the current bounces off rocks. Four steel rails spaced about a foot apart along with metal spiderweb mesh netting separate me from the icy waters below.

The breeze turns an unseasonably warm day into a chilly but clean smelling one. If only the water looked as clean.

A shiny blue Ford F350 pulls up to the bridge's far side. Onlookers stand shoulder to shoulder across the road's width. The truck positions itself perpendicular to the bridge, blocking any escape.

My escape options vanish.

"There goes that idea," I mutter.

I wish I'd worn my jacket. I blow into my hands and rub them together as fast as I can. It wouldn't surprise me if a fire lit between my hands.

Milt assumes center stage. The sun partially emerges from the clouds and shines God's spotlight on him.

"Gentlemen, a bridge challenge has been issued. You shall all bear witness. No matter the outcome, Marc's participation absolves him and his family of Axe's challenges or personal claims in the past, present, and future. That is the reward of The Bridge. Additionally, should Marc win, Axe will return his journal. Should Axe emerge the victor, Marc, if he is able, will assist Axe by all means necessary to locate Axe's missing property."

The circle of heads bobs in unison.

Milt refrains from using the word notebook. Plausible deniability on this part.

"The rules are simple. Anything goes behind the yellow line except weapons. Only grappling and boxing in the road. And no one may leave. Five-minute time limit, and it begins on my signal."

"What do you mean behind the yellow lines?" I ask.

"The space between the railing and the line you're standing on," Milt says.

"That's like three feet."

"Well, it should be easy to avoid then," Milt answers.

We stand a long distance from a car's exit off the bridge, but only an arm's length from a freefall into the water. The bridge spans thirty yards across the water, short by most standards, and not nearly enough space for me to run around and avoid Axe for one minute, let alone five.

Milt edges in my direction.

"So, how do I get out of this? Offer him money? Kiss his ring? Seriously, Milt, what's my play here?" I ask. "Fighting doesn't seem like an awesome solution."

"Stay low and try not to get thrown off." Milt smiles a non-welcoming smile. I remember Thanksgiving and his use of the phrase "test-drive." I realize he isn't trying to help. This is about our future, not mine. His future, really, and my place in it. He is using me, but why, I don't know. Milt is nothing but trouble. Plain and simple. Dad wasn't a great man, but he would never have put me in harm's way.

A chill races up my spine and convulses my body twice. I peek over the edge again. "That can happen?"

"Only seen it once before, but I bet that's what he has in mind." Milt turns to walk away but pauses, "Think you can make it three minutes?"

"Three? What about the other two?" I let my voice get out of my control, and it grabs the attention of the spectators.

"Keep your cool, Marc." Milt counters. "You've been in fights before. Do you think you can last?"

I shrug.

"You're not exactly filling me with confidence," Milt says.

"I'm standing here about to fight a guy twice my size, and I'm supposed to worry about filling *you* with confidence? Are you fucking serious?"

Milt laughs, "Not the first time I heard that. And for what it's worth, you sound like your old man. If you can make it three, then I might be able to get you out of the last two."

"But—"

He turns his back on me without another word and joins the other men.

Milt is no friend. The argument my father had with him that time he sent me to my room plays in my head. Dad understood what Milt was, what he wanted from me.

Where has she gone, my voice? My promised Kismet? She's all but abandoned me since Dad died. Could use her right about now. A low murmur in the crowd of onlookers grows into a frenzied exchange. Hands fly in the air. One man wags a finger in another's face. A push follows, and then more shouting. Milt separates the two and threatens them with his own set of brass knuckles.

Axe shadow boxes while we wait. I note most of his punches stray to the high side. He also extends his follow-through. It might leave him vulnerable if he misses, but if he connects, I'll be in trouble.

"Five minutes on my start." Milt looks to Axe. "You ready?"

"Hell yeah. Let's go. Woo!" Axe raises his fists in the air and howls at the sky.

Milt turns to me. "You ready, Cheeks?"

"Honestly, no," I say.

Milt shakes his head. "It's rhetorical. Get ready."

Optimism melts from Milt's face.

"Fight!"

Axe charges across the road. He's on me in four strides.

I duck left, but his giant paw catches hold of my shirt. I straighten my arms, bend at the waist, and free myself with two quick steps back. The move works, but I find myself shirtless.

A chorus of laughter rises from the spectators. One of them demands my shirt as a prize. The three hairs on my chest stand tall as a cold gust of wind hits my back.

Hurried strides carry me to the far end of the bridge. I want to keep running, but this was the schoolyard all over again. Maybe I could climb over the truck before Axe grabs me, but then what? There's no one out there to help me.

"Thirty seconds," Milt shouts.

Time freezes. Axe plods down the center stripe. I watch as he dips left, then right, left again, leaving me little room to squeeze by his outstretched gorilla arms. His wingspan covers half the bridge's width. He carries my shirt in his teeth like a dog with a rogue piece of lunch.

Axe slows as he approaches, stopping about ten feet from me. He removes the shirt from his mouth and throws it toward me.

"Put that on. I don't want to look at your scrawny chest." He sneers. "Any last words?"

"Dude, you got spit on my favorite shirt." I crumple the shirt in my hands.

Axe inches closer while I crouch, waiting. When he cuts the distance between us in half, I chuck my shirt at his face.

Hobbling, I sprint as best I can when the spit-soaked cotton connects with his ugly mug. He lashes his arms in every direction but only skims my bare shoulder.

I spy open road ahead with only a few potholes to dodge. Three minutes waits for me at the other side of the bridge.

My forward vision overlooks the Yeti-sized foot flung in my direction. I manage to maintain an upright stature for two steps before it evolves into a stumble, followed by a tuck-and-roll. Panicked, I don't even try to regain my footing. Instead, I crawl toward the other end of the bridge.

I feel every metal eyelet of his Wolverine boots imprint in my ribs. The kick's momentum flips me onto my back, exposing my soft underbelly.

"Two minutes."

I wish time moved faster.

Mom would be disappointed. She always said never wish your life away. No matter how bad a moment may feel, you will never get that moment again. I doubt she'd feel that way rolling shirtless across this pebble-littered pavement.

Three revolutions put me face to paint with the yellow line. I freeze.

"This is the part where you pay the man." Axe pushes my body another foot closer to the railing. "And I'm the man."

Axe slams a closed fist into my belly button, changing my outie to an innie. He follows with a left hook. My head flies back, bouncing my skull off the pavement. When I open my eyes, two Axes dance above me. Warm liquid puddles under the back of my head.

As if avoiding a single hard Axe isn't hard enough, now I'm forced to contend with two.

I do the only thing my fuzzy neurons conclude as a plausible solution to the situation; I curl up in the fetal position. My mind thinks fetal, but my heart hears fatal. It skips a few beats while I wait for Axe's next move.

He screams obscenities while alternating kicks between his right and left legs. I struggle to breathe, and the world above me won't stop spinning.

The kicks push me into the railing's webbed-metal mesh, and I lose any give my body possesses out in the open.

Thank God the mayor fixed the railing before the potholes. For the moment, his decision saved my life, even if it meant imprinting crisscrosses on many parts of my body.

"Three minutes!" A mix of groans and cheers echo from the crowd, although I can make out Milt's celebration. Those are the only sounds I hear above the thumping internal thrombosis.

Axe stops kicking my back and shuffles around to my head. I wrap my arms around my skull to protect it the best I can. Instead of feeling another thump of his foot, Axe screams. A thud on the ground follows, which bounces my curled body. "Freaking potholes." He inhales deeply as he complains.

I risk a glance. Axe sits a few feet away, clutching his ankle.

"Broken?" I ask.

He scrunches his face and growls, "What?"

"Never mind." I clamber to my feet, and he lashes at my ankle. I grab for anything I can reach as he holds tight.

I latch onto the nearest railing and pull with all my strength. It groans under my force and the additional pressure of Axe pulling on my ankle.

My chest scrapes along the pavement as I work to free myself. The section of the metal railing snaps from the bridge.

"Guess only the metal webbing is new," I mutter, but I found *it*. Old or new, that metal would not have snapped with old Marc.

I yank my foot clean, abandoning my Nike shoe in Axe's hand, and hop up. If this continues much longer, I'm liable to find myself naked.

Axe rises to his feet and limps toward me. I walk backward, maintaining a slow pace, and ready the railing piece above my shoulder.

"No weapons!" a voice from the crowd shouts.

"Easy to say from the cheap seats! Why don't you drag your ass out here and take my place?"

"One minute left," Milt announces.

I'm running out of bridge, and Axe walks with only a minor limp now. My foot sinks in the deepest pothole on the bridge. Cracks radiate in every direction.

Axe points at me and shows his canine teeth. "Enough games. Time for you to take a little swim."

I want to yell, "You shall not pass!" to satiate my inner nerd, but without word or warning, I smash the rod vertically into the pothole. A small chunk of cement lifts from the ground. I slam the rod harder the second time. Cracks crawl in every direction.

Again, I bring the slender steel down. Axe stops dead in his tracks.

"What the hell are you doing?" a voice from behind draws closer.

I lift the metal cylinder high into the air and shatter the thin layer of asphalt. Running water twenty feet below becomes visible. I kick off my other shoe in Axe's direction.

"You must not like yourself." He examines my shoe and paces forward while I fight off the growing pain emulating from the bruises on my back. "Screw the five minutes. We're going to overtime," Axe growls low enough for only me to hear.

The blood has stopped flowing from the wound in my head, but the pulsating continues. I use its rhythm.

Slam.

Slam.

Slam.

The hole widens and forces me back. Everyone from

the bar except Milt stands over my shoulder. The cracks chase Axe in the opposite direction.

"Five minutes. Time's up," Milt hollers.

Slam.

The cracks merge with other cracks and potholes across the surface of the bridge.

"You can stop now." A hand touches my shoulder. I wrench my arm and free myself.

I loathe them. They stood and watched Axe beat me without a care. Hell, they cheered. No one intervened. And when I leave here, there will be no one waiting at home for me.

I loathe them all.

I raise my silver beacon high above my head. For the first time, I notice Axe's wide eyes filled with fear.

"Dude, wait. I didn't mean—"

No part of me wants to wait. Their fear tastes refreshing, and my need for adrenaline is unquenched.

Susan crests the turn at the far end of the road from the bridge. She's the last thing in my sights before me, Axe, his friend, and the cadre from the bar, along with two tons of asphalt, plummet into the frigid water below.

THIRTY

The icy water bites my bare feet and naked chest. Try as I may, my body refuses to listen to the swim instructions my brain shouts. I can't open my eyes. They pinch tight, and I drift deeper.

Chunks of the roadway bang into my body. A hand brushes against my back, jarring me enough to realize I'm not dead. I force my eyes open, but the murky water renders me blind. No part of me wants to reach for the hand.

So many talk shows discuss how drowning reminds the subconscious of time in the womb and creates a sense of calm. What a load of crap! How can anyone be calm with sewage, silt, and grit invading their mouth and lungs?

A large piece of asphalt careens off my ribs, forcing me left, where I meet face to face with another body grasping a familiar shoe in his hand.

A dying embrace with Axe tops my list as the worst way to leave this world.

You're not going to die.

I hear her voice as if we're talking on the telephone,

but I resist the urge to answer. It seems someone winds up dead whenever I answer. Too many times, I'm that someone.

Your choice, but if you ignore me, I'm pretty sure you're going to die, she presses.

I release the last of the air from my lungs. The count-down to death hits high gear.

Fine. No offense, but I was hoping we'd never speak again. I answer with thoughts, not words.

That makes me sad. I'm only trying to help. I help you. Then you help me.

My urge to inhale swells.

Push down on his shoulders, she says. *Send him to the bottom of the river. No breath for him.*

He's already dead.

I run the phrase around every part of my mind. Concluding he's dead may help avoid guilt.

And you will be as well if you don't do what I say.

The muscles in my abdomen tense. I try to relax, but my desire for oxygen seizes control. Axe doesn't flinch when I touch him.

No guilt. Just push.

I run my hands up his arms. The Spartan tattoo flashes in my memory as my fingers pass his bicep. This was no hero's death. Fortunately, he's no hero.

His body sinks without a fight, but it provides enough leverage to shift my momentum upward. I glide through the water, and within moments my face breaks through the divide that separates my life and death. A new baby's scream fills my lungs with precious oxygen. Every time I try to open my eyes, the cursed creek throws water over my head. My mouth bobs in and out of death.

Milt's shouts catch my attention. I manage to catch a glance of him running along the bank off to my left.

A hand clenches my ankle, submerging me into the cognac waters again. I kick but find nothing below.

She won't give up on her prey easily. You have to fight. Most creeks are tributaries, givers to the bigger waterways. This creek is a taker. A taker of souls. The voice pipes into my head. I don't just hear it now. I feel it. *Fight.*

I flap my arms and kick, but the creek, she wants it more. The struggle saps my lungs faster than before. Where is the calm so I can give in and go peacefully?

My hand breaks the surface, but the siren refuses to grant me air.

Get to the right and reach, she says.

But Milt is left, I counter.

Milt is no friend. She confirms what I already suspected. What my dad tried to tell me.

The creek concedes horizontal movement without resistance. Me draining the last of my oxygen supply suits her end game. Munson Creek probably appreciates me separating myself from the one person, Milt, who can help me.

The floating pieces of asphalt descend to the depths of the water, nothing more than shrapnel the creek absorbs to devour her prey. She will spit it out into some other river a day or two down the line. I consider bargaining with her. After all, I delivered the cab driver already, plus served up another half-dozen today.

That's gotta be worth a reprieve.

No, it isn't! She's angry. *Stop thinking and start acting. In ten seconds, you need to reach high and strong.*

Never give a drowning man a countdown. I swear I'm short of oxygen by the time I hit three. At five, I expect to pass out. By seven, dying seems like a decent option. Roundabout nine, I remember Susan's face atop the hill.

At ten, I thrust my arm skyward. A sharp branch

pierces my forearm before the mental clock hits eleven. My mouth fills with watery sludge when I scream.

Warm liquid oozes down my wrist. The creek drinks my offering willingly while she poaches my body. The taste of my blood satiates her enough to release my ankle. I'm now the poster boy for Munson Creek's catch and release program.

The branch won't break. Pull yourself up. The voice jumps around my brain.

I extend my free arm out of the water but grasp emptiness. The unyielding water pours over my freezing bones. Oxygen teases me.

She won't let you go without suffering and sacrifice. You have a grip. Pull.

My freedom relies on my ability to use an impaled appendage to lift myself out of the water. How am I going to explain this one to Doc Malcolm?

I've watched a ton of movies where the hero performs one-arms pull-ups, so I convince myself if an actor can do it, then so can I.

Eye of the tiger.

A silt-filled grunt burbles from my lips. Blood flows freely from my arm. The waters relax as they lap up my additional offering. Enough room to collect a deep breath. I fear it may be my last.

With a scream, I torque my shoulder with dying strength. My shoulders break free from the water. My impaled forearm cracks as I lunge my free arm to the nearby moss-covered branch. The water remains calm as my blood drains into the creek.

Her voice calms me. *Prop yourself up and wait there until help arrives.*

"What if I stop bleeding?"

Then make yourself bleed. Duh.

Blaring sirens fill my ears a minute later. Susan points the rescuers in my direction. Milt ducks into a car driven by a familiar face, but one too far away for me to identify. Leaving me here to die.

Again.

THIRTY-ONE

"It's a pleasure to attend to your medical needs without having to revive you first." Doc Malcolm forces a laugh from under his white coat. "Considering the filth your body bathed in, you may need to shower in hand sanitizer for a week."

"What's the damage?" I resist looking at him as his cold stethoscope hops its way down my back. Nurses stare with unyielding eyes from beyond the end of the examination table, but no one says a word.

Doc Malcolm steps to the curtain and wings it all the way around the metal rolling system, cutting off the protruding eyes. He moves in close. His leg touches my knee.

"The damage?" He rubs his fingers across his forehead. "Outside of what should be half-dozen broken ribs, a fractured radius and ulna, severe blood loss, hypothermia, and death; nothing. Not a goddamn thing.

"So there's the issue. Those were your injuries when they pulled you out of the water. Everything except the hypothermia and death. Unfortunately, and I'll deny this if you ever tell anyone, we're short-staffed, and given the others who fell into the water, no one was sitting with you in the back of the ambulance on the ride here. And now look at you.

"Your arm was cut, but not broken despite a large branch impaling the thing. It was like your bone grew back through the branch on the drive back to the hospital. Either that or it was the oddest shaped branch in the world and somehow passed completely through your arm while missing your bone."

"As if that weren't enough, your back and stomach are covered with deep bruises." Malcolm lowers his clipboard, scratches his head, and points to various injuries covering my body. "These colors of plum and indigo and crimson signify there is something seriously wrong. Deep and often devastating injuries. Usually broken ribs, internal bleeding, emergency surgery stuff. And I now have to say usually, because your ribs aren't broken, and there's no internal bleeding."

I hold out my arm and notice the Frankenstein stitching. I pull the blue hospital gown over my chest and back. My eyes make their way to my feet. Everything appears normal, except I'm missing something.

"Where are my toenails? Why don't I have any toenails?" I lift my right leg to the side, so my foot comes in full view for Doc Malcolm.

"Focus here, Marc. The water temperature measured forty-five degrees. Not only were you without a jacket and shoes, but the police found your shirt a thousand yards downstream. The medics on the scene told me your temperature was one-hundred-one when they pulled you out. A fever. How do I explain that? Do you know? I sure as hell don't." Doc shakes his head and glances up.

"Say I was one-hundred-four before I fell in," I reply. Sounds logical.

Doc Malcolm feigns a chuckle. "You are your father's son, but you're different. I treated a lot of his injuries, and while I'd argue he was the fastest healer I have ever seen, but it was nothing like this."

"You still didn't tell me the damage," I say.

"Other than the fact I figure you were dead at some point under the water because that's your thing?" Doc Malcolm winks.

"Yeah, you know, let's focus on the important details."

"A puncture wound already stitched up, the toenails, which you already noted, and your fingernails on your left hand." Doc Malcolm points his red pen to my left hand.

"Guess I'll have to cancel that mani-pedi I had scheduled for Sunday. Glenn's gonna be disappointed."

Doc stifles a smile. "Keep those bandages dry. No more swimming in that cursed creek or any other water. You might be able to heal quickly from most injuries, but that cursed creek always did a number on your father, and it seems to have the same effect on you. You'll heal, but like your old man, it's going to take a bit more time. I don't even want you in the shower. Sponge bathe for now. I still need you to stay clean to prevent a staph infection. If you get an infection in a deep wound like that, you're in for a world of trouble. Drink plenty of fluids—" Doc reaches over and grabs a bag— "I borrowed some clothes from the lost and found. They've all been laundered. Twice. Sorry about the underwear. Pickings are slim. I want you to come back and see me in a week and don't tell a soul about this."

Doc punches a few times on his Samsung Tablet.

"That's it?" I ask.

"That's it," he sighs. "We're going to keep you overnight for observation. A nurse will be in first thing in the morning to discharge you. I'm sure you'll be hearing from the police as well."

Doc moves to the curtain.

I sit on the exam table's crinkling paper and fish through the bag of clothes, pulling out a pair of Star Wars underpants. I didn't know they made these in my size.

"Really?" I stretch out the pair, putting the Death Star on the backside in full display. "You trying to tell me something, Doc?"

"It's a trap!" Doc's belly shakes with his laughter. "Like I said, pickings were slim." He pulls open the curtain.

I stop him short of leaving. "Hey, Doc." I move the underwear out of view. "I think I'll pass on the underwear, but thanks. For everything."

"There is one other thing." He pauses, looking down at the ground before back at me, "Your eyes."

"Did the fall screw up my vision? Everything looks in focus." A quick scan of the room and nothing is blurry.

"Your vision is fine. The color of your eyes. What are they?"

"Blue," I reply.

"Well—" Doc steps through the open curtain— "now one's green."

THIRTY-TWO

I convince a nurse to dig through the lost and found boxes to find me a pair of sunglasses. It's not time to advertise to the world my clock is ticking. Not that I know exactly what that means.

The hospital won't let me leave under my own care, and Glenn's nowhere to be found by lunchtime, so I'm left slumming it with Milt rather than risking another meal of shitty hospital food. Our drive back to the bar takes twice as long with the bridge out of commission. The blaring music prevents any meaningful conversation.

"What the fuck, Milt?" I huff, crossing my arms and turning my gaze to the passing landscape. "Where's my journal?"

"Drop it. It's gone. We saved the notebook. That's all that matters," Milt says before cranking the bass on the Cadillac's stereo to a full-body thumping level.

I spend the remainder of the drive Googling changes in eye color. Mood. Development. Illness. All plausible, if I let myself believe, but I know the real reason. I even search the name Dollhauser and find lots of news articles about indictments for murder and money laundering, but never a conviction. Swell guy.

The lack of audible dialogue continues until we start cleaning the bar. I indulge in a basket of wings, downing about twenty Cokes along the way.

Sirens wail in the distance. Debris particles fill my nose with each deep breath. Milt wipes down the counter while I reset the bar stools. I hate being here, but my options are limited. And Milt was the name in Dad's letter.

"We need to find your Kismet," Milt says.

"You know about that, or did you read about it in the journal? That was my dad's private journal." A fire burns in my words.

"I know a lot of things." Milt slams dirty glasses into the green bucket. I cringe with every clink. "What I don't know is what the hell happened on that bridge. I wanted you to scare him, not kill him."

"What happened?" I raise my bandaged arm. "You didn't give me a freaking choice. That's what happened. Why didn't you help me?"

"Five minutes were up. You didn't need help. It was over!" Milt grinds his words. "When are you going to trust me?"

"Axe wasn't going to stop! You left me to die!" I smack an open palm on the bar top. Freshly mint cracks outlined my hand. "And you keep getting me killed."

"I'm making your stronger, but you're too dumb to see it, and—" Milt points to the bar— "you're going to pay to have that fixed."

"Whatever." I look around for anything to keep me busy. Clearing the table of Axe's food certainly doesn't appeal to me. "Take it out of my fourteen percent."

"Five, if you're lucky. I wanted you to send a message.

Now I gotta worry about Dollhauser sending more guys. Hell, I'll be lucky if I'm able to net five percent now." He rotates from slamming glasses to tossing plates in the sink. "Plus, I wasted a whole day in police interviews."

"What did you tell them?" My chest heaves, and my breathing shallows. I grab a few napkins and try to substitute them for a brown paper bag.

"Told them we were fishing. Bridge collapsed from a freak lightning strike. I had to toss my best gear downstream when no one was looking. That and a thousand bucks should keep them off your back."

"But I didn't kill anyone!" My protest falls on deaf ears. "I'm done with this. Whatever this is. And I'm done with you."

Milt sets aside the flatware, closes his eyes, and inhales through his nose. After a few seconds, he exhales before speaking, "I get it. You're angry. And I'm sorry. Maybe we could've handled that better."

"We?"

"Me. But, Marc, we still got issues to handle before you go. After that, go on your merry way."

"Like finding my journal?"

"That thing is gone. Forget it. I'm talking about a log that's clogging up the toilet and gonna flood our bathroom," Milt says, but his tone loses confidence. He looks left rather than making eye contact.

"You mean the cops?" I ask.

"You're half right."

"Can we stop speaking in riddles? My head still hurts from the fall," I say.

"The cop. One cop. Singular. The one in your house. Remember him?"

I swallow my tongue.

"Your silence is reassuring," Milt says.

"Yeah." My words carry no strength. "I remember."

"You leave, and he's your problem to deal with. All of it." Milt words escape his gritted teeth. "Plus, you need to find your Kismet. I can help with that. No more fighting. I swear."

"You can stop saying that because I don't know who that is. Why do *we* need my Kismet anyhow? I need to know not you." A helpless feeling creeps into the back of my mind. I don't know, and I don't know how to know.

"You and your Kismet can fix this mess. Make it go away. Make the cop forget. And it's *we* because I am smack in the middle of it. Think of it as a Jedi mind trick. I remember your dad telling me how you're into that sci-fi shit." Milt paces around the bar, his Wolverine work boots moving freely one minute and fighting the glue-like floor the next. "It's probably someone close to you. Someone you trust. Someone you've known for a long time." Milt looks at me. "Your eyes. Damn, it's started. Think. Someone close to you."

Tick-tock. There goes my clock. Sci-fi shit in the real world.

Susan. It has to be her. It's a female voice. I'm drawn to her. Or she to me. P3. The bridge. School. Too much to be a coincidence.

"I think I know." *But I'm pretty sure I shouldn't tell you.*

"Get 'em to your place. This ain't an audition for a dance company. Don't have eight people show up." Milted tosses me my Under Armour jacket. "Go there now. I'll be there by five. Called you a cab. My treat. Local guy. You can trust him, not like your other cab driver." Milt winks.

"Very funny." First chance I get to cut Milt out of my life, I'm starting a ride-sharing business in this town since none of the big ones will come here, and we're left with old-school, rundown yellow-checkered-cabs. Most of them have been through more than I have.

"Five o'clock. Don't forget." Milt vanishes into the storeroom.

I spy a utility knife hanging off the edge of the kitchen counter. It could come in handy if this cab driver turns out half as crazy as the last one.

Or maybe if I need a little pick-me-up.

THIRTY-THREE

"What's so important that I needed to rush over to your dad's place?" Glenn throws his black North-face jacket on the couch, usually reserved for Clyde. The fur clinging to the sofa represents the extent to which I've seen him over the past few months.

When I'm not in the hospital, I spend most of my time at the bar working, sleeping, and showering, so it stings coming home. Everything about this house rubs my soul raw. The place looks about the same, except Milt's empty vodka bottles overflow the trash can rather than Dad's beer cans. If he's been sleeping one off in my bed, I'm going to torch my room. Okay, that's a bit extreme, but the comforts of home died with Dad. Milt installed bars on all the windows along with two deadbolts and a stupid fake thumbprint lock on the door to my dad's bedroom, so it's not like I can check. At least there's no rank smell coming from under the door.

My childhood home is now a prison, a memorial, and possibly a morgue if Milt's been lying to me about keeping the cop in Dad's room alive.

Shortly before Glenn arrived, I removed the cash from Mr. Chavez's garage and moved it to the freezer's ice maker. If things go well today, I may move back in here permanently.

"As a sign of my gratitude, feel free to help yourself to my food," I say. "Just steer clear of the ice compartment. It's broken, and if you open it, a shitload of ice will fall out."

Ice. Money. Same difference.

Glenn rolls into the kitchen and opens the fridge. I follow close behind.

The smell wafting from the interior indicates eating any contents would be a game of leftovers Russian Roulette. Glenn bobs up and down from a crouched position, "There's nothing but leftover pizza and Chinese food in here."

"You love pizza and Chinese," I scoff. "And it's not leftover. It's like two hours old."

Glenn flings the door closed. "This is exactly what I'm talking about."

"Did I miss something?" I whip open the door.

Glenn raises his shoulders. "I'm a vegetarian. You got bacon on the pizza and a chicken-like substance in the General Tso."

My mouth drops open. "Vegetarian. Since when?"

"Since I started tutoring Leslie Mannis in math and she told me she was a vegetarian and would only date the same," Glenn says.

"Dude, that's crazy. Who's dumb enough to do something like that to impress a girl?" I laugh.

"You mean like becoming a teacher in a hometown you hate just to be around my sister?" Glenn replies.

"Don't judge me!" I slam the abused refrigerator door

closed. It wobbles a few times before coming to rest. "It's called loyalty."

"It's called stupidity," Glenn scoffs. "Speaking of stupid things, you look awful. Did you secretly try out for the NFL? Throgmorton did say you would make a great tackling dummy."

"More like a biker gang." I rub the back of my neck and move away from the foul odors of the kitchen. I breathe deep. "Glenn, I need your help."

The question lifts his face along with his spirits. "They all come crawling to the Glennster."

"Glad you're enjoying this." I plop down on the sofa.

Glenn's pants make a peculiar sound as he sits on the arm of the couch.

"New jeans?" I ask.

"Yeah. Leslie said all the guys in Europe are wearing this style."

"Europe?" I snicker. "Can you breathe wearing those?"

Glenn inhales. The copper buttons above his zipper strains to hold the pants.

"No sweat," Glenn speaks, holding in his stomach. His cheeks turn rosy, and his eyes bulge, matching the button on his jeans.

"This is going to sound unbelievable, but you have to believe me."

"Well, when you put it that way." He starts laughing as I fumble with my shirt.

I can't stop glancing at my arm. Showing him my wounds and explaining everything may be best. Explaining how being a good guy doesn't always mean doing what is considered traditionally good.

"Hit me with it," he says.

"I need you to go along with me no matter what I say."

"Why me?"

"After my dad died, weird stuff started happening. The school fight was only the start. Ever since then, people have been trying to fight me. Hell, trying to kill me. This guy Milt has been trying to help me. At least, I thought he was helping. Now, I'm not so sure. He's trying to help me find my Kismet. You know, like two people meant for each other. I think it's your sister."

Glenn throws up his hands. "Whoa, dude. Ease up on the sister chatter."

"Not like that, moron. If your sister is who I think she is, then I could use her help. Unfortunately, I don't completely trust Milt, so I'm worried about what he might do if she isn't who I think she is."

"And if she is who you think she is?"

"I'm petrified."

"Why not bail?"

"Because sooner or later, he'll figure it out." I pace the floor of the kitchen and family room. "Even if he doesn't, you can bet he comes to collect on your dad's debt if I vanish."

"But you said it was handled!"

"Handled as long as I keep working for Milt."

"Well, that sucks donkey's ass."

"Together, we should be fine. Play dumb, so I can feel him out. If you start feeling uncomfortable, we'll bail. Cool?"

Glenn sighs, then gives a few shallow head nods. "Cool, but first dibs on anything in the fridge or the panty until he gets here."

GLENN OPENS his mouth wide and announces, "Abandon all hope, ye junk food who enter here," before polishing off the last of the stale Cheetos.

He licks his fingers clean of the orange dust as Milt's hour melts into us waiting two. Glenn's mother put the family on a gluten-free, non-GMO, healthy food diet. Pair that with his newly found vegetarianism, and his diet to me is about as much fun as a dentist on Halloween.

Milt bursts through the front door. I notice the front wheels of his SUV rest on my front lawn.

He storms straight to Glenn. "Is this him? Is this the one?"

Glenn straightens his back and puffs out his chest. Milt squeezes Glenn's biceps and peers into his eyes. He pats Glenn's body up and down, possibly searching for weapons or clearing him for departure.

"I think so," I say.

"Think or know?" Milt's voice sounds grainy.

"I don't even know what I'm supposed to know. So, no, I don't know."

"You sure we can trust him?" Milt asks.

"Cross my heart and hope to die." Well, not today, I don't hope to die.

Glenn stares at Milt. "Who's Grizzly Adams, why is he frisking me, and what does this have to do with me?"

"This is the guy. He's here to help," I say.

"I'm not getting a good vibe," Milt says.

"Whatever, Miss Cleo." Glenn yanks his arms free. "This ain't the psychic club hotline."

Milt snatches Glenn's hand and drags him down the hallway to Dad's bedroom. I follow behind. Bewilderment seizes Glenn, but I only muster a shrug of the shoulders and raise eyebrows to answer him.

This is my first visit to his room since he died. Milt

makes quick work of the locks, presses down on the thumbprint, and swings open the door. Maybe I should have mentioned the whole person under the floor thing to Glenn, but the idea of telling him there's a cop playing a role in my live-action version of *The Tell-Tale Heart* didn't seem wise.

The weight of Dad's vacated room clouds my judgment. I want answers. And I want my parents back.

"I need you both to stand right there." Milt points his stubby fat finger at the wood boards covering my secret.

"Would someone mind telling me what's going on?" Glenn put his hands on his hips.

"I'll explain everything later." Assuming I understand enough to explain.

"Fine, but if I help you, you help me sometime in the future, no questions asked."

"Deal."

"No matter how big," Glenn adds.

"I already agreed."

"So? You gotta swear it."

I hold up my right hand. "I swear."

"And?"

"Enough!" Milt stomps his foot. "Shit, I probably just broke his nose." Milt peers at the floor.

"What?" Glenn kneels and places a hand on the board. "There's someone under here?"

"I can explain." In an instant, I dash through the Italian shoe story and the part about how the cop threatened me and tazed my dad.

The last of the day's sunlight sneaks through a small hole in the window shade. The beam catches Glenn's face, exposing his disgust.

"You don't do that to a cop. Hell, you can't do that to any person!" His cheeks flush.

"That's why I need you to help him." I look to Milt. "Right?"

Milt grunts, "Something like that."

"I'm eighteen now. I can go to jail, like real jail for shit like this." Glenn edges toward the door.

"For everyone's sake, you'd be best advised to do what you're asked," Milt says.

"What happens if I don't agree to help?"

Milt slides his hand toward his waist. "Do you really want to find out? What would Mommy say if she found out about Daddy's gambling habit? What would your father's financial planning clients think? Your financial aid and scholarship money might vanish as well."

"Um," Glenn struggles to speak.

"That's right. I know all about your folks. So, I'll ask again, do you really want to find out?"

Glenn glares at me. "We're going to help him, right?"

"Absolutely." I nod.

"This sucks donkey balls." Glenn exhales. "What do I need to do?"

"If this doesn't work, you can cut the cop free with this knife." Milt steps forward, hands a six-inch knife to Glenn, and repositions us, so we stand back to back. "Tough to say how it will work best for you two, but this position seems to create the least distractions when first working together. On second thought, I should hold on to the knife."

Milt pulls a handkerchief from his jeans and wraps it around the knife's blade when retrieving from Glenn.

"Don't want to cut myself," Milt says. "Now, concentrate. Make a connection with the man under your feet. Visualize reaching into his head and looking at his memories like you're scrolling through texts or tweets. Delete every memory you see involving Marc and his dad. All of them."

"What are you talking about?" Glenn asks.

"The police officer's mind. You should be able to get into his memories," Milt says.

"I have no idea what kind of stupid crap you've gotten yourself into Marc, but your buddy here is insane."

"Devil spit in my face and call it holy water." Milt pounds the wall. "This one should be easy. It's not him. It can't be. This is a stinking waste of time."

I open my eyes and gaze upon the newly minted hole gracing the wall courtesy of Milt.

"Wait here." Milt storms out of the room. Glenn and I turn and look at each other.

"Marc, you know this isn't right. There's a line, and there's crossing the line. Trapping a guy under the floor is way the fuck across the line. What the cop did wasn't cool, but my gut says this Milt dude is way worse than a crooked cop. Did you get what you need? Because I'm uncomfortable, like really uncomfortable. I want out of here. To protect my dad, I won't say anything, but this is it between you and me."

The weight of Dad's vacated room clouds my judgment. I want answers. And I want my parents back.

"I'm scared, Glenn. Things are happening. Changes. I can't explain them, and Milt is the only person who seems to care, to offer help. I don't trust him, but I need answers."

"First person? I don't count?"

Glass clinks in the background over Glenn's words.

"What now?" he asks.

I shrug. "No clue. Listen, I get what you're saying. If I had it to do all over again, I'd like to think I would have done things differently. It all happened so fast. I thought that guy was going to kill my dad, my dog, and probably me."

Milt hurries back into the room, carrying an arm full of liquor bottles. Jack Daniel's. Jose Cuervo. Johnny Walker Red and Black. Dad could never afford Blue.

He hands me three bottles.

"Stand back." Milt directs us to the side of the room. Glenn and I huddle in our time-out corner while Milt unlatches the floorboards, exposing the officer.

"Why is he on his stomach? When did you move him? Why did you move him?" My voice cracks.

Dale lays face down with one shoeless foot positioned most unnaturally. His uniform is wrinkled and loosely hanging from his body.

"You gotta be freaking kidding me!" Glenn pushes his back against the wall. "I'm out. You two aren't including me in your little game of torture!"

"I beg to differ," Milt says, unsheathing the knife using the handkerchief again. "Not sure how you'll explain your fingerprints."

"No!" I yell, but Milt doesn't hesitate.

He plunges the blade deep into Dale's lower back. It Jello-jiggles for two seconds before blood further darkens the navy-blue shirt around his kidney. The wound looks . . . familiar.

"And before either of you two get the idea about being a hero, you should know me and my Colt might have something to say about that," Milt says, flashing us a quick glimpse of the gun in his utility belt along with another knife and three pairs of brass knuckles.

Jesus, does this guy belong to the brass knuckles of the month club? Glenn is right about Milt. Training ends today.

Milt unscrews the cap from the Jack Daniel's bottle and jams a rag in the top. He pulls a lighter from his pocket and flicks his stumpy thumb. The orange amber dances to life in the still air. "Sorry to inform you, Officer, but the blanket you're resting on isn't what we call flame retardant."

"Milt, what the hell are you doing?" I manage to push words out of my mouth. "This isn't right. He knew my dad. Maybe he can help me understand—"

"I'm doing what needs to be done. We gotta burn this place down. They'll blame the cop's death on your buddy. His dad's in deep with his shitty gambling. No one will have any problem believing Glenn had something to do with Dudak as well." Milt reasons. "Ties things up clean. You and me can start fresh tomorrow."

The rag embraces the flame as its own. Milt spikes the bottle against Dale's skull before he slams the floorboards shut.

"Hand me another bottle." Milt waves his hand.

My body refuses every command.

"No way. No fucking way. This is insanity! How is that fair to me, Dad, or Glenn? People will label them murderers! People will call my family crazy!"

I fight back the tears. Glenn freezes. Traumatized. Tears stream unabated from his eyes.

"The dead don't get equality. They don't use the same scale of fairness compared to the living. I'm doing you a goddamn favor, so how about a little respect?" Milt says. "Go wait for me in the truck. I got man's work to do."

"I'm not going anywhere with you guys. You freaking lit that guy on fire. On fire!" Glenn repeats words like he's trying to convince himself. "He's going to die if we don't get him help. I'm not waiting in your truck."

Milt resists raising his head, but his eyes appear as if they are looking through his eyelids. "I didn't tell you to wait in the truck. Like I said, the dead don't get equality. Marc, grab him."

I set down the bottles and latch onto Glenn's bicep. There's no escape without a plan.

"Let go of me." Glenn pulls away with his whole body, but I don't budge. I squeeze harder until he winces in pain.

"Put him in the closet," Milt says.

Glenn thrashes, but I overpower him and pull him to the closet door. I whisper, "Trust me, okay?"

Milt grabs the remaining bottles of liquor. I slide my other hand into my pocket and pull out the signature pen Mr. Layer gave me. Although I've never needed it, I carry it with me everywhere.

Glenn trembles. A pale white color washes over his face. "Why should I—"

"Lower your voice." I bang the wall to make it sound as if Glenn is struggling, but Milt appears too focused on the liquor bottles to notice. "Let's get outside as quick as we can."

"What the hell are you doing over there?" Milt snarls. "Get his ass in the closet, or you'll join him."

"Milt, I can't—"

Milt looks at me. "Your old man wouldn't think twice."

I squint. "I'm not him."

"No shit." Milt shakes his head. "He's probably rolling over in his grave. I can't imagine his disappointment." Milt pauses his advance to flick the lighter and bring it to life. The flame hovers below the dangling rag. "Don't worry. You'll be able to ask him yourself in a minute."

"I'd rather ask my grandmother."

Milt cocks his head to the side. I shove Glenn to the floor and pivot towards Milt.

His eyes scream death.

I aim Mr. Layer's trinket at Milt's face, hoping to silence those eyes.

"Green," I say, pressing the light. Milt recoils.

"A flashlight?"

Glenn's facial disbelief changes to a smile once he sees Milt's facial hair smoldering.

"Why, you little shit!" Milt shields his face with his arms.

"Black!" I press the second button, and the name *Nellie Cheeks* burns itself into Milt's arms.

I advance two steps and kick Milt square in the nuts, sending him sprawling backward onto Dad's bed. The liquor-soaked rag leaks onto the sheets.

I spy a familiar set of bound pages poking out of Milt's pants.

"That's mine!" I yell, grabbing the journal.

Milt regains his footing, wraps one hand around the journal, and shoves the drenched charred oak smelling cloth over my mouth and nose.

Two torn pages remain in my grasp as I stumble away from Milt.

"You want it?" He waves the pages. "Give me your buddy, and I'll give you the journal."

Some things in life are worth dying for, but few things are worth killing for. I see Axe's bloated face on Glenn.

"I need that journal, Glenn, but . . . "

But I'm already too much like my dad.

Whatever quest Dad set me upon will have to be completed without further aid from him or Milt.

I don't give Glenn a choice, grabbing him off the floor and dragging him down the hall.

Milt yells out from behind us, "Say goodbye to your fucking journal." Coughing interrupts his words. "I'm going to burn down your goddamn house. Say goodbye to everything you know! This isn't over!"

"Let's go!" I pull Glenn. "This may be our only chance."

"Our only chance to what?"

"Survive," I say.

Glenn's wide eyes peer over his shoulders. His legs flail, and I use every ounce of strength to keep him from falling. Glenn hyperventilates as we reach the back door. He manages three words.

"Survive from what?"

"Death. The devil incarnate." I refuse to look back as we burst through the door. "Me."

THIRTY-FOUR

The crisp, fresh evening air reinvigorates my lungs as the flames and burning flesh transform Dad's room into a pocket of hell. Real estate is all about location, and unless you're a demon looking for a three-bedroom fixer-upper, my place is about to become worthless.

Did I mention the large walk-in closets and quaint kitchen? Oh, and there may or may not be twenty grand in crisp hundreds in the freezer. Literally crisp.

The sky affords us a few flares of gold, but twilight covers most of the landscape. A flash of red explodes from the kitchen.

Disregard the kitchen.

And the money.

Milt drenches my childhood in Molotov cocktails.

"He's burning down your freaking house. Aren't you going to call the police or the fire department?" Glenn paces with his hands on his head.

A cloud of smoke billows from my bedroom window.

"That's number three. We gotta move, Glenn."

I figure he'll go for the furnace with the last bomb. Milt

will flee at the first sound of sirens. There won't be time to search for us. He might check the shed or drive the block, but I already know how long it takes emergency services to arrive. Three more minutes and counting.

There is only one place to hide. "Follow me." I practically lift Glenn off the ground as we sprint down the street.

"Where're we going?" Glenn asks between exhales.

"There." I point to Mr. Chavez's garage. "We can hide there."

Flames leap into the branches around my house. There would be no solemn farewell. Like so many other things in my life, my house is ripped away from me in front of my eyes. No time for tearful goodbyes now.

"Holy smokes." Glenn turns to me. "No pun intended."

I punch in the code, bringing the garage door to life.

"Is that . . . ?" Glenn's jaw drops.

"Yeah, it's the cop's car," I say. "I disabled the tracking system on this. Pretty sure the department has given up looking for it after all this time. Hop in the car. I'll close the garage. We need to lie low for a few hours."

Glenn hesitates. "We could head to my house. My folks will know what to do."

"That's the first place everyone will look. Milt will point the finger at us if he is caught." I stand in the shadows of the garage as the door crawls lower. My eyes remain glued on the gap between the door and the ground. The chasm separating life and death. Not mine. Glenn's. "If we can't figure something out, then we'll head to your place. Cool?"

Glenn barely acknowledges with a nod and eases himself into the passenger's seat of the cruiser.

I worry the subtle white light on the opener might give us away to anyone passing by. I scan the wall of tools and grab a hoe. With a sharp jab, I shatter the potential traitor. The only remaining light shines from the dome interior of the police cruiser.

I open the driver's side door.

"Turn off the light," I say.

I toss the hoe into the back seat and hop in.

"It's going to get cold in here." I rub my hands together.

"If this is your attempt to get me to cuddle with you, I suggest you stick to bribing me with junk food," Glenn sneers. Neither of us deals well with adversity and stress, so we hide under sarcasm and snark.

We chisel our backsides deep into the vinyl seats.

"How long you figure before the firetrucks show up?" Glenn asks.

"Based on my dad's notes, less than three minutes." I check the windows at the top of the garage door for any signs of life.

Glenn glances at his watch.

"What are you doing?" I ask.

"I'm praying your dad is right. Until then, we're fish in a barrel."

"Better pray hard. Being right was never his forte." I mutter.

"It's been two minutes."

Our breathing fogs up the car windows. Glenn leans forward to wipe the windshield.

"Leave it!" I snap.

He jumps back as a siren comes into range.

"Time?"

"Two minutes, forty seconds." Glenn smiles.

"Thanks, Dad."

Tires squeal on the roadway outside, immersing us in the cover of the night as sirens draw nearer. A momentary reprieve, but from who and what exactly? I want the journal back, but it's ashes.

Ashes to ashes.

Damn irony.

The garage windows juggle red, white, and blue lights into the wee hours of the morning. Adrenaline keeps us awake the first few hours, but the sirens and lights fade as the hours roll deep into the night.

"You think the cop would've arrested your dad?" Glenn asks.

"Arrested or killed." I sigh. "He was pushing us for a fight. Me and my dad."

"But you don't know for sure. Should the cop have died for that?" Glenn's tone backs away a bit with his second question, but his eyes stare relentlessly.

I purse my lips and push streams of cold air out my nostrils.

"No, but—" There's always a but, or at least there should be.

Two wrongs still don't make a right.

Glenn refuses to accept my logic. "We stood there and let that cop die. Shouldn't we have at least tried to save him?"

"We'd be dead too, Glenn. I've lost everyone else that mattered in my life except you and Susan. I'll make it right, but I'm not about to risk your life doing it."

"Why didn't you take time to figure things out?"

"Curses don't wait around for you to figure them out, in case my house burning down wasn't an obvious clue." I toss my head in the direction of my former homestead.

"Hey, *mi casa es su casa*, dude," Glenn says in his best Spanish accent.

"I don't think they say dude in Mexico," I laugh.

"Sorry, amigo." Glenn holds out a hand.

"You want to save a life?" I fish a page from my pocket. Glancing down at the remaining piece of the journal, I see the historical names of the Cheeks' manly-family tree. "Save mine."

Glenn pulls his head back and frowns. "Dude, what are you talking about?"

I surrender the page to Glenn.

"Read," I say, pointing at the page.

I stare at the three question marks following my name. Life is supposed to be this great unknown, but those question marks mean something negative will fill the space. It won't remain blank. History says so.

No journal.

No home.

No hope, maybe.

Glenn flips the page over and continues reading.

"This is amazing." Glenn's voice breaks my moment of self-pity.

"What is?" I ask.

"Did you know there are different types of chokes? I always thought you strangled someone to cut off the air, but you can blood choke someone."

Glenn points to Dad's chicken scratch, and I read it aloud.

"Cerebral blood flow chokes involve restricting the flow of blood to the brain. A person should pass out in about 10 seconds but come back in about 30 seconds after you let go, so plan your escape before letting go."

"Your dad was kinda badass. Look at this stuff," Glenn says, running his finger along with the words while reading to me. "If body temp exceeds 107.6 degrees Fahrenheit, heatstroke can't be reversed, and I'll die. Or how about this one? If I lose more than 40% of my blood, I'll need an immediate transfusion but should be able to survive at a 30% loss. Wow. How much blood do you think that is?"

"I dunno, but I'd prefer not to find out." I remember my time in the hot-box and wonder if Dad would've let me go as far as Milt did.

Glenn continues, "Thirty-minutes max in water at 40 degrees Fahrenheit." His teeth chatter as he pulls Officer Dale's jacket tighter across his body. "I'm totally rethinking that refusal to cuddle. Don't judge."

We force a laugh.

"Once those lights fade, why don't you head home," I say, nodding toward the back door.

"No way, man." Glenn shakes his head so hard I thought he might've concussed himself. "This is serious shit."

I pinch the bridge of my nose and close my eyes. "Dude, you're not built for this. You have your whole life ahead of you, and you've seen the stuff on those pages my dad wrote. There's a reason he needed that information. There's a reason he wants me to know that information. Not you."

"Come on." The fight fades from his voice.

"I need help with one thing, but then you head home. Hide with Susan. Have your parents stash you until I can figure things out," I say. "Cool?"

"Nope, not cool." His nervous laughter comes naturally this time. "But I'll do it anyway. Promise me you won't get shot or do anything stupid."

"Cross my freezing heart and hope to die." The cold penetrates my clothing and licks my skin.

"So, you got a plan?" Glenn asks.

My heart sinks as I realize I need to put our lives into the hands of a madman: the other surviving Cheeks.

"Yeah. First, I'm gonna grab the little bit of cash I have

left stashed in here. We're not gonna sit in this garage all night," I say.

"We're not?"

"Nope. We have the perfect camouflage to drive out of here. There's nothing but cop cars all around. One more won't stand out."

"I don't love the sound of that," Glenn says. "That's crazy. Won't they be looking for that cop's patrol car?"

"Well, if you don't like the sound of that, then you'll probably hate where I'm taking you. And even if they are, the fire will distract them for now."

THIRTY-FIVE

"None of us thought you'd be crazy enough to come back," Conley says as he leads me down the hallways of P3.

"Doctor Gehringer said regular visits might help my uncle." I lie, banking on the notion the doctor doesn't discuss much with a guy like Conley.

Conley jumps in. "Don't believe anything Doc Gary says. The words that come out of his mouth some days could fill the liar's forest."

"The liar's forest?" I ask.

"The gravestones in the Forrest Cemetery." Conley flips his head left. "Behind the hospital. It's a grave of folks unclaimed or forgotten by family, but we nicknamed it that because the truly crazy, insanely desperate patients will say anything to get out of here, especially when they're near the end. So many lies. Makes for great stories, though."

I laugh awkwardly.

"Well, we've arrived." Conley waves an arm at the door.

I point to the wall. "Which handprints belong to him?"

"What?"

"Which are his? My uncle's."

Conley shrugs. "No clue. Hallsy probably knows, but he ain't here today." He pauses before he opens the door. "Your uncle is painting, but I sedated him earlier. Will that bother you?"

"He's not painting a clown face on himself or anything, right?" I ask.

Conley humors me with a chuckle. "No, although I might slip him an extra dessert to see that one day when Hallsy's working. Would absolutely freak him out. Then I could pronounce myself the true prank king."

"You guys are that close?"

"Practically brothers. I'd do anything for that guy."

Thoughts of Glenn run through my head. Would I do anything for him? I don't know, but I decide to lie to myself and say I would.

"I know what you mean," I say.

We exchange nods as he shuffles through his keyring and finds what he needs, a copper key with a small black handprint insignia. *This place is so random.*

My uncle pays us no attention as we enter as classical music plays from overhead speakers. Notes dance across the frosted wall to my right.

"Young Marc, to what do I owe this pleasure?" He sounds refined, never breaking the visual connection with his canvas.

Conley and I stare at each other.

"How'd you know it was me?" I ask.

"Come closer. Pay me the honor of sitting next to me, and I shall enlighten you. Perhaps you can critique my latest Rembrandt."

Conley gives me a reassuring glance. His eyes widen in

relief as he passes by the white steel door that separates him from the throes of potential insanity.

My uncle waves me over. "Come. Sit. It's always a joy when my favorite nephew comes to visit."

"Don't you mean *only* nephew?" I ask.

"Well, only makes you my favorite by default. Let's not spoil the moment, shall we?" He continues to lather blue on the white pallet. "What do you think of my music selection?"

"It's nice, but not my thing," I say.

"Nice? I'm sure nice is what Bach was going for when he wrote the Cello Concerto."

"Sorry. I'm not much of a music guy. I enjoy rock music from time to time."

"Rock music is garbage. Clogs up my mind, so I can't think straight."

"Holiday music has that effect on me. Gets me thinking about my mom, and I spiral," I say. In all honesty, I loved listening to the Christmas songs throughout December with her, but now they served as empty, painful reminders.

"Interesting." Lester holds the last syllable of the word for an extra few seconds, to the point I feel uncomfortable, so I press forward with a change of subject.

"What are you painting?" I inch forward but pace my approach. My instinct warns me to wait for him to turn toward me before I get too close.

"If you're waiting for a formal invitation, you're going to be standing there for quite some time. I'm in the zone," Lester says.

I look left and notice the girl holding her palms against the glass. Her cold blue eyes chill my soul. Every hair stands on the back of my neck.

"You made quite an impression on her, nephew. She requested the glass defrosted earlier today as if she knew you were coming to visit. How prescient. Salem would have burned twice over already."

I approach the glass as I did before and place my palms against hers. Icy air nips my fingertips, so I snap my hands back to my side. I watch as green seizes her left eye. It takes only three seconds for all the blue to fade.

"Did her eyes . . ." I stop my question short and put a finger to my discolored eye. My research suggested emotion caused her change, but maybe the doctors missed a cause, and by doctors, I mean my search results on Google.

Insanity?

She opens her mouth wide to scream, but no words emerge.

"I think I can see her uvula," I say.

"I think I was about sixteen the first time I saw a girl's uvula. Always good when it's with someone the same age as you." Lester laughs.

"It's the thing in the back of her throat," I say.

With Lester's arms free, I suddenly second-guess my sarcasm but focus on her.

After a deep inhale, she puffs up her cheeks and holds back her breath before slamming her forehead against the glass. The impact vibrates my body, forcing me to retreat a step.

"You did it now." My uncle follows his words with a tsk, tsk, tsk.

Repeatedly, she slams her head against the glass. A small fissure erupts on her forehead, oozing red liquid into her green eye. My face already offers a similar scar to where hers will form.

I wave my arms a few times before clasping them together in a prayer position. Repeatedly, mouthing, "I'm sorry. Please stop."

"How long is she going to keep this up?" I ask my uncle, desperate for a solution.

"Until you put your hands on that fucking glass and keep them there until she's satisfied, Nephew. You know, for a smart guy, you sure can be an idiot."

I jam my trembling hands hard against the glass. The blood trails down her cheeks and drips from her pink upper lip onto her white teeth as she smiles. She matches her hands against mine. Her blood-tainted smile almost looks pretty, but her stoic eyes ice the blood in my veins. My hands stop trembling. An eerie sense of calm washes over me.

The blood stops and recedes into her head. I blink to make sure my vision isn't playing tricks. When her face returns to normal, she removes her hands from the glass and escorts her newly minted scar to the center of her room.

"What the . . . ?" I stammer.

"Sometimes it's better not to know," Lester says. "Besides, that's not the question you want answered." Lester swivels, flashing a disjointed demonic grin and a diabolic tone. "Is it?"

THIRTY-SIX

I gaze at my uncle's hulking forearms for the first time.

"They let you paint?" I ask, stealing a glimpse over my shoulder at the girl. She retreats to her painting, tucked in a shadow protected corner.

He shifts back to his canvas. "Sometimes. At least they don't make us use those God-forsaken finger paints any longer. She——" my uncle flips his head toward the girl in the next room— "is the only one any good with them. Quite the artist, that one."

"So, how are things going?" I creep closer. "They told me you were sedated. Can you understand what I'm saying?"

"Cut the crap. I don't want to spend my painting time coddling your butthurt." Lester flexes the rubber paint-brush in his hand and, with a release of his fingers, flicks blue paint at me. "It's not like their tranquilizers last longer than five minutes unless they knock us out." He mumbles.

"I think I know who my Kismet is, but how can I be sure? Milt, maybe you remember him? He's a friend of my dad's, and he said he knew you. Anyhow, he was helping me. Was being the operative word, but now me and my friend are in trouble, and Milt, well . . . " I maintain a perimeter outside of his reach or paint flicking prowess. If the sedation truly doesn't affect him, I need to be cautious.

Lester stops painting. "Yes, I know Milt. I know him well. He tried to feed you to the river, didn't he? Fucking injuries from that bitch take forever to heal."

How the hell would Lester know about that?

"It's a creek."

He puts the plastic tip of the paintbrush in his mouth. "River. Creek. No matter. It used to be a tiny stream before Milt started feeding that thing as a young boy. He does that, you know?"

"Does what?"

"Feeds that cursed river. I've known Milt for a long time." He taps the brush against his clean-shaven chin. The end fits snug in his dimple. "Let me guess. You introduced him to your Kismet, you were wrong, and he tossed you both off the bridge. Amazing you survived. No one survives in those waters."

"No . . . " I hesitate. "No. Not like that. I pissed off a guy at the bar and fought him in some bizarre bridge ritual. How did you know about the river? Creek. Whatever. How did you know?"

"Dammit. I hate being wrong. But they always want to fight. Always. I told you. Come." My uncle beckons me to his painting. I need answers, so I risk getting close.

His painting showcases a large figure standing atop the bridge and two smaller heads in the water below.

"Who are they?" I ask.

"This is Milt." My uncle points to the figure on the bridge that is surprisingly accurate down to the wardrobe and facial hair. "And these two sacrificial lambs swimming in the cesspool known as Munson Creek are you and your friend, who wasn't actually your Kismet."

"But that didn't happen—"

"No, but . . . " Lester reveals a second canvas behind the first.

A crumbling bridge with numerous bodies falling into the murky water. Milt standing center stage, watching it all from the coast, wearing a smile on his face. Same wardrobe. Same facial hair as the other painting. And the journal sticking out of the back of his pants.

"How?" It's the only word I can muster.

"Sometimes, want gets mixed with reality. You came alone this time, didn't you?"

"Here? No." I shake my head until my uncle reaches up and puts his hand on my shoulder.

"Is Milt with you?" His eyes dart in every direction.

"No."

I inspect the painting's details. "What's this up here?"

"Not sure," he says.

"What do you mean, you aren't sure?" I ask.

"I didn't paint this one, but I did do the colors. Seeing through Milt's eye helps with that part."

I gulp. He captures the macabre bridge scene in vivid color down to the perfect shade of blood red mixed into the creek's brackish water. He put his initials L and C where my eyes should have been.

"Excuse me. Did you say Milt's eyes?" My understanding of my uncle's presence in this establishment, as well as my fear, grow. I feel a sudden urge to use the restroom. Any restroom, as long as it's in another room.

"I probably should have told you earlier, being family and all. Milt is my Kismet."

I recoil but try to lighten the subject so Lester won't detect my fear. "So, did you guys date and everything?"

"God, no." Uncle Lester spits on the floor a few times. "It doesn't always work like that. Nothing wrong when it does, but Milt isn't my type. Hell, I don't think he's anyone's type. I could land a guy far better looking and smelling than him. And one with proper decency."

"Sorry. My bad. It's confusing. I'm trying to understand. I'd appreciate any help. How do I get rid of this?" I don't understand everything yet, but I think Milt pulls the strings. First, Lester. Then, Dad. Now he wants me as his next puppet. Dead or alive.

I reach out and touch his arm, scaly, not smooth, but I force myself to maintain contact. "Please. I don't understand."

He contemplates my hand position. "You agree never to touch me again, and I'll consider answering your questions."

I withdraw my hand at an even pace to avoid appearing relieved to break contact.

"Your Kismet is your other half, your one and only. That person meant for you, but that doesn't mean it will be a romantic relationship or even a friendship. You might fucking hate each other, but you need to learn to tolerate each other if you want a chance at survival." Lester returns his attention to the canvas. "Guessing most of what you need to know is in the journal."

"I lost the journal."

"You lost the journal?" Lester rolls his eye. "If anyone ever asks, I'm not going to admit I'm related to you."

"It wasn't my fault. Your crazy Kismet torched it along with my house. I need your help," I plead.

He dabs dark blue in the creek. "You need more help than I thought. How about I help you if you help me?"

"A little cliché, don't you think?"

"I don't."

"Believe it's cliché?"

"Think. More importantly, I don't care. That's the deal."

I peek over at the girl. She's busy with her art but turns her easel, so the picture becomes visible. I can make out a group of people standing in front of a building, maybe an office building or a school. A sense of dread fills my mind at the thought of going back to work. Ever. The rumors, the stories, the questions, they will be too much for me to handle.

"Fine. Whatever," I say.

"Is that a yes?"

I nod.

"You share things with your Kismet. Love. Hate. Emotions. They feel it more than us. Much more. Emotion stays with them as strength stays with us. For most Kismets, it's too much to handle when we get out of control. You become filled with rage. They experience it times ten. You feel sad. They turn suicidal. You get angry. They become murderous. You crave respect. They demand power. Higher highs and lower lows.

"You'll learn to sense each other, especially when there is trouble. I sensed Milt last time you visited, although every time I managed to spark a mental connection with him, all I could hear was heavy metal music." He points to the picture. "These colors came through clear as day for me. Easy to see."

"Because he was worried?" I ask.

"Hell no. Because he was excited."

"Excited?"

"Do I have to spell everything out for you?" He rubs his finger and thumb together on the bridge of his nose and exhales. "Kismets can communicate telepathically. They do it best with their partner but can sometimes do it with another Stitch, if the situation is right. We stitch our bodies back together. They stitch together thoughts and emotions.

"Hell, a few Kismets can even stitch with family members. Their unspecial family members." Lester sighs. "It was never this difficult with your mom and dad."

"My parents?"

"Can you speak in more than two-word sentences?" He spikes his brush on the ground. A blob of cobalt creates a Rorschach image. "Yes, your *perfect* fucking parents. It took them about two minutes to find each other. We celebrated by going to the carnival. Those places are such a scam, but they had this one game with a baseball. For the low cost of five dollars, they'd pay you ten dollars for every mile-per-hour you could throw it over 90. Of course, they rigged the radar gun. Unfortunately for them, they'd never run into folks like us before. Your dad wanted to try, but he was new to this. I had five years working with Milt already. You know how fast I threw?"

Curiosity burns in my brain. Lester is outlining a potential something for me, but I slouch my body into a formless posture to appear only remotely interested.

"One-ten," I guess.

"Ha!" He tips his chair back to its breaking point. "Not even close. Two-thirty-five."

"That's not possible."

"After what you've seen, you're going to tell me that's impossible? Don't overthink it, Nephew. Besides, I bet I'd be closer to four-hundred these days." Lester's crooked smile returns. "Anyhow, they refused to pay. Your mom flirted with the guy who ran the game and convinced him to meet her later. When he showed up, your dad did a little of his own convincing. They were a good team. Well, at least until you came along. Baby Marc screwed it up for everyone. Me. Them. Milt. We ran this town. Headed for bigger pastures, much bigger pastures. You opened the door for interlopers like Dollhauser to step in."

I back into the wall, refusing to take my eyes off him. They blame me. All of them. Maybe even my own parents. They died because of me.

I find myself pressed against the wall moments later.

"Don't look so shocked," he says. "Why else do you think your mom was with your dad?"

"Because she loved him." I maintain a consistent volume despite my trembling chest begging to scream.

"Love. Kismet. Whatever. Some people get confused. Best I can figure, Milt wants to use you. He believed the crazy idea you get rich if you own a Stitch. And not just money rich, but rich with power. Your power. That might explain his interest in the journal."

I step away from the wall. "So, Milt is setting up something bigger. What does he want with my Kismet?"

"It's easier to control you without your Kismet around. You gotta figure out who it is because if Milt finds your Kismet before you do, then you'll end up someplace bad, and your Kismet will be in the ground."

"What if I leave town?"

Logic. Fight this crazy situation with logic.

Destinations storm through my brain. Canada, Mexico, or a small village on a tropical island.

"He'll track you down if he knows you're out there. He'll find you, and he'll kill you if you don't do what he says." Lester focuses on the canvas.

"What about my parents?" The need for answers consumes me. Information is power, and I need more strength to face Milt.

"That's it for today."

"Wait. How do I get rid of the curse? Can't I give it to someone else without, you know, dying?"

"Like I said, that's it for today. I need to finish my painting, and you've used most of my time." Lester picks up his brush and waves me closer. "And now you owe me. Come back another day." He lowers his voice to the sound of butterfly wings. "Bring a dozen sharpened pencils. I hate painting. I want to shade. You do that, and I'll tell you how to get rid of this curse. Heck, I might even tell you what actually happened to your mother."

Her smile bounces around my head and my heart. Dad never spoke of what happened the night she died, and now my uncle appears to be my last hope for answers. I want to know. I need to know.

"Agreed," I say.

"And Nephew," Lester inhales a deep, relaxing breath, "Milt would never burn the journal. My bet is it's some-place close to him. Unfortunately, you're not strong enough to challenge him, and whatever plans he has up his sleeve."

"But I could be," I say.

Lester smiles. "Now you're thinking, but be careful with that Raggedy-Andy stitch job on your wrist. Wouldn't want that busting open. Folks see a cut like that, and they think you tried to kill yourself. Put you in a place like this. You belong here. This room wants you. It needs you."

He hisses the last two words. My queue to exit.

I walk to the door, looking over my shoulder every other step. My uncle sets to working on the figure he can't explain in the drawing. I don't recognize it up close, but standing from a distance, I can see it's a girl, a girl with blonde hair. A smile lights my face. I only know one girl with hair like that, and I was right to keep her away from Milt.

The haunting girl in the next room stands near the

glass. I don't see her as scary so much as lonely, and probably a little paranoid being surrounded by crazy men. It occurs to me I might need an ally in here other than Conley. Someone who can keep an eye on my uncle's paintings. I need to step outside my comfort zone and do something crazy. I can't think of a better place to do that than here.

I detour to the glass and plant my lips on the cool surface.

She giggles.

I believe it's the first time I saw a genuine look of joy in any of these rooms.

I wink, and she hops up and down, rapidly clapping her hands.

Did I get that right?

The door slams shut upon my exit. The hall's black hands wait to greet me, curling their fingers as if to call me in.

THIRTY-SEVEN

"You get the answers you needed?" Glenn asks as I hop into the driver's seat.

"Hardly. Five hundred bucks to find out what we already know. My family is fucked up. Milt wants us dead. And if I want more answers, I need to do my uncle a favor and come back."

"If it makes you feel any better, my family is messed up too."

Internally I roll my eyes but outwardly smile, appreciating his attempt at cheering me up.

"And for the million-dollar question," Glenn says. "So, what now?"

"The DMV." I flinch, anticipating his reaction.

"Are you freaking nuts? You'd been better off staying in your house," Glenn scoffs. "While it burned down around you."

"I know a place." I quickly recall Dudak's bloody face. "There's a good chance it's empty and may even have a few of the comforts of home."

"Comforts?"

"Maybe that's stretching it, but it will work for a few days until I can get my head straight and my strength up," I say. "I should have a plan by then."

"Sure," Glenn relents. "What about my mom? She's gotta be freaking out."

"When this is over, just blame me."

"Like I was going to do any different?"

"Thanks, a-hole." I cock my arm back but stop short of punching him. The trust of control isn't there for me.

Glenn chuckles. "What are friends for?"

"Hopefully, a couple of pizzas and leftover General Tso's chicken," I say. "But this won't be easy. Everyone will be looking for us. Milt. The cops. Whatever army your mom rounds up."

"So, basically, the rest of the town," Glenn says. "At least Dad will be happy to have her out of the house for a bit."

"That's the spirit," I say. This isn't Glenn's fight, but the idea of tackling everything alone with nothing but the clothes on my back requires sacrifice. Of course, Glenn wouldn't appreciate hearing his name along with the word sacrifice. "Shall we?"

I motion to the road.

"Shall we? Really?"

"It's my first day on the run. Cut me some slack," I say. "Let's hit the road before anyone realizes we're in a cop car. We have to find a new ride, and we're gonna need some supplies. This car needs to take a dip in Munson Creek. There's a spot where its waters kiss the banks near the DMV. After that, life—" *and death*— "is about to get a bit messy."

THIRTY-EIGHT

"There's too much blood!" Glenn screams. "Why do you have to do this?"

I imagine running a blade across my wrist isn't the indoctrination into the DMV Glenn expected. I look up from the gash with a sigh. "I told you, I need to increase my strength. It's the only way to survive Milt and his bullshit so I can link up with my Kismet. Pay attention."

Glen nods, but I'm still not sure if he hears me.

"Dammit, Glenn. Just put the freaking needle through my skin where I showed you." I wait, but the only thing that moves is his eyes, wide and unblinking. "Now!"

Glenn drops the needle onto the ever-reddening mattress and steps back.

"Chill out, dude. I'm your friend. Remember?" He stretches his open palms toward me.

"Huh?" I glance at the pulsating blood flow of my right wrist, then to my left, where my arm holds the knife high in the air as if it's waiting to descend on something.

Or someone.

I release my grasp and watch it bounce harmlessly off the soaked mattress and onto the floor.

"I'd prefer not to die today." The room spins as I fish the needle off the floor. "If I get it started, can you finish? You know, before I pass out and die."

"I don't want to die either. Kick the knife away," Glenn says, pointing to the blade.

"What? Why?"

"I don't know. I always see it in the movies, so there must be a reason."

"Fine." I slide the knife across the floor with my foot. It bangs into the bottle of activated charcoal we bought at CVS on the way here. "Now get over here. I've got about two minutes before I pass out. You are the perfect example why they should still teach home economics in high school. No one knows how to fucking sew these days."

Glenn shuffles over. "You're irrationally calm. It's freaking me out."

I wince as I puncture the needle through my skin on each side of the opening. The knot holds firm as I tug it tight.

"You're gonna be off the charts freaked out if I die," I say, making another pass with the purple thread. "One more pass, then you take over."

"I thought stitches were straight lines, not exes. This looks like a scary doll," Glenn says. "Can I call you, Ken?"

"Seriously, Barbie?"

"Sorry." Glenn rubs his arm. "I'm nervous. I say dumb things. What if I make things worse?"

"I'm bleeding to death. I don't think you can make things worse."

My eyes flutter on my next pass attempt, and it requires two stabs to cinch both sides.

"I'm going to lie down so you can finish."

"On the bloody mattress?" Glenn asks.

"Well, it's my blood," I say. Peering at the stained Sealy makes me yearn for a hospital bed.

Doc wouldn't screw this up.

The needle shakes in Glenn's sweaty palm.

"Can you do one more?" Glenn asks.

I roll left to leverage my good hand and push myself up. Glenn grabs my forearm before I rock too far backward.

"Position the needle, and I'll do the rest." I slur the last bit of the sentence.

Whether I want a crooked scar or not, I'm getting one.

The Raggedy-Andy stitch work requires another ninety seconds along with two slaps in the face courtesy of Glenn and a couple of drinks of Jolt Cola.

I ease my body into the pool of AB negative and lift my arm in the air.

"So, is that it? Are you stronger now?" Glenn paces from the front door to back.

"It doesn't exactly work that way," I say, eyes closed, waiting for the pain to subside and focus to return.

"Well, how does it work?"

"I can't explain, but not like that." I search my brain for answers. "Doc said something about adrenaline. But I need to heal. Just need more time . . . "

Focus doesn't return. Blackness does.

THIRTY-NINE

My brain beats the inside of my skull. No sign of Glenn. Last of the day's sunlight peeks through the windows. I hate losing the sense of time in the void. Waking up in the future like a lost time traveler, having no idea the time or date.

Pain cascades horizontally across the threads in my wrist. Better, but not entirely healed. Maroon flakes crumble on to my fingertips as I slowly drag them across the incision.

"Getting better," I mutter.

I shift focus to the brown pill bottles on the floor. A prize I snagged from Dudak's body before disposing of that in Munson Creek along with the car. Did it myself to spare Glenn any additional horror? The kid has been through a lot.

Admittedly, I breathe easier knowing the patrol cruiser lies in the cruel waters of Munson Creek. No search team will risk their neck, even if someone witnessed me pushing the cruiser in the water. Lake Gitche Gumee isn't the only one that doesn't give up her dead.

Milt never mentioned Dudak dealing drugs, so I'm guessing these are legit prescription Elavil pills. A quick search using the last one percent of my phone's battery hints they are worth hanging onto for later. An unopened can of Jolt waits for me, along with a note from Glenn.

M,

Left to grab food. Will bring you back something. Called an Uber since our former ride is now swimming. Hope to be back before dark.

-G

MY ATTENTION TURNS to my wrist.

Better, but I don't feel strong enough. Need more. More strength. Enough to kill Milt.

FORTY

"**M**arc."

My body jostles left, then right.

"Marc."

My body is paralyzed, but my ears work. A moment later, my mouth joins the party.

"How long we been here?" I ask.

"Two days," Glenn says. "But I checked your pulse and made sure you were breathing any time I was here."

Hanging out in Dudak's DMV shack for two days appears on no one's bucket list, but it's done the job to keep us safe.

"Aren't you swell? You sure you didn't kick me in the head a few times while you were at it?"

"Headache?"

Glenn pushes a pile of Domino's pizza boxes into the far corner.

"Waking up," *or coming back,* "is the worst." I rub the hangover out of my eyes, but it returns immediately.

"How long you been back?" I motion to his note.

"Two places have our picture hanging in the window,"

Glenn says, not answering my question. "There's a phone number attached."

He shows me a picture of the missing persons sign. I immediately recognize Milt's cell phone number.

"Milt's looking for us." A low, evil tone dominates my voice. "When did you get back?"

"I dunno. Twenty-minutes ago," Glenn says. "Why?"

"When did you write the note?"

"Marc, I don't under—"

"Jesus Christ, it's not a difficult question, Glenn."

"An hour." Glenn scratches his head. "Maybe a little less."

The two kerosene lamps flicker, sending our shadows dancing across the ceiling.

A countdown clock approaches zero in my head.

"Need your help on round two," I say. "Time to throw up, and I need you to make sure I don't choke on my puke. If I don't, I'm dead-dead, and that won't help anyone. Especially me." There's enough of the drug in my system now that the damage it does will help, maybe not as much as dying and coming back, but I don't have confidence Glenn can bring me back.

"Marc, I can't do this." Glenn sets a container of Chinese food and chopsticks on the floor. "We should go to the police or something. I have to tell my parents and Susan that I'm okay."

"You can do it." I struggle to focus on his blurry face. "Don't even need your finger. We can use a chopstick."

"I mean this." Glenn spreads his arms. "All of this. Everything with your house and Milt and him killing that cop and you with your death wish. This place reeks. I bought every air freshener Walgreens had, and it still stinks in here. You could have at least put us up in a swanky hotel with all your cash."

"Except for the fact that everything not in my trust or in my pocket burned up along with most of my worldly possessions."

He paces in circles. I get dizzy watching him. "It's too much. I'm out, man."

And you didn't think to tell me this before I swallowed the bottle of Dudak's pills?

Glenn bounces the door open, testing the withering hinges.

"And my advice to you is to toss those pills in the trash and come with me," Glenn says, hovering over the doorway.

I snatch the empty pill bottle from the ground and wing it just wide of his head. The bottle bounces twice before making a semi-circle roll, coming to rest against Glenn's Sketchers.

"Throw that away for me, will ya?" I flop onto my side and poke at a chopstick on the floor. Every time I pinch my fingers together, I come up empty. "Little help?"

"You swallowed that bottle of pills?" Glenn stomps the bottle, flattening what splintered brown plastic doesn't fly off in any of four directions. "The whole bottle? When? Do you have any idea what was in there? I sure as shit don't!"

My mouth stretches to its limits, taking in as much air as possible. "I'd say sleeping pills judging by my yawn." My eyelids droop, picking up weight with each passing second.

"We have to get you to a hospital. Like right now!" Glenn grabs the pieces of the bottle from the floor and moves to me with lightning speed.

"Whoa. You're so fast," I say. "Are you the Flash?"

"What?"

"Barry Allen Flash or Wally West Flash?"

"Shit. You're messed up." He twists the pieces of

broken bottle in his hand. "Elavil. Twenty-five milligrams per day. Treatment for stress, anxiety, and insomnia. These are Dudak's prescription meds, not some drug he was selling."

I lap my tongue against the roof of my mouth, unable to create saliva.

"Up. Chuck. Need activated cool-cool first," I say, reaching my hands into the air, although I want them to grab the box on the floor. The words work in my mind, but my mouth can't say them, "I need to puke, then drink the charcoal powder. Act-a. Act-a. Vate."

"Who's Chuck? You're not making any sense." Glenn pushes my hands away. "What are you talking about?"

"Activated. Pow!" I say. "Char char coal."

Wait. What?

I thrash my arms like one of those blow-up wacky wavy things outside of car dealerships. Anything to get my body to cooperate. My left thumb snags the snitches on my wrist and pulls two free. Blood oozes from the wound.

"Pow—" My tongue flops to the corner of my mouth. I pull it back in with my teeth, sawing off little chunks of tongue flesh in the process— "der."

"Marc, you're not making any sense. Shit. You're gonna die right here. Shit. Shit. Shit." Glenn stands and spins in circles, kicking the box of powdered charcoal across the floor farther from my reach.

I lose vision from my right eye.

Sludge and bile flood the back of my throat like an overflowing septic system.

Glenn lunges for my shoulder and rolls me on my side just in time for me to heave a dozen pills and a Jolt cola on his jeans.

"Jesus Christ, that's disgusting!" He launches himself back into the kitchen area.

Phlegm escapes through my nose on my second and third convulsions. I lose all function of sight, and Glenn fades into the void.

"Activated Charcoal!" His scream of triumph passes through the void and connects with my brain. "Well, that explains you buying this at CVS. You planned this and didn't tell me. Asshole."

Then, silence, for what seems like an eternity.

Drink, she whispers in my ear. *Drink, or we'll both be stuck here in this emptiness.*

I hate the texture but don't argue.

"There you go, asshole," Glenn says. "If I weren't so busy saving you, I might kill you for putting me through this. Swallow. Swallow. Swallow."

The grit filled carbonation washes the vomit from my mouth, and I sink back into the comfortable, silent darkness.

FORTY-ONE

"So, you guys have been here the whole time?" she asks.

"He has," Glenn says. "I've made the few supply runs. Undercover, of course."

"You need to do a better job," she says.

"I don't have much to work with here," Glenn says. "And if I have to walk two miles to meet an Uber one more time." He shakes his head.

Their conversation is something born of a radio morning talk show that turns on with your alarm. Ringing dominates the sounds in my foreground, but their voices in the background remain vaguely audible.

"Is he awake? He looks awful, Glenn. How long has he been sick? Might have been the flu."

My shoulder rocks back and forth. A soft touch. Her touch. It can only be Susan.

"Marc, are you awake?"

I open my mouth, unsure about how to answer her.

"Blechhh!"

A cascade of yellowish bile and phlegm spews from every opening on my face. I crack my eyes in time to catch the projectile vomit as it lands squarely on her furry Orolay jacket.

"Well, that's awesome." Susan jumps back.

"Yup, he's awake," Glenn says.

"Oh, my God. I— I— I'm so sorry," I say, reaching a waifish arm in Susan's direction.

"Don't worry about it." Susan removes her jacket, freeing her blonde ponytail to bounce freely against her neck. "Glenn said you were in rough shape, but this is way worse than I imagined."

"How? Where?" I struggle to put together a full thought.

"She spotted me at Walgreens," Glenn says. "She was putting up missing person flyers my mom made. Right next to Milt's."

"Took me about two seconds to realize it was him. I lost him when he ducked behind some big display. Then the goof followed me into the ladies' room. I screamed at first. Thought he was a rando trying to kill me or something. Once I realized it was Glenn, I wasn't afraid, despite everything going on. I can take him." Susan holds up two fists.

"No, you can't," Glenn says.

Their volley of words provides enough time for me to sit up and clear my head. Blood pulsates through my veins, pressing against my skin as it courses through my body.

A couple of deep breaths and I stagger to my feet.

"Dude, you know she's right," I say.

"I should have let you die," Glenn says with a single laugh.

In all fairness, I should be thanking him, not insulting him, but it doesn't occur to me until after I see his eyes drop.

"Well, I'm happy you're both alive, although I have to

question your choice of living arrangements," Susan says, wrinkling her nose at the smell. Can't say I blame her. Sweat, barf, and death might make for a pretty good Febreeze commercial, though.

"Yeah, it's a fixer-upper," Glenn says.

Susan lunges forward and throws her arms around my neck. Strawberry scented hair masks the scent of smoke in the air. My whole body smiles.

She pulls back. "Tell me it's not true," she says, staring into my eyes.

Despite my foggy brain, I should know what she is talking about. "Huh? Tell you what's not true?"

"It." She pushes the word on me.

"I have no idea what you're talking about," I answer.

Susan bites her lower lip. "Your house. The cop."

"Oh yeah. That." The towering flames flash through my mind. I imagine Milt strolling out the back door of my house, smiling with a bottle of whiskey in one hand and a pair of brass knuckles on the other.

"Glenn told me about that guy Milt, the other one putting up missing signs for you. There was Milt on TV today saying my brother killed a cop that you lured into a trap at your house. Then, the two of you set your house on fire to cover your tracks. Talked all about our dad and your dad being in deep with a local bookie. And that guy is missing too. Coach Throgmorton came forward talking about how your dad attended Gambler's Anonymous meetings he hosted."

Glenn rolls his eyes. "So much for the anonymous part."

"Throgmorton runs a poker club, not GA meetings. I should know. I helped Milt collect from folks into the poker club for some serious cash. God, this town is so stupid."

"We didn't do anything!" Glenn yells. His chest heaves,

then his breathing falls shallow and rapid. "I think I'm gonna pass out." Glenn staggers back and finds support in the form of the front door.

"I wouldn't be here if I thought you did those things. But they have proof. I heard them talking about a knife and a liquor bottle."

"He's lying!" Glenn slams his fist against the wall, rattling the window. "Ow. Ow. Ow." He hops, frantically shaking his hand.

"Dude, relax. The fire would have destroyed the fingerprints."

How the hell can I ask him to stay calm when I want to ball up on the mattress and go back to sleep?

Damn, now I'm the guy willing to sleep in his own blood rather than face reality.

"Guys, the police found a bloody knife with Glenn's prints in the backyard and liquor bottles with a kerosene rag stuffed in the top lying in the driveway. That has your prints on it, Marc. Social media is going batshit crazy."

Shit. He dropped the knife outside and kept one of the bottles with my prints. Lord knows he could have had another bottle in the kitchen or stashed somewhere in the house.

"I can explain everything. I promise we didn't kill anyone, and I sure as hell didn't burn down my own house." Tears fill my eyes. I'm screwed. Glenn is screwed. Hell, his entire family is screwed. Everything is gone. My next trip into the void should probably be a permanent one. Milt outsmarted me. "That was my life, Susan. The last memories of my mom and dad. I don't have anything left."

"You still have Clyde," Susan says.

"And you got me, dude." Glenn pushes his anger aside and stands tall. Taller than I ever remember.

"Us," Susan puts one hand on my shoulder and another on Glenn's back.

"Thanks." I force a goblin's grin. Ugly, crooked, and full of snot. "But your prints are on that knife. Milt tricked you. He tricked me. My prints are on the bottles. We don't have a choice."

"But I do." Susan steps forward, pushing the door closed.

"So, you believe us?" I ask.

"My little brother can't kill a spider, so I doubt he could kill a cop. You might be different from when we were younger, but I know you aren't your dad. And we can all agree anyone Throgmorton validates is a slimy piece of shit," Susan says. "What can I do to help?"

"I need a favor, and I'm not sure you're going to like it." I kick a small pile of bloodied yarn away from my foot. "We need to get ourselves a new ride. I promise everything will make sense."

"I do too. Cross my heart, sis." Glenn makes a cross on the wrong side of his chest.

I stare at the knife on the dirty floor, then glance at my wrist.

Is the purple-black line my stitches or a request?

"Leave it," Glenn speaks to me like I'm Clyde.

"Leave what?" Susan asks.

"The Jolt Cola I haven't finished," I say. "I can come back for it later if I need a boost."

Glenn and I both know I'm not talking about the cola.

FORTY-TWO

"You think it's a good idea to be driving around in my parent's car? God, I hope it doesn't breakdown. There's a reason it's been in the garage for two years." Glenn leans over from the backseat. "And why does she get to ride shotgun? I called it first."

I adjust the rearview mirror so my eyes connect with his. "She's sitting in the front because of a forgotten tradition known as chivalry."

"Because of chivalry?" Glenn wrinkles his forehead.

"Yes." I focus on Susan. "Chivalry."

Her cheeks turn a soft pink.

"That's messed up, man. What about the long-standing tradition of bros before hoes?"

"Dude, that's your sister," I say.

"Not technically since I'm adopted." Glenn sits back, offering a smug grin of triumph on a technicality.

Susan leans over and presses down on my thigh, forcing my foot into the brake pedal. Whiplash wipes the smile from Glenn's face.

After three minutes of the silent treatment from the

back seat, Glenn joins me, explaining our story. He focuses on how crazy Milt acted and how Glenn thought he was going to die while I tell her about everything that happened with the Italian shoe, the bridge, my dad, and the cop, and Milt.

Well, not everything, but I hit the highlights.

And we skimp on the events at the DMV. So far as Susan knows, I'm sick. That's what Glenn told her. Not only have I underestimated him, but I under appreciated his friendship as well.

I pick away two blood-stained cuticles before admitting we'll need to trust someone outside of this car if we hope to survive. "Glenn's right. We can't keep driving around. We need to make a call."

"My folks?" Glenn voice cracks.

"My attorney," I say.

"You have an attorney?"

I smile wide. "Don't you?"

Susan flips her hair back as she giggles.

I balance my hands at the top of the steering wheel and transition from picking cuticles to peeling away blackened fingernails. "Sorry to drag you into all this."

Susan stares straight ahead, doing her best to maintain a straight face. "It's cool. If we get busted, I'll say you kidnapped me."

"You can't do that to family!" Panic sweeps across Glenn's face.

"But you said technically we aren't family."

"That's not what I meant."

"Relax. I'm totally kidding." Susan's eyes light up. "Besides, it's clear you need help. Everyone knows girls are smarter than boys."

"Well, I'm glad you're here," I say.

"I didn't have any solid plans for the day," Susan jokes. "And I feel like I'm supposed to be here."

"I kinda feel like you're supposed to be here, too." I need to maintain my confidence. If either of them sees fear in my eyes or concern on my face, everything could spiral. Glenn is already a peeled nerve. If I say boo, he'll likely pee all over the back seat.

"Huh?" She tilts her head to the side.

"Just saying I agree with what you said." I pause, but she doesn't say anything. "That you felt like you were supposed to be here."

"I didn't say that," Susan replies.

"You sure?" I ask.

"Yup. I'm sure."

"She didn't say it, man." Glenn jumps in. "I'm worried you spent a little too much time in the looney bin. So, what's the plan?"

We need to stop Milt. Maybe kill him.

"Marc Chesterfield Cheeks, you are not killing anyone!" Susan smacks her hand against the dashboard.

Glenn raises his hands. "Whoa. Whoa. Whoa. Who said anything about killing anyone? Who do you think we are?"

"Well, we are on the run from the law," Susan says.

"But we didn't do anything." Glenn huffs between words.

Glenn misses the big picture. I pull into the dirt-covered area behind the Exxon, pop in my earpiece, and dial my attorney.

The Exxon's abandoned gas pumps, decade-old vending machine, and overgrown weeds provide cover. A for sale sign hangs in the window, but it should say forgotten, like so much of this town.

Mr. Layer walks me through exactly what I need to do and where I need to go.

FIVE MINUTES out from Mr. Layer's office, my phone rings. My hand trembles as I turn the screen so I can read the Caller ID. The entire car holds its collective breath.

"It's just Mr. Layer." I wiggle the phone, flashing the screen in front of them. "My lawyer."

Both exhale and sink into their seats.

"Hello?"

"Mr. Cheeks. This is Ms. Holton from Mr. Layer's office. Did I catch you before you've arrived?"

"Yeah, but we'll be there in a few minutes."

"Great. Mr. Layer wanted me to let you know due to the boys in blue patrolling the area. You should park on level thirteen. Use the elevator. It will take you to where you need to go. When you exit the elevator, walk down the hall and through the double doors."

"Thanks for the heads up."

I bury the car deep in the parking garage as per my instructions. The few lights that remain throw off scant illumination. Seven or eight cars are scattered in the dark recesses of the parking garage's lowest levels. None have license plates, while most have shattered windows and a layer of dust.

"You sure this is what Mr. Layer said?" Glenn asks.

"I didn't talk to him, but his secretary said level thirteen," I say, pulling into one of the few spots with a working light above it.

"Really? Here?" Glenn asks. "I bet if we go down a few more levels, we could find one devoid of any cars. Or better yet, we'll find Satan working as a valet. We can stiff him on the tip when he brings the car back around to us."

"Just look for an elevator," I say.

"Why do you assume Satan is a guy?" Susan asks.

"The whole long, pointy tail thing. Everyone knows that's a euphemism." Glenn steeples his hands and positions his pointer fingers against his chin as if deep in thought. "Besides, Mom always tells Dad that he makes her life a living hell."

"Can't argue with that," I say.

We file out of the car and work our way along the cold, uncaring concrete wall heading toward the erratically blinking red exit sign. Glenn peers in the trash can under the sign when we reach it.

"When do you think they last emptied this?" he asks.

Susan leans over the can but snaps her head away. She waves an open hand in front of her nose. "Judging by the putrid smell, I'd say never."

"Bet you there's something valuable buried in here." Glenn tentatively reaches his hand into the opening.

"Guys, can we focus here?" I corral Susan and Glenn through the heavy steel door, and we find ourselves in front of an elevator with a single button.

"What now?" Susan asks.

"I guess we push it." I shrug. "Mr. Layer's secretary said we should see our ride once we're outside. This must lead to the hallway that takes us outside."

The shaft groans to life, and within a minute, we stare into an elevator adorned with graffiti, a few advertisements of products we don't recognize, and a utility blanket covering the floor. The red splatters make Susan shudder and retreat to the corner.

"Kaufman's 1979 semi-annual clearance sale," Glenn

reads. "Whoa, check out these funky clothes and the afro on this dude."

"That's great," I say, staring at a single button.

"Where does it takes us?" Susan asks.

"Only one way to find out," I answer.

Probably Hell.

I hope not. A female voice sounding like Susan's answers, but I never see Susan's mouth move.

"Did you?" I ask.

"Did you?" She answers with a question of her own.

Ding!

"I hate the feeling when an elevator comes to a stop," I say, waiting for my stomach to settle. Other than the pit in my belly, I feel surprisingly good. Strong. Level-headed. Healed, practically.

The opening door unveils a dimly lit passageway into a circular room with a single door set across from our elevator. We all hesitate. I reason I got us into this mess, so I should lead the way.

"I guess this is our stop." I step out first. The smell of ammonia assaults my nose. My eyes water and my throat tightens. I clench my jaw to keep from puking. Glenn isn't so lucky. His gag reflex has never been strong. Two steps in, and he bends forward, unleashing his version of hell.

He wipes his mouth with the front of his shirt.

"Gas station vending machine beef jerky and Twinkies weren't such a good idea after all," Glenn says. "I thought that stuff never expired."

"Gross. Grab the fire extinguisher off the wall and put a stop to that." Susan pinches her nose and pushes past us into the circular room. "This must be what the guy's locker room smells like after gym class."

I pull Glenn along behind me. The few lights in the room flicker randomly.

"Caution. This ride may cause vomiting and seizures," Glenn says between coughs.

"Seriously doubt anyone wants to change the light bulbs in this place." I scan the room. "I'm impressed they work at all."

A lump of black undulates in a nook to my left.

"You kids shouldn't be here," a raspy voice calls out from under the dark cloak. "If you in here, you done somethin' bad out there." A shaking finger, skinned practically to the bone around the knuckles, points to the double doors. "Real bad. But we keep your secrets safe. We keep them with your blood."

A wave of black masses rises to life around the room. One sheds his cloak. A sliver of light catches a shine to his bald head and scarred skin. A red mass of flesh leaking puss occupies the spot reserved for his right eye. The beam casts a spotlight on something else. A blade. Short and wicked sharp, like the Karambit carbon tactical knife, Milt keeps on his belt. Dangerous in the right hands, desperate ones.

"Mr. Milt didn't tell me we was gonna have company," the bald man says. He glances toward Susan and snakes his tongue. "She smells—" he sniffs deep— "pure."

I hook Glenn's arm and pull him to his feet. "We're getting out of here. Now!"

I turn my shoulder lower and sprint toward the door, dragging Susan and Glenn behind me.

The entire room shakes as the doors bounce our trio back into the field of play. Glenn grunts as Susan and I land square on his chest and stomach. The fall sucks every ounce of oxygen from my lungs, and I writhe around on the wet concrete, fighting for breath. The last two yarn stitches pull free from my wrist. No blood. No cut. Just a fresh scar now.

I scramble to my feet and perform my best pirouette, accessing the situation. Five black masses align the floor, preventing our exit, although three struggle to stand without swaying. The bald man with the knife bounces side to side effortlessly. He has more energy than I'd hoped. Five of them against three of us aren't great odds.

"Marc." Susan paws at my arm.

"Shit. This is an ambush," I say. "Do you see anything we can break the glass with?"

"You stuck, boy." The bald man motions his head toward the double doors. "That glass is the same stuff they use in the looney bin up north. And we chained 'em doors from the outsides, so's no one can get in. Only desperate folk come through here, and no one misses desperate folks much."

"Marc!" Susan's concerns escalate.

"The elevator. We aren't going to get through that glass with our bare hands." I push her too hard, and she stumbles in front of us. "Go!"

Adrenaline surges through my veins. Sweet adrenaline.

My muscles beg me to turn and fight. They want more; more of the sweet nectar, but Susan and Glenn are guppies in a lake full of mutated underwater beasts. I have to get them out of here.

Once Susan puts a few feet of space between us, I hurl Glenn across the ground and turn to face the interlopers. But it isn't them. It's us. We're the unwelcome intruders. This is their home, and we're here because of me.

"There's no button!" Susan screams.

I turn and watch her frantically bang the wall where one would find the elevator call button. Instead, she pounds concrete over and over, shrieking so loudly it makes Glenn cover his ears.

The words on the closed elevator doors above Susan's head read:

BID FAREWELL TO THE LIGHT
YOU ARE NOW BORN INTO THE DARKNESS

Pain ricochets through my ear. A warm trickle crests my sliced earlobe. I feel it separate when I whip my head around. The bald man cackles and licks my blood clean from his blade.

"I don't want to hurt you, old man." I raise my hands, protesting his advance. The knife, clean again, readies for another assault. My wrist silently taunts the old man's blade.

I've been cut by worse.

"Let us be on our way, and we won't hurt you. We won't even tell anyone you're here," I say.

The other four steady themselves behind their bald leader. Whatever hindered them before is swept away with the smell of fresh blood.

Glenn joins Susan pounding on the elevator door screaming for help. I already know no angels are coming to escort us safely out of this hell.

The bald man lashes again, striking my open palm. I retreat closer to Glenn and Susan as the bald man raises the knife with a bloody war cry. The site of me dripping crimson emboldens the other four who step forward, shedding their cloaks to reveal emaciated, pale bodies covered only by torn sweatpants, thick boots, and puss oozing boils on their chests.

I glance to my right and find my confidence in a different shade of red. Fire extinguisher red.

"Be ready to go on my signal," I say.

Again, the bald man runs the blade across his tongue, lapping every milliliter of my AB negative blood.

I lunge for the wall and pry the faded red cylinder from

its mount. The metal hook breaks free from the deteriorating sheetrock, falling to the ground. I snatch it and turn to Susan and Glenn.

"Take a deep breath and hold it. Ready?"

I don't wait for a response, pulling the extinguisher's pin, tucking the cylinder under my arm, and blasting the CO into the crowd of men. The sound of cursing and coughing signals its time to make a break for it. Nozzle in one hand, cylinder firmly underarm, and hook in hand, my plan begins whether I believe in it or not.

Glenn and Susan follow as I charge into the room, spraying fire suppressant wildly in every direction. The flickering lights and white powder transform the room into a hellacious disco dance floor.

A hand seizes my ankle, and the flash of the blade across my knee tells me who's in the haze below. I slam the canister and hear his forearm crack. Susan follows with a kick to the side of his head, flattening the leader.

I scoop up the canister and press forward, blasting in every direction. A hand flails from my left, and I toss an elbow to the side that sends someone sprawling. We barrel ahead, gaining steam and using the spray to clear our way. I don't know much about fighting beyond my recent experiences, but there is little finesse needed in a bull rush.

Almost out of breath, I charge ahead, shifting the fire extinguisher to the front of my body as we approach the sealed doors. Not holding anything back, I hit the glass full-force with my red extinguisher battering ram and my body.

Pieces spray in every direction. The plastic nature of the safety glass prevents anything more than a few cuts and scrapes on my arms and face.

They'll fit right in.

I tumble through the glass opening, pushed by sheer

momentum. Glenn's face emerges from the smoky white seconds later.

"Susan!"

I toss the canister aside and grab hold of her hand, helping her crawl through the broken glass. It crackles under the weight of our bodies, but the alleyway we stumble into is devoid of both noise and occupants.

As Susan clears the door, a hand grasps her calf. A familiar bald head and single eye comes into view. He struggles to work his broken arm as the knife clatters across the floor with each attempt he makes to lift it. Other bony, white hands decorated with jagged, yellow fingernails emerge.

"Duck!"

Susan flattens her body on the broken shards, and I swing my arm, planting the fire extinguisher wall hook into Baldy's one good eye. No pus, only spurting blood, screams of pain, and a retreat into the circular sanctuary they call home.

Glenn grabs Susan's arm and pulls her clear as I remain at the door, screaming.

"Anybody else want some of this?"

I fire the last of the carbon monoxide into the opening.

"What we do now?" Glenn rushes in circles.

I stand ready to pounce on anything following us outside, but the dark masses retreat from the broken glass. Outside of a few empty garbage cans, there's nothing in the alley, not even a piece of trash or wayward cat. The damn thing is spotless.

My phone displays Mr. Layer's incoming call. I skip the pleasantries.

"What the fu—"

"Marc, do not go down to level thirteen!" Mr. Layer screams.

"A little late for that."

"You survived? But how?" Mr. Layer stammers. "No one . . . " His voice trails off.

"We still need a ride," I say.

"If you're outside in the alley behind that cursed room, there's a black car parked a few hundred yards to the left on Sixth Street. You can trust the driver. He's my brother."

"Mind telling me what that earlier call from your secretary was about?" I ask.

"I don't know, but I'm sure as hell going to find out. My guess is Milt has something to do with it. I don't have time to explain now."

"Nothing gets by you," I say. "Might be time to pay him a visit."

"If I hear anything, I'll be in touch. Be careful, Marc. I get the feeling Milt is out to hurt you."

"You know what they say, whatever doesn't kill you makes you stronger."

FORTY-THREE

The black Lincoln Town Car ferries us back to town without incident. It matches Mr. Layer's black suit in every aspect. The backseat provides enough room for us not to be in each other's laps, but I still struggle to get comfortable. Wounds twist my thoughts. Scars want to come out and play, not sit quietly, healing.

While Glenn and Susan sit in shocked silence, I formulate a plan to surprise Milt, tie him up, then drag him down to Munson Creek until he talks. I need to know how he set us up, who's involved in this, and how we can clear our names.

Unfortunately, our picture sits in the front window of Ace, Walgreens, Target, CVS, and every other store in town. Buying anything from duct tape to rope is next to impossible. Somehow, Milt prioritized getting Susan's picture up as a *Wanted for Questioning* person of interest. He can't be working alone. There's no way he'd know about her before the trip to Mr. Layer's.

"There's nowhere to get supplies within thirty miles. Our pictures are everywhere, and there's not enough rope in the scraps of the DMV to hang a chipmunk." I slam the car door. Probably a good thing. From what I can remember, Dad's journal did not address hanging. He considered it, but he was worried about snapping his neck or not having someone cut him down. "We have to stop Milt. By any means necessary, if you know what I mean." I fold my upper lip with my bottom teeth.

"You're not exactly giving me the warm and fuzzies," Glenn says.

"I know, right?" I stretch out my forehead, temporarily smoothing the stress wrinkles. "Is there anywhere we can get rope that isn't a store likely to have our pictures hanging?"

"Chavez's garage?" Glenn poses his suggestion as a question.

"Not sure we want to risk going that close to my house. Don't remember seeing any rope there anyhow."

Susan raises her hand apprehensively. "I know a place."

I fear asking. "Where?"

"You're not going to like it."

"Susan, we're desperate," I say.

"School." She points toward the towering oak trees tucked behind the dilapidated iron mill.

"What?" Glenn says. "You gotta be freaking kidding me."

"In the gym storage closet," she says.

"People are looking for us. How exactly are we going to Mission Impossible this?" Glenn asks.

"I have my work badge. It's an in-service training day, but the training classes are being held off-site. No students. No teachers. Pretty much the only place in town that will be empty, so no worry about anyone seeing us," Susan says.

I exhale loud enough to startle the driver. "School it is."

"Yes, sir." The driver acknowledges. "I'll let Mr. Layer know I'll be longer than expected, so he doesn't worry."

Susan twirls her school badge as we wind through the backroads of town. Glenn and I slide down in the seats so only our eyes and the top of our heads can be seen through the windows. If I can't get Milt to come clean, this may be the last time I'm looking upon my hometown. The worst part is every image withers and dies in my mind before I can commit it to memory. It's like seeing everything, but nothing at all.

The car eases into the gravel lot. The driver pulls into an isolated spot far from the school.

"I should call my mom. Tell her I'm innocent. God, I bet she's freaking out. I've never gone this long without checking in. I bet she's leading the search party." Glenn reaches for his phone. His finger hangs over the bright screen. "What do I say?"

"Tell her the truth, tell her I got you into this. You're innocent." My shoulders slump heavily on my chest. "She'll believe you."

"She's gonna be pissed." Glenn dials but stops before he punches the last number. "Can you give me a minute? She's probably going to have a lot of questions. Susan, where does Mom think you are?"

Susan sighs. "At the high school, participating in helping to teach our students morals and ethics training."

Oh, sweet irony.

"I'll wait outside with Marc. Don't tell Mom I'm with you."

Susan and I file out of the car along with the driver.

"I'm going to grab a smoke if you folks are going to be a few minutes," the driver announces. His gruff voice leads me to conclude many of his rides involve the need to take a smoke break and not all on his own volition.

"Those things will kill you!" Susan calls out.

He flashes his stained teeth and gives her a quick lift of the chin as an acknowledgment.

Susan and I stand in silence.

Glenn hangs his head as he exits the car. "My mom is totally pissed. Innocent or not, I'm grounded until I'm eighty."

"Eighty? Seems a bit harsh." I shake my head.

"Well, let's see. You go over to your teacher's house. It burns down. You're accused of killing someone, and you don't check-in for a week," Glenn says.

"Yeah, you're screwed, bro," Susan says.

"Not helping," I use my deepest voice. "You didn't say anything about me, did you?"

"Well," Glenn kicks aside a few rocks. "Maybe."

"Dammit."

"But I didn't say much. Said we left before the fire, and I helped you get out of the state. I only talked to her for a minute, and it was mostly her yelling." Glenn's face turns pink. "It's not like Milt doesn't know we're alive."

"You're right," I relent. "My bad."

A soft fist bump later, we tromp over the gravel and head into school.

"Let's get in and out. Whatever we're going to do, we need to get it done before Glenn's eight pm curfew." I stick out my tongue at Glenn.

"Watch it, buddy, or I will throw that apology back in your face," Glenn says.

"I've seen you throw. I'm not worried."

Susan rolls her eyes. "Is it possible for you two to stay serious for five minutes?"

"Sorry, Mom." Glenn drops his voice two octaves.

Susan ignores him and points down the hall. "The ropes should be in the supply closet past the vending machine."

Distant laughter makes its way to our hall. The sounds of ripping paper and a woman calling out cadence pauses our advance.

My heart skips two beats. "Who the hell is here?"

"Shit, that's probably the dance committee. Sounds like it's coming from the gym. My bet is they're here to vape and drink while the school is empty. Better than risking getting caught at home; I doubt they'll realize we're here." Susan whispers.

"And if they see us?" I ask.

"This is high school. They'll probably want a selfie with you. Doubt many of them think either of you has it in you to kill someone. Plus, I'll owe them. It's nice to have a student-teacher on the hook to blackmail." Susan's cheeks puff with her laugh. Her infectious smile provides me with a small spark of hope.

"There it is." Glenn motions to the door.

We huddle around the Healthy Cakes vending machine.

"Ugh. Where did all the chips and candy go? Whoever heard of a Healthy Cake?" I peer in at one of the offerings. "Non-GMO brown rice and granola cake sprinkled with a dusting of free-trade organic cinnamon."

Susan sticks out her tongue.

"Isn't all cinnamon organic? Glad I never needed to use the student snack machine. Who the hell would torture kids with these snacks?" I ask.

Glenn stares at his shoes. "Our mom."

I stifle a laugh despite my desire for a real laugh for the first time in as long as I can remember.

"The sad thing is this stuff is still better than what we get at home," Glenn says.

After I catch my breath, I turn to Susan. "So, how do we get in?"

"Well—"

Before Susan finishes, Glenn flashes in front of us, hurling his body into the air moments before impacting the door.

The thud sends him sprawling backward across the floor. A loud groan emulates from the huddled mass on the floor I once called my best friend.

"Dude. Why don't we use explosives? How about some subtlety?"

Susan grabs the door handle. "As I was saying, it should be unlocked." With a twist of the wrist, she exposed the contents of the gym closet.

Glenn stands up and makes large circles with his right arm stretching out his shoulder. He grumbles something about me owing him a trip to Vegas.

Susan crosses her arms and winks at Glenn. "When will you silly boys learn that girls are smarter?"

Glenn joins my side as we stare at the dark, brown intertwined rope that spent the better part of the year delivering rope burns to the hands and legs of every non-athletic boy in Munson High.

We both look down at our palms, and Glenn says, "I swear I still have scars from my last encounter with Hannibal Lyncher during sophomore year."

"Are you two going to help me or stand there whining?" Susan asks.

Glenn raises a scrawny arm. "I vote whining."

"Come on, wuss." I tug his arm.

I hold out my arms, and the other two pile the rope into the cradle created. Rogue strands poke through my sleeves, scratching my skin. I stifle any complaints, trying to look tough. Hell, I am tough. I maintain bandages over my injuries, but it's only for show. Healed. All healed.

"How old do you figure these are?" Glenn sifts through piles of junky sports equipment in the back of the closet and emerges with matching tennis racquets. I'm sure they were used in the 1924 Olympics.

"Let's roll," I say. The awkward size of the rope slows my pace, but I lead the way down the hall.

"Glenn, I think you forgot something." Susan points to the tennis racquets in his hand.

"No one's going to miss these." Glenn practices a forehand. "Besides, you know how much Mom loves tennis, and she loves antiques. If I give her these, she might forget about grounding me."

"Not even the Wimbledon Plate will save your ass," Susan says.

"The what?" I raise an eyebrow.

"It's a tennis thing," both say in unison.

"Your mom's weird," I say.

"No kidding." Glenn demonstrates his backhand with the racquet, but his follow-through connects with his head. "Ow."

"Smooth." I chuckle.

"Can we move faster? In case you two forgot, we're carrying stuff that doesn't belong to us." Susan waves us along.

"This place doesn't exactly lift my spirits these days," I say.

We push open the doors to the outside and locate our ride.

"I know what will cheer you up," Susan says.

She sprints across the grass edge of the parking lot before launching into a flippity-flip, as I call it. The proper description is a front handspring into a somersault. At least, I think that's how she described it.

"Damn, girl," Glenn's jaw gapes wide, nearly touching his chest.

"How was that?"

This woman doesn't need my approval, or anyone's for that matter, but her asking is the highlight of my day. Maybe the year. "Umm. Perfect?" I say as my lips turn down at their corners.

"Are you asking me or telling me?"

"Telling. Definitely telling." I struggle to hold up all my fingers. "A perfect ten. Flawless. Heck, a ten and a half."

"Why not eleven?" she cocks her head to the side.

"Cause the Russian judge is biased. Maybe offer them a bribe?" I suggest.

"Got anything in mind?" Susan winks.

"Antique tennis racquets," I say, nodding toward Glenn.

Glenn swings off balance at a passing insect.

"I'm sure we can think of something better than that." A familiar but unwelcome voice chimes in on the conversation.

Coach Throgmorton.

FORTY-FOUR

"Surely, a vibrant young woman such as yourself has something better to offer a judge. Maybe something with that sexy mouth."

"Back off, Coach," I growl. "Shouldn't you be in ethics training?"

"A man of my stature in this community doesn't require it." Coach nods his head.

I hear the crack of metal against bone before the pain renders my legs useless. My teeth vibrate as I hit the ground. A freight train drops on my lower back. Two more on my legs. My knees push three inches into the hardened soil. The rope nestles under my chest, providing a scant area for my lungs to expand and contract.

Coach Throgmorton brought friends. Hitting a man from behind to boot. How ethical.

I don't pass out, but part of me wishes I would. Despite my prone position, when I turn my head to the side, I see Throgmorton, Susan, and Glenn in my field of blurry vision.

Coach grabs Susan's arm and motions to the side of

the school. "You're lucky me and my players are here to save you. Might be about time to finish what he started. How's the back, Mr. Cheeks?"

"You will release me this very moment, Mr. Throgmorton, if you know what's good for you," Susan says. She wriggles left and right, trying to break free.

Coach squeezes his hand tighter. "I was *trying* to be polite. I'm keeping you safe from these lawbreakers. You don't have to be such a prissy little bitch about it."

"Excuse me?" Susan's voice mirrors the annoyance on her face.

"How about a little gratitude for saving you?" Coach releases her arm, crosses his, and boasts his chin high.

Susan unleashes a backhand across Throgmorton's face, but he absorbs the blow with ease. Susan's athletic frame is no match for his boulder physique.

Coach extends both arms and launches Susan several feet backward. I feel every scratch and bruise as she hits the concrete.

"You're lucky I don't punch skirts," Coach taunts her.

"Hey!" I struggle to speak. "You can't do that."

"Look around, Mr. Cheeks. There's no one here to help you this time. There's six of us against the three of you. I'll introduce you around after your co-worker apologizes for assaulting me. Hell, if it's satisfactory, I'll even let her leave. Milt only sent me here to get you and Glenn. So, here's the deal, Miss Susan. You apologize and don't deny any rumors you may hear about me and you, and we're good."

Coach wipes his hand across his cheek and mouth where Susan hit him.

"You do not get to talk to me that way!" Susan lunges at him, but one of his cronies catches her mid-thrust.

"Feisty," Coach smiles. "Just how I like 'em. Maybe I'll

let your new friend here wipe the man juice off my baby maker when we're done here."

I wiggle an arm out from under my stomach. "How about you go screw yourself?"

I rock left, then right, but the bodies pinning me down barely move.

It's not there. I need the strength, the adrenaline, and it's not there. Fucking curse is useless if I can't learn to control it. Goddamn Milt was right about something. Irony sucks.

Two feet stroll inches past my head. I overhear someone call him Kyle. Another boy trails a few steps behind. Seconds later, two more guys come into view. They dress to match, sporting red practice jerseys with white numbers and blue jeans too tight for most high school boys.

"Hey, Coach, I see you found your favorite person." The kid behind Coach slobbers as he speaks. "And there's the dork who tutors me in math for free. Hell, most of the time, he does the work for me." He points at Glenn.

I suddenly realize what Glenn meant back at my place when he asked for my help with his big problem in math.

The group circles Glenn.

Glenn maintains his guard of the tennis racquets. I focus on the pack of wolves threatening our survival.

Coach's predator eyes turn from brown to a golden hue. "Now, about that apology."

FORTY-FIVE

I struggle to understand if Susan is my damnation or salvation.

Lester spoke of the Kismet as the other side of a coin. But every time it flips, I call tails, and it comes up heads.

Tails never fails . . . unless you're a Stitch.

Dad's notes alluded to the idea of what he referred to as sunsets being a possible answer. He spent almost as many pages detailing how to nearly kill someone as he did outlining the best methods to survive suicide attempts and not look insane. It's more of a how-to than a diary.

Sunsets, the passing of day to night. Where we live in neither. In our case, being Stitches, I believe he means the existence that is neither life nor death. Passing into the void. Like that place between sleep and awake that Peter Pan talked about. A period where we grow both stronger and weaker. Physically, I can feel it.

Mentally, I wait for the slip as I lay here with three thugs atop my body. I might kill them. They might kill me. But I desperately want to send Coach Throgmorton to this place of limbo. His last moments would be delicious.

Nothing in that journal matters if you don't figure out how to get us away from these gorillas.

Stay out of my head. Especially when I'm plotting. I whisper internally.

"Kyle lost his scholarship. Donnie's still eating soft foods, and I may not win Munson County Person of the Year this year 'cause of you, Mr. Cheeks." Coach pecks his head toward me with each sentence. "Turning you into the cops and collecting the reward money might ease my pain. Enough money to quit this lousy high school gig and really get this venture with Milt into high gear. I don't think you truly appreciate all he has to offer. Took us longer to get your dad out of the picture than I thought it would, but not going to make the same mistake with you. You're freaking cockroaches."

I can hear pebbles crunching in every direction. The circle tightens around Glenn. Coach signals the players to bring him in closer.

"My dad is dead, my freaking house burned down, the police want me for murder, and you're worried about Person of the Year for the fourth fucking year in a row?" I snarl. "You and Milt. Your life is over. It's fucking over!" The weight on my back lightens, but not because the boy sitting on it moves, but because I can feel it, something growing inside me.

"Better do what he says, asshole." Susan follows my snarl with a growl.

"Doesn't look like the Smurfette is going to apologize." Coach smiles wide and holds up a dark green metal tin with a grizzly bear label on it. "Hold her, Kyle."

Kyle steps in and wraps a meaty arm around Susan's chest.

Glenn raises his hand. "Our mother doesn't approve of tobacco products."

The players erupt into laughter. The one closest to Glenn plants a right hook into his gut, collapsing him to his knees, gasping for breath.

I scan the parking lot and surrounding woods, but our driver is MIA. Dark memories flood my mind when I catch sight of the tree where I was stabbed last fall. Adrenaline courses through my veins. I clench my fist. My nails dig into my palm, and a drop of blood falls.

Susan buries her teeth in Kyles's hand and draws blood. He yells so loud his mouth opens wide enough to show off his tonsils as he loosens his grip. She uses her newfound freedom to knock the tin from Coach's grasp.

Kyle clamps down on her quickly. His biceps flex through the jacket one-size too small.

Susan whimpers.

"Give me the can." A henchman grabs it off the ground and flips it to Coach. He plucks a pinch of flaky manure-colored leaves and sniffs deeply. "Smell that purity, Miss Susan. I only buy the good stuff. You are in for a real treat."

Coach pushes the dip into Susan's face, but she squeezes her beautiful rosy red lips together.

"Pinch her cheeks together," Coach commands. "You will never speak of this. Here's a little taste of what will happen if you cross us again. Next time, it will be worse. Much worse."

Kyle pinches Susan's cheeks, forcing her to pucker like a fish. His blood douses the front of her shirt as well as her cheeks. Coach jams the shredded tobacco past her objecting tongue. The Dr. Pepper brown pollutes her pearly white teeth. I witness her anger, but worse, I live her shame. It's new to her, the feeling of shame, but not to me.

"Leave her alone." I manage three words between gasps of air.

"Shut him up," Coach says, pointing a chunky finger away from his straight arm.

Two boys jump off my legs before I can react. Another kid kicks me in the groin before joining the other boys raining boots across my ribs.

"Memba' me?" A deep, muffled voice says.

I swivel my head and see metal bars outlining a drag smile. Donnie jumps in the air and brings the full weight of his body onto my back.

He grabs a handful of my hair, pulling my neck and head back towards him. A freshman newcomer to the football team connects his laces with my lips. Blood flows freely from my mouth and nose. Teeth swivel in my gums.

I don't like it, but I need it.

If I'm honest, I don't hate it either.

I push up as Donnie rides me like a bucking bronco. He grunts into my ear. Drools of his saliva mingle with my dripping blood. I manage to get a knee under me, then a foot.

Donnie slides his forearm under my chin and regains control by constricting his python-sized arm around my throat.

"M'arms ain't screw'd up," he mutters.

Oxygen transitions from an afterthought to a rare luxury. My fingers prevent him from cutting off my oxygen completely, but I start the clock in my head. If he cuts off blood flow to my brain, I'll only have seconds before I go nighty-night. This lug might choke me until it becomes a permanent nap.

Coach fills his fingers with more tobacco.

"As soon as you swallow like a good woman, you can go." Coach twists his hand in a rhythmic motion.

"And then we'll collect our prize!" Kyle says.

I pull Donnie's arm, exerting most of my strength, but

create room to tuck my chin. Removing the possibility of being choked out emboldens me. My strength returns as oxygen fills my lungs.

I release Donnie's arm and feel it clamp against my jaw. The pressure forces my saliva onto his forearm.

"Did ya spit on me, you wittle pa-wick?" Donnie asks.

I seize the opportunity to dig my fingernails deep into his forearm and rake downward. His sweat-soaked top layer of skin curls under my nails, leaving eight trails of blood in their wake. My thumbs anchor his arm in place. I expect him to squeeze, but the tension eases.

I explode from my kneeling position, tilting my head back and driving my skull into the base of his chin.

The metal on his face slices into my head before yielding to the force of the blow. He tumbles backward, taking the other grunt next to him down as well. Metal splices in different directions, freeing his jaw. Blood pours from Donnie's mouth as the tip of his tongue hangs dead on his lips. His jaw loses all structure.

Play-Doh jaw.

Enjoy the concussion and six more months of eating through a straw.

"Ahh!" Glenn borrows my fight and Susan's anger. He slams a racquet across the back of Kyle's neck. It splinters into two pieces but does little to disrupt Kyle. Hands paw at my back and my side, and I wail in every direction with closed fists, succeeding in putting down the most massive goon in the bunch. One lucky shot to the temple does the trick.

Left holding a splintered handle in one hand and a surviving racquet in the other, Glenn absorbs a right hook to the cheek. Both racquet and remnant hit the ground moments before Glenn joins them.

Free of Donnie's grasp, I punch Kyle square in the ear.

The backing of the small, golden ball earring pierces his neck. Instinctively, he reaches for the wound.

Don't let him breathe! The voice in my head commands.

I follow up with a second punch, this time keying on his Adam's Apple. Both Kyle's hands rocket to his throat as he gags and rolls around on the ground like he caught fire.

Susan lunges forward and kicks Coach's kneecap, forcing his leg into an unnatural angle.

Coach's squad flees in every direction.

I scurry and grab the splintered racquet as Coach Weeble Wobble rolls in circles clutching his leg.

"You stupid bitch! I'm going to make you wish you hadn't done that," he screams.

Coach's eyes morph to fear as I tower over him with the newly created wooden stake. I could justify staking his chest if only he were a vampire. Unfortunately, he isn't.

Susan doesn't try to stop me as I plunge the sharpened wood handle into Coach's shoulder.

His scream raises welcomed goosebumps on my skin.

Donnie kneels a few feet from me, focusing on stemming the blood flow from his mouth. Kyle stands five feet from me, unconvincingly making a fist with his hands.

"I recommend you get medical help for these shitheads unless you'd rather be unconscious while you wait, Kyle." I wipe the blood from my cheeks and lips. Who's blood? I've lost track.

Kyle nods a few times slowly and retreats, refusing to turn his back on me.

"Go on. Get out of here, you chicken!" Glenn yells. "And I'm done doing your math homework. From now on, you do mine!"

"Really?" I ask.

He shrugs. "Got caught up in the excitement."

I sense the shame in Susan melt away as she surveys

the scene and listens to the moans of pain coming from our attackers.

I grab Hannibal Lyncher and make my way over to Coach Throgmorton, kicking his arms away from his face so I can get a clean wrap of the giant rope around his neck.

"Milt should have killed you in the schoolyard when he had the chance," Coach groans.

"What?" I loosen my grip on the rope.

Coach's hyena laughter fills the winter air. "You didn't know? Fucking moron. You really do deserve to die."

A quick hop and I'm behind him with my foot on his back, and all my weight is leaning away, tightening the rope around his throat. A piece of me wishes I could watch see the panic bloom, the bulging eyes trying to escape his fat face, and the red cheeks fading to ghost white.

No breath. No breath. No breath! The voice in my head chants.

"Marc, don't do this," Susan says.

"Make up your mind!" I yell.

Susan tilts her head like a confused puppy.

"I know what I'm doing," The rope restricts his carotid artery, and the blood flow to his brain ceases. Coach's body falls limp.

"Jeebus, you gonna kill 'im!" Donnie's words are more blood than language.

"Please, everyone. Shut up." I say.

Nearly kill someone else. That might dampen the darkness. End the curse or fill a hole. Maybe it will work if the prey is a nemesis. Some things I need to learn on my own.

I bark orders. "Glenn, call nine-one-one. Susan, find our driver. Donnie, don't move, or I'll bash your mother fucking skull, so it matches your jaw."

I squeeze the rope hard.

"The driver is gone!" Susan's voice resonates panic.

"Do you think there are any teachers in the school?" I ask.

"What?" she asks.

"For in-service day," I say.

"Maybe. A couple. Probably."

"Donnie, limp over to the gym and find a teacher," I say. "Drool blood on them or something."

They'll probably label him a hero and have a parade in his honor.

I release Coach and watch his body roll onto its side.

I drop the rope and look at Susan. "It's time to go. You ready?"

"But." Glenn's shoulders lurch forward with the objection.

"Sorry if I wasn't clear. It's time to go. Now!"

Donnie struggles to his feet and hobbles in the direction of the school entrance. He leaves a rose petal-shaped blood trail.

"Marc, are you all right?" Susan doesn't finish her question. "Maybe we should wait for the cops and let them help us sort out everything."

"Trust me, Susan. Please." I put my hand on her shoulder and pluck a few strands of ugly brown tobacco that had polluted her golden hair. "The police in this town owe me no favors, nor are they my friends."

I sense fear and frustration replace her shame and anger as we pile in the car. No driver, but he left the keys in the ignition. I rev the engine in a way my pop would have been proud, but I let off on the gas as I shift into drive. No need to draw more attention to us.

"Did you kill him, Marc?" Susan cranes her neck, attempting to get a view of Throgmorton.

"No. No. Definitely not." I keep my eyes focused on the road.

"Then what was that?" Susan presses her body against the passenger's door.

"And what the hell is that?" Glenn bangs his hands on the back of my seat.

A shadow dangles from the noose on the Hangman's tree. Not a shadow.

A man. Hanging taut.

Dressed all in black. Like a limo driver.

Our driver.

"Holy shit, Marc! Get us out of here!" Susan screams, flailing her arms.

"Go. Go! GO!" Glenn locks his back door, then sprawls across the seat and locks the other.

I punch the lock button. Then hit it again. Double-tap. Always double tap. I slam my foot on the gas and push the red line on the limo. The tires spit gravel into the cloud of dust trailing the car. I fight the fishtailing car every inch of our exit from the school's parking lot. So much for the non-conspicuous exit.

I'll have to start outlining my epic Ted Talk on getaways and revenge, assuming my plan to take down Milt works.

If only I had a plan.

FORTY-SIX

I drive every pothole-filled and unpaved road I can find, keeping the car five miles per hour under the speed limit.

Susan keeps whispering 'why' under her breath.

"Let's grab food and drink and think this out. We need to get our stories straight, so they don't pin the dead driver on us, too," I say.

"Too? Can you even hear yourself?" Glenn sinks into the backseat, chin on chest and arms crossed. "Why does everyone around us keep ending up hurt or dead?"

"Because I'm cursed." I puff my cheeks. "I should drop you both somewhere safe. Hide until the truth comes out."

"And if it doesn't?"

"Ever thought about living in Mexico?"

"*Su curse es mi curse*, compadre." Glenn rubs his back-hand against his nose, then checks his skin for blood.

"Thought we covered that's not how Spanish works, moron." I shake my head. "I appreciate the gesture. Dealing with a curse is hard enough. Let's not insult people too."

"You really believe you're cursed?" Susan asks.

"I am, but there's still hope for you guys." I pull the car into the deserted dirt parking lot of the Iron City Coal Company. "No matter what anyone asks or says, I want you to blame me, okay? You guys have helped too much already."

I failed. Guess I am like my old man.

Susan stares into the abandoned factory. "It doesn't have to be a curse, does it?"

"W—w—what?" I stammer. "What did you say?"

She sits upright and shadows a glimmer of hope with her words. "Every curse has a cure or a hidden positive. We need to find yours. If we stop now, me, you, Glenn, we are screwed. The Milts and the Throgmortons of the world will keep on doing what they do while we end up in prison, or worse. And I'm guessing we won't have each other to lean on when times get rough if we walk away now."

"We do this?" Glenn asks.

I put my hand out. Susan and Glenn pile their hands atop mine.

"I'll take that as a yes," I say.

A short nap and lots of caffeine raises everyone's mood.

Glenn drums on his legs as we cruise down the road. I fear the button on his tight jeans might give way if he hits his legs any harder.

"You're offbeat." I yell into the backseat before leaning over to Susan and whispering, "It's so bad, it hurts my ears."

"As this is my last day of freedom, I'm going to ignore your criticism and jam out to classic Kansas."

I look into the rearview mirror and watch him belt out off-key lyrics to *Carry On My Wayward Son* into the handle of the surviving tennis racquet.

"Does this radio go any louder than ten?" I ask. "Give me some aspirin."

"How many do you want?" Susan asks.

"Three or four." I hold out a hand.

Glenn leans forward and says, "Jeesh, dude, you swallowed six when we stopped for food."

Susan pulls back her offer of four white pills. "You get two."

She dumps the pills in my hand, and I swallow them without hesitation. Glenn's disapproving reaction distracts my focus on the road, so I shift the mirror, but it snaps off in my hand.

"Shit." I toss it into the back.

"Watch it!" Glenn yells.

"What do we do now?" The helplessness in her voice digs into my bones.

"Don't know. I'm playing it by ear. We only know Milt won't be happy to see us."

"So," she sighs, "we're going to see the man who wants you guys dead, we have no plan, and we have no help because we can't trust the police."

I nod. "Yup, that about sums it up."

"Doesn't any of this worry you? I mean, it sounds crazy. You sure you two aren't embellishing this guy wanting you dead? Like dead-dead?"

Susan fiddles with the radio stations, searching for a new song that will meet Glenn's approval.

"—we interrupt Saturday Night Classic Drive to bring you an update on the breaking story from Munson High School where several teens and our beloved football coach, Bob Throgmorton, were brutally attacked. Two victims are in serious, but stable condition. The suspects are said to be two Caucasian males along with a Caucasian female. All are believed to be associated with Munson High. They should be considered armed and dangerous. Police ask anyone with information to please call—"

I click the power button.

"Is this what we've become? I thought we were the good guys," Glenn says.

"It's not you, Glenn. It's me," I say.

"Christ, you sound like you're breaking up with me or something."

"You're just guilty by association."

"I don't want to go to jail. The big guys in jail make you do more than their math homework," Glenn says. He pops his head into the front seat, looking first at Susan, then at me. "Then again, it might be better than facing my mom." He flops back into the leather seat. "The food's probably better. Can't be any worse, that's for sure. Either way, I'm screwed."

"If anyone's going to prison, it's me." I make certain Glenn can hear a straight-lined voice. He needs to know I won't let anything bad happen to him. Maybe I can convince him because I'm not sure of anything right now.

"Ain't going to matter if you're cursed like you say. Like Susan said, curses and blessings, they're two sides of the same coin. All you gotta do is flip the coin," Glenn says.

"And how do I flip the coin?" I ask.

"By doing good." Susan jumps in. "Help people. Help people who can't help themselves."

"Yeah." Glenn's voice elevates volume. "Why not do good? Beat up bullies, stop bank robberies, rescue kids trapped under cars. Hero stuff."

"I don't know where to start." Concentrating on the road and weighing Glenn's words proves difficult. I drive over rumble strips about ten times in the next mile. "It's not like kids are getting trapped under cars in our town often."

"You have money, don't you?" Glenn asks.

"Yeah, but not like Bruce Wayne, Batman had money."

Glenn ignores my objections and pushes forward. "You need a costume!"

"A what?"

"One with tight pants, a cape, and shows off your muscles!" Susan smirks.

"Don't encourage him," I say.

"She's right, except for the tight pants part," Glenn says. "Hell, you don't need to spend much money on it. You can practice sewing."

I roll my eyes and want to smack him.

"You know I love you like an older brother, but I can't go down a dark path with you. There's gotta be hope for this to work. There must be a reason for it. Susan is right; maybe it's only a curse if you don't know how to use it the right way. Not just for me, but for all of us. You especially," Glenn says. "Jail isn't our only worry. We can't lose ourselves. We can't lose who we are. I may not be your Kismet or whatever the hell you call it, but I'm your friend. It's not a curse if we do something good with this. I'm not a bad guy. I can't be, and you can't be either."

Glenn continues to reassure himself as I push the gas pedal deeper into the shadows of the floorboards. This can't end without me chasing a darker path first, but I need to maintain righteousness over hatred and vengeance.

FORTY-SEVEN

The path to Milt's shields us from the major roadways, especially with the bridge out of commission. Munson cops live for weeks without seeing this much action. Big action usually equates to a bar fight or a drunk driver running from the law after blowing through a stop sign. Dad was the one who kept them truly busy.

Between the bridge collapse, the fire at my house, one of their own missing, and the attack at the school, every available officer finds himself with the potential to earn overtime for the first time in their career. The town doesn't employ any female officers, eliminating any thought of pursuing a rational conversation with the authorities. The testosterone flows hot and heavy in town.

I know once they identify Officer Dale's unearthed remains from the ashes of my home, it won't take long to connect my attack on Throgmorton with his support of Milt's accusations earlier on television. Milt might find himself at the back of a long line of cops who want me dead.

Facts aside, my path sets me anywhere but the light. I

have to finish this. It started in the dark, and I don't see how it can end anywhere but in the dark. It might disappoint Glenn, but I need to escape, although I hope I won't spend my entire life as a fugitive from unwarranted accusations. I like the idea of being the first Cheeks man to turn this thing into something besides a curse, but first, I face a bigger issue: Milt.

The sun slides below the horizon before we make the last turn toward Milt's Bar. I turn off the headlights when the faint glow of the pub comes into view.

I pull the car behind an overweight oak.

"We can hoof it from here," I say.

The lack of housing near Milt's—plus the onset of darkness—makes staying undercover easy, but Glenn's heavy steps are bound to give away our approach.

I clench my teeth and try to keep my voice soft, "Are you wearing cement shoes?"

"It's these stupid orthotics," Glenn says.

"Orthotics?" I ask.

"You know. Inserts. I have tall arches and—"

"I know what they are, genius. You can skip the podiatry lesson," I say.

"Grandma has inserts. She's seventy-eight years old and still runs," Susan counters.

I stop and put my hands on my hips, "Really? You too?"

Susan opens her big honey eyes wide. "Sorry."

Milt's palace of death comes into view through the trees. A yellow hue illuminates the backside of the tavern.

"Quiet evening," Glenn says.

I scan the barren parking lot. Not a single car.

Susan squints her eyes and leans forward. "It looks like he's closed."

"That's impossible. Something's not right," I say.

"You know our mom thinks bars are a recruiting center for the devil. A workshop of evil." Glenn quotes his mom far too often, but for once, I agree with her.

"We need a plan." I huddle us.

"Are you sure this is a good idea? I'm all for getting back at the guy who murdered a cop and burned down your house, but this is riding a barrel over Niagara Falls crazy." Glenn stares at the pine needles scattered across the ground, refusing to look me in the eyes.

"It isn't the greatest idea, but it's the best we got." I pat him on the shoulder. His weight shifts and he struggles to maintain his balance. "Do it for Leslie."

Susan snaps up straight and tilts her head. "You like, Leslie? Skank ho, Leslie?"

Glenn brushes a pinecone away with his foot. "She's not a skank. She's fashion-forward. No idea if she's a ho, but I'd be all right with that. Can you talk about students like that? Seriously, though, can we all agree if something goes wrong, we call the cops?"

Susan and I nod.

We hide behind a large evergreen to plan our assault.

"Well, let's see," I say. "I left the rope at the school. Glenn would never let me buy chloroform, so all we have is an old tennis racquet."

Glenn clicks his tongue twice. "I left it in the car."

"You left our only weapon in the car?" I ask.

"I wouldn't exactly call it a weapon."

"Good point," I concede.

"I thought it worked pretty well at school," Susan says as she bounces her head from side to side.

"What about your wonder twin powers? Can't you make his head explode or something? That would be cool." Glenn clenches his fists so hard they shake.

I bite my lip and look around to make sure we're still

alone. "I don't think it works like that."

"How does it work?" Susan asks.

"The journal didn't outline much beyond thoughts. Milt was supposed to teach me everything. We didn't get to that part before he wanted Glenn dead. I think we have to connect and work together. We're supposed to harness each other's strengths or some shit like that. Milt has my dad's journal. We need it. It might explain everything."

"Great. Where is it?" Susan asks.

I try to lift my arm, which suddenly weighs a thousand pounds. After what feels like minutes, I point a finger at Milt's.

"The bar? His bar?" Glenn fails to control the volume of his voice. "You're telling me the answer to the question of how to stop the man who's trying to kill us is inside the bar owned by the man who wants to kill us?"

"Simple. Right?" I say.

"This is like a bad episode of the Twilight Zone," Glenn says.

"I should get the journal," Susan says.

"No way." I shake so hard I thought it might twist off.

"Why not?" Susan says, straightening up.

"Well," Glenn and I look at each other. "You're a girl."

"A woman, thank you very much, who runs faster than either of you two." Susan's index finger pecks at us with each word. "Besides, Milt isn't looking for me."

"She's got a point, dude," Glenn says.

Susan kicks a pinecone and won't look at me. "Plus, I have a reason for going there, but you're not going to like it."

I puff my cheeks, exhaling. "Spill it."

"Before all this mess happened, Milt asked me to bring Clyde over to him. At his bar." Susan covers her face with her hand. "And I did."

"You didn't!"

"I did, so that's why you need to let me do this," Susan says.

"We need more," I say. "My uncle asked me to do him a favor, but . . . "

"Does it involve killing anyone?" Glenn asks.

"No—"

Glenn jumps in. "Then go visit your uncle, dammit. Suck it up and do his favor, then ask him what the hell we're supposed to do."

I bury my anger since I don't have any better ideas.

"And who will look out for her if she gets in trouble?" I ask.

"Dude, I'm right here. She's my sister. I'm not going to let anything happen to her." Glenn says. Besides, there's no one at the bar."

I release a deep, cleansing breath.

"You sure you two can handle this?" I ask.

"We can handle it. I'll get the journal. Glenn and I can hoof it back home and hide out in the pool equipment room until you get back," Susan says.

I don't have any better ideas.

"Fine."

Susan claps her hands together, never letting them separate by more than a few centimeters.

"Where is it?" she asks.

"Honestly, I don't know," I say, but she wrinkles her petite brow, so I keep going. "Start in the storeroom. Milt had it hidden in an empty keg in there the first time he gave this to me. He likes to put stupid fake thumb scanners on things. He talked about how the obvious is the answer. The obvious place would be the same place he kept it before."

"No one would be stupid enough to do that," Glenn says.

"Then we start there," Susan chimes in. "Occam's razor."

"Look for the Keystone beer keg. There should only be one. The top unscrews."

"Sit tight. I'll be back soon," Susan says.

"Wait." Glenn holds out his arm. "Shouldn't we have a signal if you get in trouble?"

"I'll bark like a dog," Susan says, bending her hands at the wrist, holding them in front of her chest.

"You look like a T-Rex," I say.

"Most bad-ass T-Rex ever," She smiles.

"You sure you got this?" I place a fatherly hand on his shoulder.

"You trying to jinx me?" Glenn asks. "I answer yes, and that's like the kiss of death for every sidekick in any movie. Ever."

"Now you're my sidekick?"

"Who else would it be?" He asks.

I flip my head toward Susan.

"Man, that's just cold," Glenn says.

"Well, I don't want to jinx you," I chuckle.

"We wouldn't want that," Glenn says.

"Trip to P3 and back is gonna take me an hour, give or take fifteen minutes. Why don't you two sit tight for an hour? Keep an eye on the place. If there's no movement, then give it a go."

They nod.

"Sounds good," Glenn says. "Now, get out of here, Marc. We got this."

A silent, cold breeze slices through our conversation. Even nature is too afraid to make a sound.

FORTY-EIGHT

Mr. Layer's car idles in a Walmart parking lot while I take refuge in the back seat, searching for courage. I worry my fears might drown me.

The answers aren't waiting for me here. The time has come to understand who I am, not wallow in self-pity.

Time to grow up.

Glenn and Susan might need answers more than I do.

I flip open the glove compartment and find nothing but the owner's manual and a takeout menu for Peking Palace, an upscale Chinese restaurant in the city. Mr. Layer's driver stores tons of loose change in the center console of the car. I scrounge up what I can before heading into the store.

The driver's black hat provides some level of cover, and I keep my head down while walking to avoid any eye contact. I hate risking the trip in, but I have little choice.

I clean myself up in a bathroom dirtier than I am. Afterward, the silver coins jingle in my pocket as I make my way to the office supplies aisle and scoop up a box of Dixon Ticonderoga Pre-Sharpened Pencils. The $2.50

price tag fits my budget and leaves me enough money to grab a Milky Way and Mountain Dew, but sadly I can't buy a hammer or a screwdriver or anything that might serve as a weapon. I pass on the retro special of the week: Jolt Cola.

Thank God for self-checkout. For as much as I try to hide the evidence from the day's activities, I wear the bloodstains on my hands and face like too much self-tanning lotion. Crappy Walmart bathroom soap isn't much for bloodstains, I guess.

I gobble the sweet chocolate, creamy nougat, and gooey caramel before I reach the car. I'm emotionally drained but not physically weak. Two little girls fuss as their mother ferries them toward the store. Soccer jerseys two sizes too big hang down to their knees, and their black Adidas soccer cleats toss about the untethered laces. I was never that kid, and even if I wanted to be, Mom and Dad could never have been those parents.

A rusted, double edge razor blade lays next to the white line dividing parking spaces. Some people simply don't care.

I slouch lower into the driver's seat to limit my exposure. Thinking back, maybe Dad meant I could end the curse by not passing it on. I hope Lester can unknowingly steer me toward a more practical solution.

Squeezing my hand, another solution presents itself. The razor. I don't recall picking it up, but here it sits. The straight edge warped from its time on the ground, its shape redefined by neglect and weather beating down on the stainless steel. But it's still sharp, very sharp.

My forearms tense. I turn my arm slowly, exposing my wrist.

Nothing.

I exhale a sigh of relief and close my eyes. Leaning

back in the seat, I open my eyes and move to adjust the rearview mirror. I never end up looking behind me because I can't stop staring at the dotted black lines that extend eye to eye via my neck.

My hand trembles. I resist lifting my arm, but a moment later the edge of the razor sits against my neck, an inch from my earlobe.

The world around me falls quiet. Even if she tries to talk to me now, she won't get through.

A small push, pressure, and a trickle of blood traces the curves of my pulsating neck. Sweet adrenaline rushes through every cell of my being. Another few inches and my worries will fade into the blackness like so many times before. But this time, in this spot, there's no coming back. I'll miss Glenn and Susan, but maybe they'll be better off without me.

I can't stop staring in the mirror. Pain challenges my muscles to move the last eighth of an inch. The rivulet of blood turns into a small yet steady stream. Just a bit more…

Maybe I should just plunge the blade in, like I would rip off a bandaid.

HOOOONNNNNKKK!

A blaring car horn snaps me from my trance. I drop the razor and apply pressure to my wound. I grab the nearest absorbent material and the Chinese take-out menu acts as a stop-gap gauze pad.

"I can't help anyone if I'm dead," I say.

Especially not me, she echoes in my head.

THE DRIVE to P3 is a blur. Thoughts race through my mind, overlapping to a point where I think nothing at all.

I stuff the box of pencils down the front of my·jeans. I would've put them in the rear, but I bet I'd walk in such a way that it looks like I messed myself. Ripped clothes, messy hair, mud-stained jeans, and dried blood crusting my hands. This is the wardrobe I believe will get me in to see my uncle? I should have got some cash out and opted for a change of clothes as well.

I've officially crossed the crazy-insane line. The Cheeks Line might replace the Mendoza Line. Of course, there's much more at stake here than a batting average or a base-ball game.

I need help, and I know the price. I fish Conley's tattered business card from my wallet. Never thought an orderly would make business cards, but he's a unique guy. A quick call later, and I'm all set.

The entrance proves no challenge. The guard at the front gate knows my face and whoever works the other end of the camera buzzes me in seconds after I request entrance. Three trips in only a few weeks likely labeled me a regular.

I catch a dark figure out of the corner of my eye as I turn the first corner. My first instinct is to jump back.

"Hello?" I peer around the corner, but the hallway is bare.

I swing around and walk down the lonely corridor. A bell rings from a distant right hallway. A shadow flashes to my left when I look off to the right, searching for the source of the bell. I whirl around to my left and catch more shadow, but as I rotate around, I know the shadow is always there but just out of my sight.

"There you are." Conley's voice launches me two feet off the ground.

I bend over, trying to catch my breath. "You scared the crap out of me."

"Bring it in." Conley leans in close and tries to hug me.

"I'm good." I back up two steps.

"Friendly hug. Hashtag bros." Conley tosses up air quotes with his fingers.

"What are you talking about?"

He leans in again but uses his hands to cup his mouth. "Sorry," he whispers. "I applied for a gig doing social media for a marketing company, and I'm trying to stay in character for my interview tomorrow." He rolls his index finger in a fast circle. "You know you're gonna owe me double since you don't have, um, anything for me this evening? Plus, visits after sunset are generally frowned upon. Had to pull a few strings."

"I'm good for it," I say, knowing I have plenty of cash in my trust.

"Susan vouched for you, so I know your hashtag legit," he says. "Follow me."

My walk resembles a rookie cowboy after his first day on a horse. My pants yearn to betray my rule-breaking ways.

"Where's Hallsy?" I ask.

"Out sick," Conley winks and covers his mouth again. "He had an interview late this afternoon with the police department. Hoping he passed this time. Poor dude failed the psych eval last time—" he throws up air quotes— "anger issues. But I've been helping him. We'd do anything for each other."

We turn sharp left, and I make out a figure waiting by my uncle's door. Conley points in that direction. "That's Cunningham. New guy filling in for Hallsy. Hashtag people helping people. He's joining us today."

"I don't think hashtag has the same effect when you say it," I say. He ignores me.

The walk down the white-walled-hall weighs on my

mind. I stare at the handprints around the doors, every crease of every hand outlined in a harmony of black and white. As we approach Lester's room, I study the girl's door in the room next to him. Her tiny fingers dwarfed by the massive paws around it. The small hand fights through the stiffness of the paint and waves.

I shake my head and blink twice.

Conley flips a key labeled "Black Hole" over his head, catching it behind his back with his other hand.

"Hashtag nailed it!" Conley sings out.

"Did you see that?" I tap him on his shoulder. My touch startles him, and he drops the key on the ground.

"See what?" He asks.

"The small hand. It moved." As the words exit my mouth, I realize how it sounds.

Cunningham moves his hand to the base of his black-jack. "Did you say this was a visitor or a new patient?"

"Easy there, Ham. This place can play tricks on the eyes," Conley says. "You know that girl has been in there for more than a decade. The small hands belong to her. I felt sorry for her when she turned twenty-one. We don't celebrate birthdays here, and twenty-one is a big deal, so I snuck her in a margarita cupcake with a candle on it for her birthday last November."

"That's awesome," I say.

"I thought so too," Conley clears his throat. "Until she tried to shove the burning candle down my throat." He pulls back his shirt collar and shows me a spot barren of hair and pigmentation. "She got me right here. Hurt like hell. Last time I try to do something nice for her."

I glance back at the hand on the wall. All is well. I silently curse myself and run my fingers through my hair. A few tiny pieces of debris fall to the floor. *Damn, I need a shower*. The pencils tuck in my crotch pinch my delicate parts when I turn away from her door.

Things go from bad to worse when my eyes meet fifteen hands simultaneously shooting me the bird. It seems while her door greeted me, the door across the hall isn't as welcoming. W*hat the hell is this? I'm losing it. Insanity must be in my genes.*

"Conley, who's in that room?" I ask, pointing across the hall. The hands return to normal by the time Conley and Ham look.

"Transfer. Don't know much about him, but he shoots me the bird every time he sees me."

Conley grabs the key from the floor and inserts it into the door of my uncle's room.

"Wish me luck. Hope I can get answers."

"You wouldn't need luck if you had Jesus by your side," Ham says.

"Not this again," Conley says, putting his hand on his forehead and closing his eyes with a sigh.

"It's cool," I say. "I've been to church a few times."

Ham laughs. "Man, you're an idiot."

"Excuse me?" My blood starts to boil, and I press my fingers tight against my palm.

Ham pulls the blackjack from his belt and smacks it against his hand a few times. "This is Jesus."

Conley turns his head in my direction. "Every day since he started. Every-freakin' day. Guy's going to get struck by lightning. Hashtag blasphemy."

"One day, you'll be happy I walk with Jesus. Jesus saves." Ham swings the club through the air a few times, showing off his forehand and backhand before banging it into the wall. "Ow!" The club clangs on the floor as Ham hops up and down, shaking his wrist.

"I'd say Jesus is punishing you. You need to ask Jesus for forgiveness," Conley snickers.

"Real funny." Ham curls his arm across his stomach. "I'm going to head to get ice for my wrist. Is that cool?"

"Do what you gotta do, man." Conley waves Ham away. He redirects his eyes to me.

Conley half-heartedly pats down my sides and asks me to empty my pockets. He quickly takes inventory.

"Keys, empty candy wrapper, and forty-six cents.

Ham wiggles his arm and flexes his wrist. He stops walking about thirty feet down the hall.

"I gotta check on Ham. You think you'll be all right without anyone watching over you for a minute?"

"Hey, Conley, can you make sure Ham doesn't tell anyone I was here? I'll throw in another five Benjamins."

Conley clicks his tongue and winks. "I like your style, kid. Hashtag class." He nods. "Ready?"

FORTY-NINE

Kneeling in front of a floor easel, Lester exemplifies Zen. He faces the door this time with the picture turned away. I play the curious cat, intrigued to see what picture he has for me today. The school? Milt's bar? A boring visit to Walmart? He even has an empty rubber chair waiting for me, like he expected me to visit. Although, I guess Conley could've put it there after I called.

"She had them defrost the glass this afternoon. I thought she wanted to admire my artwork. Clearly, that's not the case." My uncle beckons me with the enthusiasm of a child. "Come, Nephew."

I steal a moment to see what she is doing next door. I expect hands on the glass and the usual grin, but today, her hands never stray from her art. Her squinted eyes connect with mine but quickly return to her work. I stop a few feet behind Lester's poster.

He lowers his voice to a whisper. "Did you bring them?"

"What?"

"Did you bring them?" He repeats without moving his lips.

I nod.

He clenches his fists. "All of them?"

"Why do you need a dozen?"

"It doesn't matter. Give them to me." He doesn't raise his voice.

"Fine." I fish the box of pencils from the front of my pants and glance back to the door to make sure neither Conley nor Ham is watching. After housing a box of sharpened number twos where only the twig and berries should live, I'm glad to get rid of them. "Here."

"Thank you. Thank you." His snicker chills my bones.

"Okay, you have your pencils. Now, what about me?"

"Huh?" His eyes shift left and right before he tucks the box under his shirt.

"Our deal. Remember?" I know he didn't care for Dad, but I don't believe he's double-crossing me.

"Right. Our deal. Tell you what I know." He bounces his head up and down rapidly, but his chin appears to stay in the same location the entire time.

"You said you'd tell me everything I wanted to know," I say. "Tell me about Mom."

"Don't you have more pressing issues?"

"You said—"

"Fine." He withdraws the pencil box from his shirt and strokes it like a kitten on his lap. "Your dad didn't kill your mother."

I clench my jaw and squint, trying to make myself look intimidating. "I never believed he did, but I'm starting to think you killed her."

"Me? You're crazy." Lester shakes a fist. "The car wreck was her idea. The tree spoke to her, or some nonsense. Your dad wouldn't agree to it, so Milt knocked him out and tossed him in the trunk. A drunk in the trunk. Tee-he-he." Lester's laugh pushes his smile off-center.

"And you agreed to kill her?" I remain stern but refrain from yelling. It seems risky to yell without Conley close.

"Kill her? Heaven's no. That was never the intention. Milt, though. Maybe. I guess I underestimated him. Poor boy. Hates competition. Delusions of grandeur. Thinks he's in control. He's nothing more than a messenger. Stitches are gods. Evolution beyond the common man."

My mouth runs dry.

Words scrape the desert landscape of my tongue to escape. "This was Milt's plan?" I ask.

Lester puts his head in his hands. "Milt, feeble-minded Milt. Too focused on the short-term picture. Greediest S.O.B. you'll ever meet. Why was I cursed with a weak Kismet? Why couldn't I have someone like her?" He points to the next cell. "The plan was perfect. We agreed. Your mom agreed."

Lester snickers as he extracts a pencil from the box.

"And then the cop showed up. Out having an affair, I think. Friends with Milt, so I left Milt in charge of cleaning things up since I had to get back here before anyone noticed I was gone. Yes, even Doc Gehringer can be bought. Not money, though. He gets my brain to study when I die." Lester holds the point of the pencil an inch in front of his eye. "Little does he know I plan to outlive him. Usually works that way when you kill someone."

I wait for someone listening in on the conversation to burst into the room, but nothing happens. Conley succeeded in getting me exclusivity. A little too well, maybe.

"I'm kidding!" Lester roars with laughter. "But you should have seen your face. Anyhow, we bribed the cop to keep him quiet. Your mom's life insurance golden goose would splat like Humpty Dumpty if the word suicide found its way to the insurance company. That fat cop was squeezing your dad ever since."

"But why? Why would Mom or Dad agree to any of that?" Tears bulge my eyelids to a breaking point.

"Why is the question, isn't it?" He snaps a pencil in half with just one hand. "Your mother wanted out. I think she wanted to spare you from ever seeing her true self. Once you were born, all she ever wanted was a normal life, but your dad couldn't control his rage, and she couldn't resist her old ways. It was your mother who paid the ultimate price."

I whip my head to the side, but he reads my eyes before I can disconnect them.

"You didn't know she was a dark force? I'm impressed. She must have protected you well." He eases another pencil out of the box. "From what I know, you've almost died any number of times now. I can see the straight line scar on your wrist. When Conley grabbed your arm last time you were here, he exposed the scar on your back right above the kidney area. Nasty place to get stabbed. An Uncle Milty favorite. Often fatal, even for a Stitch, especially if you don't get medical attention right away.

"You're stronger now, and you know it. I'm guessing you fantasize about how you can almost kill yourself every day. Instinct, initially, then a need. It's a drug, you know. Makes you feel sooooo good." He snaps another pencil in half, using only his thumb and index finger.

I jump.

Drool drips from my uncle's cracked lips; his glossy eyes highlight a Cheshire grin.

Dopamine. Doc's word echoes through my mind.

"We become strong. Almost invincible if you survive long enough. Unfortunately, it has a cost. For some, it's their temper. Your grandfather became apathetic to everyone and everything. Journal says his darkness was cancer, but I contend it was apathy. Both eat you alive from the inside. For *my* uncle, it was control of his bowel movements. Downright nasty to be around. For your uncle, well, you can see where it landed me. Wonder what the wheel of fate has in store for you?"

Lester taps his finger against his temple.

"My stinking deuce dealing uncle was so desperate to fix himself he found something interesting in the family history."

I lean in on his words and almost slide off the chair. "What did he find?"

"He first theorized almost killing another person provided the opposite effects of almost dying. It would reverse the curse. Never worked for me or your dad. You probably know all this already from reading the journal. Bet your dad even led you to believe he wrote it all himself." Lester scoffs. "He was so drunk half the time he didn't even realize what he was writing. Drunken scribes make great storytellers but terrible historians.

"Your dad missed the fact your grandfather held the answer, but he was too cowardly to go through with it. On the bright side, his weakness helped my uncle figure it out. He found the cure. Unfortunately, my uncle met an untimely fate before anyone realized it. But I know." Lester's sing-song voice snaps me back to reality. "After all, how could anyone else know if two pages of the journal my uncle entered were missing? Pages removed and burned by a crazy man, but they locked me up before I could execute my plan of escape." A fire lit in my uncle's eyes. "Without anything more to offer Gehringer, I was stuck here. I needed to manipulate your father into thoughts of escape and then make Milt believe he could control Stitches for everything to fall into place." He sets the two broken pencils on the ground next to him. "It would lead a clueless Marc to his uncle. Alone."

"Dad told me it doesn't have to be a curse. You—"

A pounding on the glass grabs my attention. "Soulmate" stands with a picture in her hand. I see myself racing from the storeroom of Milt's bar with a bloody handprint and a message scrawled on the hot-box. Glenn's bloodied silhouette hugs the edge of the paper while Susan watches over him, her eyes black and a crooked smile that resembles Lester's.

That isn't a picture of my past.

"Oh shit," I mutter.

I jinxed him.

FIFTY

The door to the room bursts open, and I hear Conley's panicked voice. "You can't have pencils, Lester."

My uncle lunges at me with a sharpened number two. His arm flashes with a speed barely matched by my reaction. We tumble off my chair onto the floor. I use both my arms to hold off his one. No matter how hard I resist, the pencil slowly descends toward my chest. His face takes on a yellow glow with anticipation. The pitch-black pupils consume his once green irises as his nostrils flare.

He wraps his free hand around my throat. Airflow to my lungs cease. My eyes widen, and I swallow every ounce of light in the room.

Would I rather be stabbed or choked to death?

I wriggle wildly until I catch enough room for one word. "Why?"

The sharpened tip of the pencil reaches the shirt covering my chest. "It's not *our* curse. When my uncle put *his* father out of his misery, he became free. His mind and body returned to him. It was stupid misfortune that got him hit by a train. Everyone blamed a curse. The curse. No one paid any attention to his two pages in the journal, but me." His words quicken with anticipation.

"Almost killing someone does nothing, but killing a Stitch family member from a different generation allows us to be our own person, free from our Kismets. The darkness lifts, the bond breaks, and the best part is you keep your strength. So, father kills son. Grandson kills grandfather. Or, in our case, uncle kills nephew."

The graphite spear tip pierces my skin. Death dances on my skin, wanting to drink more of my blood. I kick my legs up with all my strength. Even with all my new strength, I can't fight one so strong.

"Your father would have known this if he wasn't so consumed with saving your mother," Lester's deep, unearthly voice growls. "He could have saved himself and your mother by simply killing you."

"Get off him!" Conley flies over me, body slamming my uncle to the ground. A quarter-inch-deep hole spouts blood from my chest. My mouth draws in as much oxygen as my lungs can handle.

I sit up as Lester tosses Conley aside. Graphite and wood reside deep in Conley's chest with only the eraser tasting light.

Lester grabs the remaining broken pencils and stands over Conley. Ham bursts through the door, waving Jesus high in the air with his left hand, and charges my uncle.

I want to help, but I sit, coughing and wheezing. Ham's awkward attack with his non-dominant hand hits nothing but air. My uncle retaliates, slamming broken pencil pieces into Ham's face.

Ham's legs buckle, and his convulsing body hits the floor, springing Jesus loose.

I use both my arms and scoot back across the polished floor.

Ham screams, "My eyes! My eyes! I'm blind! Jesus, someone help me!" A pencil half protrudes from his eye, making him look like a candied apple. The blood trickling down his caramel-tanned face adds to the illusion.

My uncle empties the remaining pencils from the box as I retreat toward the door. Staring right at me, he straddles Ham. "And sometimes you'll find you don't want to stop at near death." Despite his bare feet, my uncle stomps on Ham's face, driving the pencil into both his foot and Ham's eye socket. The screaming stops. "Because it makes no difference to a Stitch in the end."

Lester flashes three pencils in his hand. "Ever wonder what pencils thrown at three-hundred miles per hour can do to a person?"

Two armed guards and an older woman in nurse's garbs reach the door. Pencils slice through the air as I cover my head with my arms. Two small thuds and the guards collapse in a heap next to me. The old woman flops back into the hallway. The handprints around Bowfinger's door creep lower toward the pooling blood around her body.

Lester takes one stride in my direction, but his other foot refuses to move. The pencil merged his foot with Ham's face. Wood sticks out through the top of Lester's foot.

"Well, that's inconvenient." He grunts deep and pulls his hind leg forward, dragging Ham's corpse with him. "Damn things are made not to break." He shakes his head. "At least you bought the right ones. Show me your face, dear nephew, so we can get this over with."

I hear another grunt.

It doesn't have to be a curse.

Dad's words run through my mind. I uncover and jump to my feet.

"I'm not your answer. You're mine." I frantically search for anything I can use as a weapon to kill Lester. To free myself.

A pencil whizzes by my head. A bevy of curse words flies from Lester's mouth as he tries to regain his balance.

"Stop right there, Lester!" Four guards crowd the entrance to the room. A quartet of shotguns threatens him.

I glance over at Soulmate. She flashes a picture of me hoisting one of the dead guards onto my shoulder with the armed living guards stand behind me. She doesn't draw anything other than Lester's head and a floating pencil. Somehow, she still manages to capture his fury.

I hear Dr. Gehringer's voice protrude over the guards. "Drop the pencils, Lester, and raise your hands in the air. You don't want to do this. I can help you."

Lester looks toward me. "Quite the family reunion, eh, nephew?" He cocks his shoulder back with a pencil in hand.

I sling a fallen guard over my shoulder, using his body as a meat shield.

"No!" I scream while rushing forward.

Fire rips through my shoulder. My uncle crumples, spewing fountains of red from his chest. The shotgun blast from the guards in the doorway, combined with my forward momentum, launch my body ten feet across the room. I land next to the very man intent on killing me. The guard's head over my shoulder resembles a Gallagher watermelon after the show, but it may have saved my life.

"Keep eyes on him while I get help," the largest of the guards says.

Even though getting hit by a shotgun is new to me, I

maintain my wits. My heart sinks as my chance of making Dad's words true lay dead inches from me.

The largest guard moves over toward us as all four men reload their weapons. "Hey kid, stay with me. We're getting help."

A girl appears at the door and yells something to the guard. Her screams won't stop until I hear her gasping for air between the words, "Nurse Lang! Nurse Lang!"

Lang? Shit. Glenn and Susan's grandmother.

The guard rambles toward her but doesn't cross the seal of the room.

The old woman waves the girl toward Soulmate. "I'll be okay. Check on my granddaughter."

I stare at my uncle's face. Blood drips from the corner of his mouth, his eyes shut. Crimson covers his chest, and the pencils roll free from his hand.

Soulmate taps on the unbroken glass and waves me over. Despite several shotgun blasts, the windowed divide between the rooms remains undaunted. Not a single scratch on it, unlike me. It hurts to move, let alone walk, but I struggle to my feet and lug my war-torn parts in her direction.

Soulmate lays out dozens of drawings on the floor. Each done in vivid detail with uncanny accuracy. My eyes jump between pictures of my unauthorized biography. The bridge incident, me swallowing the pills at the DMV, the first fight at the school, the fight behind Milt's bar. I scan the row from left to right as they appear to be laid out chronologically. It ends with a picture of Lester sitting up, smiling, and twirling two broken pencils in his hand, all while I'm staring into the other room.

Oh shit.

I spin around.

A finger twitches. His finger. Blood pulsates from the wounds.

I struggle to talk. I find my raspy voice, but no one can understand. "His eyes should be open. His eyes should be open!"

They open with a blink. They aren't glazed over.

Adrenaline surges. I leap across the room and snatch the four pencils once held in his murderous palm. Soulmate pounds on the window, but I ignore her. I know what I need to do. I know where I need to be.

"Aaahh!"

Four tools to write my father's words into legend from lore. Four pencils driven deep into the heart of a soulless man. I baptize Lester's heart with all four pencils.

"I am not a curse!"

I withdraw my weapons and enjoy a surge of relief.

That all you got?

He blinks again.

I plunge the pencils deep into his chest again. And again. And again. I snap the pencils to the side, leaving four halves in his chest. I ram the remaining splintered pieces into his neck and twist. Blood showers my face, neck, and arms.

A curse lifting Christening.

"What the hell are you doing, kid?" A guard waves his arms. "He's already dead!"

I pull out the pencils from one side of Lester's neck and hammer them into the other side, making certain I hit every artery. Two remain in his neck for good measure.

He blinks again.

I thrust the last two into his eyes and smash them deep with pounding fists.

The blinking stops.

"Holy shit, kid. What did you do? You're freaking nuts.

Batshit crazy like him. Crazier!" The guard recoils against the wall, pumps his shotgun, and points the barrel at my head.

Lester's right. This is where I'm supposed to be, but not quite yet.

I exhale, wiping blood from my forehead. "I may be crazy, but I'm not insane."

FIFTY-ONE

I inventory the room. Lester, two guards, Ham, and Conley comprise the dead, or as Conley might say, "Hashtag massacre." Nurse Lang rests in a puddle of community blood. Alive. Barely.

I roll onto my back and allow pain to seize my body. The room fills with voices. In minutes, the live bodies outnumber the dead ones.

Gehringer steps forward, under the guard of three gigantic, heavily armed men, and injects me with a warm liquid. A halo-haze clouds my vision, but Gehringer underestimates how much it takes to incapacitate me.

The plain, unmemorable girl kneels next to Nurse Lang, sobbing until she hyperventilates. Once she catches her breath, she turns her bloodshot eyes toward me.

"You!" she screams. "How could you be so goddamn stupid?"

The medics push her away.

"Her pulse is fading. We're losing her!" the medic yells.

"We've got to move her!" The other medic screams

directions, and a flurry of white-clad folks whisk her grand-mother out of sight.

Soulmate positions her hands on the glass in a familiar way and stares at them.

I place my blood-caked hands against the glass. It takes a moment to keep them from sliding around. I leave streaks of red in their wake. Soulmate looks up, smiles, then closes her eyes.

Dad's words run through my head.

It doesn't have to be a curse.

I have no family left. No family left to kill to end the curse.

Goodbye, Crazy. Hello, Insanity.

Insanity's forever.

But it might just be what I need to survive.

Visions of my body convulsing fill my thoughts. I make them a reality, writhing on the floor, pushing my body to the brink.

Paramedics ferry me from the room. The gurney bounces off every wall as they race me down out the door. The chaos of frantic guards, crying workers, frenzied patients, and darkness provides the perfect camouflage. Dr. Gehringer is too busy laying claim to Lester's body. No one but Soulmate realizes I'm gone.

As they load me into the ambulance, the two white-clad men offer little resistance to my escape. Thankful for their quick patchwork on my shoulder and wounds, I can't avoid making an awful mess of the supplies in the back of the ambulance, but I do stop short of breaking any bones in either of their bodies while knocking them unconscious.

The two will have to share a gurney on the ride to Milt's.

Sirens on, I'm fortunate no one thinks to look at the ambulance driver as I exit P3.

FIFTY-TWO

The cloak of the ambulance's sirens and flashing lights provide quick passage to Milt's. While I would prefer to be anywhere but here, I don't have a choice.

Soulmate's last drawing.

My trembling hands struggle to park the ambulance. I position it farther away from the bar than even where the Lincoln Town Car had been. Although I haven't been gone long, I don't want to startle Glenn into doing something dumb seeing a vehicle like this pulling up near him. That is, if they are even still here.

I cross my fingers they already finished up and sat waiting for me to get back.

I hop from the ambulance and push forward. Emerging from the evergreen branches, I cross my fingers the black car is gone so I can head to Susan's instead, but there it sits. Quietly. Only the sound of a bark emulating from the shadows behind Milt's permeates the night air. The bark is familiar.

"Clyde!"

The good news is Clyde wasn't part of Soulmate's

picture, so there's hope. The bad news, that asshole has my dog.

My legs carry me down the hill's gentle slope to the side of the bar faster than ever. The melting snow softens the ground around Milt's, helping to silence my footsteps. I work my way, inch by inch, along the textured concrete wall until I can see the field behind the bar.

I peek around the corner and see two figures. The shorter, chubby guy struggles to maintain hold of a leash. A moment later, the second man comes into clear view. I recognize him before I even blink.

"Milt," I whisper, but no sign of Glenn or Susan.

Clyde barks as the overweight man holding his leash complains about him.

"Look, we need the dog as a failsafe," Milt says.

The fat man's arms flail as he struggles to maintain hold of Clyde.

"Should've killed that shit in the schoolyard when we had the chance." Milt's partner snorts. Something about his familiar voice grates on my nerves, but with his back to me, I can't get a good look at him.

"Don't I know it, Dale." Milt nods. He takes a drag from his unfiltered cigarette. "But Lester wanted him alive for some reason."

Dale?

I think back to Dad's room. Milt. The body. The body in the floor with a crooked ankle, a foot twisted in the wrong direction.

Wearing Italian shoes.

"Milt killed the Italian shoe guy," I say. The weight on my failure steals most of my confidence.

He's not a hack. Milt set us up to fail. On top of that, Lester played him. He played me. Shit. He played us all.

Even if Glenn had been my Kismet, we would've been

trying to read the mind of someone different. Milt killed the guy Dad fought with earlier that day, then he let Dale out and put that guy in the floor. Dressed him to look the same.

Anger. Hate. Betrayal. Revenge.

Blindness.

A trap. All of it. How could I be so stupid? Milt wants us here. All the leverage on me he needs, and I brought it to him.

First, I need to find my friends. Then, I can deal with Milt and Dale.

I hurry to the front of the bar. The sign out front reads "ilt's Bar." The "M" burned out a few weeks earlier. Milt told me there were more pressing issues than fixing a sign, and there are better ways than an orange neon sign to get people to know your name.

The dirt cedes ground to the cold, empty parking lot. The rough gravel and pavement serve as a reminder Milt's battlegrounds are always uneven.

The bar welcomes me without a challenge. Milt hasn't touched the front of the building since we sparingly cleaned after the bridge incident. Flies swarm a plate of chicken wings, probably the same chicken wings that led to the destruction of the Munson Creek Bridge.

The soft buzzing of the bar's only clean-up crew infects my ears. I tiptoe as not to disturb anything, including the cadre of flies.

The pitch-black path through the kitchen requires caution, not speed. I close my eyes and concentrate on Susan's face, the gentle curves, the rounded chin, and the sprinkling of a few freckles on her cheeks.

"Nothing," I mumble aloud. It's comforting to hear a sound beyond insects feasting on decaying meat.

I use my hands to see through the darkness. The grease

on the countertops extends to the floor, so I stop tiptoeing and *skate* to the storage door instead. My memory of the place serves me well, and for the first time, working here provides a benefit.

Once I find the knob, I put my ear against the slimy door and use my hands to steady myself. I can hear an off-balance click of the fan every few seconds.

I turn the brass knob with as little force as I can. It occurs to me I don't know if the back door is open or closed. By walking into the storage room, I might expose myself to Milt's line of sight.

The door clicks. I ease it open. The hateful thing creaks the entire arc.

I let out a sigh, seeing the closed back door shielding me from the outside. The fan continues its assault on my ears. I flinch with each wobbling spin. The two small square windows on the high side of the back wall let in enough light for me to make out shapes. The kegs sit piled off to my left.

"Susan?" I whisper, but a poorly timed one as it coincides with the click of the fan.

Click . . . click . . . click.

I bob my head with each rotation.

"Susan."

Click . . . click . . . click.

"Susan." I raise my voice.

"Shhh!"

Her voice rises from the collection of kegs.

"Where are you?" I ask into the nothingness.

A bright light temporarily blinds me, and I jump into a fighting stance.

"Relax, killer," Susan says. "Over here." She traces a path for me to follow with the light, so I hunch low and waddle over.

"Thank God you're here," she says. "I've been trapped hiding in here."

The familiar pages of the journal lay sprawled in Susan's lap. Milt's sloppy handwriting pollutes the open pages. She almost looks comfortable sitting crisscross on the floor, snuggled amongst the silver cylinders. I squeeze into the small space next to her.

Now isn't the best time to discuss what happened with her grandma. Besides, I left not knowing her full diagnosis. Probably nothing more than a superficial wound. It's easier to tell myself that.

"Some light reading?" I ask.

"That's one way to put it," Susan says. "But I think of a few other less cheerful ways to describe it as well. Wait, is Glenn with you?" she asks.

"No. I thought he might be hiding in here with you. He's not out back." I toss my head toward the backdoor.

"Bet he's hiding in the woods. Did you check?"

"Shoot. I didn't even think to look." Makes sense Glenn would hide behind a group of trees. Practically the same as us hiding in Mr. Chavez's garage. I point to the pages of the journal. "So, what did you find out?"

FIFTY-THREE

The soft light through the window highlights her silhouette. Her eyelids flutter from the slight breeze of the fan. The indentation on her upper lip is more pronounced as a shadow.

Mesmerizing.

" . . . and that's about it," Susan says. "Now, how the hell are we going to get out of here without getting caught?"

I shake my head. "Huh?"

"Did you hear one word I said?"

Nope.

"Sorry, I thought I heard something outside." I feign a concerned glance toward the back door.

The worst lies are the ones that come true.

The backdoor knob jostles.

"Did you lock the back door?" I ask.

"I came in through the front," Susan says. "I have no idea if it's locked."

"Give me the journal." I finger the book from her lap. "And turn off that light!" I whisper yell.

Susan uses her manicured nail to punch a button on her phone, leaving us with only a wisp of light. The door swings open. Milt fumbles with the keys in the lock. I peer through a small separation in the kegs. Susan huddles next to me.

"And you're sure the dog can't escape?" Milt asks.

"Nah. Tied 'im up good," Dale says.

"And you took care of that fancy lawyer's driver?" Milt asks.

"I hung his body on the noose tree. Lifted the kid's prints and put the gun where the cops will find it."

Milt twists his hips and launches a backhand with full force. Dale crumples to the floor before Milt even completes his follow-through.

"Why didn't you throw him in the creek like I told you!"

"Planting evidence never works on a wet body. Trust me," Dale whimpers.

"Me and that creek got an understanding, Dale. I don't tell her secrets, and she don't show mine," Milt says. "You disobey me again, and I'll end you."

I freeze. Susan fans her face. Her breathing becomes shallow and erratic. For all the symmetry in noise the clicking fan offers, Susan's breathing epitomizes chaos.

"As. Ma." She puffs out between inhaling attempts.

All this time, I thought her perfect, but this flaw, maybe her only flaw, might expose us.

"You hear something?" Milt puts out both his arms like an eagle and circles, tilting his head to the side. I survey the immediate area for a weapon.

"Quiet." Milt darts to the room's light and plunges us back into darkness.

"What?" Dale asks.

I have a straight line of sight to his face. Dad's memory lives on in Dale's purple bruises and blossoming scars.

Susan's wheezing escalates. I cup my hands over her mouth, imitating a paper bag. She swats them away. Tears and panic fill her eyes as she looks at the L-shaped Advair inhaler in her hand.

Milt's voice grows louder as he spews a string of profanities.

Susan eases the cap off the inhaler, and the metal edge reflects the dim light onto the inhaler's lavender neck. I cringe at the popping sound. I wrap my hands around her wrist and shake my head.

She mouths the word, "Please."

I stare at the dark side of her beauty. The illuminated side of her face remains forever out of my view.

Milt opens the back door and beckons Dale. "Follow me. No more waiting. I think it's time we encourage our new friend to talk."

My eyes connect with Dale's as he starts to stand. I pinch them closed, hiding their white.

"Hey, Milt . . . " Dale's voice wanes.

I want to open my eyes, but I feel his look would turn me to stone. I perform my best impression of a statue as it's my best hope of making him doubt what he sees.

"Dale, get your donut lovin' ass out here!" Milt demands.

Susan's wheezing morphs into a slight whistle.

"But, Milt."

"Get out here now!" Milt slams the door into the metal shelves. The falling cans jar my inner Golem.

I open my eyes.

Cans roll where Dale once sat.

I reach over and squeeze Susan's inhaler. She fills her lungs like a newborn baby.

"Oh God," she says between two huge breaths. "I thought I was gonna die."

Commotion out back cuts short our moment of relief.

"Bring him over here," Milt says.

"Don't hurt me. I swear I won't say anything to anyone," the voice pleads.

My heart sinks. I know that voice all too well.

"Glenn," I say. "Shit, they got Glenn."

I abandon my hiding spot.

"Marc, they'll see you." Susan tugs on my shirt.

"What did it say in the journal? How do we beat Milt?" I ask again.

"I don't know. It doesn't say," Susan begins. "That's what I was trying to tell you earlier. There's nothing in there titled *How to beat Milt*." Susan stands next to me. I push a keg to the side to give us more room. "There's stuff in there about how long it takes an ambulance to get to your house. And I found a bunch of chapters about how much blood you can lose before dying and how many minutes you have to get your stomach pumped after swallowing a bottle of aspirin."

"Yeah." I rub my eyes. "I read that stuff already."

"What is this thing, Marc? It's pretty fucking creepy. Your dad was screwed up." Susan throws her hands in the air. "I think you might have skimped a bit on your explanations. There's a page in here where your dad thinks he'd be cured by almost killing someone. And the more he cared about them, the better the chances. I mean, what the hell does that mean? Is this why you did what you did back at school?"

"I can't explain everything right now." I point toward the door. "We have a bit of a situation to deal with here. We can do this together. You're my Kismet."

"Marc," she lays her fingers on my forearm. "I'm not so sure."

"Where is he?" Milt's raspy demands interrupt Susan and me.

I can see Glenn's feet elevate off the ground. Milt holds him by his throat with a single arm and directs Dale with the other. Even if he wants to give us up, I don't think he can speak.

"What are we going to do?" Susan whispers. "He's going to choke him to death." Panic sets in with her words. She crouches behind me as I peer out the door.

Clyde barks and pulls at the chain.

I grab two cans of Bush's Baked Beans from the floor and rear back. I unleash a rainbow arc throw, and the can sails five feet over Milt's head.

The clank of the can against a rock catches the attention of everyone and everything outside. Fortunately, they look in the direction of where the can landed with a thud.

"You throw like a girl," Susan says, snatching the other can from my hand. "Move." She pushes me to the side.

An effortless dip, arm extended, and then an explosion of her hips. The can rockets from her hand, hitting Milt in the back of the head seconds later.

"Whoa. I love you," I say, donning the look of a doe eyed puppy dog.

"What?" She whirls her head around.

"Like a moth to a flame." Milt drops Glenn onto the damp grass and points to the open door. "Get him!"

"Hide!" I say. "They don't know you're here."

"But—"

"Hide now!" I strain through gritted teeth. My voice becomes more hiss and air than words.

Dale wobble-sprints toward the open door on the backside of the bar. He skids on a patch of freshly minted night dew. I turn to confirm Susan has made herself invisible among the kegs.

"I wonder . . . " I wrap my fingers around the handle of the Coors Light keg. Milt skims beer before selling it to local teens, but I know it will be three-quarters full. I rock it to the side and slide my hand under the base.

A grunt emulates from deep in my chest. I might argue I birthed it in my soul with help from Mom and Dad. No matter the origin, it proves useful.

As Dale reaches the three stairs offering access to the storeroom, I offer him a welcome gift.

I scream and step forward, extending my arms. The keg leaves my grasp with a very different trajectory than the can of beans. No arc. No speed. Minimal distance. But unlike the can of beans, I don't need pinpoint accuracy. The keg permits a great deal of room for error, and its brute force doesn't disappoint.

The misnomer light beer takes hold in keg form. The one-hundred-pound projectile meets Dale as he steps through the door. His feeble last-second attempt to shield his chest with his arms fails.

The sound of bones crunching fills the air before intense cries of pain. The doorway halts the keg's brutal assault as Dale tumbles backward down the trio of stairs.

Beer sprays from the broken nozzle. I hurry to the door to stop Dale's retreat. He lies on the ground, rolling left and right on his back. His arms are bent at the elbow, as well as the mid-forearm, creating a U-shape. Fear dominates his blood-filled eyes.

"You broke my arms! I'm going to kill you!" Dale screams.

"Don't let him." A female voice pipes in over my shoulder. "Take care of him. Don't let him breathe."

"Susan . . . " I lose my ability to answer her or keep her out of my head.

"No breath. Do it," she says in a monotone voice.

Or am I only hearing it?

"I'm not going to kill him," I say.

"Well, I'm going to kill you!" Dale shouts. "But before I let you die, I'm going to make you watch me drown your mutt in that cursed river."

I pick up the keg spitting beer. This time, it comes easily. I walk down the steps and stand over his body. Milt moves in behind Glenn and uses him as a shield with a knife to Glenn's throat.

"I wish you hadn't said that." I tower over Dale.

Did he say it? I don't know anymore.

"Listen, kid, walk away, and I'll call us even. Explain to the police this whole thing has been one big misunderstanding. You know they'll listen to me. Okay?" Dale pleads. "There's no need—"

I drop the silver keg on his midsection evicting, every ounce of oxygen from his lungs but sparing his life. Dale may come in handy later if he's telling the truth, but I don't trust him much more than I trust Milt.

Which is to say, not at all.

Susan joins my side. I glance over and notice her pearly white teeth filling a wide, sinister smile. Her glassy eyes remind me of every inmate at P3.

"No breath," she says.

FIFTY-FOUR

"Not another step, or I spill this kid's Kool-Aid down his shirt," Milt says, pulling the knife tighter against Glenn's throat.

I stare down Milt, scanning for an opening. The gurgling sounds from Dale cease. The weight of the keg and damage from the smashes cut off his oxygen supply. His ashen face and empty eyes hint at his last moments on Earth.

"You let Glenn go, and I'll flip this keg off Dale's chest. Deal?" I ask, crouching next to the keg and putting my hands on its underside.

"Let him die. Don't matter to me," Milt says. "I should thank you for doing my job. I planned on tossing him in the creek when this was over."

I flip the keg off Dale. It topples end over end twice before settling on its side. Dale's eyes let life's light in, and color returns to his face.

"Looks like you'll have to do your own dirty work," I say.

"Hell, this whole thing was his idea; you should want him dead."

I feel the weight of the keg as if it's on my heart.

"I know you're lying." I snarl. "Lester already told me your plans. Kill my Kismet, then kill me."

"And why would I do that? You and me belong together. I realize now, I ain't supposed to be with Lester, and you ain't supposed to be with no one else. You'd be dead by now if it weren't for me. Lester and Dale wanted to kill you when you was just a boy. They wanted to right after they killed your mom. She was alive after the accident. Then they smothered her while I was tending to your old man."

But Lester said he left the scene to return to P3. Left Milt and the cop to clean up. Unless he lied to me. Or maybe Milt's lying to me now, hoping I'll be content with getting revenge on Dale.

"Ask him yourself," Milt's smile snakes up his cheek.

"He's lying," Dale gasps. "I'm a police officer. I swore an oath. Protect and serve. Protect and serve!"

I serve up a soccer-style kick to Dale's temple.

"This conversation isn't over," I say. It doesn't matter who did what in the end; they're all guilty and deserve the same fate as Lester.

Dale no longer poses a threat anyhow. Best I figure, he has two broken forearms, a cracked sternum, and a bunch of broken ribs. If he doesn't get help soon, Milt probably won't have to do any dirty work.

Milt relaxes his knife-wielding arm for a moment and points the blade toward Susan. "She your Kismet?" He raises his chins and sniffs the night air deep. "Smells like it."

I wave Susan back to the bar. She refuses and stands with a can of beans in each hand.

"Why does it matter?" I ask.

"I'll swap you him—" Milt licks his leathery lips— "for her."

I watch him flex his biceps. Maybe it's some bartender mating ritual, but it's also an opportunity. His arm retracts a few inches when he pushes his bicep to the brink of bursting through his shirt. The blade of the knife rests on the side of Glenn's neck, a few inches from his jugular.

"What would you do with her?" I ask, taking two small steps in the direction of Milt.

"Train her. Take her under my wing," Milt says. "We're always helping people like you, but nobody's helping us. Nobody's there for a Kismet."

I point to Glenn. "But you were ready to kill him at my house."

"Heat of the moment. No pun intended," Milt snickers. I inch closer when he loses focus on me during his laugh. "Perhaps my thoughts were a bit misguided earlier."

"Misguided? That's the understatement of the century." There's logic in his thinking, but I doubt his words hold any truth or sincerity. "And you won't hurt them?"

"Two is better than one. Her. Me. We both work with you. Keeps me from having to be everywhere at once. What do you say? We'll be a family. Your family. Glenn can be our pet."

"Fuck you," Glenn screams. His squirming in Milt's arms accomplishes little other than to allow me to step closer.

"Fine. An awkward cousin," Milt huffs.

"It would be the most dysfunctional family ever," I say. If I can keep Milt under control, it might work.

"Marc." Susan shakes her head no.

"I have no family." I look at Glenn, then pivot to Susan. "It's not the worst idea in the world."

I think, and mouth, *throw a can*, hoping Susan can read my lips in case she can't hear my thoughts.

"No, because it's the worst idea in the entire freaking universe!" she says.

"You want him to die?" I ask. The verbal games allow me to close the distance several feet between me and Milt. "He's your flesh and blood. He's your family."

And you are both my family now.

A voice inside my head shouts, *Duck!*

Susan rears back and fires the can directly at my head, using my body as a screen.

Grace never bestowed herself upon my body, but fear serves as a great motivator, and I fear taking a can to the face. My crouch, turn, and dodge showcases all the elegance of a newborn pony trying to walk for the first time. I use my hand to steady myself in a three-point stance as the can sails past Milt and Glenn.

I explode from the ground. I'm only one step away when Milt's hand rakes the knife down the side of Glenn's neck. I foresee the three of us tumbling in a shower of Glenn's blood, but a quick glimpse of the cut tells me Glenn's jugular remains unscathed. Milt panicked, trying to avoid my tackle, and pulled the knife back rather than across.

Glenn folds over my shoulder. A moment later, our trio rolls to the ground in chaotic harmony. My head smashes into something hard and painful, halting my momentum. The world around me spins. In my rotating view, I see Susan holding more cans. Her mouth moves, but I can't hear what she's yelling. In fact, I can't hear anything at all. My arms and legs remain limp.

I'm dead, lying here with hollow eyes. My arms and legs have given up fighting and surrendered to the Grim Reaper, but my brain hasn't realized it yet.

That's gotta be it.

Her voice once told me it's hardest to keep fighting when you feel like dying, but what do you do if you're dead?

FIFTY-FIVE

*I*t doesn't end like this. I am not spending the rest of my life trapped in your head. Wake up!

Sloppy wetness runs up my cheek. My eyes shoot open. "Clyde!"

Pain pulsates through my forehead. Rushing blood races to my head while adrenaline spikes throughout my body.

Moonlight on the offending rock reflects my crimson blood. I never noticed all the different shades of red my blood could showcase.

A couple of blinks and my vision returns along with audio. Glenn screams about bleeding to death while Susan grunts with each projectile she hurls in Milt's direction.

Legs tucked to his chest, and Milt lays folded near me. Susan throws rocks, not cans, and connects on more than a few throws. My blackout probably lasts only a few seconds, but time passes like a human year to a dog while unconscious. Ten minutes might feel like ten seconds when your world is static, but ten seconds feels like ten hours with my life at stake.

A reflection of light exposes the knife's sheltered place among the short grass and rocky ground. Milt pops to his knees and uses a forearm to shield his face from Susan's assault.

"I'm dying. Call nine-one-one!" Glenn wails. He rolls on the ground in the short space between Milt and me. If he isn't careful, he'll roll onto the knife.

I crawl toward the blade. The sharp pebbles on the ground bite my hands. I ignore the pain and lunge for the knife, but Milt's hand secures it first. I abandon my crawl as he raises the blade over his shoulder.

The same rock that knocked me unconscious a moment ago halts my roll. A projectile whizzes past Milt. Susan's aim doesn't save me. I connect a jab into Milt's jelly-filled gut, but he barely budges.

"Maybe you should've studied harder. A knock to the head like that always did your dad's strength in for a few minutes as well," Milt says.

A silver streak of death plunges through the night, seeking my chest as its final resting place.

I close my eyes. I've already witnessed enough anguish.

A second scream overpowers Glenn's. Not mine, but Milt's. The pure terror causes me to open my eyes.

Clyde buries his dirty white fangs into Milt's black and blue forearm. I see the familiar crimson again. Fortunately, the red blood cells pouring from a body aren't mine. I can't make a sound thanks to the one hundred plus pounds of canine on my chest, but I can't keep my eyes closed either.

The knife clangs off a rock and bounces out of reach. I eye it momentarily, but Milt's hammer-fist to Clyde's back draws my full attention.

"Get this fur-covered piece of shit off me!" Milt rages. "Get up, Dale!"

I roll over and stagger to my feet. The world wobbles

for a few seconds before my vision comes into focus. Power surges through my muscle and bones.

"You."

I plaster Milt's face with fist and bone.

"Leave."

Another punch.

"My dog."

I channel my dad and smash my fist on Milt's scalp.

"Alone!"

I drive my knuckles into his ear. Blood gushes from my shotgun shoulder. Lester is still messing with me even after he's gone.

Milt flails his free hand at me, all the while wearing Clyde like a ripped sleeve. As he twists to try to block my strikes, Clyde's chain entangles Milt's chest.

"No breath!" Susan hisses. "Choke him." She points at his chest before moving over to Dale and planting her heel on his chest. "Now!"

I swing behind Milt and pull Clyde's long-chain past Milt's shoulders. He tries to tuck his chin, but a yank on a fistful of greasy hair opens him up like a cookie jar. The metal links slide over his Adam's Apple before a small chunk of hair comes off in my fist.

His cursing turns to grunts, then voiceless gasps. I create silence as I tighten the chain around his neck. My adrenaline overpowers my pain.

"Release!" I command Clyde.

I use my foot as leverage, pushing back against Milt's spine.

"Drag him to the water," Susan says. She stands right on top of us, having left Dale motionless on the ground.

"Check on Glenn," I say between labored breaths.

Milt clutches at the chain but can't slip his fat finger under the metal links. His muscular arms offer no flexibility to reach behind him and grab hold of me. Now on his knees with a chain around his neck, Milt is no better than a turtle on his back.

"Doesn't feel good being chained up, does it?" The wrath in my bones pours into my words. "You better pray Clyde isn't hurt. If he is, I am going to end you."

"Do it. Do it. Do it," Susan chants.

Milt's arms thrash over his head, but the stretched chain shields me from his reach. Clyde releases his arm as Milt collapses in a heap.

"Drag him down to the water," Susan says as she yanks at the chain's post. She looks at me. "I can't get this out of the ground alone. Help me."

"But I have to—"

"Help me." Her voice sounds flat and dark, yet stern.

"Fine." I toss the chain on the ground. Milt's chest rises and falls at a slow pace, but it's his only movement.

I use five long strides to approach the post, but I only need one pull to free the twelve-inch steel stake from the wet ground.

"Little help over here!" Glenn's panicked voice calls out.

"Glad to," a dead man's voice answers.

My heart plummets into my stomach. That voice shouldn't be speaking.

I whirl around to see Milt atop Glenn.

"Time to sacrifice a virgin," Milt chuckles. "Got any weather requests to the Gods?"

"No!" The veins in my temples bulge.

Milt plunges the knife into Glenn's stomach before I hit my second stride. He poses with the blade in Glenn like it's a photo opportunity, smiling at me all the while I run at him.

Glenn yelps and coughs blood into Milt's face. Milt laps

up what he can from his cheek with a reptilian tongue. When I'm in range, I don't hesitate jamming the stake deep into the meaty part of Milt's shoulder. The post punctures his back, cutting his grunt short. I pivot and run in the opposite direction.

As I pass Clyde, I clap my hands and yell, "Come on, boy. Come on."

Awkward but powerful, Clyde's bruising paws sink deep in the mud until he finds traction. The chain races along the ground behind Clyde. He never breaks stride, even when the chain becomes taut.

Milt's head whips back, and his body follows. Clyde drags Milt across the grass like a rag doll until Milt's husky frame hits a bigger rock than the one that kissed me good-night earlier.

Clyde breaks free, dragging the chain, the post, and a chunk of Milt's shoulder behind him. I want to keep running, but I know once I start, I can never stop.

FIFTY-SIX

"Is he breathing?" Susan asks.

I kneel next to Glenn.

"Yeah, but he doesn't have much time if we don't do something."

"Not him." Susan flips her eyes and head in Milt's direction. "Him."

"Don't know. Don't care. But he's not getting up this time," I say.

Glenn folds his hands around the knife. The concern about his neck shifts to his stomach.

I debate running up the hill and back down the road to the ambulance for bandages, but there are needles and thread close. Plus, we have the added benefit of two unhappy paramedics in the back of the ransacked ambulance who may be awake and unhappy to see me.

"Stay with him. I'll be right back," I say.

"Where are you going?" Susan grabs my arm.

"The truck."

She squints. "What truck?"

"Milt's SUV." I point to the two-toned champagne

beast parked across the way. "Keep Glenn awake. I'll be right back."

Clyde escorts me to the Cadillac Escalade. The chain rattles behind him while Milt's flesh gathers pieces of dirt and dormant grass.

I need Jacob Marley's chains because Milt religiously locks his truck. I reel in the links to get a hold of the hook and bait end. In a single motion, I launch the post at the window. It bounces off and falls to the ground.

"What the hell?"

Looking at the post, I realize the skewered chunk of Milt protects the truck's window.

"Stupid symbolism. Guess you can't catch a truck using bartender as bait," I complain to Clyde.

I put my foot on the chunk of shoulder and pull the chain upward. The flesh squishes under my heel.

Tonight's special: Milt kabob.

Things that would have disgusted me six months ago now feel commonplace. Either I'm growing up or going crazy.

Crazy, but not insane.

Milt stores his intricate tackle box in the backseat. I figure he won't be casting a line anytime soon.

I hurry back to Glenn with a tacklebox in tow.

"He's barely breathing," Susan says. "We should ease his suffering and get out of here."

I stop in my tracks. "What?"

"You know. Help him pass into the next life. Smother him or something. Then we can dump him and Milt into the water." Susan circles her hands. "Circle of life."

"He's your brother!"

"Only by technicality of paperwork."

"This isn't you, Susan." I push her away so that I can focus on Glenn. I peel his hands away from the knife.

Blood trickles into their shadow. I remember what my uncle said about my mom, my dad's Kismet, being a dark force. Is that true of all of them?

"I'm going to need more than fishing line to stop the bleeding," I say to Susan. "We need to split up. There's an ambulance parked a little way past where we had the car." Susan raises her hand, but I don't give her the opportunity to speak. "Don't ask. In the back, grab whatever you can find. And if the two paramedics happen to be awake, drag them down here with you."

"Umm, okay."

"And if they seem a little upset, just know it's because of me, not you."

"I'm sensing a theme here, Marc, and it's not a good one."

"Just go!" I snap.

I'm sure there are more helpful items in the ambulance, but I need to act fast. There's a chance neither paramedic will physically be able to help if I overdid it during my escape, so I head for the bar while Susan sprints up the hillside.

I fly up the stairs and through the storage room into the kitchen. I grab a few utensils and turn on the gas burners. The blue flames jump to life after a few clicks and kiss the serving spoon and butter knife I'm holding.

The silver metal morphs into glowing orange as it hovers in the flame. Sweat forms on my hand, and I worry about losing my grip as the metal turns white-hot. I curse Milt for not having a phone within reach of the stove. It's time to call for backup paramedics if my calculations are correct, but Glenn won't make it without me or a miracle.

I snatch a bottle of 151 Rum on the way out the storeroom door.

As I race back to his side, I pause by Dale. His pupils

have overtaken most of his iris. The black reflects the moon without interruption. Blood streaks from both sides of his mouth down his cheeks.

"Holy shit," I mutter.

He's dead.

I think back to Susan standing with a foot on his chest. Her other foot wasn't on the ground. Dale's crushed windpipe makes me realize that I couldn't see her standing on his throat from my angle.

Unfortunately, I don't have time to try to save Dale. If the torched utensils cool too much, they won't be of any use to Glenn. Plus, the transparent look on Dale's face indicates there isn't anything I can do for him.

I read about cauterizing wounds in Dad's journal. It seems he was quite proficient at the task. The knife and spoon return to the pulsating orange I need for the procedure. A real-life Indiana Jones swapping out the hunting knife in Glenn's stomach with the fiery butter knife.

I rehearse the procedure in my head twice. Dad's voice runs through my head. "Measure twice. Cut once."

"Not gonna lie, this is going to hurt," I say, but Glenn doesn't hear me. The combination of pain and loss of blood renders him unconscious.

The night turns silent. She holds her breath along with me as we listen to the music of the sizzling metal and the beat of the dripping blood.

I wrap my left hand around the blade's handle. The cold radiates through my arm and down my spine. I hesitate as I withdraw Milt's knife from Glenn. Precious blood gushes from the wound. I've grown accustomed to the sight of my blood, but the sight of Glenn's is another story.

The hot steel sizzles against his flesh. I withdraw the butter knife and lay a spoon on Glenn's stomach to seal the wound completely. I can't speak for any internal bleeding, but hopefully, this will keep him alive until we can get him help.

Glenn releases nary a grunt. Maybe I'm too late. I unscrew the top of the bottle of 151 Rum and empty the liquid contents onto his stomach.

The stench assaults my nose. Burning flesh and hot alcohol could just as easily be rotten eggs sprayed by a skunk.

I flip open the tackle box. Milt always kept pre-threaded hooks, although I could never figure out why since it weakened the line. Then again, he and Dad also said fishing was more about drinking and dynamite. Pre-threaded hooks are the best friend of a drunk fisherman.

Glenn's neck looks worse than its actual severity. His hands wiped blood everywhere, but Milt's knife didn't penetrate deep. The blood renders the skin soft and easy to poke. I only need five loops with the hook, and the wound closes well enough, for now, to stem the bleeding and lessen the chance of infection. Glenn needs real medical attention, though. My patchwork stitches won't help him for long.

"Com 'ere, Clyde."

Hobbling physically but not in spirit, the big furball bounds to my side and licks my face despite my resistance. I unhook the chain from his collar and give him a giant hug. My arms become lost in the jungle of blood-and-honey-colored fur. Once free of the chain and my arms, he shakes himself back to a dopey look and panting tongue.

Susan runs down the hill. "Paramedics are on their way." Tears flow over her cheeks as she approaches. "Both are pretty banged up, so they called another unit to assist."

"Thanks," I say. "Rough night, eh?"

"I guess. I don't know. People are dead, and I don't

understand why any of this is happening." She collapses to her knees and buries her face in her hands.

I lean close. "No one said being my Kismet would be easy." I sigh.

Susan wipes the tears from her eyes and gathers her composure. "How do you know it's me?"

"Milt seems to think so." I smile, trying my best to reassure her. "We're continually meeting in random places. Popping in and out of each other's thoughts. It's fate."

Susan doesn't return a smile. "Marc, I don't think I'm your Kismet. When's your birthday?"

"Thinking of throwing me a surprise party?" I say with a slight grin.

"Seriously. When?"

"November seventh."

"And I'm March twenty-eighth." Susan flops her hands over her knees.

"And?" I stretch out the question.

Susan sighs. "And Kismets have the same birthday as their partners."

Just when I believe I have the curse figured out, it kicks me in the nuts and steals my girl.

FIFTY-SEVEN

S usan sits vigil next to Glenn with his head in her hands.

"You gonna be okay if I leave you here with him?" I ask.

Her head shoots up, and her eyes open wide. "Alone? You're going to leave me here to explain all this?"

"It'll be fine, but someone needs to tell the paramedics what happened to Glenn so that they can treat him properly." I put a bloodied arm around her shoulder. She doesn't flinch.

"And what happens if Milt gets up and attacks me? Or that guy over there stands up—" Susan looks over toward Dale— "He's dead, isn't he?"

She fumbles for her inhaler between hurried breaths. Puffs from her mouth into the cold night air create small clouds that encompasses her head.

When the cops arrive, they'll discover Susan's footprint matches the injury on Dale's throat. A comforting arm around her isn't solving that problem. Self-defense likely won't fly on a killing of that nature.

"Wait here for a minute. I need to take care of a few things before anyone gets here. For your own sake, focus on Glenn."

"Do I want to know?" A few tears well up in her eyes as she asks.

"Just focus on Glenn, okay?"

She manages a small nod, but her smile fades quickly.

Ten minutes ago, I hesitated leaving Susan alone with Glenn, but now I'm not concerned. Something is different. Maybe she'd fed off Milt's negative energy. Maybe mine or the energy projected from whatever dark force I'm becoming.

It's time to set this right.

I sprint back toward the kitchen, pausing only to grab a collar full of Dale's bloodied shirt and drag him with me. Soon, sirens will come into range, so I don't have much time. I throw his body on the floor next to the stove before heating a spatula. Milt is about to receive a taste of what Glenn experienced mixed with a concoction of his own medicine.

I let the gas burners flow as I prop Dale against the oven.

"The Court of Cheeks has found you guilty of conspiring against my family and ultimately leading to the death of my father. I hereby sentence you to an eternity in the fiery pits of Hell." I say to Dale's corpse. "Don't go anywhere. I'll be back."

I head outside and march toward Milt. Mud squishes under my feet.

Milt lay face down, shirtless and motionless. Blood covers every inch of skin from his shoulders to his waist. When I tap his side with my foot, a small gurgling emulates from his throat.

I lean in close, confident he isn't going to spring to his feet. "Why?"

Patience left me long ago, and I don't wait. I plant the white-hot spatula on his back. Steam feathers into the air against the backdrop of the trees hiding the creek.

Milt huffs and wheezes until I remove the searing hot instrument.

"You were wrong about everything." I sit crisscross next to him. "You know that's gonna scar. Really bad. The tissue's gonna be dead. Long, painful rehab for your shoulder. Oh, and your place of business is going to need a major overhaul when I'm done." I arch my back and toss the spatula well out of range. "Here's what you should know, Milt." I suck in deeply through my nose before continuing. "Doesn't matter whether you live or die. It won't make me weaker. It won't reverse this . . . this curse." I resist calling it a curse, but I can't find an alternative.

Milt gulps, "Your uncle. He knows how."

I shake my head. "No. No. No. No. No! No cure is worth the cost! You are all wrong. Using this for your benefit, hurting others, killing, stealing. You all made it a fucking curse." I smash my fist into the ground, creating a small crater. "It didn't have to be, but you made it that way and drug me down the fucking hole with you!"

Milt fights for each breath. "Didn't get it wrong, just different opinions on right and wrong. It didn't finish the way I wanted. Your dad was easy. Disable the airbag. He always crashed into that tree when he wanted to build his strength. Predictable. I didn't think you'd be in the truck to help him. Guess I got lucky there." Blood trickles from both sides of Milt's gaping mouth. "But this fight isn't done."

"Not yet, but it will be," I say.

"This was your uncle's idea. His grand plan. Your

mom's death. Your dad's. Yours. But he wanted yours, and I couldn't let that happen. You're my leverage. You. Alive. I don't want you dead."

I palm the back of Milt's head like it's a greasy basketball and shove his face into the softening earth. The dirt thwarts my initial attempt, but with persistence and leverage, Mother Earth accepts Milt's face into her bosom. I wait until he stops squirming before I allow him another breath.

"Lester's dead!" I demand. "You want to live through the night, you better talk. You better show me something right now!"

"See for yourself. Surely your uncle told you about this." Milt manages to grasp my thigh and squeeze. "Kismets can share words and even visions with their family and with other Stitches. Welcome to my Hell. Best to keep arms and legs inside at all times, but it don't matter because this is going to hurt like hell."

Dad didn't mention this in the journal. Lester didn't tell me either. The two missing pages. He didn't want me to know. If I got into Milt's mind, I could've stopped all of this before it started. Now, I didn't have a choice if I wanted in his head or not. It's happening.

Every memory of Milt flees as his mind and assaults mine. They flicker like an old movie projector. A childhood filled with abuse and nightly beatings. Milt wears facial hair to cover scars made by his father's Swiss Army blade. His romantic life saw only two girlfriends, one in high school and a more serious relationship in his twenties. The second crumbled when Milt met my uncle. Murder will put that kind of strain on romance.

A slideshow of bodies flashes through my eyes. Neither Milt nor my uncle showed any regard to age, sex, race, or religion, and never did they attempt to nearly kill a person after the first attempt went awry. My uncle may have been the bus, but Milt did plenty of driving.

It cuts to all white. I can practically hear the spent reel smacking the end of the movie against the projector, but like many movies, there's an after-credits scene.

SUDDENLY I'M DRIVING down a dark, familiar road. I can't quite make out the words coming from the seat next to me. I look to my right, and there is a soft, lovely female shadow of a face. Mom's eyes bounce from fixed to all white as they roll back into her head. She keeps flicking her eyebrows high, trying to open them. My focus returns to the road rolling faster and faster underneath the car.

The words next to me come into focus for my ears, "Not this sunset. It's not beautiful."

I reach over and unbuckle her seatbelt and pull the wheel hard left. Three rough bumps, and I find myself face to face with a bloody thirsty tree that claimed the life of my mother. The same that stole Dad from me.

Moments later, I pull my badly beaten and unconscious dad from the trunk and place him in the driver's seat of the wrecked car that acts as Mom's initial coffin.

A police officer arrives on the scene as I finish positioning Dad in the car. Dale. He grabs a pillow from his cruiser, places it over Mom's face, and finishes off what the tree started. Dale and I converse around a burning pillow as a third silhouette flitters in the background.

I recoil my hand in horror. My heart races, and I can't catch my breath.

That's the first and last time I ever want to live through Milt's eyes.

"Why?" Tears flood my face. "Why her? Why my mother?"

Rage, not adrenaline, surge through my body. I reach my arm high, torquing my shoulder to its maximum, and stiffen my talon fingers.

"Answer me!" I scream.

"Marc! Stop!" Susan cries out.

"I never wanted your curse. I want power. Real power. I want people to cower at the sight of me as I did at the sight of my father. I want an army. We have it for the taking. Your father and uncle had it and blew it, but we still have a chance. You and I and your girlfriend over there can lead this wasteland of townsfolk." He swallows hard. "Hell, it almost sounds noble. And your mom was along for the ride until she wasn't. She wanted it to end, to have a normal life. You see, all the evil you Stitches do sinks into your Kismet tenfold. You make us. Somehow your mom found a moment to resist it, and she persuaded your dad to walk away. She convinced the authorities to lock your uncle up in the looney bin. This is her doing."

Milt's breathing hastens.

"You're not my enemy, Marc. She was my only real enemy. Now I know a Kismet, any Kismet, is a viable threat to me and my ideals. Sometimes those ideals came at the price of blood and innocence. I let your uncle think he was in charge, but I can't have another Kismet, like your Kismet, stopping me from controlling you." Milt's words rake across my soul. "Either she falls in, or she needs to go."

The sirens reach the far side of Munson Creek. The morons are in such a hurry, they forgot the bridge no longer exists.

"It's not noble. Someone needs to pay. Retribution." My shriek becomes a war cry. "Your blood should pay for it. All of it!" The anger-filled screams of my soul aren't the only sounds in the night now as sirens race around Munson Creek.

I plunge my claws into the soft, newly scarred warm flesh of Milt's back. It tears from his skeleton like perfectly cooked baby back ribs. I hurl the charred meat toward the creek.

"If there's a heart in here, I'm going to rip it from your body and bury it in the creek with your victims so that they can feast on it for eternity."

Warm wetness entrenches my hands. Milt's body twitches twice before it snaps me back into reality.

Not here. There can't be any evidence to bury Susan or Glenn.

Finding a bone in Milt requires fishing, but I latch on and drag him across the wintry ground into his bar. I drop his failing body next to Dale and duck outside. Red and blue lights dance on the other side of Munson Creek. The clock continues to tick.

I locate Milt's tackle box, remove the top layer to expose a hidden compartment, and fish out three sticks of dynamite. He loved to toss these bad boys in the water and scoop the dead fish into his boat.

Milt's Fresh Catch of the Day.

I stuff the red sticks of dynamite into my pocket. Susan's voice calls out, but the shadows of night overpower her words. Those shadows drive me back to Milt.

Shadows or ghosts?

For Milt, they're about to become one and the same.

"I have a special treat for you, Uncle Milty," I say.

Neither he nor Dale has moved. I grab Milt's ankle and drag him into the storeroom. "No," Milt pleads. "Told you what you wanted. Let's cut a deal. Fifty-fifty. Your friends live."

"My parents too?" I ask.

"You can't change the past, Marc." Milt's raspy grunts ring hollow.

I cram his large, ravaged body into the hot-box. "No, but you can avenge it."

With a flick of my wrist, I snap the safety regulator from the box and crank the temperature to one-thousand degrees.

Milt paws bloody fingers against the window.

I return to the bar's kitchen, pull the three brick-red dynamite sticks from my pocket, immerse their fuses in the blue flame of the burner, and wait for the crackling sound. Sparks dance down the fuse, so I toss the rods of destruction into the front dining room and sprint to the storeroom.

A last glance toward the hot-box shows no signs of Milt. No doubt, he's succumbed to the heat already, but he somehow still manages to freeze me in my tracks.

On the glass, in blood, sits Milt's handprint and the words:

'C |_|'"
~Su'on)
=> :x

Streaks of baked red make it impossible to read. No time to decipher. The sparking wicks aren't stopping for anyone.

"You might want to cover your head!" I scream as I race toward Susan.

I dive onto the ground and take cover.

Everything stops. The dark sky yields to a bright white flash. Shockwaves and sound reverberate across my body, threatening to shatter my eardrums. A shower of debris litters the battlefield.

A minute passes.

Susan sits up, huddling with her arms wrapped around her legs.

I gather myself and make my way to her, patting Clyde as I pass. He whimpers. A few pieces of debris or the sound may have furthered his injuries. The overprotective mutt assumed a guardian stance behind Susan.

"You okay?" I ask.

Stupid question.

"Everybody's dead," Susan stammers. "Are we dead too?"

Flames dance in the background with more life than Susan or Glenn. I grab both her shoulders and shake her gently. "Susan, help is on the way. You'll be okay. Glenn will be okay. Look after Clyde for me, will ya?"

"He's a good dog. I won't let anyone take him. If someone takes him, they'll probably end up dead, too," she says, giggling from an empty soul.

"I'll be back, Susan. I promise."

"Not if you're dead."

Been dead plenty of times, yet here I am.

Two paramedics sprint toward me, and I point them toward Glenn. Susan's sobbing drowns in the hands over her face, and the crackling fire of the bar's remains.

As I walk into the broken dark to meet the incoming flashing red and blue, Susan remains by Glenn's side even as the paramedics begin to assess his condition. An orange glow outlines their bodies. Her words run around my head.

Not if you're dead.

I think I've died enough.

FIFTY-EIGHT

"You sure you want to plead guilty but mentally ill?" Mr. Layer asks. "The sentence may be the same."

"I'm sure," I say. "I'll take my chances."

Plus, I know a particular doctor who would love to get his hands on my brain, and he happens to have a recent vacancy.

Anyone who heard my story might think me insane for letting Mr. Layer represent me, but he proved it was his secretary that secretly helped Milt. It wasn't him.

The state accepts the plea with little media fanfare. My case quickly moves to sentencing. Munson County wants the case buried like the rest of the town's history, and Valentine's Day is when they will put me into a dark corner to forget I ever existed.

I shift uneasily in the courtroom chair. Mr. Layer pats his hand on the table and directs my attention to the judge.

"Why four?" the Judge asks. Her arms swim in her black robe.

A pencil for each chamber of the heart is what I want to say, "He was still alive. He blinked." I tug at my collar. Way too much starch. "And spoke."

"Son, witnesses made it clear he was already dead."

What could I say? I shrug. "I know what I saw."

"It is the opinion of this court that your actions demonstrate a troubling trend. You have a history of attempted suicides and risky behavior. You willfully disobeyed the rules governing the hospital where your uncle was a patient, and it resulted in five deaths. Furthermore, you maliciously and severely injured several Munson High School students, not to mention several incidents of destruction of property. One witness contends your actions were in self-defense." The judge leans forward on her elbows. "I understand you lost your mother and your father, and I sympathize with you. I do, but you need help, son. Unfortunately, I believe the serious nature of the mental treatment you require may sit outside the realm of the traditional penal system."

She sits up straight and centers her glasses to her crooked nose. "An offer of treatment has been made to and accepted by this court and agreed upon by Mr. Cheeks. Therefore, it is the decision of this court, Marc Cheeks will enter Piedmont Plains Psychiatric Hospital for a period of no less than sixty months for evaluation and treatment under the care of Dr. Jonathan Gehringer."

Another awkward reunion.

No family. No freedom. No friends.

I don't care, because I need to go. My future is in that cell.

If there's hope to be found, it's there.

"At least it's not prison." Mr. Layer tosses a stack of paper into a folder. "As long as you remain there."

"I got nowhere else to go." I look at the generic black tennis shoes on my feet. "How's Glenn doing?"

"The doctor said his outlook is improving, but he's still

in a medically induced coma." Mr. Layer says. "They expect it could be months, but he should survive."

This is the part where I'm supposed to express my sadness, but I can only find sarcasm.

"Do I get a discount on your services since your secretary was passing information to Milt?"

Mr. Layer stifles a laugh but smiles with closed eyes. "Always with the humor? I guess I might deal the same way. You're gonna be all right, Marc. Your friend Susan is going to watch over Clyde." He places the folder in his walnut brown leather Berluti briefcase. "I've never been able to replace your old man since he died. Perhaps we can connect after your release."

"I think he'd want me to be my own man," I say, extending my two hands to say goodbye. "I'll expect plenty of visits."

Mr. Layer returns the gesture. "Now, those are rates you can't afford." He places a hand on my shoulder. "This isn't the end, Marc."

"No, it's not, but it is the end of us," I say.

If life shapes us and death becomes us, what happens when we refuse to accept what either offer? Where do we stand? My uncle said cursed and doomed. The courts declared insanity and institutionalization.

I prefer to think of it as untapped potential.

FIFTY-NINE

For the first time, I enter the Piedmont Plains Psychiatric Hospital from the rear. Dr. Gehringer waits for me as a trio of armed officers escort me from the van nicknamed "Crazy Hearse."

Dr. Gehringer greets me with the calming, warm liquid. The painful pinch from the injections fade in seconds. We walk to his office, where he points me to my seat, and every muscle in my body melts into the chair.

The man learned his lesson about dosing.

I check out mentally while he rattles off the procedures and policies of life around P3. He snaps his fingers several times.

"Marc, I asked you a question," Gehringer says.

"Huh? Sorry. What?" I'm not dazed. I'm . . . apathetic.

And there it is. Violent and apathetic. Blessed with traits of my dad and my grandpa. Oh, and possibly insane.

Marc Cheeks card for the win.

I move my handcuffed hands around my seat, touching and squeezing every piece of fabric and cold steel. "Are these chairs new?"

"Marc, I need you to focus so that we can complete your intake. I want to begin treatment immediately." Gehringer jots a few notes on the papers in front of him.

"Is that a brain?" I squint, attempting to focus on the corrugated and grooved frontal lobe swimming in what I could only assume is formaldehyde or ethanol.

Gehringer interlocks his fingers and rests his chin on his folder hands. "You might recall your uncle and I had a deal, but that's not important. Four employees died. Your uncle died. A valued and long-time nurse almost died too."

"I guess it's better than dying. Isn't it?"

"That isn't the point, Marc."

"What's the point?" I fire back.

"Innocent people died."

"Innocent people die every day."

Return volley.

"But these people died because of you."

"I killed them?"

"No, but your actions led to their deaths."

"Because I stabbed them?"

Gehringer slams his pencil on the desk. It doesn't break.

"Is that a Dixon Ticonderoga?" I ask.

Hallsy arrives in the doorway.

"Looks like my ride's here," I say.

I hear Gehringer mutter something about "I don't want his brain" before we exit the room.

The chain anklets force me to fall behind Hallsy and the lead guard, but I manage to remain a half a hall length ahead of the two guards behind me.

We turn a familiar corner and head down the hall. As I pass each doorway, the handprints clap but halt their action if either Hallsy or the guard glance back. Every door applauds except Bowfinger's, which offers me a one-fingered salute as Hallsy fiddles with a small contraption he carries.

Hallsy turns and opens a giant green rectangular box, unveiling a soft matte surface. Black ink.

"Here's the drill, pat your hands on this and place your prints on the wall outside the door."

"This is my door?" I ask.

Hallsy affirms.

"You're putting me in the Black Hole?"

"Yup, but hey, we removed the pile of my dead friends you killed."

"But I didn't—"

The black stock of the guard's shotgun collapses my stomach. I fold in half before falling to my knees.

I cough a few times before I can speak. "I'm not putting my handprints on that wall."

My head snaps back when the guard buries his knee in my jaw. The white ceiling flips in my vision as I flop onto my back. I roll to my side and spit blood on the floor. The normal dark crimson appears pink against the white tiles.

Breathing and talking prove challenging. "Will you show me which handprints are Lester's?"

"About a foot away from your head." Hallsy points above me.

I scan the hallway and note only one other set of prints this low. Soulmate's. Her dainty prints look out of place compared to the other adult-sized handprints around the door to her room.

"Okay." I exhale and wave Hallsy down to me.

Hallsy presents the green box, and I sacrifice my hands to the soft, spongy material. I wait a few seconds, then push down hard, freeing the box from Hallsy's grasp. My hands sink deep into the mesh, and black ink oozes up past my wrists.

I twirl and sprawl to Soulmate's door. The guard grabs for my legs, but I tuck them into my body before he can get hold. Hallsy smashes his nightstick against my outstretched arm. I fight through the clubbing, slathering black ink until her handprints are no more than a Rorschach inkblot.

"You're going to regret that!" Hallsy screams as he continues beating me. The guard straightens my legs, and Hallsy pummels them until he can no longer catch his breath.

I crawl back to the green box and dip my hands in again. Hallsy raises the club above his head.

"I'll do it right," I say in a timid voice. My head hangs low.

If my hands weren't handcuffed together, I would not have been able to lift my right arm. Hallsy's last strike snapped my radius or ulna. It's difficult to tell, but bone moves freely under my skin. My pinky and ring finger dangle like a worm on a hook.

I shuffle to the wall on my knees and place my hands atop my uncle's handprints. They're a perfect match except he had shorter, stubbier thumbs. I offset my fingers and palm ever so slightly to create a shadow effect on his handprints.

"What the hell are you doing?" Hallsy asks.

Hallsy's club reigns down hard on my skull and scrambles my brain, but I refuse to lose consciousness.

"That the best you got?" I spit a puddle of blood on Hallsy's white shoes.

"Drag him in here!" he says as he opens the Black Hole's door.

The guard clutches the collar of my white jacket and drags me across the floor. I don't pose any resistance. My blood acts as my trail of breadcrumbs, a path no one dares follow. The bright incandescent bulbs blind me as I skid across the floor on my back.

"Leave him right there," Hallsy says.

The guard drops my upper half, and I catch my breath moments after the thud. I want to sit up but need to rationalize my situation.

"I'm sorry about Conley," I say. After all, he seemed like a good guy. "Was the funeral nice?"

"What?" Hallsy's face flushes red. He grips the nightstick so hard his hand turns white. "You don't get to say his name. He was my best friend. He was family. I turned down my dream job so I could keep this job and make you suffer."

Hallsy turns his shoulder and pivots at the waist. I know what's coming next and roll onto my back, tucking my arms under my body.

There's no finding a good place for me. All the good places in life are gone. All the friendly faces are gone.

All—but one.

I manage to open my eyes in between blows and catch a glimpse of Soulmate. She presses her hands flat against the glass. A tear trickles down her face. A small smile pushes her cheeks higher, and the tear traces the outline.

Soulmate mouths "thank you," but I hear it as if she whispers into my ear. The eerie darkness about her fades. I can't find the same sadness I'd witnessed in her eyes on previous visits despite the tears.

"That's enough!" Gehringer's voice bellows from the hallway.

Hallsy ceases pounding on my back and kneels next to me.

"Get used to this, lunatic, because every day instead of arts and crafts time, you're going to get something extra special. I'm going to beat you to within an inch of your worthless life." He spits on the side of my face.

"Hallsy, my office. Now!" Gehringer enters the room.

I rotate to my side and gut down a mouthful of blood before turning my empty stare toward the door. The guard swings his arm over Hallsy's shoulder and walks with him to the doorway.

Hallsy presses, but the guard blocks his way and pushes him out of the room. As Gehringer closes the door, Hallsy screams, "Within an inch of your life!"

All part of my plan.

"Make it half an inch," I mutter.

SIXTY

A frost darkens the glass between Soulmate and me. I want it gone, but Gehringer refuses my requests. He does allow me my choice of music.

Christmas music. All day. Every day. I need to eat the darkness alone.

Dr. Gehringer vacates most of the cells adjacent to mine within days of my arrival. He explains the fear of me careened in a palpable wave through almost every patient near me. It makes his job impossible.

Soulmate refuses to leave her cell.

Minutes. Hours. Days. Weeks. Months. They melt together.

Beat. Eat. Sleep. Beat. Eat. Sleep. Over and over.

On the bright side, I can discern the hours from days when Hallsy works. A beating during the first hour of his shift. A few kicks to the head during his mid-day break. And a royal pummeling on his way out.

Hallsy tries to convince a new guy to carry the torch during his vacation, but that ends when he drops his black-jack, and I snap it in two. It's not his fault he's too weak to stand up to a pawn like Hallsy. I let him leave without punishment.

Truth is, Hallsy doesn't realize he isn't breaking me down. He's building me up.

Some days, I'm more monster than man, but thanks to Hallsy, I'm no longer scared of my curse.

HALLSY's latest fascination has been black eyes. He'll make both of my eyes swell to the point I can't see. Every day, both eyes, for months on end until Gehringer finally slowed his roll a few weeks ago.

My door creaks open. Hallsy's shit-eating grin walks into the room one step ahead of him.

Just my luck that the first thing I see when my vision finally returns is him.

"Music off," I yell. Wham's Last Christmas fades into silence.

"You ain't gonna believe this, but I have two presents for you today," he says. "First, Doc Gary approved a glass defrosting for the day. He said he'll let you know the cost later. And, second, you have a visitor."

"Knock knock."

Seeing Susan causes me the first real pain since I arrived.

"You dyed your hair," I say.

"I thought a change might be good after everything that happened." She tosses her hair and smiles. "Do you like it?"

"Ginger, eh?" I say, getting to my feet.

She immediately retreats two paces and stiffens.

"I'm not going to hurt you," I say.

"I know. I'm sorry. It's going to take time."

I bow my head. "I understand."

"Glenn's awake. About two weeks now. Doctor Malcolm said he'd need a few months of physical therapy, but there's no permanent damage."

"That's great." I miss Glenn. "You think he'll visit."

"He wants to. I swear, but you know our mom," Susan says.

"Speaking of which, how's your grandma?" I ask.

"She's doing better. Volunteers at a children's hospital now. That's a whole different crazy."

We stare at each other in silence for about thirty seconds when Susan turns, and Hallsy hands her a white Kleenex-sized box.

She walks with confidence, head high, and wide eyes.

"I made this for you."

Susan opens the lid, unveiling a pink frosted cupcake with a purple candied 23 on top.

"Surprise! Happy birthday!"

"Shh." I put a finger to my dry lips. "Don't you know you aren't supposed to yell at the patients?"

"Oh my God, I'm so—"

My laughter drowns out her words.

"You little jerk." She smacks my arm. "I thought . . . "

"Thank you. Seriously. This is way cool. But how did you get this in here?" I ask.

She smirks. "Having your grandma almost murdered gets you a few passes."

"Look, I'm . . . I mean." My words trail off.

"I know," Susan says. "How about we just focus on your birthday today and save the apologies for another day?"

"November already? I didn't even know it was my birthday. Time loses meaning in this place." My eyes bounce between the two cupcakes as I try to decide which one to take. "I can't decide. Which one do you want?"

"The other one's not for me. It's for my cousin." Susan waves to Soulmate, who isn't paying us any attention, buried in another art project. "It's her birthday, too."

Son-of-a-bitch. I must be the stupidest Stitch alive.

SIXTY-ONE

I struggle to find comfort laying on the floor. Hallsy's morning beating hurt. The emotional trigger from Susan's visit woke me. Less monster. Less man, even. I miss the simple life of learning how to adult.

It must have stirred something in Soulmate as well because she stands at the defrosted glass divide. Unwavering. Whenever I feel a little surge of energy, I inch toward the glass.

My room's door room swings open, and Hallsy enters carrying my lunch tray. He whistles as he saunters to the area between my body and the glass wall.

"Oh, and you're so close to your girlfriend." Hallsy teases.

"She's not my girlfriend," I snap.

"Whatever. Here's your lunch." Hallsy fishes a bowl from the tray and dumps cold pea soup on my head. "You gonna want crackers with that?"

"Are they gluten-free?" I guess Glenn's mom rubbed off on me.

Hallsy bursts out laughing. "You are crazy."

"Crazy, but not insane," I say.

"Enjoy your afternoon." He moves behind me and plants the sole of his foot on my backside, using all his force to push me forehead first into the glass. "You're welcome." Hallsy chuckles. "See you tomorrow."

I don't have an opportunity to stop the impact with my arms, so I tuck my head and let momentum do the rest. The entire room, floor included, shakes when my skull connects with the glass wall divider.

Hallsy pauses when he reaches the door. "Holy shit, did your head crack the glass?" He hurries through the door and slams it shut.

Once I regain my vision, I examine the crevice. A lemon-sized hole, not a crack, centers a spider web of faltered glass in the pattern of my skull.

Soulmate slides down the wall and seats herself on the other side of the broken glass.

She leans her mouth close to the slivered opening and says, "I'm Cammie."

"Marc." My name stabs the rawness of my throat.

"I didn't think you'd come," she says. "Like . . . to stay for more than a visit."

Cammie pushes her hand toward the opening, but it's too small for her hand to fit through.

She pushes harder, like trying to wear a glove too small for her hand. Jagged edges slice into her fingers and palm. Blood cakes the opening, but she refuses to stop. Soon her fingers and palm resemble a melting red waxed candle, but the smile remains plastered on her face. She wiggles her fingers once they emerged from the glass canyon. Blood drips from the tips and nestles in her knuckles.

"Go ahead." She eyeballs her fingers as she speaks.

I match mine against hers and all the sadness, the emotional pain, fades from my mind. Trapped, but happy.

"Thank you," she says.

"For what?" I ask.

"Whatever you did, it helped. The day you arrived here to stay. For the first time in forever, that day, I could breathe again. The dark thoughts fled from my mind, and they haven't come back. It's like I'm me again. I've been trying to figure out how to say thank you, and Susan helped me figure it out." Cammie holds up a picture of a cartoony cupcake beating on Hallsy with its burning candle. "Cupcakes. The one Susan brought made you smile."

I realize what my uncle meant. This isn't Cheeks' curse. This entire time, I've been chasing a lie, thinking I'm cursed.

We're not cursed. We are a curse. We're the cause, but Dad understood we could be the cure.

Mom felt Dad's actions tenfold. She wasn't dark like Lester said. Mom was cursed. A magnifying glass of Dad's violence. If he knew it, he didn't know how to tell me.

Cammie suffers my actions. All the sadness for my parents. All the violence and hate. All the death and darkness.

Dad meant the relationship between Stitches and Kismets. He meant us. Me.

I don't have to be a curse. Do something for her, something kind, something self-less.

Maybe something like covering her black handprints on the wall outside her cell. It's a start.

"I like your cupcake picture," I say.

"That's not even my best one!" She reaches back with her free hand and grabs an elaborate drawing full of vibrant color. "This is my favorite. See? There's you and me running out the back door of this place. Santa's on the roof. He brought us extra special gifts, that gun in your hand, and the smile on my face." Cammie brushes away a pencil shaving. "I didn't get the shading perfect on the Glock." Her finger slides across the page. "And over here is Doctor Gehringer setting the hospital on fire, not knowing Hallsy's trapped in your cell. I love how the orange flames complement his skin tone."

I curl my fingers, and she responds in kind but quickly retreats.

"Wait," she says. She unearths something from the floor before pushing her hand through the opening. "You'll need this for Christmas."

Our hands tangle again until a sharp prick jabs my palm.

A shard of glass.

Cammie passes me a razor-sharp apple-peeler size of glass my head freed earlier. I push through the pain in case Gehringer is watching us.

"Who's the little girl way up in the corner?" I point to the small, blonde-hair, blue-eyed child in a pink dress.

"That's my niece. My brother's daughter. She needs us," Cammie says. "Promise me you'll help."

While I'm not drawn to the idea of fire or more people dying, freedom holds appeal, and I'll have no love-loss if anything happens to Hallsy.

"I promise." And I mean it. "We need to help people. Not just the others in here, but out there. People like us."

"Like us?" she asks.

"There's a lot I need to tell you," I say. "But I'm meant to be here. I needed to find you. I need to help you."

"Because I'm your soul mate?" She smiles.

"No, because you're so much more." I smile back. "You're my Kismet."

SIXTY-TWO

December 25th
        The fire alarm's piercing sound breaks the silence of my Christmas dawn. I wake with a smile.

Today, we escape. Cammie and I. Tomorrow, we start helping those who can't help themselves, but first things first.

My hand excavates the broken glass hidden in my mattress. The lock on my door clicks. I race to position myself behind it. Hallsy enters, gun in hand, unaware of what awaits him. That I await him with an uncle Milty special.

Today, I escape. Tomorrow, I prove Dad right.

It doesn't have to be a curse.

I don't have to be a curse.

ACKNOWLEDGMENTS

Bringing together the final draft of a book is about far more than an author writing it and making some edits. I want to thank Rachel Tamayo and the crew at Foster Embry for helping me bring the Stitch Universe to life, Rusty Marcum and Maria Tureaud for keeping me grounded and helping me fight Imposter Syndrome, and the greatest community on social media, the writing community for supporting myself and every author putting our worlds out there for the world to enjoy.

ABOUT THE AUTHOR

By day, Tim Collins covers the world of finance, and by nights and weekends, he's building the Stitch universe. He currently resides in Austin, TX with his wife, Stacy, their three kids, and three dogs. Hobbies include, oh, who are we kidding, with three active teens, there isn't time for hobbies, but you won't hear him complain...much.

facebook.com/Darknovelist

twitter.com/DarkNovelistTim